DARKTHORNE CHRONICLES

SHADOW

OF THE

SOUL BLADE

JAY ROLAND

Author: Jay Roland
Cover Layout & Design: Jay Roland
Editor: Nicole Zoltack
Editorial Proofreader: Belle Manuel
Internal Design & Layout: Jay Roland
Cover Art: John Ric Detoon
(https://www.artstation.com/johnricjezzad03)

ISBN: 979-8-218-13077-0
ISBN: 979-8-218-14439-5

Printed in the U.S.A.

Typeset in 12 pt Baskerville and 36pt Trajan Pro

Dedications:

I would like to thank my wife and children for their unyielding support and belief in me. Without them, I would not be the man I am today. So, for your love, patience, and understanding, thank you, Nyssa, Darius, Sydney, Alexa, Jaxson & Savannah.

I would like to do a shout out to the original ITG Team. The memories that we forged are one of the cornerstones of my imagination, so thank you, Abbey Hunter, Robert Nink, Connie, AlleyCat, Jon, Ricky, Matt & all the friends we made along the way.

Ratings and Trigger Warnings:

This book is intended for mature adult readers because it contains gratuitous violence of a visceral nature. This book contains graphic descriptions of violence which could be considered disturbing to some individuals.

While it is not the aim of the author, or this book, to celebrate the existence of violence, I have done my best as an author to place the proper gravity on the nature of violent actions through the process of apt and thorough descriptions.

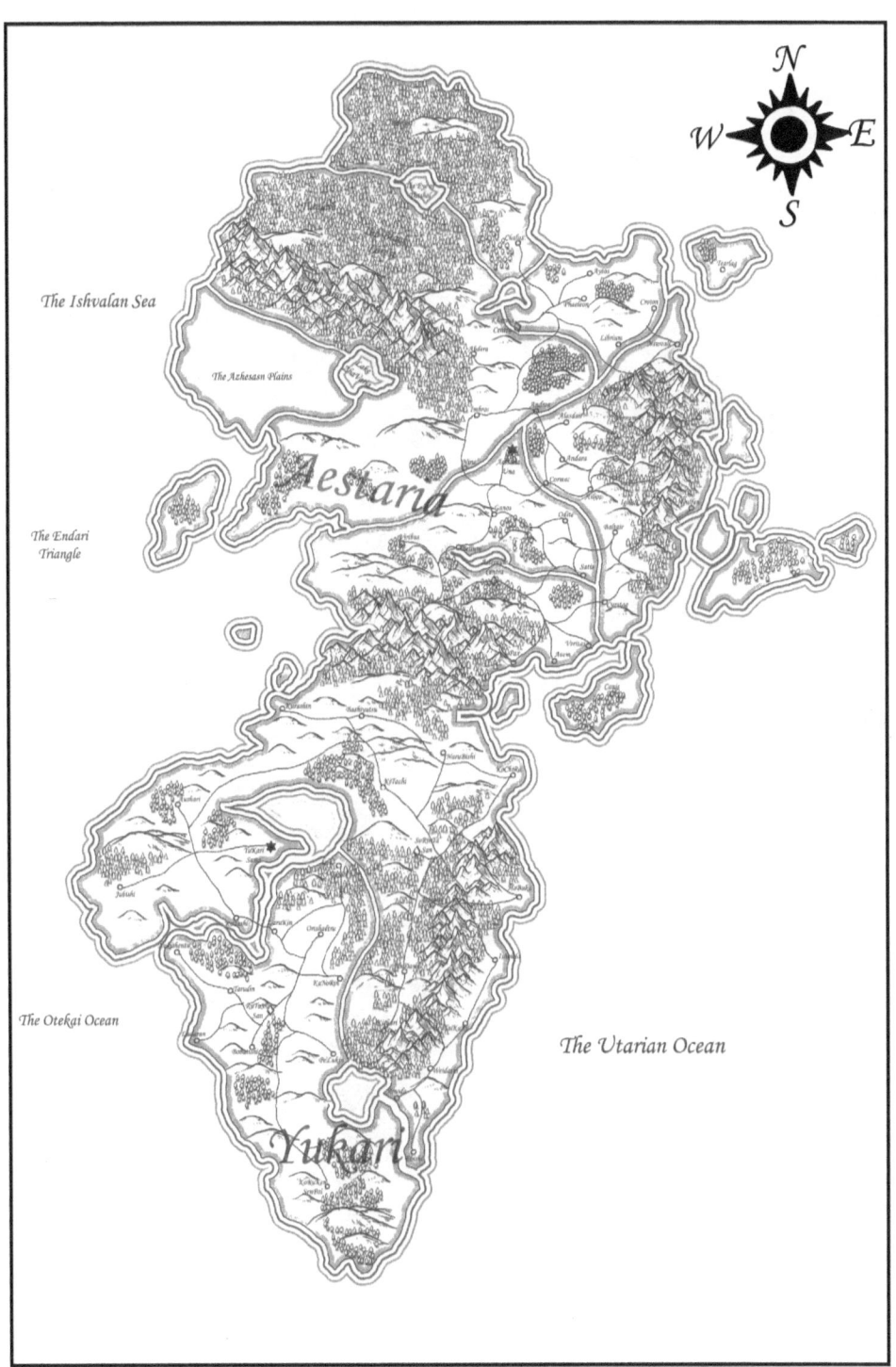

1

Silver needles of fresh moonlight pierced the trees of Ashana's black forest. High above the canopy, the first of the night's nocturnal otabi ventured to soar through the early evening air hunting for food. Held aloft by thick, leathery, trisectioned wings, the creature's armor-scaled body glistened against the lunar glow overhead. The beast would be absolutely fear inspiring, except that it was no longer than a large forearm. Flapping its wings, it flitted about, swooping and circling while filling its mouth with anything that would fit.

In a clearing far below, a tribe of feral Selece gathered around a large stone circle. On one side, a female Selece stood on a thick tree stump, her attention focused on the two hulking males embroiled in combat within the stones. The two warriors clashed with a deafening roar, their claws and fangs bared.

Bastian dodged, stepping back with his right foot. The feline whiskers on his feral face twitched as the claws on Doksha's foot sliced through the air in front of him.

Expecting that attack to connect, Doksha landed off balance. Bastian rolled forward, right leg reeling, his heel aimed at Doksha's stomach. With a smirk of confidence, Doksha twisted away.

Using his momentum, Bastian got to his feet. Instantly, a sharp sting bit into the back of his ankles as Doksha swept his legs from beneath him. Bastian's spine landed squarely against the dirt, forcing all the air from his lungs.

A brilliant light consumed the large Selece's sight. Moments later, the blinding illumination behind his eyes dissipated, leaving him in pitch darkness.

Bastian opened his eyes to find himself lying suspended in the netting of his hammock. He peered through the window beyond the treetops, where the evening sun hung low in the sky. Today was the first of the chagontha trials, where he would fight for the honor of being chosen as a mate.

Looking around, everything appeared to be just beyond a dull haze. Lifting his nose, Bastian inhaled deeply, taking in the scent of spiced lappes fruit drifting through the air. Just beyond that was the bouquet of fresh meat.

He crept out to the kitchen, prowling toward the cutting board to sneak a hind quarter from the small, freshly killed jora while his mother's back was turned. A vicious snarl froze Bastian in place until her sudden laughter broke the tension, permitting him to continue.

When she turned to face him, the honey-colored tones of her fur shined beautifully against the dark browns of her undercoat, shimmering between gold and brown in the sunlight pouring in through the window. Her light brown mane fell in waves just above her shoulders and was just long enough in front to touch her triangle nose, split diagonally between pink and black. The material securing her more sensitive areas was a medium tan, thick quality leather, rough around the edges from years of wear. The fur around her eyes creased with joy, brightening her face.

"Eat up. You have a big day today." She walked past him, gently combing her fingers through his mane.

Bastian tore into the jora leg, his sharp fangs ripping at the meat more than cutting it. Each bite extracted the aroma of raw flesh. His teeth split the fibrous muscle into individual strands, further sating his hunger. Every morsel he swallowed sat heavier in his stomach than the last.

His mother brought over a stewed bowl of spiced fruits. Bastian reached past the sweets for a bowl of fresh water. He put it to his lips and swallowed the cool refreshment. The flavor of his meal diminished with every drop.

With his palate cleared, he reached for the spiced lappes fruit. Examining the bowl's contents, he broke the silence. "I don't know that I can defeat Doksha. He's always overpowered me in the stone jaga circle." He looked down, head hung low, one claw toying with the squishy lappes fruit in his wooden bowl.

Shifting her eyes downward, his mother's face revealed her concern. She grunted in dismay, distraught by his anticipation of inevitable defeat. "Your father almost lost the chagontha. He chose your Uncle Jareth to be his opponent, and he was nearly defeated."

Bastian looked up at his mother, his eyes wide and mouth agape. "What would you have done if father lost?"

A heavy pair of clawed hands clamped down on Bastian's shoulders when a jovial laugh bellowed from behind. "She would have chosen me anyhow!" The large, gravelly bass voice continued its assault on the peaceful calm.

Bastian's father reassured him with a squeeze of his shoulders and moved to the cooking counter. The towering Selece reached for the jora's hind quarter on the cutting board. The sun gleamed off the dark sheen of his tree-bark-colored coat as his forearm muscles rippled beneath his fur.

"Nuratha!" His mother's voice snapped like the crack of a whip.

The only thing more impressive than his father's strength was his mother's speed. Her hand became a blur, tagging the back of Nuratha's wrist before he could touch the jora or pull his hand clear in retreat. A small drop of blood beaded to the surface.

A curious sense of déjà vu overcame Bastian, as though he'd seen this before.

"Shala?" The sound of Bastian's mother's name rolled like

warm molasses from his father's tongue. Nuratha raised his injured paw to his mouth.

Her lithe female form padded over to her mate, embracing his hand in both of hers and drawing it to her lips. She worked at the wound, cleaning the red blemish from Nuratha's paw under the watchful eye of his loving gaze.

His father gently ran his fingers through Shala's mane. "From that day forward, she's made all my dreams come true. Don't worry too much about the outcome of the chagontha."

After drawing her lips away from Nuratha's hands, Shala's soft tenor voice echoed, "It's not about who wins. It's about what she sees in her own heart while you engage in the contest. She will see the truth buried within your heart, so long as you're willing to do everything in your power to overcome the obstacle in front of you. If you give her your all, she will give you her heart."

His father's thunderous bass rumbled again, but something was wrong. Nuratha's mouth wasn't moving. "That's the beauty of dreams. You can sleep all night in the blink of an eye or experience a lifetime in a moment."

The constant haze in Bastian's sight suddenly became a dense, luminous fog. The world around him started glowing, the light from the window becoming so brilliant it flooded the room, overwhelming his senses.

Moments later, Bastian found himself on his back in the center of the stone jaga circle once again. The fur on the left side of his body twitched with anticipation. Bastian rolled in the opposite direction, away from Doksha's clawed foot careening toward the ground. The impact landed with a sharp crack. When the Selece sidestepped to assume an offensive stance, the remaining imprint was impressively deep.

Raising both legs skyward, Bastian rolled backward into a handstand. Gracefully, he allowed one foot to touch the ground, followed by the other, lowering himself in a crouch. The ball of Bastian's foot pressed against the dirt, claws pushing into the ground to provide greater traction.

Tension grew in the stillness between the two fighters facing each other within the jaga circle.

Doksha sprinted across the circle. Bastian lunged forward, using the claws on his feet to great advantage. Intercepting the lunge, Doksha grabbed Bastian's fur and rolled backward, locking his legs around Bastian's hips. Their fur meshed together with Doksha's arms held tight around his opponent's upper body.

Bastian pushed his hands firmly against the dirt on either side of Doksha's torso, lifting them both off the ground. After pressing his forehead against Doksha's chin, he thrust his hands to the side. Both bodies fell, sending Bastian's head careening into Doksha's jaw.

With his opponent stunned, Bastian laid back, sliding his arm down Doksha's leg. Moments later, he wrapped his own legs closed around Doksha's hips and locked his feet into position. With Doksha's foot ensnared in his massive biceps, Bastian leaned back, putting pressure against the center of his opponent's ankle.

Doksha cried out before his ankle popped. "Kamonesh!"

Bastian released his grip before doing any lasting damage.

His success came at the cost of all his energy. After struggling to his feet, Bastian padded over to Shamira and bowed before her. Collapsing to his hands and knees, he waited within the reverent silence of the stone circle.

She climbed down from the stump and placed her hands on his head. Her body went limp over his, tangling their fur together in an all-consuming embrace. An excited breath escaped her lips. "You will be mine."

2

Rector Agani stood at the front of a classroom, her rector's rod in hand. Every student sat frozen, eyes forward, gazing upon an imposing female figure of small stature surrounded by an enormous air of authority, clad in a black rector's robe with white trim. Her light brown skin nearly matched her light brown hair, pulled taut into a tightly woven, braided bun. Her light blue eyes matched the color of the noon sky on a clear day. Wherever she went, the scent of moon flowers and sweet morning dew followed.

The rector stood beside a wall imbedded with a blackboard. A large scroll hung down from a lesson roller with four images. All the children recognized these images to be small clay disks imbedded with gems. Their parents would exchange these tokens with other adults for food or services. The first on the left was brown, imbedded with a single clear gem in the center. Under the image was the word *'uni'*. The next was red with two orange gems, labeled *'chen'*, followed by a grey disk with three blue gems, *'sune'*. The last read, *'shal'*, beneath a black disk with four red gems.

The rector's eyes scanned the class while deciding her next victim. She selected a simple-looking creature in the middle of the room. The student's long unbound hair was a dark matte brown in contrast to her pale skin and dark blue eyes, every strand perfectly in position. The frail child would look out of place in her purple robes trimmed in silver if they hadn't been neatly hand tailored by the family's seamstress. Like the other children in her class, the daydreaming little girl was no more than eight harvest cycles old.

The rector's voice, silky smooth and firm as the smith's anvil, filled the stillness. "Meraina, what is the exchange rate from chen to uni?"

The small, anxious girl looked around the room. The words stumbled from her lips through the air in choppy bits, like an unfinished wooden puzzle still missing pieces and in need of some assembling. "Te-ten ten un-uni o-one ch- one chen. Ten uni to one chen."

Meraina winced at the snickering from the far corner of the room. The young girl searched for the source until the heat of her gaze settled on Jera. A bitter anger crept into her blood just thinking about him. *Jera is a useless little swamp skreetch*, the girl thought, *all he does is pick on me and make funny faces when he thinks I'm not looking.*

Even with her eyes closed, she recalled his long blond ponytail and the annoying dimples that sprouted on his smiling face every time he made fun of her. The thoughts poured in, causing her stomach to flutter and tightening her throat, making it difficult to swallow.

"Silence!" the rector's voice thundered. Stillness consumed the classroom. Rector Agani spoke again. "Jera, what is the exchange rate from uni to shal?"

The small boy quickly replied. "Ten uni equals one chen. Ten chen to a sune`. Ten sune` equals one shal."

"And the extended exchange rates?" The teacher pressed further.

Jera cleared his throat. "One hundred uni is one sune`. One hundred chen is one shal. One thousand uni is equal to one shal."

The rector returned to the blackboard, wrapped her fingers around a red cord hanging from the chen scroll, and gave it a quick tug. The scroll retracted itself back into the roller. Her hand reached over to a blue cord, and in a fluid motion, she pulled down to unfurl a giant map from the scroll roller.

The instructor stared at **Meraina,** clearing her throat to get the small child's attention. "What is the name of our planet?"

Sighing in disappointment, **Meraina** scowled at the teacher in frustration. "Ash-Ashs-Ashana. We live on the planet Ashana."

"And where on Ashana do we live?" The rector's gaze fell to the map.

The little girl's stammer sent words stumbling from her mouth. "W-we live in the kingdom of A-Ae-Aestaria in the city of Aestaria Un-Una, the capital of Cen-Central Aestaria."

The rector pressed further, asking, "And who are our neighbors to the south?"

The girl played nervously at the silver trim of her robe, mumbling the words in response to the teacher's question, "Aet-Aeternum."

Rector Agani turned her attention to the room's far left corner, near the back wall. "Abriel, what can you tell me about the land to the west of Aestaria?"

Clad in green robes trimmed in gold, a small child with short, dark, curly hair sat in the corner. The silken material glowed in contrast to the boy's ebony skin. His voice held a smooth swiftness edged with a slight Ignatian lilt.

"The western lands are filled with Selece. Savage upright beasts that do nothing but mate and hunt. There are two types of Selece—tree walkers in the north and plains stalkers to the south. While they seem stronger and faster than Kandari, they are nothing more than vicious animals."

A muffled snickering came from the direction of Jera's desk. "Show off."

Rector Agani set her gaze once more on **Meraina.** "And what can you tell us of the land south of Aeternum?"

The child's voice squeaked something out, hardly audible over the ringing day end bell. "YuKari."

Children scuttled about fiddling with indexes and pages. A crack roared over the commotion, and everything froze. The air went thick with authority issued from the rector's atonement rod connecting with her thick wooden desk.

"You do not leave until your rector dismisses you. Do you understand?"

The class replied in unison, "Yes, Rector Agani."

Looking at the class with disapproval, the rector forced the word forward, "Dismissed."

3

On either side of Bastian's room, a board with four holes and a stick anchored his net woven bedding to the thatch-work walls. The Selece lay in his hammock admiring the sunset through the window, thinking to himself, *when the sun finishes its journey through the sky, the hunt will begin.*

Raising his left hand, Bastian rubbed at a blank patch where fur had not grown for nearly eight cycles now. The ache of the phantom pain where the ombashi spike pierced his palm radiated from the bones within. His mind was filled with visions of his uncle Jareth lifting him by his leathers, to pull him from danger, and the blood dripping from the ombashi talon piercing his uncle's chest through his back. Bastian ran while the ombashi was feasting, but what else could a Selece cub of just ten cycles do?

Suddenly, the chagontha drums' deep tones resonated off the trees. While all could hear them, the echo of rumbling drums called for him. The rhythm of the night beckoned.

Bastian grabbed his bow before sliding a set of chatta claws into the straps around his waist. One had to be careful how they secured the chatta with their two claws. He had to take them, though they would be of no use during the ritual hunt. What they symbolized was most important.

Padding out of the thatch-work wooden dome, he gazed down and knew the ground beneath him was a distance of ten fully grown Selece.

Finding secure footing, Bastian rushed forward along the tree branch until he found his favorite spot and descended. The movement was so relaxed it appeared almost clumsy or accidental. Instinctively, his body went vertical, and his hands clasped a branch. The large Selece whipped through the trees from limb to limb with preternatural grace. Bastian continued his course, tumbling through the air while locks of his light brown mane whipped across his face and into his eyes. Clutching one last branch, he flung himself forward, soaring end over end before his feet firmly connected to the ground with a thump. Sliding his fingers back through the locks of his tousled mane, Bastian walked forward toward the unrelenting drums' thunderous call.

Bastian strode into the chagontha circle, eyes locked on his parents, standing tall on the other side. Their out-stretched arms beckoned him closer. With a confident gait, he closed the distance. Drawing near, he raised the bow from his shoulder and placed it delicately into his mother's open paw.

Moments later, he retrieved the chatta from their leather holsters, and their razor edges gleamed in the moonlight. With a firm grip on each, he held the blades, tips pointing towards his own flesh. With a steely gaze, he offered the chatta to his father, Nuratha, who took them with the same grip he would use in battle. Slowly, the elder Selece lowered his arms to his sides, a silent acknowledgement of his son's readiness to begin the trial.

His parents turned their backs to each other, placing the objects into two separate boxes. Reverently, each opened a wooden chest on the ground before them, placing Bastian's objects inside. Once closed, they slid a row of wooden toggles along the lid's edge, locking the boxes shut. When they rose to face their son, he looked past them into the woodland tree line.

When the moon rose to the center of the nights sky, Nuratha broke the silence. "It is time!"

Bastian padded toward the tree line. He scanned the area beyond the evening moonlight and observed a shift in the forest hue. The foliage under the forest canopy shade radiated a luminescent green more brilliant than the midday treetops, with echoes of color reverberating from their center in an iridescent aura.

Starting forward in a light jog, the dark wilderness glowed more brilliantly the deeper he went. Ahead of him, to the right, was an old tree with a thick trunk and sturdy branches, outstretched as if to embrace him. Once Bastian closed on the tree, his claws dug into it with the ease of a chatta blade piercing an overripe fruit. Bastian made his way upward with nearly the same swiftness he'd been moving on the ground.

From fifty paces behind Bastian came the sound of intense huffing. The heavy breathing was not the cost of expending energy, but a deliberate increase to generate more.

Bastian continued to find solid footing on boundless tree branches nearly the thickness of his own torso, yet he wouldn't be able to maintain this lead for long. *Staying ahead isn't the goal,* he thought, *but it's still fun.*

Between two branches, he shifted his body midair to tumble end over end. His feet thudded against the next tree limb, and he raced forward along the natural wooden framework toward the trunk. In an instant, a large, ominous figure emerged from the shadows. Beneath the creature's thick hide, massive muscles rippled and bulged, a testament to the raw power that lay beneath. Its razor claws glinted with a menacing sheen in the darkness.

Running too fast to stop or change direction, Bastian hit the creature so hard the air exploded from his lungs in a choking gasp. The figure's dense mass sent a thought reverberating through Bastian's head, *Why couldn't I have hit the tree trunk instead?*

The stunned Selece nearly fell until a deadly hand wrapped itself around his wrist and forearm. Bastian hung in midair at the mercy of this shadow-covered beast.

"You've gotten faster," a gravelly voice rolled out with a jovial undertone of laughter.

"Thank you, Father." Bastian's tight voice escaped his constricted throat, still stinging from the sharp gasp that escaped his lungs when colliding with this force of nature.

Nuratha lowered the young Selece, until he was steady on the branch. The elder Selece looked on silently while his discombobulated progeny stretched toward the sky, muscles and tendons popping back into place. Once the young Selece regained his center, Nuratha broke the silence. "Have you found the trail yet?"

Bastian grunted in affirmation and gestured toward the trail with his nose.

"Well, what are you waiting for? I'm just here to watch. This task is yours to complete. This is your hunt. I know you'll make me proud."

Bastian set his body toward the trail he had picked up earlier and shifted his weight to gain traction. Like a moravian steed, Bastian shot forward and maintained a steady stride. His father lurked in the shadows, effortlessly keeping pace. Even when he couldn't see or smell Nuratha, Bastian knew the rathan, leader of all northern Selece, was there.

The two sprinted for nearly half the night with the full Evening Moon high overhead, though only flecks of it pierced through the dense forest's thick canopy.

Bastian's instincts pushed him to press forward toward his prey, but something was amiss. Something pulled his attention in another direction. He felt a disturbance in the forest. After rounding a mound of thick brush, Bastian came upon a sight confirming what he already known in his heart.

Looking on with curiosity, Bastian watched nearly hairless, pale bipedal creatures encumbered in swaths of dead plant life dyed with bush berries walk around in his tribe's forest. They appeared lost, especially the largest in front. He was also the one with the longest sharp metal stick. They all carried boxes in one hand which held glowing flames. The harsh brilliance flickering in the darkness flared aggressively against the smooth backdrop of night, forcing Bastian to shield his eyes. The young Selece stayed perfectly still, crouching on the tree branch, watching.

Nuratha's presence crept over Bastian like a shadow shifting in the midday sun. Nuratha placed his mouth just behind Bastian's ear before speaking in a low whisper. "These are the Kandari the elders and I spoke of. The peace pact we made with their people forbids these actions. We must confront them and tell them to remove themselves from our land. They cannot be allowed to search the Kaitan caves, or everything our people love will be lost."

Bastian tilted his head back slightly. "What will we do?"

Nuratha put his hand on Bastian's shoulder. "You will approach openly from the front peacefully. You will speak their language as you have been taught."

Bastian's face puckered into a visage of sour disdain.

With a long sigh, Nuratha's face became perplexed. *I know it's difficult,* he considered, *but he must.* His gaze hardened. "As you are the future rathan, we taught you the ways of the Kandari so you could keep the peace and uphold the pact. The time has come for you to call upon that training. You will speak with them peacefully in the Kaanish tongue and do nothing to harm our mutual oath. You will state our rights to ensure the pact is honored. Tell them you come on behalf of Nuratha, Chief of Theshal, the Northern Selece. Tell them we wish them no harm, but they need to remove themselves from this land. When you approach them, face them head on, and shift your eyes away slightly. This will lessen your discomfort from the lights. What they're holding are lanterns. They do not see in the darkness as we do, so they bring the firelight with them."

Bastian's eyebrows raised. "They're holding fire? On purpose? Without being burned?"

Nuratha smiled wider. "That is what the box is for. It stops the fire from escaping and engulfing the one carrying it. We need to move now. I will stay in the shadows and only show myself if they present danger."

Moving along the tree branches, Nuratha vanished into the darkness, while Bastian descended toward the forest floor. Trudging along the trail, the adolescent Selece reflected on his past lessons, practicing his best Kaanish in his head.

4

A man standing seven feet tall, with long light-colored hair woven into a herringbone braid down his skull and clad with mahogany leather armor, stood at the mouth of a cave. His face was covered with light stubble from days of travel and no access to a shaving blade. His left hand rested on a crest imbedded into the pommel of his sword protruding from a wire-wrapped handle with an elaborate bronze hilt. The Master-crafted blade was secured in a scabbard muddled between maroon and brown with the wear that comes from years of faithful service in the field. Scanning the perimeter, his eyes saw though his mind wasn't yet aware of.

"Jorgan!" a scratchy, masculine voice barked from behind.

The well-armored man snapped his head towards the sound of his name.

The abrasive voice continued like nails pulled across a rector's teaching board, "What are we even looking for here anyway?"

Jorgan's voice bellowed in a rough baritone, throat filled with the gravel that comes from years of yelling commands and too much pipe smoke. "Continue the course, Miles. We were told we would know what it is when we see it, and our benefactor would not provide any further instructions beyond that. Remember, don't touch it. The object must be placed into the bag without being touched. Anyone who touches the stone will be cursed to suffer an agonizing death."

Miles turned back into the cave, taking his lantern to light the way. He stood a head shorter than Jorgan and was clad in poorly fitted brown armor on his average size form over a green tunic. His light brown pants were threadbare from years of wear and layered with dirt, both new and old. A small blade hung from his side, and a crossbow, preloaded with a bolt and already cocked, hung on his back. The only thing stopping the crossbow from firing was a small wooden block on a hinge lever.

Pressing further into the cave, Miles worked at the spool on his belt, letting out a length of white rope while barking out orders, which sounded like mumbled echoes. They had tied the rope to a thick log anchored into the ground, adding to an assortment of thin ropes, each a different color, all leading into the caves.

From the shadows beyond the light came a large, hulking form. It was a bipedal beast covered in medium brown fur and a wild, dark brown mane blowing in the wind. The creature wore only a leather loin cloth, which was a darker shade than its own fur. Around the creature's legs and arms were thick leather bands tied together and secured by leather string, one on each leg and one on the left arm. Beneath these straps were thick, well-defined muscles with substantial definition. It appeared to be an unusually lean figure for a creature with such an athletic build.

The form stood at the light's edge, just beyond sword reach. It was completely unarmed save for a ferocious set of claws extending from its hands and feet and a slightly snouted mouth, which would no doubt bear rows of razor-sharp teeth.

The creature opened its lips, and through a string of growls and long guttural grunts, Kaanish words crawled out. "Greetings. I offer you no harm. I am Bastian. I bring word from the chief of the northern Selece."

The large Kandari's mouth agape, Jorgan stumbled back in surprise at the creatures mutilated Kaanish. The large man placed one foot securely on the multicolored ropes, while his other heel gave the bundle a sharp kick, tugging at his comrades on the other end. Jorgan continued to step back past the ropes until he steadied himself on the post that was securing the lines.

"I'm Jorgan. Tell me, what message do you have for us from your chief of the north?"

Bastian took a moment to process the man's words. It sounded new coming from the mouth of a Kandari.

Bastian's mouth distorted at his best effort to make the strange Kaanish sounds. He tightened his throat trying to remove some of the gravel from his voice and stretched out his neck. The sounds came smoother this time.

"He wishes for peace. We offer peace if you leave."

Jorgan's one eyebrow turned curiously upward. "And if we stay?"

The feral mouth moved slowly with grave intent. "If you stay, we bring death."

Jorgan smirked at the sound of workers' voices echoing from the caves. From the corner of his eye, the ropes shuffled about the post.

Stroking the stubble of his chin, Jorgan reached across, resting his palm on the pommel of his blade. "Well, leaving isn't an option, friend, so I guess I choose death."

Jorgan's fingers tightened, and the naked blade rang from its sheath, flashing in the firelight. The mercenary spun the steel through the air in a playful flourish. With his opponent two lengths away, Bastian was in no danger.

Bastian permitted the man to close the distance. When Jorgan was within striking range, his blade lashed out in a slanted arc. Charging forward, Bastian ducked low, closing the distance in a blink. The inner ridge of his bestial hand swung high, attacking Jorgan's grip. The Kandari's fingers opened, sending the blade flying forward.

Clasping onto Jorgan's vest, Bastian stepped back with a hard twist, sending his enemy ass over teakettle careening toward the ground. With a tight grip on Bastian's leathers, the Kandari brought the large Selece down with him. Landing atop the barbarian, Bastian drove his elbow into his opponent's breastbone. Jorgan thrust his feet into Bastian's hips, sending the Selece sprawling behind the prone Kandari. With a flick of his tail, Bastian Landed on his feet, coiled into a crouch.

Nuratha emerged from the shadows behind the stone mound to intervene, when seven Kandari exited the cavern. Five men and two females, but that made no difference on the battlefield. These foes would be considered larger than normal amongst the Kandari people, but to Nuratha, they were mere pups.

The first closed in, sword drawn, hand sweeping down, bringing the blade with it. Nuratha's lithe form sidestepped away. When the sword found the end of its path, Nuratha kicked the man's wrist. The weapon went loose, twirling through the air before clattering against the cave's stone entrance.

Continuing his momentum, Nuratha's leg swept through the air, slashing his foot's razor-sharp claws through the front of the enemy's throat, now dark red with four razor thin lines of separating flesh. Eyes glazed over, the Kandari thudded to his knees, life's blood pouring from his neck in a macabre waterfall.

Jorgan lay on the ground a length away from Bastian, feet pointed away from his bestial opponent, poised to strike. Jorgan rolled to his stomach and heaved himself up, clutching at the ground. The Kandari warrior charged forward, his long braid flailing in the wind, as he hurled the dirt out in front of him.

When Bastian lunged, his hands came up in a failed effort to shield his eyes. Jorgan sank his hands into the crook of Bastian's knees and planted his large shoulder into the center of Bastian's torso. The embroiled figures crashed hard to the ground.

Clutching his opponent's knees tight, Jorgan had the Selece held secure. The searing anguish from shards of debris raking across the back of his eyelids left the feral warrior momentarily blind, pulling all of his focus to what he could hear and feel. Jorgan crawled forward to straddle his heavy legs over the Selece's midsection. Bastian felt the mercenary shift from side to side as the sound of a metal blade chirped from its sheath.

Raising his hands, Bastian intercepted the attack, and the blade slid through his fur. The razor edge bit flesh, just before his forearm collided with Jorgan's wrist. Bastian entangled their arms, holding the blade at bay, while preventing his foe from rising up.

Unable to free himself, Jorgan dropped the blade into his other hand, when Bastian's foot wrapped around Jorgan's ankle. The Selece thrust his hips skyward and sent Jorgan sprawling. The reeling Kandari unintentionally flung the knife into the shadows beyond the tree line.

Bastian mounted the Kandari infiltrator, thrusting his hands forward to bury his claws into the Kandari's flesh. Jorgan grabbed both of Bastian's wrists, crossing his vicious adversary's arms.

In the distance, Bastian glimpsed Nuratha attacking the Kandari invaders in sweeping circular motions. The Selece Chieftain's long legs prevented his foes from coming in close.

A female warrior clad in brown leather over black cloth slashed forward with her blade. Nuratha rushed forward inside the weapon's arc. Entangling his opponent's arm, twisting it in the wrong direction. With a wet crunch and a pop, the woman went limp with a shriek of pain.

Another Kandari lunged, and his blade bit at the side of Nuratha's right leg. With the Kandari's diminutive size and lack of coordination, the sharp edge merely wounded the outer layer of Nuratha's flesh. The attack left the man's body sprawled out on the ground. Nuratha stomped on the man's forearm, and his bones cracked. The Selece chieftain shifted his stance, to thrust a clawed foot into his opponent's stomach. The feral talons slid effortlessly through the leather armor, finding their way home into the red sanguine layers beneath.

Nuratha pulled his foot from the fallen mercenary's torso and stepped hard onto the wet grass. Foot slick with blood, he slid down to one knee. The hulking Selece was now eye-to-eye with Miles, who frantically swung his sword with everything he had.

With the flick of a wrist, Nuratha deflected the blade skyward, causing Mile's desperate thrashing to turn him away. Nuratha raked his claws across the back of the invader's knee. Miles stumbled forward in agony, tripping over a prone comrade. His body timbered to the ground like a felled tree. Miles' face careened toward a long-jagged rock near the cave's entrance. His forehead collapsed inward, chest thudding against the dirt.

The impact shifted the loaded crossbow's locking mechanism aside, pushing the string from its notch. The thrum of the bow rode the air like the voice of death itself, and the fatal bolt flew. Nuratha collapsed to the ground in a languid avalanche of fur and muscle.

With heavy eyelids, he saw the remaining figures flee. One man carried a satchel betraying the shape of a large, flat stone. Nuratha watched the three remaining Kandari rush over to Bastian and Jorgan's struggle. Looking on, as Bastian hunched over Jorgan, ready to strike, the rathan lay helpless while a female Kandari slammed a large branch it into the back of his son's thick mane.

When Bastian's limp body fell to the side, the band of raiders pulled their leader to his feet and regrouped. One of Jorgan's cronies handed him a sword. He slid it into his scabbard and ambled over to his fallen opponent. The large mercenary slammed the flat of his boot against Bastian's still form. Satisfied by the lack of response from the motionless creature, Jorgan signaled to move east. The four remaining Kandari walked off into the forest, taking with them the fate of all Selece.

The pull of coming darkness was too much to resist, and Nuratha closed his eyes. Memories flashed. Visions of Shala dancing under the stars. Playing resch in the woods with Jareth. His first ombashi hunt. Sitting in the woods peacefully listening to the spirit of Ashana.

Nuratha was floating in an ethereal darkness when everything began shaking. Silent bolts of lightning tore apart the abyssal void around him. His fur-covered eyelids cracked open, pierced by shimmering slivers of early morning moonlight.

The Selece Chieftain sighed in relief at the sight of Bastian's face looking down on him, wet with tears. The slightest breath sent a searing jolt surging through his core. Nuratha's body wanted to convulse in response to the pain, but he shut it out, refusing his natural reflexes their normal allowance of control.

"Father! Don't move. Let me go back and get Mother and the Nanguh. The Nanguh can bring the herbs to heal you."

Nuratha gazed softly on Bastian's troubled face. "It's too late for that, son. My time here is done. I hear the Ashuun calling, saying it's time to join our ancestors."

Bastian's tears fell. "No! I won't let you. You must fight this. You always taught me to fight and be strong. Why can't you follow your own lessons?"

Nuratha's gaze hardened. "I've fought this long because I have to give you a message. I must give you a duty. You have completed your chagontha, and you are now the Rathan of the Northern Selece, the Selece of Theshal. Take the ombashi tusk necklace and lead our tribe."

Bastian shook his head in protest. "No, Father, it isn't your time. You're too st—"

"Shh," Nuratha whispered. "I don't have long now. You must retrieve the Spirit Stone. Without it, our tribe is lost."

Nuratha's breath shifted the arrow around in his chest sending a surge of agony through his body, its only manifestation the rippling of his fur rolling over his torso. His face remained statuesque.

"Take the ombashi tusk necklace," Nuratha grunted, "and lead our tribe. Before we started this hunt, I told you to make me proud. The truth is, I have always been proud of you, my son, and now to watch you become the rathan…" Nuratha's breathing went shallow, and his eyes got heavier still. Two words accompanied his final breath. "Love… Shala…"

Tears streamed down Bastian's face like a river of hate. The brilliant pink of dawn pierced the night sky, heralding an eternal mourning. His throat opened in a bellowing roar at the rising sun cresting the horizon beyond the trees. The sound Bastian unleashed shook the trees throughout the forest.

"Wake up! This can't be! Wake up!" he pleaded. The wailing Selece pounded his hands against his father's limp body before collapsing in foreverwhelming sorrow.

A thunderous roar crashing through the forest echoed in the fleeing Kandari's ears. Jorgan dismissed the sound. Pressing forward, his uneven gait favored his injured foot. To ease the pain in his shoulder, the large Kandari's hand rested on the handle of his sword. Metal ridges chaffed at Jorgan's palm. Looking down at the pommel, he discovered it lacked the brass fitting etched with the winged moravian steed against the setting sun. *Oh well,* Jorgan thought, *I'll just have it replaced when I get back to Aestaria Una.*

The group of Kandari journeyed onward toward their homeland, following their fearless leader, Jorgan, with not a care or worry in the world. In fact, with only four left, they would each get a bigger slice of the pie.

5

Bastian's body lay heavy, slumped over Nuratha's corpse. Where his limbs touched the ground, blades of grass pushed through his fur, provoking his muscles to twitch. The morning bird's song echoed in his ears. Bastian's eyelids sat like giant boulders obstructing his vision, forcing him to strain to open them. Dried blood fused his right hand in the matted fur. Nuratha's fur. His father, his mentor, his rathan...

The image of Jorgan's face, with his golden braid, reverberated in the obsidian looking glass behind Bastian's eyes.

His mouth opened with a low rumble. "Jorgan..."

Waves of heat surged through Bastian's body, rippling out from his core. His fingers tensed, and the claws on his toes pierced the soil beneath him. Bastian shot to his feet, eyes wide. Save for the corpses littering the ground, he was alone.

Near the mouth of the cave stood a post the width of his forearm anchored deep into the dirt. When he approached to investigate, Bastian pulled at a mess of different-colored ropes tied to the base. Following the thick cords led him no farther than the cave's entrance.

Bastian explored the caverns, but they all reeked of Kandari, each tunnel as rancid as the next. The large Selece came out of the cave, searching the landscape. *Why were they here?* He wondered to himself, *what do they want with the Spirit Stone?*

Bastian made his way back over to Nuratha's still form. Reaching around his father's neck, he untied the ombashi tusk necklace with great care. Bastian sat upright, holding the piece aloft to examine it. The thick leather braid was strung through a collection of ten white piercing tusks, each the length of a Selece finger and claw together, with the center tusk being the longest.

A word crept out of Bastian's mouth like a faint whisper from a ghost. "Ombashi."

An image of the black forest's legendary terror flashed through Bastian's memory. A profound sense of foreverwhelming dread filled him, pushing the thought deep into the recesses of his mind. When the image faded, Bastian slid the cord around his neck and knotted the two ends.

The ombashi tusks weighed heavily on Bastian's chest as he knelt by his father's side. The Selece reached forward and gripped the shaft protruding from Nuratha's fur. With a quick twist, the bolt snapped in half, and Bastian discarded the piece behind him. He stood and walked around to the front of Nuratha's supine form.

In a swift, fluid motion, Bastian rolled forward onto his father's body, latching a hand behind Nuratha's knee. The momentum brought them both up off the ground, leaving the young Selece in a kneeling position, bearing his father's weight on his shoulders. With a grunt, Bastian forced himself to his feet. He trudged six or seven lengths into the cave before making a single turn. Using all the fluid grace he could muster, the Selece slowly sank to one knee, and lowered his father's corpse onto the cave floor.

Bastian rose and walked back to the cave entrance, emerging into the brightness of the morning sun. A yellow glint on the forest floor ahead caught his eye. Padding to the spot, the young Selece knelt slowly. He raked his fingers through the thick grass and clasped the weighty metallic bobble. After pulling his clenched fist from the lush green overgrowth, he unfurled it to reveal a small round brass ornament, polished to a mirror shine, sitting in the center of his paw. The object looked like it should fit inside something, but he wasn't sure what. Upon close examination, he recognized the etching to be a moravian steed with leathery wings shaped like those of the otabi. The creature's etched silhouette was flying away from the backdrop of a sunset. Bastian had not known of a moravian that could fly. Such an enormous beast would need a wingspan many times larger than the otabi. *This is the same emblem from Jorgan's armor,* he speculated, *this came from Jorgan's blade.*

The pile of bodies near the caves entrance rolled and shifted, and a choking sound sputtered from beneath. Bastian tucked the metal piece into a small pouch when a cough rattled off the stone walls, pulling his attention toward the cave's entrance. Something moaned, making no recognizable words in either Sele or Kaanish. The sound was one of pain and torment.

A Kandari female crawled from beneath the other bodies before shifting her weight to prop up on one arm. A rasping cough wheezed and popped with broken breath as the woman spewed saliva and angry words.

Bastian slowly walked over to her. More sounds came, and Bastian halted.

"Kotching... shaat!"

He stood stone still, contemplating the sounds meaning. *The first word is the derogatory for mating. The second word is the derogatory for defecation. How odd. What do those words have to do with each other?*

Bastian's brow furrowed with puzzled curiosity until he looked past the woman to the cave. His father's current resting place. His dead father.

Heat radiated through his core in waves of painful tension rippling through his muscles. Bastian leaned forward, digging the claws of his feet into the ground. He pushed off hard, sprinting toward the newly animated foe.

Bastian closed the distance with a quick stride, his eyes fixed on her one good arm. In a sudden flash, he spun. His foot arced out with deadly precision, smashing against her limb with a bone-jarring impact. Her head cracked against the woodland floor, her senses reeling. When his foot returned to the ground, Bastian was facing away from his victim. With a fluid motion, he arched his back and lifted his legs high into the air. The hulking warrior flipped backward, landing with a grace that defied his massive frame. He hovered over his prey, ready to finish the job.

Her spine popped under the steady pressure of his bent knee pressing into her back, while the fur from his foot brushed against her ribcage where her torn, disheveled clothes left her torso bare. Bastian's hand balled her shoulder-length dark brown hair into a fist and jerked back her head. One claw on his free hand lay still on the opposite side of her neck, ready to be drawn. He pulled his claw across her skin, and the razor-edged tip bit into her flesh. A light trickle of blood beaded from the line separating the top layer of skin.

Bastian's mouth was tight, his voice full of gravel and pain. "Why did you come?"

"I don't..." The effort of responding through a split lip caused her to flinch. "I don't know."

Bastian's hands flexed, and his clawed finger slid closer to her throbbing vein. "Lies!"

The woman shrieked, her face contorting with pain and fear. "The stone! We were supposed to get the stone. Jorgan said we'd get paid in buckets of chen if we got the stone."

"Which stone? Why?" Bastian pressed her, his anger and pain ready to burst through the surface of his control.

"We didn't know. We weren't told. He said that we'll know it when we find it. Just before Jorgan called us out of the cave, we found a glowing yellow stone etched with strange carvings. The men said they're taking it to Jorgan's boss."

Bastian's hand shook. "Who is Jorgan's master?"

The terrified figure collapsed, choking on sobs of agony. "I don't know! I told you everything I know! Everything! Please don't kill me. I have a family."

Bastian's fist clutched her hair so tightly it trembled with pure hatred. He stood, pulling the woman up with him. She hung limp, like a ragdoll getting dragged around by its locks of yarn. Her feet touched solid ground, and she pushed her toes down just enough to take the slightest pressure from her skull.

Immediately, Bastian slogged toward the cave, clutching her scalp while she scrambled to keep up. They walked for what seemed to be an eternity until they rounded a corner. Bastian thrust his hair-entangled paw toward the motionless mountain of muscled-covered fur lying on the stone floor.

"That is my family. That was my father! That was my chief!" The heat of his ominous words echoed off the stone walls. "Who killed him? Was it you? A scrawny little bog skreetch?"

"No, it was Miles." She pointed toward the cavernous exit. "The one on the rocks."

"Yes. Blame the dead man!" The voice was so coated in anger the Kaanish was barely coherent from his snarling muzzle.

"I can show you!" she choked out, gagging on her own saliva.

Bastian lowered his mouth to her ear, and the heat of his heavy breath rippled across her cheek. "Show me."

When he loosened his grip, the woman's hair slipped through his fingers. She tripped at the sudden change, slamming into the floor. The collision caused her right shoulder to pop, sending bursts of pain through her body. A gasp escaped her lips as she held back the tears.

Suddenly, the woman came up in an explosive circle with a small thin blade in her hand. Bastian gracefully retreated. Her next attack was more panicked fury than forethought. She drew her right arm down hard, the shining sliver of steel protruding from the bottom of her clenched fist.

Bastian held up a defensive arm. On contact, he slipped his second arm behind her biceps, clasped his hands together, and wrenched forward. The Kandari woman's entangled arm bent backward at the shoulder with a swift wet crunch. A shrill note of agony exploded from her mouth, overshadowing the metallic rattle of the blade skittering across the floor. The large Selece stepped back, unclenching his hands to allow the mercenary's arm to slide through. His attacker slumped to the floor, her face wet with tears of agony and dread.

Bastian looked down in stoic apathy. "Show me."

The woman's head scraped against the floor, nodding ever so slightly in compliance. Her attempt to push herself up faltered when she put weight on the injured wrist Bastian had kicked earlier. The Kandari slumped forward with her right shoulder sagging against the stone floor. Her mouth tensed, and the only sound she could make was a high-pitched whimper of defeat.

With great care, Bastian slowly placed his hands around her hips. Flinching at his touch, she hesitantly allowed him to lift her to her feet.

"Show me." Bastian's voice echoed from the cave walls, his tone cold and steady.

Fear dripped from her words. "What will you do to me?"

"That rests on what you show me."

The only sounds to be heard were the muffled echoes of their footsteps leaving the cave.

Her arm flopped in Miles' direction. "There. It was him. When he fell, his weapon killed your father." She turned, shifting her gaze to where Nuratha had stood when the arrow had struck. "The Selece—"

Bastian's hand reeled through the air. With a crack, white-hot pain seared across the female mercenary's face. Her body fell under the agony and when she opened her eyes, Bastian's face was in front of hers.

His breath was hot with anger. "His name... was Nuratha."

"Nuratha!" she panted.

"He was the rathan!" The heat of his breath crawled across her face and down her neck. "Rathan Nuratha."

"Rathan Nuratha," she squeaked. Her left arm lurched in the direction where Nuratha had stood. "Rathan Nuratha was standing there when Miles stumbled over my body and the crossbow fired," she sobbed. "I heard the arrow fly and watched Rathan Nuratha fall."

Bastian took a few steps and turned toward the cave's mouth, contemplating the weapon's trajectory. His outstretched claw pointed toward the ground where he'd found his father. Bastian's eyes turned glassy as he was confronted with spectral images of the rathan's last battle. The hulking Selece's shoulders went slack, head nodding in morose affirmation.

"You believe me?"

Chest reverberating with an angry grunt, Bastian regained his composure. "No, you are a lying thief, but I see the truth, even out of the mouth of a swamp skreetch like you."

The woman shivered, fearing the answer to her next question. "What will you do with me now?"

Bastian's gaze fell over her with a level of disgust normally reserved for the smelliest shaat that could come out of an ass. "That will be for Shala to decide."

"Who is Shala?" the terrified voice whispered.

"My mother."

Bastian crouched and began sliding his fingers through the cords that lay on the ground. He worked at them until they became a solid braid of rope. The pain and exhaustion brought her in and out of consciousness as she watched him work. Soon enough, the weight of her fatigue overcame her, and she surrendered to sleep.

6

Reinhardt's eyes opened to the morning sun. A sliver of golden light penetrated the curtains of the eastern balcony. He lay relaxed, the coils of his shoulder-length burnt auburn hair slack on the pillow under his head, his right hand between his head and the pillow, his left occupied by the Lady Ras'Burgess. Her jaw lay firmly against his chest while his fingers traced the edge of her ear before traveling down to the lone jeweled stud adorning her earlobe. His eyes wandered from her raven hair pulled tight into a high bun down to her grey eyes flecked with lilac. He could get lost in the depth of those eyes against her pale skin, but it was her dimples that left him breathless. Every time the corners of her lips drew into a bow, shifting those two points inward, his heart skipped a beat.

"Are you sure you're not just a dream?" she asked, touching the end of his nose with her forefinger, breaking the focus of his intense gaze.

"Why would you ask such a silly thing?" he replied, a light chuckle in his voice.

"Because you only come at night, and you're gone before daybreak." Genuine sorrow crept into her words.

"You know why that is. If there were any other way..." The proper posh accent of his rich medium tenor nearly faltered with sorrow.

"I know." She sat up, gathering the lavender-colored silk sheets around herself, leaving him fully exposed. Her eyes wandered across his bare skin before she glanced away.

Reinhardt occasionally thought to himself that he should feel guilty, but he didn't. If the Lord Ras'Burgess paid more attention to his gardens at home rather than tending to his distant fields, Lady Ras'Burgess wouldn't need to find herself another gardener with a steady plow.

The two lay there, lost in each other's arms for what could have been minutes or hours. A ringing bell echoed through the keep, shattering the calm. First one bell followed by a second and finally, a third sounded. Three bells meant the master was coming into the keep. The pair scrambled.

"I thought he wasn't due back until mid-morning." Reinhardt collapsed to the stone floor, pulling on his maroon leather pants.

"His lordship returns as he does everything else! At his leisure!" she let fly in an exasperated tone. "Here! Now go!"

She flung a grey tunic into his face while he fumbled at his bronze belt buckle. He fastened the sheath of his crescent-hilted dagger to the mirror-polished clasp on his belt. Reinhardt walked toward the balcony, pulling on the tunic and stepping into his black boots. With haste, he climbed down the inlaid sculpture with a proficiency that only came from familiarity. When his feet hit the cobbled road, he looked up at the balcony to meet the duchess' gaze.

"My Lady is so beautiful," he shouted up toward the opening in the keep's stone wall. "She's stolen my heart away."

She quickly turned to rush away from the window.

Walking backward, he continued, "She could turn the darkest night into the brightest day!"

As the last word escaped his lips, his legs reeled out from beneath him. Reinhardt stumbled backward over a stone structure which had escaped his attention, bringing water crashing in around him. The young trelliseer sat up to find himself in the town square's fountain.

The crowd began laughing, but the merriment quickly turned to shock when his disastrous attempt at a boisterous recovery reared a passing horse. Holding onto the reins with a fierce grip, the rider made it to his feet.

Reinhardt again righted himself, planting one foot solidly on the fountain floor while still on one knee. People giggled, watching the water from the fountain's spitting fish splatter squarely on Reinhardt's head. It was as though the great Ashiere themselves had taken the time to piss on him.

From behind, a stern voice cracked like a whip. "In the future, I'd advise you to look in the direction you're traveling, so you're less likely to go astray."

Paying no attention, he stepped from the fountain.

"You! Boy!" snapped the horseman.

Reinhardt turned to find himself faced with a local lord in medium plate armor. There was no battle or tournament this day. He couldn't imagine why anyone would wear such a thing, other than to show it off. With the vestigial shield emblem showing black, red, and silver, he knew this was a lord from house Han'Durial, though which lord was of no concern.

"Apologies, My Lordship, I'll watch better next time." Reinhardt bowed only slightly, showing just enough deference required by his apparent station. The truth was, Reinhardt was a member of House Vos'Korendel and in good standing, but he didn't wear his house colors of black and white trim on a field of blue when he climbed trellises, lest he bring ill repute on his family name.

"Rise you up," barked the noble, lifting his hand.

"Thank you, Lordship." Reinhardt rose and started away.

"I did not dismiss you!" the noble lord spat.

Reinhardt stopped in his tracks.

"I think you could use a lesson in manners before you go."

Reinhardt pleaded, "I assure you that is not necessary, Your Lordship." His eyes averted toward the Lord Han'Durial's feet in feigned deference.

"Oh, but I think it is." The noble lord clicked his tongue against the top of his mouth three times, as though he were calling a pet or contemplating a trivial task.

"Please, Your Lordship, I beg of you—" Reinhardt implored.

"Oh, you'll beg, and you'll learn. You shall have a lesson before you go!" the offended lord scoffed in a condescending tone.

"And who's going to teach me? Is it you?"

Reinhardt stood tall for the first time in his encounter with this local jackal in noble colors. His height was even with the pompous peacock standing before him. He squared his shoulders, remaining calm.

"It will be me indeed." The Lord Han'Durial sneered, taking a step forward.

Both men's eyes flicked about, looking for a color. Would it be red? Yellow? Green? White? Their eyes landed on a yellow silk scarf tied around a flagpole about twenty feet up. Not impossible to post up, but just high enough to make it difficult for authorities to take down. They had ten beats for this incursion. It would take the kalash ten beats to arrive from the time steel rang against steel.

Reinhardt stood relaxed and slowed his breathing, drawing out his breaths like he had done a thousand times before. He unfocused his eyes with his gaze set in the general direction of his opponent, just as his training dictated. The swell of heat crept from Reinhardt's core up to his ears. Time began to adjust, and moments stretched on. His heart pounded like a smith's hammer against the anvil, and the space between beats shifted from moments into minutes. A leaf on the wind blew between the two of them, so slowly he could count the fluttering foliage's veins. His opponent's muscles flexed beneath their shoulder armor, putting a hand to steel.

Beat one. The lord stepped forward, drawing his sword from its scabbard with a slash. The fast strike had tremendous power, but the arc was wrong. *Was this a bluff?* Reinhardt Wondered, *why would he waste time on a feint with only ten beats? Amateur.* Staying stone-still, the blade passed in front of Reinhardt's face two finger-widths from his nose.

Beat two. The Noble's blade soared gracefully through the air, redirecting its way down, and now there were two hands grabbing the handle to add extra power. He directed the vicious two-handed attack at Reinhardt's left side, intending to sweep across his neckline with fatal intention. Too strong to block, Reinhardt would have to deflect. The air hummed around the steel blade, soaring horizontally through the air.

On the same beat, in a single motion, Reinhardt's right hand drew his dagger with the point directed down. His blade's crescent-moon guard intercepted the edge of his opponent's weapon. He lifted his knife, redirecting the sword over his head. His opponent attacked with such force the defensive maneuver threw him off balance, and Reinhardt found himself face to face with the ass of this... ass. What else was there to do but give it a kick? It wasted a beat but needed doing. Reinhardt thrust his foot, landing firmly and sending the lord jolting forward.

Beat four. The furious nobleman turned on Reinhardt. He still gripped the sword, the pommel set back, ready to thrust the blade forward. In the space of a blink, the nobleman changed his hands, gripping just above the weapon's pommel with his right hand. This technique extended his enemy's attack range by a foot or more. It was nearly imperceptible, but nothing was too small to escape Reinhardt's awareness in combat.

This was the reason for the original feint, to make Reinhardt underestimate the length of his enemy's blade. Reinhardt figured his enemy was used to his length disappointing someone.

The blade thrust forward. Before the point was within a foot of Reinhardt's flesh, he stabbed down in its path, locking the hilt of his dagger on the steel's upper edge and pulling it to his right side.

Beat five. Once again surprised by the lack of resistance, his opponent stumbled forward, his blade passing by without ever posing a danger. The nobleman came to a jolting stop when his shins collided with the edge of the stone fountain. To keep himself dry, the noblemen thrust his sword tip against the fountain floor and leaned on it with a sigh of relief.

After turning, Reinhardt found himself face to face with his opponent's hindquarters once again. Being a skilled swordsman, he couldn't resist such a perfect target. Just ask Lady Ras'Burgess.

He slammed his foot forward into his opponent's rear end and listened to the crowd explode in laughter when Lord Han'Durial spilled face first in the fountain, water crashing down around him.

Before the noble's pompous mouth was clear of the water, Reinhardt Vos'Korendel took his leave. He sheathed his dagger while his stomach groaned, hunger pulling at his attention. Moving into the flow of foot traffic along the buildings, the famished rapscallion faded into the flow of foot traffic along the buildings in search of an alehouse to satisfy his hunger.

7

The jostle of traveling through the forest stirred the female mercenary awake. She was slung over Bastian's shoulders like some prized animal to be taken home as a trophy. Allowing her body to stay limp, she silently endured the agonizing pain in her shoulder, made worse by her arm's unnatural position. She flexed the muscles of her legs and feet to find they were not bound tightly, but something prevented them from coming completely apart. The feeling of the rope was just the other side of a tingle. Her legs were numb from lack of use, bad position, or both.

A low rumble reverberated from Bastian's chest. "Your breathing has changed, and it stinks like the breath of a Kandari. I know you're awake."

Bastian tilted forward, releasing the woman from his stiff, fatigued back. When her feet hit the ground, she winced in pain from the pins and needles plaguing them. The Kandari's ankle rolled, forcing a frustrated grunt through her lips. She twisted her face with anger and determination. Fighting against the momentum was no use, and she staggered backward, slamming her spine against a small tree. "That could have been much worse," she groaned, as a look of relief shimmered across her face.

When Bastian pulled on the rope connected to her braided cord binding her hands, she lurched forward. Searing agony radiated from her wrist to her shoulder, and she let out a small, high-pitched bark that turned into a whimper.

Her feet shuffed forward with a heaviness, bound by the elaborate knotwork. A memory flashed through her mind as she recalled the awkwardness of the burlap sack races from her childhood.

Bastian slowed his pace, keeping the tension on the rope constant, and forced his exhausted muscles to push through the ache of overuse.

"We've been walking half a day, and the village is just up ahead." His voice came out in a low dejected growl, forcing its way through teeth clenched together in pain.

She continued playing at the rope around her wrists, internally contemplating her own fate. *Will this creature's mother let me live?*

Minutes passed like hours. Eventually, an arrangement of elevated wooden domes made of thatch-work sticks came into sight as the pair exited the darkness of the dense forest. It was a colossal construction of independent structures, supported by massive tree branches. Webs of interconnected ropes made from vines and other natural fibers connected some sections, while others left her uncertain how anyone could ever reach them.

A roaring howl echoed from a Selece perched on a high tree branch. Those who were diligently minding their own business stopped to watch the incoming travelers. Some rushed over, all with variations of brown and light brown fur coats, covered in an assortment of leathers with different textures and shades of black or variations of brown.

One approached, standing a full head taller than her enormous captor, exchanging low growls randomly intermixed with sounds she was unfamiliar with.

Another Selece came forward, growling at her captor, "Ha Shontha bash. Soth Nuratha. Soth Rathan."

Bastian's eyes landed on the largest Selece, wearing dark tanned leathers over dark brown fur mottled with white patches.

He looked Bastian over. "You look and smell of death. Where is Nuratha? Where is the Rathan?"

Bastian's face went stiff with anger before he regained control and relaxed his visage. "Shothun, I need to speak to Mother. Soth Shala?"

The large Selece's face frowned with a worried anger. "She is in the spirit hut, awaiting your return with your father."

Bastian's words came out hard and fast. "Ready the council. They will be needed when she calls."

Shothun became indignant. "Only the rathan or rathana can call the council, boy. You know that!"

The large Selece's gaze fell to the ombashi tusk necklace on Bastian's chest.

Bastian glared at the hulking figure. "She will call the council. You tell them to be ready."

Bastian continued towards the trees, absent-mindedly clenching the rope in his hand. The sudden jerking motion caused the Kandari woman to cry out and stumble forward. Her limp made it a useless effort to try to catch up through the distress, but she had no other options.

Remembering he was pulling an injured beast; Bastian slowed his pace; *She won't talk if she's dead,* he considered, *then she'll be of no use to anyone.*

Bastian passed by one of the female Selece cubs and addressed her in a soft snarl, "Chuuna, go to the spirit hut and tell the rathana that I have returned. Ask her to meet me at our shelter."

The small creature stumbled back, eyes wide. In a blink, the Selece cub turned to race forward in a blur so quick, Bastian's prisoner gasped in surprise. The small, fur-covered Selece hit the massive tree trunk and went vertical like an insect crawling up a wall. She spiraled around the base of the tree before disappearing like the setting sun at twilight.

Bastian and his captive slogged on despite the pain and exhaustion. The Selece kept his eyes pointed mostly skyward while the pair continued trudging around the tree.

Bastian stopped suddenly, motioning to the woman to come closer. "Up." His voice came with no inflection.

Her face shifted in confusion, and the question chirped out like a cough. "Up?"

"Get on my shoulders, we're going up there." He pointed to the canopy above.

"And if I refuse?" Her words rang with false bravado.

Bastian's visage remained ominously calm. "I cut your throat where you stand, and the young ones feast, picking the meat from your bones."

She relented to her captor's demands with a submissive expression of defeat betraying her pride. She cried out in a chirping gasp as Bastian slung her over his shoulders. With an exhausted sigh, she settled into place.

Bastian's left shoulder was tight against the center of her body between her legs. She moaned in anguish, her mind racing with possibilities of what would happen next.

Bastian ran at the tree, his claws sinking in while he made his way upward to the first branch. She jostled about with her body affixed to the large Selece, ascending the ancient tree. He moved along the branch until he clutched a hanging vine. Gripping it tightly, he his feet pushed off the bark's rough wooden surface. The pair soared through the air in an arc. When Bastian's feet found another branch, he released the vine. It stuck to the branch, adhering by some unseen force. Bastian sprinted to the tree trunk and climbed to the next set of branches. There hung another tangled set of intersecting rope vines.

Supported by the massive vines and two immense tree branches was a domed hut made of thatch-work walls held together by a thick twine rope. The dome reminded her of a large bird nest, primarily constructed of large interwoven sticks the width of her thumb knit so tightly a sliver of light couldn't peek through.

Bastian continued toward the hut. When they entered, he

shifted left, leaning over until she stood steady on the thatch-work floor. She shuffled her feet around to acclimate herself to the structure's sturdy yet flexible flooring. Uncertain where to go, she inched back to a corner.

Standing in what appeared to be the cooking area, she remained statuesque, while her eyes flickered about. A collection of stones held smoldering coals within them. Over that stood four thin stone pillars locked into the floor, supporting a stone cooking slab. In the middle of the room sat a dining table. It was an assemblage of planks interlocked together with a few strategically placed wooden dowels. At its base were two pairs of wooden crosses, just thicker than her upper arm, lashed together with fibrous rope. The two crosses intersected each other and used the tabletop's weight to interlock themselves into a stand.

Light footsteps and whispered throaty growls came from beyond the door. Three large figures entered. The closest silhouette walked forward to reveal a lean, elegant form with supple muscles rippling under a coat of light brown fur, highlighted by waves of dark brown shimmering across its body. Finely crafted leathers covered the creature's pronounced breasts and nether region, indicating to the prisoner that this Selece was female. The mercenary's throat tightened, stomach churning, and her heart raced at the realization she was facing her captor's mother.

Shala looked to Bastian before her gaze fell toward the bound Kandari woman behind him. Glancing around quickly, his mother's nose turned up. The sound of growling snorts rumbled from her nostrils, followed by one long inhale.

Shala looked at Bastian's right hand. Taking it into her own, she raised it to her nose. With great effort, she drew in a lung full of air, overwhelming herself with the fragrant essence infused within. Immediately, her breath went ragged as realization set in.

Shala took a step back to observe the scene before her. Her eyes went to the ombashi necklace sitting on Bastian's chest. They then flicked to the corner of the room at the Kandari prisoner, standing the height of an adolescent Selece. Her fur stood on end, ears back. The sound of tendons crackling beneath the Selece's thick hide was audible over the silence, followed by a deafening roar. The Selece's eyes turned glass and a stream of water flowed down the fur on either side of her pink and black nose.

A second deafening roar tore through the room, engulfing the Kandari in the heat of Shala's palpable anger. Reverberating within her chest, the sound consumed her. With a sudden pop inside her left ear, the prisoner collapsed, clutching at the side of her head, clenching her eyes shut. A piercing ring consumed her senses when she became overwhelmed by the feeling of a red-hot poker skewering the side of her head through her ear. Time passed, turning the searing pain into a dull ache. When the Kandari opened her eyes, all the Selece were gone save for her captor.

The female mercenary collected herself into a submissive pose on the rough thatch-work wooden floor, digging into the skin on her knees. Her own face twisted into a visage of suffering and sorrow. Her eyes welled up, overcome by the realization of what she'd done.

"I'm so sorry. I just need... There was... My..." Each word was broken by sobs. She continued choking out the beginning of a sentence that her sorrow would not allow her to finish.

Bastian looked down in disgust. "Sorry that you've been captured, or sorry that you took something precious from someone else? Something irreplaceable." The words came out with the calm heat of a creature ready to kill.

"Why am I still alive?" she whimpered.

"The council will decide what to do with you." Bastian stepped back to give the prisoner room to regain her feet.

Her deferential gaze remained averted to the floor. "I thought you said your mother would decide my fate."

Bastian nodded. "All in due time." Gesturing to his neck, he added, "Up."

"Fine," came the exasperated voice from the floor. "Where to now?"

The woman shambled to her feet. The rope binding her ankles together left a foot of slack between them, with intricate knot work on each ankle, not unlike fibrous manacles. Without the use of her hands for balance, she stumbled slightly over the rope at her feet. The rope between her wrists and her captor's clenched fist snapped tight, preventing her fall. She winced at the burst of pain shooting through her elbow and up her arm.

Bastian's steady gaze remained cold and stoic. "Up."

Bastian leaned to hoist her up, and the woman sighed at what was now an all-too-common experience of the Selece's shoulder in her guts. Moments later, he stood upright, throwing her over his shoulders with the ease of a woman putting on a shawl for a dinner party. A very savage dinner party.

Departing the hut, he climbed the tree until he found a branch. They were so high in the air, her stomach fluttered when she looked down. The woman jostled about while her captor climbed the trunk, swung from vines, and traversed branches to continue their ascent. Her eyes remained squeezed tight until they were still for more than a moment.

When she opened her eyes, they were in another hut. This one had no rooms and was secured by vines. There were no tree branches beneath, only the tree's trunk far out of reach with a set of branches high above, holding the vines suspending her aerial prison.

Bastian's voice came out quick. "Stay here until I come and get you."

He looked around, glancing from the floor to the ground

below. A hint of sympathy flashed across his face on her behalf at the realization she would have no other choice unless she suddenly grew wings or claws. Bastian gestured with his hands to reinforce his expression, implying her only option was to do as she was told.

The female Kandari walked into the room and collapsed from fatigue. The last thing she saw was Bastian's silhouette vanishing from the doorway. Her eyes went out of focus, and the all-encompassing darkness of exhaustion consumed her consciousness.

Bastian descended from the isolation loft and made for the spirit hut. Before entering, he placed his hands together in front of his heart and touched the tips of his longest fingers to the center of his forehead. "Ancestors hear me," he silently whispered in reverence while walking through the door.

He entered the structure, twice the size of his family's hut. At least two dozen male and female Selece surrounded his mother. She lifted her nose with a snort, and her eyes snapped to him. Shala's sadness transformed into anger, then gave way to sympathetic sorrow. With a sigh, her gaze softened. Her arms opened to her little cub with the world's weight suddenly thrust upon his shoulders.

After padding his way over to her, Bastian navigated through the host of kneeling bodies. She embraced him softly, and their bodies became a mingled mass of fur and sounds of sorrow. They stayed locked in the same position, only shifting their heads to allow room for the continuous flow of tears. Moments stretched on and on until a quarter day had passed and their well of tears ran dry.

Shala pulled her head back, regarding her young one softly. "Come now. Tell us what happened. Was she responsible?" Her voice came out firm and smooth.

Bastian's face turned down, shifting his eyes up to his mother.

"She was with the pack of Kandari that felled Father, not the one to strike him down."

A voice yipped out, filled with gravel from old age, "Come now. What happened? Start from the beginning."

Shala's head whipped around toward the gibbering source. Her eyes landed on Elder Nathenga, who immediately averted his gaze. She turned back to Bastian with a soft, low purr. "Come now. From the beginning."

Bastian's voice came out hard from exhaustion as he recounted the events resulting in his father's death and the loss of the spirit stone.

At the mention of the Spirit Stone, the elders gasped.

A voice barked. "Without it, we can't contact the ancestors!"

"Without their guidance, we're all lost!" another pleaded.

"We are aware!" Shala snarled, glaring around the room. "And the woman?" She turned her gaze back to her son. "What was her part in it?"

Bastian looked up toward the Kandari woman's prison. "She was one of those in the cave that surprised Father. She came from the cave with the others and attacked. Father struck her and left her unconscious. I thought she was dead until she stirred. I took her to show her father's body so she could see what she had done."

"My sweet, sweet cub. The wonder that **is** your father... will not be found in his eternally resting body, but in the vitality of his people." Shala looked into Bastian's eyes, sorrow overcoming her face. "Where is your father's body now?"

"Inside the Kaitan caves," Bastian whimpered.

Shala looked to a corner of the room. "Cherith, go to Shothun. Tell him to recover Nuratha's body from the caves." Shala looked at Bastian, raising an inquisitive eyebrow.

Bastian cleared his throat. "You can track it from the cave's entrance. It's only seven or eight lengths into the cave and around a corner."

Shala looked back at Cherith and spoke with graceful authority. "Go."

In a blur, the messenger bolted out the door, dark brown fur whipping in the wind.

A wave of hushed murmurs rippled through those still present.

Shala's head rose as she addressed the elders, "I call for a gathering of the council of elders."

"On what matters?" came the voice from Elder Nathenga in an official tone.

"First, on the matter of acknowledging our new rathan."

An interruption came from the back. "He doesn't have a mate. Who would the rathana be?"

"And he hasn't even officially completed the chagontha yet. There is no new ombashi tusk on the necklace," another faceless voice growled.

Others murmured silently in agreement.

The rathana's low growl swept the room. "These are difficult times, but Jareth is gone and left no heir. Nuratha is gone, leaving a single heir created under the full Evening Moon of Ashara with the rathan and his mate, the rathana. Bastian is the heir and will have a quest far greater than the chagontha to complete. He has the spirit quest of the ashagontha to complete. He must retrieve the Spirit Stone, and he must be the rathan to do it, for only the rathan can touch the Spirit Stone."

The crowd began mumbling in disagreement.

Shala's hand flashed through the air, pulling the ombashi necklace from Bastian's chest. The thin leather strip securing the piece gave way. She held it out toward Elder Aganshi. "Do you want to travel to find the Spirit Stone and retrieve it?"

The elder cowered in fear, submitting to her dominance.

She held her hand toward the remaining elders. "Do any of you?" She padded over to Elder Thamenga. Speaking softly, she placed the ombashi necklace in his hands. "Then I expect you to acknowledge our new rathan at dusk because with no Spirit Stone, we are lost, and with no rathan to complete the ashagontha, there will be no Spirit Stone. I will continue to be your rathana until I am finished educating Shamira on her future duties. As your rathana, I will lead our people in the rathan's absence, until Bastian returns with the Spirit Stone to take his place and be bound to his mate."

"They must be bound before he goes," Elder Aganshi chattered.

Bastian's soft baritone came out with an air of authority. "Elders, I appreciate your concern, but in these challenging times, there is no way for us to balance all the traditions. Each one conflicts with another because our ancestors, in their wisdom, did not plan for this. I wish nothing more than to be bound to Shamira, but we must put our tribe before our desires. My father's last words, Rathan Nuratha's last words, were clear. Save the Spirit Stone to save our people. We will hold those words above our blind obedience to tradition, lest that tradition leads us all over a cliff."

A hushed murmur of agreement swept the room.

"What other business have you for the council?" came Elder Thamenga's voice.

"I seek justice for the death of my husband, our rathan, Nuratha. I seek the council's wisdom in deciding the fate of the one who helped murder my husband, Rathan Nuratha."

The elders in the room nodded in consensus, murmuring in agreement.

"Finally, I ask the council to confirm the ashagontha and send our new rathan on the spirit quest to save our people. These are my reasons for calling the council of elders."

Elder Thamenga let out a low toned guttural sound. All eleven council members raised their hands, with his own making twelve.

"At dusk, we decide the fate of our people and the fate of the Kandari prisoner."

The elders shuffled around the room, meandering about.

Shala padded back over to Bastian and pulled him close for a warm embrace. The mother and son made their way to the door and descended. When they arrived at the front door of their hut, Shamira was waiting on a branch just outside. Consumed with grief, Shala ambled towards the door, oblivious to the girl's presence.

The Selece girl dropped to one knee in submission. "Rathana, my humblest to you."

Shala peered down at the girl with a warm gaze of sincere affection. "Shamira, you look and smell nice, and your thoughts are appreciated. I will leave you two to speak." Shala continued into the hut.

Bastian looked at Shamira. "My father has fallen, and now I'm to be the rathan."

Shamira pulled her fingers across her cheek to wipe the tears from her fur-covered face. "I heard. I've cried for hours over what our tribe has lost." She looked at Bastian with a gentle consideration. "What you have lost." The girl hesitated before choking out the next question stuck in her throat, "What will become of us?"

Bastian gazed down with an air of authority until the appearance of exhaustion broke through in his demeanor. "My mother will show you the ways of the rathana. When I return from the ashagontha, we will be bound." He took Shamira's hand into his own. He turned her palm skyward and licked it gently. "You have claimed me, and I have won your heart. I am yours, but now I must comfort my mother."

The Selece girl, just one cycle younger than Bastian, gave an understanding nod. Shamira walked backward along the tree branch, keeping her eyes locked on his, before dropping out of sight.

Once in the hut, Bastian entered the room where his mother lay sound asleep. Her bedding was a round sack constructed from a collection of stitched animal hides filled with crushed dried hay and straw.

The young Selece silently prowled over to nestle himself within his mother's embrace. She lay behind him with his back to her, her arms limp over his torso.

Bastian's words came out in a whisper. "What will you do with her?"

In a voice just this side of sleep, she breathed, "That is a question for tomorrow. Now is for dreaming of brighter days and sweeter nights."

The pair lay in a soft embrace as sleep took them.

8

A gravel baritone broke the silence within the thick darkness of her suspended wooden prison. "It is time."

Before her was the all-too-familiar silhouette of her captor, the son of the fallen rathan. His form filled the doorway of her aerial prison cell.

The Kandari woman rose to her feet entirely without the use of her hands or arms, which was challenging on the hut's thatch-work floor. With a relenting sigh, she positioned herself the best she could, knowing what came next.

Bastian's motion was quick and predictable enough to ease some discomfort. In a single motion, she was on his shoulders, and moments later, they were bounding through the trees. Her arm became swollen while she rested, turning the pain into agony now that the exhilaration of battle had completely cleared her head.

The two landed at the edge of a dark clearing. Bastian leaned forward, placing her on her feet. She stayed statuesque, observing all she could through the darkness to find her bearings. In the dusk's shimmering twilight, the elders knelt to form a semi-circle, each remaining two lengths from a large, polished stone. The centerpiece was half the height of a Selece and the width of a wine barrel. Most of it was matte orange, shimmering into swirls of iridescent yellow from its base to the smooth flat top.

The Kandari prisoner played at her ropes, to no avail. Thyrian sailors couldn't tie knots this tight.

The Evening Moon came over the horizon of the black forest. When the first rays of silver light pierced the surrounding woodland canopy to touch the stone, the drums echoed low and deep, resonating off the tree line. Between the four drummers, a huge bonfire roared to life. They played slowly, each keeping a unique rhythm. Every tone formed a thread in the fabric of a larger, harmonious tapestry, as ominous as it was beautiful. The Kandari prisoner observed a Selece elder with poor posture, amble to the middle of the circle. When he touched the stone, the playing stopped, and the echoes rumbling off the trees faded to a dense stillness.

Bastian looked on, watching Elder Thamenga walk forward to touch the stone of Theshal. The elder's fingers touched the stone, and the playing stopped. When the echoes died down, the elder spoke. "This gathering of elders has been called by Rathana Shala, and we are to address her three matters." The elder gestured to the rathana.

Shala gracefully entered the circle with an unmistakable air of authority. Elder Thamenga stepped back from the rathana's path. She laid her hand on the stone.

Looking forward to addressing the elders, she said, "I have come seeking acknowledgement of the new rathan. I have come seeking justice for my husband, the fallen rathan. I have come beseeching the elders to send the rathan on the ashagontha spirit quest to save our people." Shala stepped back.

Elder Thamenga moved forward toward the stone. Placing his hand firmly on the stone, the elder's voice sounded. "Regarding the new rathan's acknowledgement, who here is in dispute?"

One hand raised, and Elder Aganshi made his way forward to the stone. Elder Thamenga relinquished his control of the stone, permitting Elder Aganshi to make contact and voice his concerns.

"We should be concerned with acknowledging a rathan who has not yet completed the chagontha."

The elder's hands traded places, allowing Elder Thamenga to reply. "Can the Selece tribe of Theshal survive without the Spirit Stone? Or any Selece anywhere?"

Elder Aganshi placed his hand on the stone. "No."

Their hands shifted again, and Elder Thamenga continued, "Do you, Elder Aganshi, have a way to save our people without making Bastian the new and rightful rathan?"

Again, Elder Aganshi gripped the stone. "No."

Elder Thamenga's hand would have pushed the other out of the way if it hadn't moved swiftly enough. Saliva coursed through the air, accompanying his words. "Who among you finds merit in Elder Aganshi's objection?"

Bastian looked around to observe the elder's stillness, hands remaining at their side.

"I propose we acknowledge Bastian as the new and rightful rathan. Rise if you agree."

Every elder stood to their feet save for Elder Aganshi, who retook his seated position.

Elder Thamenga regarded Bastian, hand remaining firm on the stone. "Come and be acknowledged."

Bastian moved with a commanding grace, nearly rivaling his mother's, but the effortless majesty he exuded hinted at the need for more practice. The elder's hands slid away from the stone. Bastian rested his paw on the stone, lowering himself to kneel before it.

The elder reverently hung the ornate string of ombashi tusks around Bastian's neck before fastening the two ends together with a solid knot. He clutched Bastian's shoulders respectfully before breaking the silence with the other elders. "Asha rathan! Asha rathan! Asha rathan!"

The new rathan stood tall, and the elders all knelt reverently. Bastian's gaze settled on Elder Aganshi, who was kneeling but with less enthusiasm than the rest. *One day,* he mused, *you will see.*

Bastian withdrew from the circle, relinquishing the stone to Elder Thamenga. He then made his way towards the Kandari prisoner.

From behind him, the Selece elder spoke once again. "Next is the matter of justice for Nuratha. Shala, what do you seek?"

Shala moved forward to place her hand on the stone. "I seek the life of this Kandari woman. I wish the right to do with her as I please and the authority to prevent the interference of any other Selece." She stepped back, relinquishing the stone to Elder Thamenga.

His words came swiftly, with the rasp of old age. "All opposed?"

All eyes fell on Elder Sheranti with her hand in the air. She made her way to the stone and placed her hand on it. "If we seek vengeance, then we should all agree now. If it is justice we seek, then we should hear the prisoner first." She reached her hand out to the Kandari prisoner, beckoning her to step forward.

The woman standing just one length from the circle looked on with uncertainty.

Bastian's commanding voice came soft, but it was not a suggestion. "Go."

With her gait restricted by the rope connecting her ankles, she hobbled toward the center stone within the circle. Her muscles were hesitant to move, constricted by the fear running through her mind and the ache of her current condition.

The Elder Selece woman took the prisoner's left hand, placing it on the stone. She winced in agony at the swell of pain stabbing through her wrist.

Kaanish words came from the elder's mouth in a growling rasp. "You speak." Gently, the elder removed the woman's hand and replaced it with her own. "I speak." She reached over and grabbed Elder Thamenga's hand. Slapping it on the stone, she pointed at him with a stern finger. "Shaat for brains speaks."

Swallowing a laugh, the Kandari woman let slip the tiniest cough. She couldn't help but notice Elder Thamenga's disapproving stare in Elder Sheranti's direction.

Thamenga, hand still on the stone, croaked out a Sele growl. "Watch what you say! This is an official—"

Elder Sheranti swatted the old Selece's hand away, replacing it with her own. The Kaanish words came out in a warble, and her eyes went overly large, wobbling her head from side to side. "I'm sorry, old shaat for brains!"

Overtaken by the inevitability of her fate, the Kandari woman belched out a laugh. The absurdity of the situation struck her like a barbarian mace. There she was, laughing in the face of the beasts who were about to put her to death. Reason scattered like ashes in the wind, her emotions erupted forth like a dam bursting under the weight of a flood. Overcome with laughter, each jostle of her diaphragm reverberated through her torso, causing something to hurt, but she no longer cared. She carried on for what seemed like a lifetime.

"Silence," Shala snapped in Kaanish.

Everything went still in the wake of her authority, resonating through the evening air. For a moment, Shala and Elder Sheranti glared into each other's eyes. Their shoulders shifted and their brows flexed ever so slightly until Shala's face softened in submission. She graciously dipped her head just slightly to Elder Sheranti. The elder gently padded back to her place in the circle and resumed her position.

Shala looked down on the prisoner. "Do you understand?" Authority from the rathana's supple voice rode the silence. She removed her hand from the stone, looking down at the prisoner expectantly.

The Kandari placed a hand on the stone, hastily chirping, "Yes."

The rathana laid her hand on the stone. "What is your name?"

"Why does it matter? Just get it over with and kill her!" someone barked out in Sele from Elder Aganshi's side of the circle.

Shala gazed toward the sound. "You will respect the stone or remove yourself, and I will know the name of the beast that killed my husband."

She snapped her head toward a cough that came from Elder Sheranti. Shala took a thoughtful breath, looked back at the Kandari woman, and gestured at the stone.

The female Kandari prisoner placed her hand on the stone. Two syllables escaped her mouth in a defeated murmur. "Teulah." She cleared her throat gently and repeated, "My name is Teulah." Her hand slid from the stone. She attempted not to further aggravate her injuries with limited success.

Shala infused her ice-cold words with restrained hatred. The Selece monarch laid her hand on the stone, gaze locked on Teulah, the Kandari mercenary. "Why were you at the caves?"

Once Shala withdrew her own, Teulah lugged her hand back onto the stone. "Jorgan promised me chen. Lots of chen." Her voice shook. "In exchange, we were supposed to get a special stone. He didn't give us any more information except that we would know it when we saw it."

Shala's hand reached for the stone, swiping Teulah's hand away. Teulah gasped at the surge of pain shooting up her forearm. A smirk of satisfaction grew on Shala's face. The rathana's ear flicked at a rasping cough from the circle of elders, beckoning her to be gracious. *I hear you Elder Sheranti*, Shala brooded, *please allow me this moment of primal satisfaction.* She wished the old Selece could hear her thoughts.

"What part did you play in the death of Rathan Nuratha?" The question hung in the air, like the darkness of a new moon.

The two stared hard at each other for a long moment before their eyes respectively glassed over, Shala because of what she'd lost and Teulah because of what she'd taken.

Their hands, once again, exchanged control of the stone. All eyes focusing on Teulah grew wider with each word. "Rathan Nuratha encountered intruders on his land attacking his son. I was one of those intruders. I moved in and attacked Rathan Nuratha. He quickly defeated me, but it gave others time to overwhelm him." Her eyes swelled with moisture before the drops became too heavy. With the falling of her first tear, a dam broke from within the guilt-stricken woman. A shower of tears fell like rain. She hit her knees and spoke through sobbing gasps. "I know I don't deserve your forgiveness, but know that whatever happens, I know I was wrong. I know I took something from you that cannot be replaced. I know I was wrong."

Shala's eyes fell on Elder Thamenga.

The old man popped his hand onto the stone, quickly barking. "Any objections?"

All the elder Selece in the circle sat stone-still.

Bastian entered the circle and hunched down next to the Kandari prisoner. "Come." He pulled Teulah to her feet before firmly leading her beyond the circle's edge.

"To the next matter then," Elder Thamenga continued. "The Spirit Stone has been taken and, with it, the ability to contact our ancestors in Ashara. Their wisdom has proven critical in helping to guide our people for as many moons as I have hairs. Without the stones, that wisdom is lost. Without the stone, our tribes are lost." The elder maintained contact with the stone of Theshal, his predatory eyes roaming across his audience, looking for weakness. "We all understand that the rathan's place is here with his people.

He and the rathana together lead and protect our tribe, but there are times when the quest set before them is of greater importance to our people than their presence among us. According to the elder spirits, this is when the elders must call for the ashagontha." Thamenga's back straightened, and his chin lifted in pride. "To recover the Spirit Stone, I call for the ashagontha. Who amongst us is opposed?"

Elder Sheranti rose and walked to the circle's center. The old Selece, with his hand still on the stone, looked on in contempt at the elder female making her way to the center. His eyes demanded her silence, but she appeared not to notice or care about his disapproval.

Her hand gently replaced his, and she spoke. "I call for the ashagontha to retrieve the Spirit Stone." Elder Thamenga's eyes went wide with confusion as she added, "And to retrieve the reason it was taken."

Murmurs of agreement flowed through the circle of elders.

"We all know the Spirit Stone can only be touched by the rathan or the rathana. If it is of no use to the Kandari, then why did they take it? We must know the reason." Looking around the circle, she sensed no disapproval. Her eyes gaped in mock surprise, falling upon Elder Thamenga as though she didn't expect to see him standing there. "Who contests the ashagontha?"

The elders remained still.

Thamenga's hand gently covered that of Elder Sheranti, his fingers resting in the empty spaces between hers. "We, then, call upon the rathan to pursue the ashagontha. He will retrieve the Spirit Stone and the reason it was taken."

Elder Sheranti gestured to Bastian. The new rathan shifted his torso into a posture of pride before padding into the circle.

Elder Thamenga addressed him, "Do you understand the tasks before you?"

"I do." Bastian looked down upon the elders, their hands

together on the stone, each standing half a head beneath him, the natural consequence of age and fatigue.

Elder Sheranti looked up at the young new leader. "You understand the risks and accept them willingly?"

Bastian's eyes hardened. "I do," he said, considering the risks of failing the ashagontha.

Each elder placed a hand on one of Bastian's shoulders before their voices let out a synchronous echo. "Then go, and may Ashana guide you and Ashara bless you."

Sheranti pulled her hand from the stone and returned to her space in the circle.

Elder Thamenga's voice rang out. "She who called us, please come forward." He waited for Shala to pad over to the stone of Theshal and looked up at the rathana. "Have all your matters been addressed?"

Shala nodded, placing her hand on the stone. "Yes, all of my matters have been addressed." Her eyes swept across the circle before bowing her head in reverence. "Elders, I thank you for gathering this day. Your responsibility to our people has been met."

On her last word, the drums sounded and the Theshal elders rose to their feet. The council members all ambled in different directions, dispersing the circle. The drums' echo faded into the layers of the surrounding forest.

Elders Thamenga and Sheranti treaded intersecting paths. When they were within reach of each other, their fingers interlaced as they walked past Bastian.

"Chormish stew for morning meal?" Thamenga inquired.

"Do you even have to ask?" Elder Sheranti's hand slid gently around Thamenga's arm while they strolled side by side.

Shala approached Teulah. "You will come with me." Suffused with stoic tranquility, her silken voice possessed only a hint of a growl.

Teulah was visibly taken aback at hearing the melodious Kaanish language come from the Selece's mouth.

"What will happen to me?" Teulah stood in the bonfire's light, a slight squint to her eyes as she tried to obscure the flames from her line of sight.

Stoic indifference saturated Shala's next words. "Whatever I want."

Bastian made some guttural sounds toward his mother while pointing at Teulah's shoulder, which Shala casually waved off. Before Teulah was aware, the Selece woman had her arms around the woman's midsection in a feral embrace. The rathana threw Teulah over her shoulder like you would a baby you're trying to burp but don't much care for. The pair of them disappeared around the tree trunk.

Shamira walked toward Bastian from between the crowd. When she was within arm's length, she knelt in deference.

He lightly placed his finger under her chin, and she rose at the beckoning of his gentle touch. "No, my future rathana. You bow to no one."

She slowly wrapped her fingers around his hand. Bringing it to her mouth, she lightly licked the center of his palm. They stood exchanging a gentle stare until her gaze became curious.

Shamira's voice filled the silence. "What is the risk the elders spoke of?"

Bastian gazed down, every word carefully chosen. "If I don't complete the ashagontha..." His voice broke.

Her eyes went wide with understanding. "You can't return?" Fear quickly turned to heated anger, and she snarled. "Why? How? What are they thinking? Why would they do this?"

Bastian pulled her head into his chest. "If I don't succeed, we're all lost. If I fail, there will be nothing to return to."

The two stood clasped in a gentle embrace under the brilliance of a breaking dawn.

9

The morning sun shone through the dome's kitchen window. Shala toiled over a pile of fruits and vegetables, dicing them into bits while Teulah sat observing from the corner. Her arm throbbed with heat after the way the rathana had bundled her on the trip to the dome hut.

The boiling pot on the stone slab blooped and blurped while Shala dropped pieces of diced vegetation into the water.

Eventually, Teulah's voice pierced the silence. "Why am I still alive?"

The words hung in the air between them long enough to grow stale. She continued gazing up at her new captor, unsure of what to expect.

"Because I wish it." Shala's voice snapped quickly with a soft lilt over a harsh growl.

"Can I ask why?" Teulah rubbed her shoulder to ease out the ache, but it was no use.

"I want to kill you. It is what you deserve, but if I kill you, you will never truly understand the severity of your actions. You would never come to know what you've taken from our people." Shala continued chopping and dropping pieces into the pot. "If you were a Selece, your eyes would be ripped from your head, and you would be made to wander the lands. With no eyes, all would know you were exiled, and the ombashi would find you and kill you."

"Ombashi?" The word came out of Teulah's mouth with a curious tone.

"The bringer of death living in the forest. There has been only one struck by the ombashi tusk who lived. The tusk's poison turns their prey's insides to liquid. The ombashi then hovers over its prey, a slender..." Shala paused to find the word. "Vine? Comes down from the ombashi. The vine connects to the victim's chest, and it feeds."

A gust of wind blowing through the door accompanied a hulking form bolting into the hut. Once inside, Bastian swept his gaze across the room, hardly acknowledging Teulah's presence as he fixed his attention on his mother. It was as if the entire world had faded away, leaving only the two of them. "I need to leave now." Authority and confidence resonated in his words.

That authority cracked and fell flat against her response. "You will rest."

Bastian's look was infused with supplication. "I need to go now. The Kandari and their people have already gained a significant lead."

Teulah's eyes flicked between the two Selece, listening to them growl back and forth. They continued the snarling exchange, their body postures constantly shifting, like two beasts competing for a piece of raw meat. Eventually, she watched Bastian's form became submissive in compliance.

"Too many traditions have already been broken," Shala declared. "We will hold to this, and you will use the time to feed and rest. The ashagontha will begin at dusk, as always. You leave when the drums call!"

Bastian's mother sliced furiously at the vegetables while the boiling water in the cooking pot rolled. She grabbed a wooden bowl from the wicker countertop near her cutting board. Taking it to the pot, she filled it with a steaming helping of mixed fruits and vegetables. Shala sat the vegetables down in front of Bastian while he obstinately stood behind the chair. Turning her head, she narrowed her feral eyes in his direction. In that one look, he relented. Bastian pulled the chair out and sat down. A clump of white fur stained red, sat next to the vegetables.

Bastian looked down at the raw meat. "No eshuthi?" He stared at the food curiously.

"There is no time to gather eshuthi." His mother continued cooking with a sigh.

Bastian dug in with purpose, tearing into the fur-covered meat with his teeth. Between taking bites of the meat, he devoured bits of steaming vegetables from the bowl. He stopped occasionally to take a drink of water, helping the meal down.

Once the meat was gone and the bowl was empty, Bastian stood. The chair scuffed back across the thatch-work floor. He used his forearm to wipe the excess from his muzzle. "I will rest until the drums call."

Shala moved over to him and nuzzled the side of her muzzle against his. The two stood for a long moment before she enveloped him in a maternal embrace. A nearly invisible exchange occurred between them. Pain, sorrow, gratitude, and understanding, each breath accompanied by a shift in their mutual tension. In that stillness, mother and son communed in solace. In that timeless exchange, they shared thoughts and feelings in a way ten thousand words would have failed to convey.

When the embrace dissolved, Bastian retreated to the hammock in his bedroom. The warm light from the late morning sun coming through the window brightened his fur. In the stillness, every twist or turn caused his injuries to ache and joints to groan. The breeze carried the scent of sweet flowers over a savory musk of ripe berries.

Bastian awoke to the sound of drums roaring through the forest, touching the spirit of all in their wake.

Bastian stood up from his hammock and made his way into the kitchen. There his mother stood on the far side of the table where the two chagontha boxes rested. Behind her stood the new servant, Teulah.

Bastian and his mother each approached the chagontha chests. After adjusting the lid's wooden toggles, they opened their respective boxes. In Bastian's box was the pair of chatta. The young Selece chieftain wrapped his fingers around the handles before sliding them into the straps on his thighs. When he closed the lid, his mother reached out and handed him his bow. Bastian took the bow and casually held it down to his side.

Bastian's face went wide with a memory of something forgotten, and he bolted back to his room. When he returned, he was wearing his arrow quiver over his right shoulder, the arrows just within reach of his right hand.

The three of them exited through the doorway in single file. Bastian moved freely while his mother was bound to carry the Kandari, rendered helpless by her injuries.

Bastian reached the edge of the stone circle, recently consecrated by the elders for the ashagontha. He stood quietly, looking around the gathering of elders standing solemnly around the circle. Other Selece looked on, speaking in hushed whispers. Shala softly padded up behind Bastian. Teulah followed, being led by an invisible chain of guilt and sorrow.

"Be careful, my son, but come back to us. To me." Shala's visage remained stone save for her eyes. Moisture crept into them like a lake of sorrow fed by a stream of fear.

Teulah's words came out awkwardly, breaking the silent tension between the pair. "I should go with him. I could show—"

Shala's hand whipped through the air, cutting off Teulah's words. The rathana's claws froze a hair's width from the Kandari's cheek, a simple demonstration of her authority and potential for violence. "No, he must go alone."

"Besides, if you came with me," Bastian added. "I might make the mistake of trusting you."

"But I could help you find Jorgan and his employer." Teulah

looked on with a meek disposition and no attempt to hide her sincere regret and shame for her actions.

"You see, I'm already making that mistake. You'll stay here and see to the rathana's needs. I must do this alone." Bastian fiddled at the feathered ends of the arrows resting in his quiver.

Shala took a sharp breath and exhaled slowly. "You are Rathan of the Theshal Selece from the north. I know you will not fail our tribe." His mother looked upon him with a stoic tranquility. For a brief moment, she closed her eyes, embracing this cub who was so small only a few moons ago. When she opened them, her arms were empty and the young rathan was padding confidently into the circle.

Bastian approached the two elders standing at the circle's edge. They represented the pillars he would walk between to begin his journey.

Elder Thamenga spoke first. "Do you accept the responsibility of the ashagontha?"

Bastian regarded the elder with a swift nod.

"Do you accept the risk of failing the ashagontha?"

Bastian's head turned to face Elder Sheranti, and he gave her a sharp nod.

As the last sliver of sunlight set over the horizon, the two elders spoke in unison. "Ashana, be with you on your journey."

At the utterance of the last word, the drumming stopped.

Looking onward with a stoic demeanor, Bastian walked in the direction of the Kandari territories of Aestaria. His walk became a canter, accelerating into a steady run. Once he broke the tree line, the forest's deep underbrush shimmered in an array of iridescent greens and yellows.

Bastian maintained this pace for ten minutes before noticing an echo to his feet pounding against the ground. Something behind him kept pace.

Bastian quickly maneuvered left while drawing an arrow into his bow. His muscles froze when he saw Shamira directly in its line of fire. Bastian shifted the arrow away and gently removed the tension from the bow string. Shamira approached with lightning speed, her hand flying up to his face. His head jostled ever so slightly as a sharp crack echoed through the trees.

"How could you not say goodbye?" Shamira looked up at him.

"Because this is not goodbye. I will return with the stone, and on that day, we will be bound." Bastian regarded her affectionately.

Looking at her beloved, Shamira's eyes mirrored his. She wrapped her arms around him in a gentle embrace, which tightened to an almost violent constriction, her affection and fear overcoming her all at once. Standing in the stillness, Bastian's hands remained gentle, stroking the fur along her shoulder. Her entranced stare offered nothing but hope and love. Bastian's gaze was deeper than the ocean, reflecting her own love back to her, like still water on a warm summer night.

Shamira took his hand in hers, gently pulling her tongue across the center of his palm. Without another word, she walked away. The forest floor buckled under the pressure of her foot, and with swiftness he'd only seen from his mother, Shamira was gone. The plants where she stood shook in her wake.

Once again, the young Selece chieftain started toward Eastern Aestaria. Moments later, Bastian became one with the forest, sprinting through the underbrush, while the green-glowing silhouettes of the plants flashed in the periphery of his feral eyes. Rushing through the forest's glowing green haze cleared Bastian's mind. In this moment, there was the run and nothing else.

10

"Stop, thief!" a tenor voice shouted in the middle of the town square.

The hulking masculine form pushed past the crowd in pursuit of a small, hooded figure in a cobalt cloak. In his efforts, the man collided with a Ganoshian guard.

The squadron was just rising from an outer table of a local pub after enjoying their evening meal. The remaining five guards, each clad in identical blue and grey uniforms, bolted to their feet.

Meanwhile, a slender female figure remained calmly seated. Clad in white, she sat statuesque save for her platinum hair waving in the breeze, glowing against her dark brown skin.

"What seems to be the issue here?" The recovering guard straightened his uniform.

The hulking man, composed mostly of muscle with generous portions of padding, looked down in apologetic fear. "Guardsman, I... My apologies. A thief stole a loaf of bread from the window ledge of my bakery. They went that direction." The large man's red eyebrows pleaded for aid, his hand raking through his short red hair on his head.

The guardsmen all simultaneously shifted their collective gaze toward the woman in white. Her stone-still form returned their stare. Her gaze quickly swept across the squad until she gave a nearly imperceptible flick in the direction the man pointed.

Without further hesitation, the men moved out with clockwork precision. Three of them detached small crossbows from their back while three others clasped the silver handles of their short sabers sheathed in blue scabbards. The bowmen pull the levers on their bows, inserting shafts with barbed arrow heads.

They maneuvered their weapons with timed precision, only rewarded to those who had endured years of repetitive training.

The woman in white pushed out a chair with a single foot. "Sit."

The baker lowered himself into a newly empty seat.

Her whispering voice floated easily above the din. "Come to the station at your leisure to make a full report. You will be immediately reimbursed for the loss of your goods under my authority."

She handed him a small white card. The embossed writing on the back lightly chafed against his fingertips. The baker flipped the card over to find, *'Ganoshian Guard, Captain Gailya, Squad: 10642'.*

"Thank you," the man sniveled.

When he looked up, the woman was already gone. He hadn't even heard the chair move. Shifting about in his chair, he looked around, but there was no sight of her. The only proof that she existed was in his hand.

The man slumped back to his store. He entered through a doorway under a sign which read, "Grom's Bakery."

In a shady back alley a few blocks away, a form blurred, cobalt cloak whipping in the turbulence. Three Ganoshian guards were nearly within arm's reach of the figure when the thief swiftly rounded a corner.

After circling back, the three guardsmen turned into the passage where a motionless, demure form stood frozen, facing a dead-end wall. Nearly out of breath, the archers nodded to coordinate the timing of their shots. When their chins dropped, bolts launched from their crossbows into the back of their helpless target's knees. Upon reaching their target, the lethal projectiles caused the shadowy silhouette to ripple. The guardsmen reached the victim of their crippling assault to find a two-dimensional fabric cutout, strung up by translucent threads, attached to nearby anchor points.

The guardsman with the blade searched the corners of the corridor, stroking his deep red beard in thought. After a few moments, he broke the silence with a sigh.

"What is it?" the other guard asked, clicking his crossbow into the latch on his back.

"We get to go back to Captain Gailya and tell her we were fooled by a kid with a bedsheet and some scissors."

His two compatriots snap straight in unison, heels together, hands down, chins up.

"You can tell me now, Traymier," came a feminine tenor of authority earned from years of issuing orders to subordinates and smoking a pipe.

The white-clad figure with platinum hair tread confidently between the men. Guardsman Traymier snapped into a rigid posture of deference mirroring his company. The guardsman remained still, watching the captain inspect the silhouette and examine the corridor walls. She clicked her tongue against the roof of her mouth while running her finger along the one wall.

"Look," she said, shattering the silence with a gentle command.

The guards eased their respective postures and leaned forward to inspect the area in question. Knife marks ascended in pairs like climbing spikes leading over the dead-end ally's wall.

"How did they..." Another guardsman ran his fingers across the damage done by the blade.

The captain went over to inspect the silhouette, letting out a small hum of acknowledgement. Pointing to the form, she asked. "Who can tell me what this is?"

Traymier touched the fabric while inspecting the string. "How are we supposed—"

A dark hand lashed out. His mouth slammed shut, head sent reeling backward. The contact reverberated through his body. The man lumbered backward, clumsy from the immediate disorientation. Traymier landed on his right side with a thud, body twisted from the force of the attack.

Another man exclaimed, "Captain, please educate us, and do us the honor of removing our ignorance." The beseeching phrase came out sharp and respectful.

"This is the body replacement technique used by the Kai-Sho family of the Nepharen people from YuKari, the empire to our south, beyond the barren wasteland."

The captain's razor-sharp blade rang out as the steel cleared her sheath. She waved it through the air, pulling the edge across the nearly invisible threads holding the form aloft. The thread gave way, allowing the form to float gently to the cobbled stones below. Captain Gailya raised her hand slowly, holding a small flat stick aloft. Suspended from the small flat stick were threads linked to different connecting points in the silhouette, supporting its form. The stick connected to two strands now dangling in the wind, suspended from random objects hovering over their heads. The captain sheathed her blade and rolled the cloth around the stick. In all, it was less than two feet long, with a width no larger than a thumb.

"This is how it's transported," the captain added, placing the silhouette into a satchel.

Across the stone cobbled road, a demure Nepharen form, engulfed in a hooded indigo cloak, crouched within the shaded corner of an abandoned building. The figure drew the cloak's hood over black hair wrapped tightly into a bun held tight by two thick steel hair pins. Almond-shaped emerald eyes looked through a brick hole toward the end alleyway. *The darkness outside should obscure me enough that no one will notice,* the rogue thought.

"Dead end," Kumori scoffed in a medium alto tone, speaking Kaanish with the slight choppiness of a Nepharen accent.

The exhilarating chase had brought a rosy glow to the rogue's hazel cheeks. Kumori inspected the indigo cloak for damage, expecting to find none. It was then turned inside out, displaying its red interior lining, fitting well over Kumori's lithe, muscular form. The hooded figure took a breath of confidence before stepping from the doorway.

Walking back toward the Ganoshian town square, Kumori passed a group of minstrels. The picker strummed gleefully to the flautist's quaint folk melody, both in time with the drummer's rhythm. The rogue reached into a cloak pocket and tossed a couple uni into a black hat sitting near the group.

Noticing a stirring in the crowd headed in the same direction, Kumori darted into a nearby back alley. Someone in the street called out, "The thief is this way. I saw 'em go down this alley."

Kumori sprinted silently ahead of the pursuing footprints echoing from behind. The soldiers chased Kumori down a side alley, bringing the shrouded rogue face-to-face with a heaping pile of garbage and no time for tricks. Three Ganoshian guards closed into the alleyway, now standing between Kumori and freedom, two with swords and a third with a small crossbow ready to fire from behind his comrades.

The first guard engaged swiftly, slashing down with grave purpose. Kumori intercepted the blade with a dagger and pulled a second blade across the opponent's inner forearm. Muscles tore, and blood spilled. The man's fingers went slack, sending steel clattering against the narrow stone road. He exhaled in a shriek, clutching his forearm, trying to stem the bleeding.

Kumori dashed toward the second adversary. The soldier's horizontal slash was awkward in this narrow passage. Ducking below the sword, Kumori passed the attacker in a low spin, pulling a blade's razor edge across his heels' rear tendons. His knees slammed into the brick-paved road with a crack that reverberated off the alley walls.

Rolling forward into a kneeling position, Kumori clenched the cobalt cloak's seam tightly, holding the otherwise unsoiled fabric at arm's length. The thrum of a loosed bolt pierced the air. Kumori's unyielding cloak encased the incoming bolt within its rugged fibers, and the rogue responded with a flick of a wrist, sending a cord with two weighted ends toward the attacker. When the line wrapped itself around the bowman's feet, Kumori tumbled forward, landing both feet dead center in the guard's chest. The soldier toppled backward, head colliding against the road with the sound of a dropped melon. After pocketing a set of fallen weapons, the wiry rogue pushed off from the guard's motionless body and bolted out of the alley.

Slowing to remove the iridescent cloak, Kumori turned the cloth inside out and flipped it in half. The bottom seam opened to reveal a second set of colors. The Nepharen's demure hands shifted the cloak around until it turned into a yellow skirt. After fastening the skirt, Kumori played at the buttons of an uncomfortable vest until it came off f The fabric inverted to become a yellow bodice with faux lacing in the back and hidden front buckles. Kumori slipped an arm through, followed by another, before setting the buckles into place. Finally, Kumori pulled the pins from a bun, allowing black hair to cascade down. After the disguised rogue rounded the last corner into the Ganoshian town square, a vendor at a fruit cart looked over and waved.

Unable to take his eyes from Kumori's enchantingly symmetrical features, the man behind the cart held up an ovular maroon fruit, just larger than his fist, topped with a green stem. "Free Turandi? It's fresh." The edges of his eyes creased over his jubilant smile.

"Thank you." Kumori graciously accepted the fruit without stopping. Once past the fruit merchant, the rogue sauntered on with an impish grin.

11

Bastian was resting comfortably in his hammock secured by two thick tree branches until the sun setting over the horizon stirred him awake. After rubbing the sleep from his eyes, he stared down toward the forest floor, judging the ground to be ten or so lengths below him. The young Selece warrior stepped onto the tree branch below and loosened the knots securing the hammock to the tree. With a few quick motions, he turned the bedding into a medium-sized carry pouch. He slung the pouch over his shoulder before securing the rest of his belongings and continuing his journey.

A quarter of the night passed by, and the pull of hunger tugged at the Selece's stomach. Bastian continued toward his quest for a few more moments when a blur on the moonlit ground caught his eye. He perched on a limb downwind from a small four-legged creature. It resembled a chomba, but instead of hopping, it walked at a brisk pace, its tail flicking back and forth rapidly. The animal's medium-length fur coat was a mix of reds and dark browns separated by lines of white, starting just behind its black nose, streaking down to the end of its tail. A small metallic disk with etchings that glistened in the moonlight hung from a lash of hide around the creature's neck.

Bastian slid his hands into the grips of his chatta and silently made his way to the ground. Shrouded in stealth, the Selece pressed forward toward his midnight meal. The creature was one length away as Bastian sat perched on his haunches, ready to pounce.

A high-pitched tone rang through the air, shattering the

silence and spooking the prey. Instead of running from the sound, the small animal ran toward it. Bastian assumed it was hunting for the source of the piercing screech to find a meal of its own.

The animal broke through the tree line into a clearing, and Bastian followed it. In the clearing, Bastian found himself face-to-face with an opponent, a small Kandari man who stood two heads shorter than him. The man's shoulders slumped with age, and his pale skin had a weathered texture, as if it had been left in the hot sun for too long. Completely covered in cloth, he wore a light brown shirt reminding Bastian of Shala's leathers and trousers the color of Elder Thamenga's dark grey fur.

Bastian took a long inhale through his nose, drawing in the sweet odor of fresh jora meat mixed with fire and wood smoke. The tendons in Bastian's fingers flexed tight, wrapping around the symmetrical dual bladed weapon's bone handles.

Lowering his voice, the man infused as much gravel as he could into the guttural sounds. "Maat, uush jontha Kaanish?" His hand reached down, caressing the fur of Bastian's previously prospective meal.

"You're Sele is horrible. How did you learn?" The Kaanish words came out chopped and guttural.

"You're not the first Selece to come out of these woods, and I suspect you won't be the last." The man chuckled nervously. "Besides, my Sele isn't much worse than your Kaanish."

Bastian flinched at the man's fur-covered companion, compounding the tension with a rough yelp, somewhere between fear and warning.

"Everything's ok, Stomper," the man eased out, switching back to his native Kaanish language. "This is our new Selece friend here." The man shifted his gaze from his pet back to the Selece before him. "What are you called?"

The tension in Bastian's fingers evaporated, causing him to

loosen his grip on the chatta. "Bastian." He paused. "I am called Bastian." His Kaanish words rolled out in the gravelly baritone of a Selece growl.

"I am called Urma." The man patted at his animal companion. "And this is my pet dog, Stomper. Come with me, Bastian. Let's get you some jora while we talk." The man started to turn.

"How do I know I can trust you?" Bastian took a hesitant step forward.

The small man faced the young Selece, pulling at a thin leather strap that hung around his neck. "Juranga." He finished tugging, and a single ombashi tusk spilled out from his shirt collar, dangling on the end of the leather cord.

Bastian's eyes shot wide with surprise. "Grandfather?"

The man gave a knowing look before giving Bastian his back and walking away. "Come on. We'll talk while we eat."

The two trekked on, followed by Stomper, who wagged his tail, unaware of how close he had been to being Bastian's next meal. They walked in silence until they came upon a log house surrounded by a circle of rocks set into the ground, all connected to each other. Bastian looked up in awe at the log house standing four lengths tall. To reach the entryway, the two of them would need to walk up a flight of steps half a length in height. Bastian lightly padded on the steps, uncertain they would hold, not seeing any rope or understanding their construction.

Urma turned back to him and let out a mall chuckle. "Don't you worry. They'll hold." He turned to continue toward the door.

Bastian followed, and his eyes wandered about, landing on a section that came out over the landing at the top of the stairs. There was no wall to hold it up, aside from a single beam at the end supporting the corner. Between Bastian and the beam sat a wooden chair, rocking in the breeze.

"What do you call this?" he asked.

"Well, this," the man said, his lanky hands gesturing around, "is a house." He pointed toward the steps and the awning. "This is a porch."

"And that?" Bastian gestured at the chair.

"Is a rocking chair," the man said with a smirk, thrusting his chin toward the corner with the rocking chair. "Go ahead. Have a seat." He gave a knowing smile.

Bastian strode over to sit in the chair. He connected with the seat, and it leaned forward before reeling back under the full weight of the Selece's overlarge frame. Bastian's face twisted in surprise, arms flailing on each side, trying to gain his balance and stop from falling. The large Selece lurched forward, trying to get up, only to be rocked backwards when the chair buckled beneath him, sending him sprawling to the porch floor.

The man let loose a jolly laugh before ambling toward the Selece, sprawled onto the wreckage of wooden debris. He held his hand out, and Bastian accepted. The man's unyielding arm and steady frame were unusual for one with such a frail demeanor. "Not to worry, I'll build another."

After helping Bastian to his feet, the two continued back toward the front door. The pair walked inside, and Bastian had to duck to enter comfortably.

"Ma! We've got a guest," the man bellowed in a raspy tone after coming through a small corridor.

Urma gestured toward the woman standing at the hearth. "This is my wife..." The man paused. His eyes shifted up, searching his memory for the word. "Shontha." Urma growled deliberately before ambling toward the dining room. "My mate," he said in Kaanish with more conviction. "She is called Maxina."

Standing in the main room, the ceiling stretched half a length above the Selece's head. The man yelled something, but Bastian's senses were overloaded. Across the room, a fire roared inside a stone fireplace. Sitting over the flames was a large pot hanging from a crane and a spit, the short stout woman turned by a handle on the hearth's far left side. Bastian's face shifted in mild discomfort at the aroma of cooking meat and raw vegetables.

"Are you heating the jora meat?" Bastian's hand slid over the leather hide of a large chair sitting in front of the fireplace.

"Yes, that's how we do, but I'll ask Ma' to leave some jora meat extra rare for you." Urma looked at Bastian for a still moment. "That means not cooked. I take mine medium rare. That means just cooked a little but still pink in the center."

The stout figure working the fire turned and gave a beautiful smile from her round face and warm olive complexion. Her salt and pepper hair was tied into a tight braid, falling halfway down her back. Her hazel eyes glowed bright above her rosy cheeks joyously, displaying two rows of brilliantly white teeth. The woman wore a long burgundy dress trimmed with deep browns with a green ribbon wrapped around her waist tied in the back in the shape of a bow. From a thin metallic brown chain around her neck hung a bronze eye adorned with a ruby in its center. She presented a solid demeanor with no hint of the softness Bastian expected from the Kandari.

Maxina gestured to the chair in front of him. "Won't you please sit?"

Turning her back to him, she stepped toward the hearth. Picking up an iron poker, she resumed playing at the fire. Maxina grabbed a wooden spoon to stir the pot of cooking vegetables, wafting an aroma into the air that reminded Bastian of home.

The large Selece stood behind a large chair covered in glossed, dark leather, shimmering between the color of dried blood and pitch black in the firelight. The chair and its twin sat half facing each other, half facing the fire. Bastian sat down to a small growl escaping his stomach. Pretending he didn't hear the sound, the Selece stifled the urge to react.

"These leather hide chairs do make the funniest noises sometimes," the woman said through her smile, "but let's get you some food." Maxina filled a blue clay bowl full of cooked vegetables and took it over into the next room.

Upon entering the room, Bastian's appetite was taunted by a table full of food. A slab of raw Jora sat on a clay plate next to the bowl of steamed vegetables.

The three of them sat down. Bastian immediately started tearing into the food. After two or three bites, he froze in the tangible awkward silence consuming the room when his hosts did not join in.

"Don't worry, Bastian. You'll learn soon enough." Urma chuckled, giving Maxina a knowing smile.

The couple simultaneously closed their eyes and touched the center of their foreheads with two fingers. While they spoke, their hands made huge sweeping circles over their own bodies with their hearts at the center. Their words echoed with a timing that comes from years of practice, both ominous and beautiful.

"Theshana guide us. Inara teach us." Their hands both made a single movement, touching their hearts while they finished the phrase. "And Aurora bless us in Ashara's name." Bringing their hands together, Maxina and Urma simultaneously vibrated a single word. "Ashuun."

Once the ritual finished, they took a drink from their small clay cups and started into the food on their plates. Each cut the cooked meat, used utensils to stab the vegetables, and placed it into their mouths.

Now it was Bastian's turn to sit still in awkward confusion. His stomach's announcement that it was still empty quickly interrupted his disorientation, and there was food in front of him to remedy that problem.

Bastian looked down at his plate while his stomach groaned. "Eshuthi?" he asked, glancing toward Urma.

"Sorry. Eshuthi isn't found this far east, and even if it were, we don't really have a taste for it."

"Eshuthi?" Maxina inquired for clarification.

Responding with a subtle wave of his hand and shake of his head, he gave Maxina a knowing glance, thinking, *you don't want to know.*

Bastian shrugged before tearing into the jora meat. It had the texture of a front quarter, but over his hunger, it was irrelevant. A growl fought its way out through a mouth full of food. "How did you know my grandfather?"

Maxina coughed to cover up a small chuckle, and Bastian's eyes flicked to her in curiosity.

"We don't speak with our mouth full when we're eating." Urma said politely. "The way of the Selece is as beautiful as it is different from the ways of the Kandari, but unless I miss my mark, you're not headed back toward the Selece territories. You're headed right into the heart of Aestaria."

Bastian nodded, continuing to chew his food. He fumbled with the tool, having two pointy prongs on the end to eat his vegetables.

"If you go into Aestaria, you're going to need to make some adjustments so that you can blend in. This way, you'll have an easier time of it. There are actually some Selece in the Aestarian territories."

Bastian froze. "There are?" he said curiously.

Urma finished swallowing a large mouthful of vegetables. "Some. At least enough that your presence won't be entirely new to them. You'll get some stares here and there, but just ignore them and everything should be fine. What brings you from the forest, anyhow?"

Bastian cleaned his face with the fur of his left arm. "Some Kandari have taken a sacred relic from our people. I am charged with retrieving it and understanding why it was taken. I tracked the group of Kandari, who took it in this direction. They would have been through here seven or eight nights ago."

Urma looked at Maxina to get confirmation. "We haven't seen anybody come out of those woods for some time. Most Kandari aren't fool enough to go into Selece territory, let alone steal anything that the Selece would want back."

Maxina nodded in agreement.

"How did you get the ombashi tusk? And how do you know my grandfather's name?" Bastian let the question hang in the air while taking another bite.

"Many years ago, when I was just a boy, Juranga came and spoke with my grandfather. He established a peace at the border with a number of us that live along the Selece territories. We do what we can to keep the peace, but it never feels like enough."

"What do you get in exchange? What is the benefit to you?" Bastian looked on with a puzzled expression.

"We get to live," Urma stated confidently. "Until then, the rite of passage for some Selece tribes was to hunt the Kandari and bring back one of our dead bodies. It was Juranga who changed that. He gave us the ombashi tusk as a symbol of peace and said that we could use his name to show that we are keepers of the peace."

Their Selece guest finished the rest of his meal in silence, allowing Urma's words to sink in.

When the food was gone, Maxina stood up and called Bastian into the large room. "Come on. Let's get him sized, Pa'."

"Sized?" Bastian stood and went into the other room, following the small woman.

"Yeah." Maxina turned around, shaking her head at Bastian. "You'll have a tough go of it if you try getting into Aestaria Una like that." She gestured at Bastian's general lack of clothing except for a loincloth and some straps.

Urma came over, and the two fiddled around with a strap of leather embossed with unknown glyphs throughout. They overwhelmed Bastian with pokes and prods. It made his skin crawl and tingle.

Bastian's arm retracted back, reacting to Maxina's unintentionally prodding the slash on his arm.

Her words came out soft and thick. "I'm sorry. What do we have here?"

"It's nothing, just a small gift from the Kandari I fought. I intend to return the favor when I see him again." Bastian rubbed at the wound, which provided a sense of comfort, even if it didn't ease the pain.

"That said, this simply will not do."

Maxina tenderly cupped his elbow in one hand while slowly petting down his forearm with the other. When her soft caress reached the wound, Bastian hesitantly removed his paw. An aethereal hum filled the air, and a glowing green light radiated from between her palms. Flashes of bone shone through the fur and flesh. A gentle warmth consumed his forearm, reminding him of lying in his hammock and letting the sunlight wash over his sleeping body.

A green glowing light radiated from the beneath her eyelids. When she suddenly opened her eyes, the lights faded, and the sound dissipated to stillness. She removed her hand covering the wound while holding the bottom of his forearm with the other. She tilted her head back and forth, examining his arm.

"Hmm, now that's much better. How does it feel?"

Bastian ran his fingers through his fur to inspect his wound, unable to find any scars or traces of damaged fur. He gazed down at Maxina with gracious reverence. "Thank you."

She looked up at him, her face glowing with joy. "Of course."

Taking up her leather strap, she continued to move it about

poking, prodding, and calling out numbers for her husband to jot down.

As they finished, Urma pointed to the staircase. "You're welcome to sleep upstairs in one of the extra rooms, or you can take to the trees outside. The choice is yours."

Bastian considered it for a moment. "I'll need to get accustomed anyhow. Best to do it in a peaceful environment."

"With a mind like that, he'll do just fine Pa'." Maxina smiled, taking her guest's hand, leading him over toward the stairs.

Bastian laid awkwardly between the blankets and the mattress, consumed by the uneasy feeling of his feet being trapped by the sheets and the consistently firm bedding. He wasn't sure what it was made of, but it was nothing like the sleeping sack his mother had. He shifted uncomfortably with his eyes open while time passed drearily by. After a while, he allowed thoughts of home to take him to that place where echoes of his mother's voice spoke about dreams of brighter days and sweeter nights.

Bastian's eyes opened to the sounds of large birds croaking and cawing just outside his window. He collected his things and made his way downstairs, where the scent of freshly cooked spiced lappes fruit wafted through the air. Urma and Maxina were already at the table enjoying their breakfast when Bastian entered the kitchen.

Maxina jumped up excitedly and rushed into the large room to hand Bastian a stack of folded fabric.

"Bastian, just go ahead and set those down. Come on in here and eat. We can deal with that after." Urma gave his wife a moderately disapproving look. "Let the boy eat first, Ma'. Then we can handle the necessaries."

"What is this called?" Bastian picked up the small piece with a wooden handle and two metal points coming out of one end.

Maxina shifted her utensils position into a gesture of display. "This, my dear, is a strad."

"Strad?" Bastian repeated, stabbing at the lappes to place them in his mouth.

"Yes, it has two points to help control the food when we eat." The woman used the strad to place bits of fruit in her mouth and chewed through a grin before continuing, "The ancient Kaanish word for sharp point was 'stra' and multiple 'stra' is represented by ending the word with a 'D' sound, so the eating tool with two pointy ends became 'strad'."

Bastian nodded confidently and repeated, "Strad." Plucking his strad into the lappes, he ate with almost as big a grin as his host.

Maxina stood again, going to the stack of clothes sitting on the chair in the next room.

Urma handed Bastian a small square cloth. "Wipe your mouth and hands with this, then go and play dress up. She worked at it all night, so just smile and nod."

When Bastian walked into the main room, Maxina handed him a stack of clothes. A piece of folded burgundy cloth embroidered with light brown intersecting vines forming a lattice weave sat atop a folded swath of rugged light brown material. Bastian took the stack into the side room and closed the door. After a few minutes of bumping and crashing, the handle turned, and the large Selece stepped forward. Walking over to take his hand, Maxina's face glowed while she pulled him to a large mirror hanging on the side wall of the large room.

Standing in front of the mirror, the creature returning his gaze was the embodiment of discomfort. The shirt's brown collar itched against his fur while the seams at his shoulders bound and pulled, restricting his motion. Bastian continued wearing his leathers beneath the loose-fitting light brown pants held up by a black hide belt. He reached into the pockets on each side to find holes within, allowing him to slip his fingers around the chatta handles. The shirt matched the burgundy Maxina had worn the night before, trimmed in a light brown. A black hide vest worn outside of the clothes was the most uncomfortable contraption of the entire ensemble. The shirt sleeves went down to the wrist, with the ends rolled back halfway up his fur-covered forearm. Looking down, Bastian admired the appealing pattern of the fabric's colors against his skin.

"Just wait one minute," Urma said, shuffling by toward the back room. Moments later, he came out with a black pair of boots.

Bastian's perplexed eyes widened in comprehension. "You want me to put those on my feet?" Irritation saturated his voice.

Urma chided, "Without something on your feet, you're more likely to draw attention to yourself. That's the last thing you'll want if you're going to find this stone you're looking for."

"Why are you both going through all this trouble, anyway?" Bastian furrowed his brow.

"Our family was charged with keeping the peace. Consider this our way of showing you that we're not all like the first Kandari you encountered." Urma handed Bastian the boots. "These belonged to our son, but he's been gone many cycles. He was a large lad. They should fit you well."

Bastian examined the boots, unable to hide the distress on his face. "Where is your son now?" He sat down on the long bench, placing his feet into the boots.

"His name was Genod. He passed in the Trillium war between the Kandari families. Genod fought for Yeugurith. Eventually, the families called for the triumvirate of peace, but not before our son was lost on the front."

Bastian stood watching Urma and his wife gaze at the floor in reverence.

Each placed their hands on their foreheads. "Ashara keep him."

"That's all in the past now." Urma clapped the Selece on the back.

Bastian almost fell over in his disorientation. He shifted his feet, stepping around to catch himself. When he got his balance, he started walking around the wooden floor.

"Well, son, as much as we've enjoyed your company," Urma started, "you have a trail to track and a quest ahead of you."

Maxina strode over to Bastian and gently grabbed his hand, lifting it to turn his palm skyward. His face betraying a nervous tension within, Bastian turned to Urma. The old man gave a jolly look and shrugged. Bastian froze, paralyzed by the awkwardness of the situation. Suddenly, a small cloth bag filled with small ceramic disks landed firmly in his palm.

Bastian's tension dissolved so abruptly he nearly fell over. "What is this?"

"This is money." Urma walked over, grabbed the bag, and pulled out a few coins. "We trade these in exchange for food, or lodging, or anything else we may need."

Urma placed the coins back in the bag and cinched it tight. He took the bag and showed Bastian how to loop it on his belt. Bastian reached through a strap pouch to retrieve the small gold pommel piece with the emblem on it. He placed the piece into the sack, where it would be more secure.

Maxina walked over, handing Bastian the satchel he'd been wearing when he first arrived. "When you get to Aestaria Una, ask for Zhannah. She is a friend. Tell her Maxina sent you."

Bastian took in a gasp. "Zhannah, that's a—"

"Selece name." Maxina nodded.

Bastian gazed down cautiously. "That name is of the Azhesan Selece from the south."

Maxina smiled up at him. "This is a whole new world for you, Bastian, and such things don't hold as much weight in Aestaria."

Urma opened the door, and they all walked out to the porch. "What matters is that the Selece unite as one. That's the only way to overcome the challenges you'll face."

Bastian walked down the steps timidly in his new boots. After reaching the bottom, he turned to face his gracious hosts with a polite nod. Looking back at him, the couple reverently traced circles in the air. Their fingers completed circles before they gestured down to touch the center of the invisible circle.

"Ashuun bless you."

With this, Bastian turned to press on toward his destination.

12

A short, thin girl with long black hair clad in purple robes trimmed in silver ran from one of the smaller campus schoolhouses. Overjoyed to be free from her rector's glare, she charged forward full steam ahead. "Brother!"

Moments later, she crashed into a tall, wiry figure in his late teens with pale skin and a medium-length mop of dusty brunette hair. He was dressed in a similar set of purple robes trimmed in silver over matching trousers. She wrapped her arms around him in relief, smushing her face against the right side of his robes, just under his arm.

Despite being jostled back, the figure maintained his footing. He placed his arms around the girl, pulling her into a warm embrace. His lips gently touched the center of her scalp, where her hairline parted. He caught the scent of their mother's teaberry hair wash with a hint of sedentary frustration.

"Rector Agani picking on you again, Meraina?" he asked, taking her hand, and they put the small grey schoolhouse behind them, strolling idly toward the large brick road.

Her nose scrunched up, sensing he had been using their father's smelling oils again. "Well, of course. She's always expecting me to miraculously turn into you one day, and that just isn't how things work. We can't all be the great and powerful—"

"Xander!"

The pair turned toward the voice shouting from behind.

A tall, muscular boy holding a tangu ball was walking toward them. He appeared to be half a head taller than Xander with dirty blond hair kept neatly above his ears. While the boy appeared two or three years Xander's senior, in truth, he only had his friend by a few moons. Something about the glimmer in his eyes betrayed the truth of his age. His deep red silk coat was short enough not to be considered a robe, embroidered with interwoven black flourishes trimmed in yellow. He held a round white leather ball about the size of his own head filled with air.

"Torga. Hey!" Xander smiled at the boy.

Torga suddenly launched the sphere in their direction, careening toward Meraina's face.

Reflexively, Xander channeled his asha into his palm, drawing it in from the surrounding air and the ground beneath. In a blur, Xander's hand thrust forward as he shouted, "Cha'Sora!"

A small, spectral blue bolt flew forward, piercing the ball. The limp sphere flailed off course, thudding into a nearby wall.

"Shift, Xan! You were supposed to catch it!" Torga went over to examine the lifeless hide material, picking it up with two fingers the way he might handle a small dead swamp skreetch.

Xander scowled. "Hey, language! My sister's right here!"

"Ooh!" Torga covered his mouth, feigning a mock apology.

Xander's scowl transformed into an indignant glare.

"Okay, seriously," Torga said, flailing his hands in frustration, "I'm sorry for my language, but you were supposed to catch it, not kill it."

Now it was Xander's turn to cover his mouth in mock apology. "Oops?" He shrugged with an impish smile.

"Anyway, skreetch face, you coming to the tangu game tonight or not?" Torga kept playing with the stitching on the ball, fitting the wound together as though he expected it to spontaneously heal itself.

"No." His head gestured toward his younger sibling just a few feet away, who appeared to pay them no attention, perched on her haunches face down toward the brick road as she used a stick to toy with a small bug. Xander sighed, raising his hands in a helpless gesture of mandatory compliance. "I have... obligations."

Torga shrugged. "It's your loss. I heard Kera's going, and she'll be looking for you."

Xander turned away, cheeks flushing a light pink. "I'm sure she won't miss me. Even so, as I said, 'responsibilities.' Anyhow, we need to get home."

Torga lobbed the lifeless hide through the air past Xander's head. The nebulous blob landed squarely in a school yard trash bin. "Okay, genius, whatever you say, but don't forget you owe me a ball." He sauntered away, shifting about to settle his shoulder satchel over his coat.

Xander crept up behind his crouching sister, in a world all her own. Her head whipped around, and he flinched when she shrieked. "Boo!"

The surprise sent the boy rocking backward, his voice caught in his throat. Xander scrambled to get his feet underneath him. In a sudden burst, Meraina sprinted forward. After finding his legs, Xander chased after her, and the two dashed toward the university's stable. Once she was within reach, Xander's hands danced along his sister's ribs, sending her flailing in laughter. Before she hit the ground, he wrapped his arms around her, collapsing to the cobblestone road with her on top of him. Xander continued to poke and prod until she relented.

"Korda! Korda!" the girl shouted through her laughter, squirming in submission.

The two lay exhausted in the road, obstructing the path of daily foot traffic. Meanwhile passersby stared down at the pair as if they were wild howler jiblans gone mad.

Xander rolled to his feet. Taking his sister's hand, he helped her up. The two strolled forward.

Meraina pulled strands of straw from her hair, running her fingers through it to orient each strand back into its place. "So, is that all I am to you? An obligation?"

"Come on, Meraina, you know better than that." Xander's hands came up in frustration. "I don't want to seem like a complete doof. Besides, how bad would Torga feel if I told him I'd rather hang out with my little sister because her company is more entertaining than his? I just couldn't bear to see the pain in his eyes if he knew how much more awesome you are."

"If I'm so awesome, then why don't you take me with you to the tangu game? Hmmm?" She peered over with a side-long glance.

"Tangu is boring, and the games are just crowds of people cheering while a bunch of meatheads smash into each other trying to get the tangu ball into the korda circle. I'd rather not waste my time."

"Mother says you used to love tangu when you were little, and Father took you to the tangu games," she pleaded.

"That's different. I was a little kid." Xander's frustration began showing on his face.

"I'm still a little kid. What's wrong with that?" Meraina jabbed an elbow into her brother's hip.

Xander ran his hands through his hair. "Maybe next time. Just not tonight. I have a huge assignment from Rector Koldanre` due Amsday and will take the entire weekend."

"Fine!" The exasperated girl reached into her satchel and pulled out a book. The title on the cover read, *The Wizard's Prophecy*.

Xander scanned the street to plot their course. "We need to stop into Jaspers so I can get some supplies for my project." Unsure if she was listening, he glanced down and rolled his eyes. "You're still reading that?"

"I enjoy it." Meraina licked her finger and turned to the next page.

"The whole concept of prophecy is completely antithetical to logic and reason. It's entirely kid stuff." He led the way, keeping a brisk pace.

"I am a kid!" She stuck her tongue out in her brother's general direction.

"As you keep reminding me." He huffed, crossing the street.

"It's not my fault that it stays relevant." She flicked another page, following close behind.

The pair arrived at a door under a placard that read, "Jaspers Exploratory Emporium."

Xander pushed the door open to the sound of a ringing bell hanging from the corner.

Following behind him with her nose in her book, Meraina dodged the rare customer and even her brother, when he occasionally retraced his steps.

Xander scurried about the store, gathering an assortment of tubes and vials filled with a powder or shimmering vibrant liquid.

Another page fluttered with the flick of Meraina's finger.

A deafening explosion came from behind the counter at the far end of the store, followed by the thud of a falling body crashing into the wooden floor.

"I'm okay," wheezed a raspy voice with the last bit of air left in its lungs.

Xander's gaze turned toward the sound. He shook his head in vicarious embarrassment, watching a puff of smoke billow from behind the counter. "The entire concept behind prophecy makes no sense. It's not possible to reconcile the ability to predict the future and freedom of choice."

A figure with wild cloud-white hair and a long grey coat jumped upright with a vigorous sense of zeal. "I almost had it!" boomed the voice of an elderly gentleman, a finger of determination waving in the air.

Meraina giggled so hard she almost closed her book and lost

her page. "Mister Jasper is Funny." She chuckled to her brother.

"Almost had what, Mister Jasper?" Xander reached into his pouch and pulled out a handful of chen.

"Bottling thunder, my boy! Bottling thunder!" The scrawny pale man proudly puffed out his chest while making change in his money drawer.

"For what?" Xander placed what little change he received into his pouch.

The man's eyes went wide, bulging slightly from his head. "Because we can, young man, so we do!" The man's lips exaggerated the last sound he made.

Meraina laughed while Xander picked up his supply-filled box. She followed him out of the door, and the pair strolled toward the university's stable.

Before the door closed behind her, she continued, "The Nepharen spirit talkers from the school of DoTotSu predict the future."

Xander rolled his eyes. "This argument again? The spirits don't perceive time the same way we do. As a result, when the students of DoTotSu channel their asha, the spirits they connect with provide a brief glimpse into what could happen based on how things stand. If they ask the spirits the same question half a day later, the answer could change. Unlike the prophecies in your fantasy stories, which remain unchanged for hundreds or thousands of years."

"It's still fun to read, so I don't care." Meraina scoffed.

"I just don't understand wh—"

Before he could finish, a blurred form crashed into the young mage, sending him reeling toward the ground. His box of supplies vaulted into the air, tumbling end over end with its contents raining down around him. Each vial and tube crashed down on the brick-paved street, the sound of shattering glass piercing the air. Continuing to read her book, Meraina sidestepped one of the larger tubes spiraling in her direction.

While the mage struggled to his feet, he saw a small figure in a dark azure cloak sprint away into the crowd. In an eager pursuit was a figure clad in burgundy with a black vest and a golden mane. If Xander wasn't mistaken, it appeared to be a Selece.

He stood and immediately checked Meraina for wounds. "Are you all right?"

Meraina thumbed another page in her book as if nothing happened. "I'm not the one with dirt on my bum. Serves you right for making fun of my book."

Xander checked himself for wounds and found none. Turning about in confusion, he realized everything he needed for his project surrounded him in a collage of broken chaos.

He gave Meraina a stern look of concern. "Across the way is Mrs. Paolo's bakery. Go inside and wait for me there."

Xander watched the small girl enter the bake shop before pursuing his attackers.

13

For a day and a half, Bastian followed Urma's directions, taking the trail east toward the main roadway into Aestaria Una. When dawn transformed into a sweltering morning, Bastian broke through the tree line to find the highest perch he could under the soft shade of a natural canopy. He liberated his feet and cursed the leather boots for their discomfort. At the simple feeling of freedom, moisture swelled in the corners of his eyes. The Selece secured his hammock to the treetop before lying back, surrendering to the forces of exhaustion.

Hours later, the crisp night air crept over Bastian's resting body. The sense of comfort embraced him, summoning thoughts of being a young cub lying in his mother's arms. Bugs chirped and hummed from the forest floor. The sounds of the wild echoed from beneath, resonating into the distance.

On the woodland floor below, a pack of shivathi circled the base of the tree, hoping he would fall to his death. The beasts' dense muscles rippled beneath brindle brown scales against a sheen of dark green, flecking black in the evening moonlight. Four massive paws supported the muscular bulk of their hulking bodies, each with five razor-sharp claws. Their horizontal torsos transitioned into thick heads and serpentine snouts brandishing sabre-tooth fangs. The pack of shivathi licked the air with long split tongues to find their prey. Bastian's father had taught him of the shivathi's ability to taste the fear of their prey, tracking a scent for days. They looked so small from this height, but if confronted by an adult male, its head would be level with Bastian's chest.

Steadying himself, he took a breath. *I know you're just hungry,* Bastian considered, *but it's not my time yet. Please don't make me kill you.* This beast had only one weakness, but Bastian couldn't help but feel a stirring of sympathy at the thought of it. He knew if forced, he would have to kill them all in a single strike or die himself.

Bastian secured everything into his hammock pouch and wrapped it around himself. For now, he wore only the natural fibers traditional for a Selece, with his chatta anchored to the hide straps on his thighs. He tugged on his gear to ensure it was secure.

Leaning forward, he let the tree limb slide from under him. He descended in freefall toward the pit of sabre-tooth viper fangs. Halfway to the ground, Bastian gripped a long sturdy branch. His horizontal form swung hard. The exhilaration of his heart dropping into his stomach forced a smile onto his face. Once the tension eased, he let his fingers slip off the branch. Pulling his knees to his chest, he tumbled through the air until he spotted the next long, thick tree branch. His graceful landing left every flake of tree bark undisturbed.

Without stopping, the Selece sprung forward, dashing across the branch, away from the tree trunk. He hurled himself to the next tree, outpacing the ravenous shivathi snarling below. Sprinting along the largest branches in the forest, Bastian stayed ahead of the shivathi pack. The beasts continued their hunt, driven by their hunger for flesh and thirst for blood. It was said that the skrattle birds never followed the shivathi because these beasts left nothing behind for scavengers to pick.

Racing through the trees, Bastian spotted the next large branch in his path. When his foot landed hard, he grimaced at the sound of cracking wood. His hands reached for the remaining tree branch, claws digging at the bark. Bastian attempted to swing himself onto the next branch, with no success. His body flipped through the air, with nothing between him and the forest floor.

Landing with a thud, Bastian planted his shoulder firmly into the dirt and rolled forward. The faint sound of snapping wood tugged at his senses. Ignoring it, he rounded on his predator. The adolescent shivathi leading the charge lunged at him. In a single motion, Bastian rolled backward to catch the beast with his feet. With a hard kick, he vaulted the animal behind him. Bastian recovered his stance, tightening his fingers around the chattas' bone handles.

His heart and mind raced, slowing his perception of time, allowing Bastian to harmonize his movements the actions with that of his aggressor. Bringing the chatta up hard, Bastian caught the large female shivathi under the jaw. He thrust upward, until the tips protruded from the skull with a slick crunch. Gravity pulled the black ichor down from the point of his chatta blades back toward the source. The four smaller shivathi pups let out wild shrieks in fear before scampering off into the forest.

When the tension in Bastian's muscles evaporated, he reverently laid the animal's body on the forest floor. A solitary tear of sympathy streamed from one eye at the thought of the pups' fate mirroring their mother without the guidance of a pack leader. With a gentle respect, the Selece softly closed her eyes. "Ombatha shivathi Ashana surasha."

After a moment of contemplation, Bastian stood upright and straightened himself to continue his woodland trek. Retracing his footsteps, Bastian felt something was missing. Moments later, he passed the spot where he had first fallen, and his heart sank. Imbedded into the soil were two fractured pieces of a bow connected by a long string.

A voice came to the front of his mind. "It's a tool, not a decoration," his father's voice echoed in the rathan's trembling bass. "A true warrior will become one with his weapon."

"Some rathan I am." Head hung low, he buried the wooden pieces. After he finished burying his fractured weapon and smoothing the ground over, Bastian carried on.

He continued forward another half day before finding the forest tree line. Across the clearing was an unimaginable sight. Stone city walls standing twenty lengths high protected buildings beyond topped with spired rooftops soaring two or three times higher than walls. The city's entrance was less than a quarter day's walk, guarded by a large door and men appearing no larger than bugs from this distance.

Before starting toward the giant door, Bastian took the time to dress himself in the clothes Maxina had gifted him. He sighed when it was time to place the boots on his feet, but reluctantly, he endured.

After he crossed the clearing, Bastian approached a line leading into the city. The guards were speaking with people before they entered, and some were showing small pieces of cloth with different symbols on them.

Bastian slowly ambled toward one of the guards, asking questions.

A sudden roar of contention came from those who had been waiting their turn, overpowering his attempt at a greeting. "Back of the line, mongrel!" a voice jeered in anger.

The guard's face twisted in discomfort at the word before a heated glare fell on the source. "You'll keep a civilized tongue in your mouth, or I'll 'ave it removed."

In one smooth motion, the guard's fingers wrapped around his sword handle. The shouting Kandari cringed in fear before disappearing into the crowd.

The soldier regarded Bastian with a natural confidence. "You don't need to take that, least of all from the likes of 'im. First time in the city?"

Bastian nodded, absolutely devoid of conviction. "Yes."

The guard looked up, doing his best to reassure the Selece. "Right. Head to the rear, and when it's your turn, we'll let you in."

The guard raised his arm to point toward the end of the line, just about nine lengths away, curving around a stone cobbled road three lengths wide.

Taking his place, Bastian glanced over, noticing a separate queue for carriages. Some were drawn by horses, while others were pulled by an entirely different creature, large black four-legged beasts standing a full head taller than a horse. The creature had a bestial physique with four long horse-like legs, each ending in three thick razor-sharp talons. A natural obsidian armor of impenetrable kaitanous plates covered its body. Each black plate reflected like a pool of moon lit water at midnight. Over the beast's hind legs protruded a set of thick scales tapering into a bulky tail equal length to the creature's torso. The carriage rigging was built to prevent the tail from getting caught under the wheels.

Bastian shuffled forward, keeping his eyes fixed on one of the beasts. In a blink, its head shifted, and their eyes locked. The smaller plates covering its feline-shaped face shifted in an expression Bastian couldn't interpret. Between the plates were two shadowy eye sockets, in which glowed a set of ruby-colored embers.

A single word escaped under Bastian's breath from his barely parted teeth. "Moravian."

Suddenly, the image from the emblem of Jorgan's crest flashed into his thoughts.

"Move on!" someone shouted.

Suddenly finding himself at the front of the line, the disoriented Selece looked back toward a jeering crowd. Bastian turned to face the gate, where the guard from before beckoned with the wave of a hand.

As Bastian approached, the man's gaze lifted to meet his own. "What's your name?"

"Bastian," he replied.

The guard pointed past the walls beyond the gate. "Here's what you'll need to do. Go to the chamberlain's office and speak to the cleric for working papers. It'll most likely be Sophie or Rhoda. Tell 'em Kaden sent ya over."

Bastian's eyes went blank with confusion.

"Oh, 'at's me! I'm Kaden." The man held out his hand, and Bastian's clasped onto the man's forearm in a rote form the way he'd learned from his father. In return, Kaden's grip tightened confidently, giving a quick jolt with a cheerful smile on his face. Squinting up Kaden inquired, "Who's your advocate?"

"Advocate?" Bastian replied with a curious look on his face.

"You got friends in the city that'll speak for ya?" Kaden clarified.

A name floating in the back of Bastian's memory drifted its way to the forefront of his mind. "Zhannah."

"Zhannah?" The man's shoulders rose in affirmation, as if it were the only obvious answer Bastian could have given. "'Course it's Zhannah. It's always Zhannah."

Kaden's movements became hurried after his fellow guardsman grumble something inaudible, having processed fifteen or more people into the city in the same space of time.

"All right, mate, tell you what." Kaden handed Bastian a small wooden placard with a thin fabric imbedded into it. The cloth had the image of a white rose set against a yellow background. "Take this to the chamberlain's cleric. Tell 'em Kaden sent ya 'n your advocate's Zhannah. Take this road straight in and turn left on Vas'Graddon Street. It's the second street down to the left. Halfway down on the right, it's the chamberlain's office. Remember Sophie or Rhoda." Kaden clapped Bastian on the back, ushering him forward into the city gates. "Ashana guide ya." Kaden let out a muffled word about pillars, but the noise blended into the din of the Aestarian capital city overwhelming Bastian's senses.

Bastian made his way through the large wooden doors standing over five lengths high. He ambled forward, focus shifting between his new card and the merchant signs. Wooden placards with symbols and pictures swung over the shops' doors while people came and went. *How do I find Zhannah?* he wondered to himself. *And where is Vas'Graddon Street?*

On his right, a group of men stood in front of a shop with an image of a hammer. He stepped into the ring of bodies and spoke. "Hi, I'm looking for Vas'Graddon Street."

The words fell flat into the lot, all now staring back in silence.

One man had long ragged hair kept tight to his head by a dark cloth that lay flat against his head and was tied in the back. He wore a ragged long-sleeved yellow shirt under a dark orange vest muddled in soot. A black leather belt with a grey metal buckle held up a pair of threadbare light brown pants.

"This mongrel's gonna walk up and butt in like this? Who does he think he is?" he piped up.

"Yeah, Radnor. He obviously doesn't know his place yet, but he'll learn soon enough," spouted another man dressed similarly in mostly grey tones with red trim.

Bastian gave them a confused look, unaware of what a "mongrel" was.

"Shut your pie holes, you two!" A larger man standing just outside the group stepped forward.

He had a thick black beard and a black vest which exposed a well-defined physique beneath. Under a brown belt with a bronze buckle was a pair of red pants and black boots. Standing a mere half a head shorter than Bastian, he carried a massive hammer in his right hand. The immense weight seemed feather-light in this man's grasp.

"Hassig, w-we didn't see you—" Radnor stammered.

Hassig interrupted, "I'm sure that's true. You don't have

enough wits to rub together to start a small campfire, let alone venture from here to the Selece territories."

Trying to interject, Radnor's words fell flat against Hassig's booming baritone.

"Say one more word, and I'll open a new cake hole right to your gut, so you won't even have to bother chewing."

"At least he wouldn't have to taste his wife's cooking again," the man in grey added.

"Like you're any better. Look at you, scurrying to the stronger side, like the bog skreetch you are. Kelna, you're the first skreetch off a sinking ship." Hassig turned to Bastian. "Don't worry about these halfwits. Vas'Graddon Street is just ahead. Turn left at the bakery there on the corner. Are you looking for the chamberlain?"

Bastian nodded. "Yes, thank you."
Hassig clapped Bastian on the shoulder reassuringly. "Left at the bakers and halfway down on your right. There will be a placard like this one." He pointed to the blacksmith sign hanging over the door. "But it will have two pillars and a yellow star between them. Ashana be with you."

Bastian ventured off toward the bakery to the sound of Hassig chastising the rabble.

"Radnor, you don't have enough brains to find your way home at night, let alone talk scrape to someone who made it here walking across the whole of Aestaria on foot."

Bastian rounded the corner at the bakery and inhaled its exquisite aromas. He caught the sweet scent of something reminding him of his mother's spiced lappes, with overtones of new fragrances. They were softer somehow, covered by something that smelled light and neutral, obscuring the other fragrances. Bastian made a mental note to return when he was finished at the chamberlain's office.

Strolling along, Bastian continued checking the signs hanging over the shop's doors. He smiled triumphantly when he finally stood three lengths from a sign with two pillars and a star. Bastian walked through the door, to find himself in a massive empty room divided between the front and the back by a waist-high wall. When the door closed, a small bell chimed somewhere from beyond the far wall. Attached to the door was a cord strung along the upper corners of the room. The vacant room held a disturbing aura of emptiness within, being large enough to hold so many people.

A large, hulking man in a blue shirt and brown vest came to the clerk's countertop. His short hair was dark wherever it didn't have streaks of grey. "Can I help you?"

Walking toward the counter dividing the room, Bastian noticed the Kandari's eyes were level with his own. His words erupted in an awkward enthusiasm. "I'm seeking Sophie or Rhoda. Kaden sent me. Zhannah is my advocate." With a wide smile, Bastian energetically displayed his yellow placard ornately decorated with a white rose.

The man let out a jovial chuckle. "I'm Rhoda, but you'll have to come back when Sophie is here. She processes all the Selece." The man glanced at the clock on the wall. "Sophie will be back in half an hour. You can come back and see her then."

"Thank you." Bastian nodded and ambled toward the door. Suddenly, he froze, turned back around, and regarded the man with a pleading expression.

The man cocked his head toward the pendulum clock on the wall and walked over to it. Bastian met him at the device. It ticked away as the pendulum swung.

The man pointed at the clock. "When this needle moves from here to here, then it will be time for Sophie to return."

The two stood watching a minute pass and then another.

Bastian took a mental note of the larger hand's small

incremental movements. He focused for the duration until the small needle made a full rotation. "When this needle points to here," Bastian said, pointing at the six then the twelve, "then I can come see Sophie."

"Oh, I think you'll do just fine!" the man said in a cheerfully booming bass. "I'll let Sophie know that you're looking for her if she comes back before you."

"Thank you." Bastian padded to the exit, carefully examining the string on the open door before walking out.

After exiting the shop, Bastian meandered across the road. The sweet aromas from the bakery down the street wafted in the air, pulling him that direction when he brushed against a hooded figure in a blue cloak. The slightest tugging at his belt caused him to reach down, only to find the pouch of chen Urma had given him was gone.

Bastian gave chase as the rogue sprinted away. Crossing the main intersection, the thief crashed into a young man in purple robes trimmed in silver before bolting off into the crowd. The box the young man had been carrying flew through the air, its contents soaring in every direction.

Bastian rushed forward in pursuit of the cloaked figure, dodging a torrent of falling glass.

14

Xander weaved his way through Aestaria Una's bustling city streets in pursuit of his quarry. Blurred images of crowds standing stone-still flashed by. With his view obstructed by the large Selece, Xander could barely make out the indigo cloak whipping in the wind, its wearer leading the chase.

The three of them sprinted through the city, weaving and dodging between people and buildings. Xander fixed his focus on the Selece. They raced down a long corridor toward the entrance of a large estate, and Xander gained ground.

Without warning, the cloaked figure nearly appeared to take flight. After nimbly scaling a colossal statue of an ancient king, the hooded rogue ascended a diagonal staircase railing and jumped atop a balcony. Vaulting with one last leap, the thief found sound footing upon a rooftop.

To continue pursuit, the large Selece bolted right, clawing vertically up a tree beside the main house. Xander focused his will, directing all the asha he could summon to his feet. With a mumbled utterance, the energy pushed him forward, increasing his speed until he reached the house.

Xander vibrated a single word, "Cho'Raka!"

Instantly, a burst of energy thrust from his feet against the ground. In a single motion, he ascended to the rooftop. Xander landed awkwardly, fumbling forward. With a focus of will, he gracefully turned the fall into a roll and maintained the chase.

The three ran across adjacent rooftops, jumping from one to the next. Xander scowled and grunted in frustration before extending his right arm. With a focus of will and a nearly inaudible mantra, a blue bolt of energy flew from the mage's fingers. The bolt soared toward the Selece's back as the feline form bounded gracefully through the air.

A spectral thrum whirred from behind Bastian. Midair, the large Selece shifted his weight to roll away, allowing the bolt of energy to pass beneath him. Continuing forward, the bolt of energy struck the shrouded Kumori square in the back, bringing the ground up with critical speed. The Nepharen planted the balls of both feet firmly on the ground, landing in a crouch before rolling forward and continuing on.

Bastian advanced, landing on a soft patch of dirt along a stone wall in what appeared to be a courtyard. Chanting a word, Xander soared off the rooftops, slowing his descent with the asha channeled through his feet.

Kumori launched a blade at the Selece. Bastian deflected it with the flick of his chatta blades. The Kandari mage landed to the sound of ringing steel piercing the air. Bastian's chatta blades batted away the second of Kumori's knives. The razer edged dagger flew tip-first in Xander's direction.

The young mage threw his hands up, shouting, "On'Daka."

A shield of translucent azure energy shimmered to life around him with arcs of lightning where the blade struck. The dagger's edge bounced off the field. The handle thumped into a nearby tree before falling to the ground.

Xander stepped forward, straightening his fingers. He held his arms out, while the mystical chant rolled from his tongue, "Tu'Razo!"

Blue flames sprang from his fingertips, solidifying into razor-sharp blades of blue energy.

Bastian brought up his chatta blades. Kumori drew a pair of long daggers, and the three raced toward each other.

Before anyone could strike, the sound of echoing thunder erupted between them in a white-hot light. Shockwaves rippled through all three bodies, sending each flying backward away from the intended melee. All three lay limp on the ground, their vision obscured by a blinding veil whiter than the lightning at midnight. Each of them moaned in agony at the deafening silence ringing in their ears.

15

The sound of chains rattling against iron bars echoed from the stone walls. A cursory glance around the corridor had a unique appearance from the perspective of one lying on the ground, hands chained behind them. The ache in Xander's shoulder let him know it had been dislocated and, at some point while he had been unconscious, forcibly corrected. Closing his eyes to focus his will, Xander realized the asha would not come.

From a catty-corner cell, a muffled snarl rumbled from the Selece regaining consciousness.

The Kandari shifted about awkwardly to get his legs beneath him. Xander let out a weak sigh of triumph, now able to sit crossed legged on the hard-stone floor. He squinted about as his eyes adjusted to the twilight corridor of cells. The arid aroma of stale shaat wafted through the air, filling his nose. The corridor appeared thirty feet wide, with metal bars running lengthwise on each side, ten feet from the stone walls, resulting in two rows of bars forming a central walkway. Running the other direction, a set of intersecting bars were placed in rows every ten feet throughout, resulting in two rows of ten-by-ten cells running the length of the corridor. A small, barred slit scarcely illuminated the stone chamber from the top of each cell, while hopeful slivers of light crept in through the large steel door at one end.

Bastian broke the silence with an exhausted growl. "Where are we? Why are we here?"

"We are here because you two taki faces wouldn't part with a few chen!" Kumori chirped in Kaanish with a choppy Nepharen accent through a whisper that rasped in frustration. "And now we are stuck in prison!"

Xander sighed in exhausted disappointment. "I'm here because you two shaat heads assaulted my sister and me, destroying fifty 'C' worth of equipment, and I chased you down to retrieve it." He turned to face Kumori. "And this isn't prison. This is just the holding cell at the Magistrate's Hall of Justice. Soon enough, they'll sort all this out."

Metal bolts slid out of place, allowing the door to open. Light poured into the corridor, followed by pitch darkness after the door slammed shut. A proud-looking figure strutted down the center section between the bars, making his way over to Xander's cell. A pompous voice bellowed from the towering, dark silhouette. "For the crime of using aggressive magic in public, you are to be put to death."

Xander's eyes went wide. "You can't! I haven't even had a trial. Nobody's heard what happened."

The ominous character remained statuesque; his face obscured in shadow. He stood in a halo of light shining through a slit in the opposite wall, forcing Xander to squint. "You will have a trial, but it will be a mere formality."

Xander's eyes glazed over while he contemplated his fate, given the severity of the man's grave words. The young mage gathered his emotions and calmed his breath, allowing his focus to drown out the bellowing baritone. Xander reached down deep into the wellspring of his asha, beckoning it forth. With the focus of his will taught to him by the Shao-Ra masters, he called the asha to his hands, yet none came.

As Xander sat in contemplation, the booming voice echoed, "Thou art therefor and thusly condemned to suf..." With all the enthusiasm of a wilting flower, the voice suddenly deflated to an elegant yet dismayed tenor. "You tryin' to cast on me right now, Xan?" The shadowy figure's arrogant posture went suddenly flaccid, as the formerly menacing silhouette barked out a laugh, buckling over in amusement.

"Rye?" Xander questioned without disguising the heat in his voice.

The form ambled slightly toward Xander's cell, just enough to let the light shine on his face while he continued to bark out laughter.

"Reinhardt, you shaat-eating kotch face! You can shift right to the void."

Taken aback by Xander's language, Reinhardt stood up straight with a seriously imposing posture before buckling over once more in uncontrollable laughter. "Your face! The look on your face." His laugh echoed like a wild howler jiblan.

"What is going on?" Kumori murmured.

"It appears they know each other," Bastian responded in a low growl from behind an apathetic visage.

"What is so funny?" Grunting in discomfort, Kumori shifted around to make the chains more comfortable.

"What in the void is going on, you shaat-brained skreetch face?" Xander surged to his feet, lunging at the bars before the chain connecting his wrists to the floor pulled taught. He winced at the bolt of pain jolting through his injured shoulder.

"Cousin." The word dripped slowly from Reinhardt's lips like thick honey. "I thought we were friends."

"Yes, we _were_ friends until you decided to come here and mock me with that ludicrous display!" Xander's rage-fueled struggle sent the chains rattling, going slack and then tight against the floor anchor. "And why can't I cast?"

"First and foremost, we are still friends, but seriously, what is a humble cadet in the service of his majesty's guard to do when he sees his cousin's name on the local magistrate's docket? I couldn't help but come have a laugh, though I'm ever so sorry that it was at your expense."

"Yeah, right! So I noticed." Sweat from the struggle and discomfort trickled down Xander's forehead.

"As for the casting..." Reinhardt pointed a finger at Xander. "You were seen using aggressive magic in public amongst the people, knowing such actions are forbidden for acolytes. Only the magus who have undergone the ceremony of sorrows have that privilege."

"I know that, Rye! I'm not a neophyte." Xander squinted at the salt from his sweat sliding into his eyes.

"Then you know it's forbidden, and you know why you can't cast." Reinhardt shuffled back to rest his weight on his opposite leg. He stroked his chin, as if to allow Xander the opportunity to vicariously exploit the reflex.

Xander's mouth fell agape. "No!" came out in a hushed whisper. "The Tor'Quari?"

Reinhardt's eyes shined wistfully at Xander's realization. With a pensive nod, he confirmed the disturbing notion. "I'm sorry to tell you, Cousin, but he has already been to see you once. He left his mark on your right hand."

A defeated Xander slumped to the ground. "And until it's gone, my connection to the asha is broken."

"That's true enough, and he has a whole list of questions to ask, particularly of this one." Reinhardt pointed a thumb back at Kumori.

"So, what am I to do for now?" Overcome with exhaustion, Xander hung his head low in the darkness of his prison cell.

Reinhardt's chest puffed up ever so slightly. "Just sit tight, Cousin, and I shall come to save you. We both know I can't help myself when there's a damsel in distress." A hint of concern crept through his melodramatic false bravado, and he started toward the door.

"Rye!" Xander yelped in a worried tone. A thought suddenly struck him like lightning. "Meraina—"

He continued toward the exit. "Is already safe at home. Mrs.

Paolo personally escorted her to the Vos'Gannon estate after she was done at the bakery for the day. Though the state she was in...." Reinhardt froze, letting the last statement hang in the air.

"State?" Trembling at the thought, Xander's voice cracked with concern.

Glancing back, Reinhardt gave his cousin a mischievous grin. "The poor child stuffed herself full of spiced bread pudding. She'll likely not eat until the next full moon or the one after."

Xander's shoulders went slack, and a sigh of relief escaped his lips. "You're an ass, you know that, right?"

"Guilty as charged, Your Grace. Oh, and Mrs. Paolo said she'll make the bill out to you personally, and on that account, we both know she'll settle up."

"I'd rather cross the Tor'Quari than an angry Mrs. Paolo," Xander quipped.

The pair of them chuckled before Reinhardt turned back to the door, taking his leave.

"What do we do now?" Bastian growled, pacing about his cell. One by one, he examined each bar, giving it a quick jerk.

"Now, I get released..." Xander's words stopped abruptly. "Hey, what the void? Why aren't you chained to the floor like me?"

Bastian slowly raised his arms into the air, pointing all of his fingers at Xander. With a mock smile, the Selece wiggled them as though he were casting a magic spell. Xander's shadow-covered face shifted in comprehension. Bastian threw his arms up in mock resignation, his gaze betraying his indifference.

"Don't chauf at me!" Xander squirmed in frustration, chains clanking together.

"Chauf?" Bastian asked.

"Yes! Chauf! To raise your arms in indignant mock resignation pointing out that I'm the idiot for not figuring out why I'm chained and you're not." Xander's voice rose in pitch and volume, his frustration growing with every word. "Because of the two of us, I'm the one with magical abilities. Chauf!"

Bastian's arms fell to his sides. He looked over at Kumori before glancing back to Xander's cell, chauffing once more at the impotent mage.

Xander looked at Kumori's cell, scoffing in frustration. "At least tell me that you're chained too."

Kumori's hands raised, innocently holding up a pair of steel shackles. "I was."

The shackles fell from the rogue's fingers. The chains rattled against the floor, sending up a small spark where the shackle struck a stone. Bastian looked over at the flash in excited curiosity. Kumori gestured toward the shackles and chauffed in Xander's direction.

"Would you stop it? As it is, I'm in here because of you!" Xander looked toward Bastian. "To answer your question, I will be leaving shortly because I'm innocent. You will most likely be getting exiled from the kingdom for causing trouble, and this one...." Xander said, flexing his good shoulder in Kumori's direction, "will probably lose a hand or two."

Bastian charged forward with a roar. "No! I will not be exiled. I cannot return home until I find the Spirit Stone!" His finger wrapped tight around two of the cold bars forming his cage.

"You should have thought of that before you made a scene." Kumori sneered at Bastian.

A voice shouted through the iron door's sliding window, "Hey, pipe down in there!"

"Stone? What stone?" Xander's voice was soft, with a curious tone.

Holding the bars, Bastian slid his hands down the metal shafts, lowering himself gently into a seated position on the cold stone floor. "The Spirit Stone. I'm only here because the Spirit Stone was stolen from my people. I came to find it and return it to my people, but not before I find out why it was taken."

"When was it taken?" Kumori crept up to the cell bars.

Bastian played at the fur on his leg, trying to distract himself from his inevitable failure. "They took it on the full moon before last."

"That was when someone stole the ancient relic from my village." Kumori's voice went flat, tears betraying a collection of hidden thoughts.

"That's convenient! You can't even have your own excuse, so you steal someone else's." Xander scooted back to position himself so he could lie against the bars. "What's this stone that was taken?"

Bastian turned toward Kumori, ignoring Xander's question. "What did they take?"

Kumori stared off at nothing, morose voice maintaining an even tone. "They took the ShenTaka. In broad daylight, they walked into the healer's sanctuary, shooting arrows and stabbing people. When the killing finished, they left with our greatest treasure."

"ShenTaka?" Bastian inquired.

Kumori pushed out a dejected sigh. "In Kaanish, they would call them healing circles or healing bracers."

The sound of metal sliding across metal filled the dank room, replacing the hushed whispers with the unbolting of an iron door. Light spilled into the corridor. Two soldiers came in carrying spears roughly seven feet in length. Light flecked off the gold trim on their red coats, displaying the traditional colors of Aestaria Una.

The guards stopped in front of Xander's cell, one tall and blond, the other taller, with short brown hair receding under his uniform cap. While the blond guard unlocked the cell door, the taller guard stood back and prepared to strike. Once inside, the shorter guard unlocked Xander's chain from the floor anchor and clutched the links in a firm fist. "Stand!"

Xander sensed the stern look on the guard's face by the sound of his voice. Xander stood as nimbly as anyone weighed down with twenty stones worth of metal and no use of their arms.

"Move." The guard used the butt of his spear to urge Xander forward. The soldier held the chain, much like that of an owner taking an unruly pet for a walk.

Xander remained calm and sauntered on, his indignation on display for all.

16

Xander's feet shuffled forward through the door into the light. The tingling sensation in his legs devolved into that dull ache that typically followed.

The two guards directed him down another passage that opened to a large galleria. He remembered being in this room before, to accompany his father during a property dispute with a member of House Han'Durial. Recalling the look on the viscount's face brought a laugh to Xander's throat that he couldn't stifle.

The room was filled with official-looking de sks, wh ere sanctioned arbiters sat on one side and disputing parties sat on the other. If two individuals were unable to come to a civil understanding, they hired an arbiter who would decide the matter. The defeated party always pays the entire cost, regardless of who brought the dispute to the arbiter.

To Xander's left, people bickered back in forth, debating about property rights, carrying on with civil disputes in the most uncivilized tones.

The distracted young mage slowed, and the rear guard's clenched knuckles prodded the prisoner in the back, urging him to continue his trudge along the wall. Just as his ears latched onto a decent dispute, they jerked him down another corridor under a placard labeled *'Officiator's Hall'*.

Reinhardt stood attentively just outside one of the officiator's offices, his eyes locked in the forward position. At the sight of his cousin, Xander's eyes filled with hope.

When Xander and his guards passed Reinhardt the cadet

remained stone-still, appearing unaware of his cousin's presence. Confused by Reinhardt's demeanor, Xander stared on.

Turning to face forward, Xander caught sight of a soldier walking in his direction. His skin was tanned like a smooth leather hide over lean muscles made from stone. He had well-oiled short dark hair, just long enough to fall freely, and a well-kept beard exuding a distinguished demeanor of authority. He wore the red and gold colors of Aestaria, with a mirror-polished archon's medallion hanging from a thick chain on his neck.

The thought of his gaze falling on the young mage sent Xander's organs into a cyclone of nausea. It was Serantes himself, King Dailan's head archon.

Xander continued looking back, his eyes following the famed figure. Serantes just passed the magistrates' office when Reinhardt gave a subtle wink, placing a finger over his mouth. Instantly, Xander's heart felt a touch of relief.

"Eyes forward. Keep movin'." The guard jerked the chain holding his wrists, sending a flash of white-hot pain through this shoulder.

The motion didn't dislocate his shoulder again, but it was so close he almost wished it had.

After going into another corridor and taking a sharp left, they faced an ominous, hard wooden door engraved with a menacing glyph—three interlocking tridents, all pointing in opposite directions. Reading the word under the symbol sent Xander's skin to crawling. *'Tor'Quari'*. These were the chambers of silence.

The guard on Xander's left knocked three times. Nothing happened. Slowly, the guard pulled the handle on the door. It opened to a desolate chamber illuminated by a red candle glowing orange. Strange bobbles, old books, and archaic trinkets cluttered four shelved walls. The room's primary feature was a large chair constructed of black iron, held aloft by a single metal pole anchored into the stone floor. The center piece was embellished with modest bits of crimson padding, leather straps, and steel manacles throughout, brandishing polished metallic leavers attached to each adjoining section of the chair.

Xander's eyes fluttered around the room while the guards urged him toward the center. The candle's glow sent flickers of amber through the shadows, revealing the guards' terror-stricken faces. They walked him to the chair in the middle of the room, despite being overwhelmed with dread.

One guard stepped toward the entrance, shutting it with an unsettling crash. The scrape of a large steel bolt sliding into place sent shivers up the young mage's spine.

Suddenly, Xander's hands were unshackled. Before he could enjoy his newfound comfort, the guards pushed Xander into the chair, slamming his wrists into the metallic restraints bolted to the furniture. Clicks came from somewhere beneath as they snapped metal locks into place. He examined the conditions of his wrists, investigating the locking mechanism within the shackles integrated into the chair. With a metallic clink, steel tightened around Xander's ankles, with his calves resting uncomfortably on a jagged metallic extension protruding forward from beneath him. *This quite reminds me of a barber's chair,* Xander reflected, *if it were constructed by a sadist.* He laughed at the thought. The rapping of three sharp knocks at the door forced him to swallow his amusement.

The guards unbolted the door. When it opened, an ominous form attired in black robes with a red collar appeared to float in with menacing grace. The candlelight glistened off the man's bald pate. His compact frame was in direct contrast to his imposing presence. An unnatural wake radiated so strongly from his fluid stride, the candles across the room shuttered with dread.

Xander gazed upon the Tor'Quari, who, despite all reason, seemed taller than the city walls. Logic told the young mage that if he stood on his feet, he would easily be a head taller than the robed inquisitor. Still, the imposing figure's aura of majestic height and ominous demeanor evoked a level of dread Xander had never known.

Xander wriggled around, desperately looking anywhere else. Meanwhile, the guards pressed themselves tightly against the chamber walls, disregarding any sense of dignified composure.

The Tor'Quari politely raised his right hand in a dismissive gesture, unleashing three simple words into the silence. "You may go." The words, infused with preternatural undertones, echoed off the stone walls in a perfect tenor.

Conflicted between paralyzing dread and the urge to flee for their lives, the guards exited the room with an unusual clockwork stride.

"It appears you have your own fan club," Xander quipped, clenching his bladder to keep from pissing himself.

"Maintaining a sense of humor, I see. I like that in a subject. So many people come in and wet themselves before we even have an opportunity to speak. Honestly, it's ridiculous how often I require the guards to clean secreted waste from this chair." The robed figure gracefully floated about, gathering small bobbles and trinkets to set them on a small wooden tray next to the chair. He lifted his nose into the air, taking two quick sniffs. "But not you. Not thus far, anyhow."

His voice was so sweet Xander couldn't help but want to hear the words, yet the content was such, he fought the urge to vomit. Xander's lack of ability to rationalize the dichotomy between the voice and its subject matter resulted in a powerful mental anguish.

"What are you going to do to me?" Xander's muscles tightened, actively rebelling against the instinct to squirm in discomfort.

"Nothing really. We're just going to have a casual conversation." The Tor'Quari's voice flowed forward in a warm, soothing tone. "Let us not forget our manners. I am Tor'Quari Pluvias, and you are?"

"I am Xander Danos of House Vos'Gannon." The words extracted themselves from Xander's throat involuntarily. His eyes went wide in confusion. "What happened? Why did I say that?"

Tor'Quari Pluvias stepped into the corner between his table and the chair. He looked down at Xander with the eyes of a mother, embracing a helpless newborn. "Because it's the truth."

"You can make me speak?" The words warbled from Xander's weak voice.

"My dear boy, I am the Tor'Quari supreme in the capital Magistrate's Hall of Justice within the Aestarian Kingdom. I could but whisper your name, and your life would simply snuff out. It would be easier for me to extinguish the light of your life than it would be to smother one of these candles along the wall. All that I require is your honesty."

The ominous figure reached toward his table, wrapping his long fingers around a small, sharp implement. With a steady confidence, he reached toward Xander's right hand.

"What are you doing?" Xander tried squirming away, and the shackles tightened around his struggling limbs.

"The examination, my dear boy."

Tor'Quari Pluvias steadied Xander's hand, bringing the tool's sharp point down to pierce the tip of the boy's middle finger, causing a red bead to well up to the surface. After grabbing a small glass vial full of clear liquid, he squeezed four drops of the young mage's blood into the tube, replaced the cork, and gave it a rapid shake. Xander's face went colorless, watching the Tor'Quari uncork the vial and lift it to his nose as though he were checking the bouquet of a fine vintage. With a slow turn of his wrist, he consumed the sample, savoring each drop.

Xander's face contorted in disgust. "What do you want to know? Just ask me, and I'll tell you."

"Of that, I am certain." The Tor'Quari used a cloth from the tray to wipe the remnants from his lips.

"All this for casting a stupid Cha'Sora spell in public? Just tell me what you want!" The chair shook under the weight of Xander's body, shifting in anger.

"That wasn't exactly a wise decision, but it's hardly the reason someone finds their way to *my* chair." The man folded his hands, interlacing his unusually lengthy fingers.

"What then?" Xander demanded.

The Tor'Quari traversed the room, floating back and forth. "There has been a string of murders in the past two weeks."

"Were they killed with magic?" Unable to avert his gaze, Xander stretched his neck around, eyes locked on his interrogator.

"No. It does not appear so," Tor'Quari Pluvias answered in a flat tone.

"What does that have to do with me, then?" Xander unwillingly relented to his exhaustion and gently slumped back in the chair.

The figure came once more to the chairside, looming over Xander's helpless body. "The murders were committed with a knife by an unknown stealth figure in a cloak able to swiftly climb walls, leaving no trace."

Xander gawked, in comprehension. "What does that have to do with me? The one you're looking for is the Nepharen in the other cell."

"At first, we didn't know how the targets were being chosen, but after seeing the two of you together, everything has fallen into place. The first victims were the highest members of House Han'Durial, followed by those from the house of San'Durin and Ras'Burgess. It can't help but be noted that none of those from the houses of Vos'Gannon have fallen, and house Vos'Gannon has the most to gain from these deaths, and now you have been seen with the murderer..."

"I didn't! We didn't!" Xander bucked, jostling the chair. "My father is a fallen hero from the Trillium wars! House Vos'Gannon received the medal of vitari from the high king on his behalf. Being honor bound to uphold his memory, we would never do such a thing!"

"Of course not. That's why you hired your little Nepharen friend in there. Everyone knows the Vos'Gannon don't do their own dirty work." The Tor'Quari squinted, regarded the helpless young mage.

"We are good people, loyal to Ashana, loyal to Aestaria." Xander's proud words came out radiating with heat.

"So you say—" A timid rapping sound from behind interrupted the inquisitor. With a sigh of disappointment, he walked over to open the door's sliding window. "Why am I being disturbed?"

"Your Grace, Archon Serantes, has requested your immediate presence in the magistrate's quarters," the disembodied voice apprehensively stated through the small opening.

"Very well. Take this one back to his cell. I'll summon him again when he has more strength." Tor'Quari Pluvius unbolted the door and stood aside while the guards entered. "Don't worry, Xander Danos of House Vos'Gannon. I will see you again soon."

The ominous figure floated from the room, and three guards entered. Two of the guards worked at unlocking the shackles, while a third stood out of arm's reach with a spear at the ready. They placed Xander's wrists back into another set of shackles before removing the restraints on his ankles and brought him to his feet. One guard grabbed the chain, and the other moved him along almost sympathetically.

As they exited the room, Xander was overcome with a sudden sense of confusion. "Where am I? Why am I here?"

"This is the worst part," one guard disparaged, hoisting Xander's arm up to keep him steadily moving forward.

"Yeah, I hate it when they get like this," the other guard agreed, matching his compatriot's pace. "Just follow us, mate, and everything will be fine."

The three of them continued awkwardly shuffling forward, retracing their steps back under the placard, *'Officiator's Hall'*, passing through the same set of open doors. Xander looked about, catching flashes of desks and chairs next to blackboards in each room. Head wobbling about, the mage's stare was cast beyond everything in sight. Outside one room stood Reinhardt's stone-still figure.

Passing by his cousin's station, Xander glanced into the room where Serantes and a little bald man in black robes were engaged in serious discussion under hushed tones. Unable to make out the details of their conversation, he had just enough sense to hope it wasn't about him.

They walked down the corridors back to Xander's cell. The two at his sides sat him on the wooden bench against the wall, while the other reconnected his chain to the floor anchor. A metallic crash echoed from the cell doors with a sense of finality before the guards turned the key, locking the deadbolt into place with a click.

"D'at one's, slush brained as a slug head, he is," one guard commented on their way out of the corridor.

Overcome with fatigue, Xander slumped off the bench. His shoulder hit the hard-stone floor, sending flashes of white-hot pain through his arm. The agony overtook his vision, and he surrendered to the darkness of exhaustion.

17

Bastian's head rested uncomfortably against the metal bars. Kumori's voice continued fading into the background while the Selece nodded in and out of consciousness. A thought crept into Bastian's mind from nowhere, igniting a flame that consumed his weariness.

Bastian interjected over Kumori, "Can any use your healing bracers outside the Nepharen people?"

"I don't understand the question." Kumori shrugged, bearing a visage of uncertainty.

Bastian ran his fingers through his mane in frustrated exhaustion. "If I wore the bracers, could I use them?" Bastian pointed at Xander. "If he wore the bracers, could he use them?"

Kumori's head shook. "You're not Nepharen." The rogue pointed at Xander. "He's not Nepharen, so they would not work."

A moan echoing from Xander's cell lingered in the air as he tried to push himself up from the floor, only to find his arms still restrained behind his back. "Holy kotch eggs. My head feels like it's been through a wood splitter." He forced out a grunt of determination. Pushing off the wooden bench with his feet, he hoisted himself up against the cell bars, a sigh of triumph, his only reward for achieving this minor victory. "What are you two idiots going on about?"

"What does it matter if we're idiots?" Kumori sneered at Xander's cell.

Emanating a low rumble, Bastian's growl evolved into Kaanish words. "The relics stolen from our people can only be used by our people. Both of our lands were attacked by Kandari raiders to take relics that only our people can use. Both attacks happened on the full moon before last."

The door jolted and the metal latches on the iron door clicked. The door burst open, sending a chirp from the metal hinges before thudding shut with haste.

"Xander, are you ok?" Reinhardt whispered, creeping with purpose through the cell corridor.

"Yeah, my head feels like it was used as a tangu ball, and I don't remember what happened. I was taken away and brought back, but I don't remember anything in-between."

"That's the Tor'Quari Thaumaturgy. That's how they keep it a secret. The room uses magic to hold the memories of whatever happened inside. Listen! We have to get you out of here." Reinhardt walked through the next open cell to get behind Xander. There, he started fiddling with his shackles through the bars.

"What are you doing? Are we going to see the magistrate?" Xander shook his hands to wiggle the shackles loose. Moments later, they rattled to the floor. He pulled his hands in front of him, bringing his free hand to massage his injured shoulder. The attempt failed to stem the pain of the inevitable ache already setting in.

"That's not going to be an option at this point." Reinhardt opened the cell. "There have been a string of murders of high-ranking lords and nobles all across Aestaria Una. They think your friend over there is the killer, and they're alleging that you've been selecting the targets. Soon, they'll be bringing in your family for questioning to see if they are conspiring with you."

"This is absolute madness! My father received the medal of vitari for his part in Aestaria's Trillium war victory." Xander lunged at the cell bars, pulling at them in frustration.

Reinhardt withdrew a small, polished flask decorated with flourishes all around it. "That's irrelevant at this point. I overheard the Tor'Quari speaking with the archon, and your whole family will be taken in for questioning."

Xander's mouth went agape before his eyes flashed with anger. "Meraina?"

Reinhardt reached through the bars to put a reassuring hand on Xander's forearm. "Don't worry. I sent a Tapi-gram to let them know. Your mother and sister are being escorted to the Vos'Korendel stronghold."

"Thank Ashana for those little sprites and their love of sweets, but won't your family come under suspicion?" Xander started rubbing at the Tor'Quari's mark, hoping to restore his connection to Ashara.

"That won't work. You'll need this." Reinhardt held up the small flask full of liquid. "This is the Tor'Quari's sombra oil. You need to remove the mark with this, or it will remain indefinitely, and no, the archon will have no desire to engage with the forces of House Vos'Korendel. He'll need to handle these matters with civility, and that should give us all the time we need." Reinhardt held out the flask over Xander's hand.

"This better work." Xander held his marked hand out under the flask.

"By the void, it better. I had to dump two hundred chen worth of Baltairan liquor to get this." Reinhardt poured the black inky oil over Xander's hand.

Xander worked the tincture into the skin. A freezing pain shot through his hand. He shook his arm out, trying to prevent the numbness from setting in. The mage took a step back. Allowing the feeling to creep back into his hands, he placed his palms together. In a motion, he extended his hands, chanting, "On'Daka."

A shield of asha came to life with arcs of blue lightning shimmering through the air. Just as quickly, the shield was gone.

Xander gave Reinhardt a curt nod. "Okay, what's the plan?"

"After I get you free, I'll take you to see Adriel. You'll be safe there." Reinhardt played at the set of keys, examining each one.

"Now? I'm going to meet Adriel? You've told me for years how much he hates company, and you pick now of all times to introduce me?" Xander approached cell door.

"What about us?" Bastian growled from his cell, leaning up against the bars.

"What about you?" Reinhardt retorted, chauffing at Bastian.

"I need to get out of here to complete my quest and save my people." Bastian's grip tightened around the bars.

"How's that my problem?" Reinhardt sneered.

Kumori walked to the corner of the cell. "We can certainly make it your problem. We'll be happy to tell them where you've gone."

"Shaat!" Reinhardt smacked his head against the palm of his hand in embarrassed frustration.

"Never one for the bigger picture, Rye! Besides, it is our problem. I don't know how yet, but this is all connected." Xander pointed at Kumori and Bastian. "They both came here to retrieve artifacts stolen from their people, not to go on a noble-killing spree. We both know I'm innocent, and the best way to prove that is to prove their innocence." Xander struggled to stretch his shoulder, attempting to work it into a comfortable position. "Speaking of which, if we're not going with the magistrate's blessing, how are we leaving? It's not as though we can walk through the front door."

Reinhardt regained his composure and puffed out his chest. "That's the genius part." He walked to the end of the corridor, pointing at a hatch. "This is the shaft that leads to the waste tanks outside."

"We're going through the waste chute? That's original!" Xander rolled his eyes at Reinhardt.

"Genius, isn't it? Wait. That was sarcasm! How is my plan not original?"

"Oh, it's original." Kumori chided.

Reinhardt twisted one of the jailer's keys within the deadbolt connected to the inner waste hatch.

"So original only an idiot would think of it." Xander examined his cell door and looked back at Reinhardt with a blank stare.

"Oh, sorry. The cell doors need to stay shut until it's time in case there are any surprise visitors." Walking by each cell door, Reinhardt carefully examined the keys.

"All right, so your idea... Aren't the waste chutes filled with shaat and directed toward the incinerator?" Xander leaned up against the bars, favoring his bad shoulder.

"Yes, but I'll open the cleaning hatch so you can get out that way." Standing in his most confident posture, Reinhardt's nose came level with the top of Xander's head.

"Ya know, standing like a rooster won't make this idea any better." Xander scoffed.

Kumori interjected, "If it's filled with shaat, can you just use your magic to make it explode and we can just escape through the front door?"

"It doesn't work that way." Xander sighed. "It's not fire or heat. It's pure ashareal energy. But that gives me an idea." He looked up at Reinhardt. "We *are* walking out through the front door."

"How?" Reinhardt walked up to Xander's cell and unlocked the door.

"Unlock the cells. We're all getting out of here, and give me your knife." Xander took the knife from Reinhardt and cut a strip of fabric from the bottom his robe. "Go around and unlock the shaat hatch like you planned. Then crow three times to let us know it's done."

"Crow three times? But I'll look like an idiot standing out there, yelling cock-a-doodle-doo." Reinhardt walked over, putting the key in Bastian's cell door. "I'm going to unlock this, but you need to stay inside until it's time. Do you understand?"

Bastian responded with a slight nod.

Reinhardt turned the key, and the door latch popped with a click. The air went still, with a palpable tension growing between them. Neither moved for what seemed like an eternity. Reinhardt backed away slowly, keeping eye contact before walking over to Kumori's cell.

"You've always acted like a cock, Rye. Nobody who knows you will ever be able to tell the difference." Xander snickered at Reinhardt.

Reinhardt walked up and put the key into Kumori's cell door. "Do you see the gratitude I get for saving his life?" The lock turned, sliding the latch out of place with a click.

"Wonderful! Now unlock the waste hatch door, and don't forget to crow three times when you're done. Oh, and leave it closed. We'll meet at the alley behind Hassig's forge." Xander spoke while playing at the fabric.

"What's the plan?" Reinhardt asked, walking toward the massive iron door at the other end of the corridor.

"Oh, and remember to leave the big door unlocked as well." Xander's one hand took a momentary break from playing at his fabric to point in the direction Reinhardt was heading.

Reinhardt stretched out his cousin's name like a tightrope between two distant trees. "Xander?"

Xander struck his most arrogant pose, imitating his cousin's voice as he said, "Trust me. It's absolute genius."

Reinhardt chauffed at Xander and exited through the large steel door. The door clanged shut, filling the room with silence. Bastian and Kumori continued waiting by their cell doors in anticipation.

A few minutes later, Xander held up a piece of braided rope with frayed ends on each side, folded in half. "And done!" he exclaimed, declaring some exciting victory.

"What's done?" Bastian squinted at the object in Xander's hands through the twilight coming in from the windows.

"This is our key out of here." Xander held the cloth up in Bastian's direction.

"It doesn't look much like a key," Kumori scoffed.

"Oh, it will be. Just wait and see." Xander sat on the bench in anticipation of his cousin's signal.

Time passed, filling the room with a palpable stillness. Seconds felt like hours, and minutes stretched into proverbial years while the prisoners contemplated their inevitable fates should this plan fail. Through the silence, a ridiculous warble echoed from a Kandari throat, a best attempt at an unpracticed rooster call. The shrill screeches were laughable enough that the imprisoned trio chuckled.

Xander walked over toward his cell door and knelt down to pick up the shackles. The mage held the makeshift torch in his bad arm, striking the stone floor with the steel cuffs. Flying into the fabric, sparks turned thin threads into ashen red embers that quickly faded away. Striking the ground once again, Xander sent flashes of fiery sparks into the fabric. The embers glowed red once more before trickling to nothing. He tried again and again to no effect, the ache of fatigue slowing his arm. The image of Reinhardt pouring black sombra oil onto his hands flashed through Xander's mind, and he glanced around the room, searching for the flask.

"He took it with him." Kumori's Nepharen accent came out flat. "This was your genius plan? Maybe if you would have told us, I would have said to use the oil, but now it's gone."

Xander tried again, attempting to will away the futility before slumping back, defeated by his own hubris. He was so overcome with grief he didn't notice when his cell door opened. A large fur-covered hand reached down and slid its fingers around the cuff. Xander looked up at Bastian's sympathetic face.

"Let me."

Their eyes locked in a moment of mutual understanding. After placing the cloth and the cuff in Bastian's hand, Xander's fingers slipped away wearily.

Tensing his fingers firmly around the material, Bastian knelt to the cell floor. He shifted the cloth to his off hand. "These stones aren't all the same." He pointed to a stone in the middle. "This looks like the stone we make our cooking fires with."

Holding out the makeshift torch, the Selece scraped the steel circlet against the stone. Sparks flew across the ground, lighting the cell in a flash like lightning. The sparks hit the frayed ends, and they began to smolder. Bastian slowly drew the cloth to his lips in a cupped hand and gently blew on the cloth. Xander and Kumori looked on in amazement, watching the embers come to life.

Bastian walked to Xander, who was now standing between the row of cells. The Selece reached out, offering the burning cloth to his new Kandari friend.

Xander took the flame carefully. "Excellent, let's get out of here."

Kumori walked out of the cell toward the others.

The mage pointed to the enormous iron door. "Stand over there."

Bastian and Kumori made their way to the exit.

Walking to the maintenance hatch with the flaming piece of cloth, Xander pulled the hatch open just enough to fit the burning fabric inside. After slamming the hatch shut, he ran the locks shaft through the latch and dove away in a forward roll. Coming up facing the hatch, the mage shouted the mantra, "On'Daka."

Azure strands of magically charged light spread across the air as the energetic shield flickered to life. With a roar, the building shook, and the hatch flew off its hinges toward Xander's head. Arcs of blue lightning flared to burning white within the ashareal barrier, protecting the trio from the metal plate. A stream of fire poured long and hot from the stone shaft, slamming hard against Xander's shield. The impromptu furnace's flames licked around the shield, lashing at Xander's arms and legs. The fire gave out just before Xander collapsed from exhaustion, both having spent all of their fuel.

Bastian picked Xander up and carried him the way a mother would hold a small child. Kumori opened the door to the sounds of absolute chaos echoing through the building. They navigated their way along the walls of the large hall toward the sound of mayhem until they found an exit. The only guards they could see were bolting toward the exits.

"My cloak. I need my cloak and my knives," Kumori muttered, following Bastian toward the front of the building.

"I also need my chatta blades, but more than that, right now, we need our freedom. The rest can wait." Bastian trudged forward, lugging the incapacitated Kandari closer to the exit. Making his best effort to walk calmly, he pressed steadily toward the freedom of fresh sunlight. They walked down the large municipal building steps when a voice rang out in their direction.

"Hey, you there! Stop!" Two guards rushed over, spears in hand. "What are you doing with that boy? What happened?"

Kumori faded into the background, appearing to be a random bystander of whom the guards took no notice.

Bastian looked around nervously. "I... When the ground shook, he fell and hit his head. I'm taking him to..." Searching for the word, Bastian looked about, leaving an awkward silence hanging in the air.

"To the medicus? Is that where you're headed? If so, you'll

need to go that direction," the guard said, pointing down the road, "and take a right on Bellatori Street."

Agonizing screams from the rear of the buildings caught the guard's attention, and they bolted toward the pleas for help.

Bastian walked in the direction they pointed.

Kumori suddenly appeared at Bastian's side, walking along as if nothing had happened. "Where are we going?"

"To the healer. The medicus," Bastian growled, marching forward.

"That is not the wisest course of action." Kumori followed, taking swift smooth steps to keep pace with the Selece's long stride.

"Yes, but we must, so we will." Bastian jostled Xander's still body, repositioning his arms and legs in a threshold position to make him easier to carry.

"Mother. Meraina," Xander mumbled in his half-conscious state.

Looking around, Kumori discovered an obscured place where the three could rest. "Come this way."

Kumori led the encumbered Selece through a corridor while Xander wriggled in his arms. The rogue led them down an alleyway with a patch of grass behind a clothesline filled with hanging linens. Bastian gently sat Xander on the ground up against a crate next to the rear of a building.

Xander's head wobbled unsteadily. "Did it work? Are we free?" He groaned.

Bastian stuffed a clump of linens behind Xander's back to help him sit up straight. "Yes, we're out. We're free."

"Hiding from authorities is hardly free," Kumori added.

Xander slowly struggled to stand upright. Bastian stepped in to assist, but Xander raised a hand in protest. "No, I don't need help. I'll be fine."

Bastian backed away cautiously. "You are still weak, Kandari. You should see the medicus."

"What we need right now is to find Reinhardt." Xander pushed himself away from the wall, stumbling a bit before he regained his balance.

"You are burned." Bastian pointed to the scorch marks on Xander's clothes where the fire had reached around his shield.

Xander examined the burns. "It's only medium rare. I'll be fine."

A stillness grew between them in a bubble of awkward silence until burst by Bastian's rumbling chuckle. "Just cooked a little, still pink in the center."

Doing his best to ignore the pain, Xander shambled forward with a nod. "We need to make it to the back alley behind the smith's forge. Follow me."

Bastian and Kumori followed the mage into the din of people bustling about their usual day strolling through the thoroughfare.

18

Reinhardt stood behind the smith's forge, surrounded by the ringing of steel striking steel. Hammers hit home time and time again as master smiths grunted away, sweating over their anvils. Reinhardt's nose scrunched up at the tang of soot wafting through the air. Shifting the bulky satchel on his shoulder, he pulled a small pocket dial from his vest. The sun was still high in the sky, but much of the day was gone.

One word crept from Reinhardt's lips while he looked up at the sky, observing a black ring round the daytime moon. "Onsday...."

The repetitive crash of steel on steel resonated monotonously in the air, keeping time with an unending clock when three figures rounded the corner into the back alleyway. Reinhardt started toward them, when his stomach dropped at the severity of Xander's injuries, with dark bruises and burns on one side.

Upon closer inspection, he noticed his cousin's stride favored one leg. "Xander! what happened?"

Xander approached with a slight limp, leaning to one side. Grabbing the Selece's large forearm, he used Bastian for a makeshift crutch. Xander gave Reinhardt a flat look and responded in a slow, intense monotone. "Someone... blew up... the jail!"

Reinhardt's face twisted, betraying a frustrated anger. Xander let out a chuckle, only to wince at the shock of pain rippling through his body from his ribs.

Reinhardt collected his posture, perfectly harmonizing pompous and condescending into a symphony of arrogance. "Serves you right!"

After exchanging glances of frustration with Bastian, Kumori spoke up. "Will you two ever stop?"

Both heads turned, shooting their gaze at the lithe Nepharen figure. "No!"

Bastian interjected, "Whatever you do, you'll have to do it on the move. He needs a healer."

The large Selece shifted about, allowing Reinhardt to take his cousin. With his former charge secured, Bastian stepped back to consider the taller Kandari's words.

Reinhardt infused his tone with heated determination. "What we need is to get out of this city. I know where we can go, but we need to leave now to get there before nightfall."

Shifting his shoulder under Xander's weight, Reinhardt slipped the satchel onto the ground. The metallic pieces within crashed together, clattering against one another.

The group looked to the satchel, but Bastian spoke first. "Is that—"

Kumori's eyes lit up, choppy alto voice pushing aside the Selece's words. "Are those..."

The two dropped to their knees around the bag, pulling the fabric down around its contents. With all the speed of a starving Selece skinning a jora, they pawed at the contents within. Bastian retrieved a leather sheath, clutching a row of throwing blades. Kumori grabbed at the blades and pulled Bastian's strapped chatta claws from the sack, replacing one for the other in the Selece's enormous paw.

The Nepharen dove back in, pulling out a large cloak shimmering between sovereign blue and gallant purple over a crimson lining. Wrists flicking with the slightest movement, the rogue became shrouded within the cloak. The fabric settled over Kumori's lithe form, melting away a sense of tension.

The two picked through the rest of the pack, exchanging and

trading bits and pieces back and forth. It wasn't unlike watching a pair of children trade candies and sweets at a Drokenalia festival. Their gaze locked on each other as Kumori's hand clutched a small pouch full of chen. The rogue's hand lifted slowly. Bastian's paw clutched the small sack, and an unspoken understanding exchanged between them. Bastian then secured the pouch to one of the leather straps on his waist.

Reinhardt regarded the two, eyes tensing with greater and greater frustration at the passage of time. "Are you two done yet? We need to make our way out of the city."

Bastian's eyes narrowed in anger, shifting his gaze skyward toward Reinhardt's dreary expression. "No! I'm not leaving tonight. I must find Jorgan. I came for Jorgan."

Reinhardt looked to Bastian curiously. "Jorgan? There are hundreds of men named Jorgan in this city and likely some women. Why do you need to see Jorgan, and why does it have to be now?"

"Jorgan came to the Selece territories in the night and stole our Spirit Stone." Bastian turned his face stone cold to suppress the well of rage boiling within.

"So, they stole a rock. What of—" Reinhardt began.

Xander interrupted, "No, Cousin, I think it's bigger than that." Xander motioned Bastian to continue.

The Selece nodded, his mane shimmering a light golden brown in the midday sun. "Without the Spirit Stone gifted to us by the goddess Theshana, my people are condemned to death."

Reinhardt's eyes flickered about, searching for lurking passersby or leering onlookers. "What would Jorgan want with the stone? Why take it, and to my original question, which Jorgan?"

Bastian rooted through a pouch on his belt. "I don't know. I need to find him so I can ask him." Bastian answered the last question by holding up a small, polished brass emblem etched with a setting sun behind a winged moravian in flight.

Reinhardt's eyes stared blankly at the small brass embellishment, trying to focus on the moving target.

Xander lifted his head, glancing toward Bastian's raised hand holding the shiny brass piece. He coughed out a sound as the tension fled from his neck, sending his gaze back toward the ground. "Oh."

Reinhardt's eyes focused. "Shaat!" His mouth fell agape, and his shoulders lifted, making no attempt to hide his reluctance to help.

Bastian's expression hardened in frustration. Shifting his gaze between the two Kandari, he pointed at the glistening brass emblem. "This is why I'm here. This is why I've come. If you won't help me, I'll go myself."

Bastian stomped an angry march, pushing his way past the two, taking care not to cause Xander to lose his footing. Descending from a rooftop to follow, Kumori moved at a medium jog to keep up with the large Selece.

"We'll leave you to the Aestarian Guard and the Tor'Quari." Reinhardt's words followed Bastian down the street, hitting him square in the gut.

Bastian stopped so quickly, Kumori nearly crashed into the large bestial figure. Moments later, Bastian sloughed the comment off, and the two continued forward.

"Cousin, we need them!" Xander's imploring voice echoed off the ground, his gaze forced toward the alley floor.

Bantering like an old married couple, the bumbling duo staggered down the alley. Reinhardt pulled Xander along at a brisk pace, making an effort not to step faster than necessary.

The foppish Kandari's posh voice rang out again in a high tenor, with a delicate tone running through his sympathetic plea.

"The two of you, please wait. I was… If my cousin says we should stay together, then that's what we'll do, but if Jorgan kills us all, I'm beating the shaat out of both of you."

Bastian and Kumori exchanged a confused look, then turned in unison and chauffed at Reinhardt.

Reinhardt indignantly raised a single finger. "Pain! Lots of pain!" His anger resolved into an exhausted chuckle.

Bastian ran a paw through his mane in confusion. "How does one dead person beat another dead person?"

Kumori looked up at Bastian. "I think he was trying to be funny."

Bastian stared back. "Jorgan killed my father. That is not funny!" Bastian shifted his gaze toward Reinhardt. "My father's death is not humorous."

Reinhardt's face softened sympathetically. "No, you're right. It isn't funny. I was trying to break the tension, but you're right. This isn't a time for jokes. Just follow us, and we'll take you to Jorgan, but you need to be aware Jorgan is related to the archon of Aestaria Una. He's nearly as protected as the royal family when he's not operating as a mercenary on the archon's behalf."

The group silently pressed forward toward their destination.

Kumori kept pace to match Xander and withdrew a hand from an inner pocket of the indigo cloak. The rogue held out a clenched fist, offering the injured Kandari a small twig. Xander accepted the herbal stem, nearly half the length of his own finger and a quarter the width.

"What's this?" The injured Kandari inspected the small stick.

"For the pain." Kumori pantomimed chewing a similar invisible piece to imitate what Xander should do with the bit in his hand.

Following the instruction, Xander began chewing. It wasn't altogether unpleasant, tasting of citrus and mint.

With Xander's arm slung across his shoulders, Reinhardt led the group. While the unlikely alliance crossed the occasional major road, they usually ducked into a side street or walked through a back alleyway.

Reinhardt maintained the pace, occasionally inspecting Xander until less and less support was required. "Feeling better cousin?"

Xander's eyes shifted to Reinhardt. "I'm not ready to run the Uraton, but I'll manage."

The Kandari regarded the rogue with an appreciative look. Kumori acknowledged with a swift nod, exchanging an unspoken understanding between the two.

Brilliant hues of twilight pink and dusk purple painted the sky when Reinhardt motioned for them to turn left at the next crossing. They continued down a road with a street sign labeled, *'Veronis'*. The group pressed forward along the lengthy stretch of road flanked by dense woodlands at either side until they came upon a final placard, *'Han'Shoden way'*. This new cobblestone road ran crossways, and their quarry lay just beyond.

A black iron gate stood closed before them. Facing the barrier, they stood between two stone pillars. By Bastian's measure, each pillar was two lengths high, adorned at their tops with large flaming lamps. At the gate's center was a round golden disk, brandishing an embossed image of a winged moravian steed against a setting sun.

Standing two or three lengths back from the gate, Bastian pulled the small bobble from his pouch. He held the polished brass piece in a position to obscure his view of the larger ornament. He shifted the smaller etched adornment in and out of his line of sight, comparing it with the larger seal to confirm what he already knew. Large glyphs above the gate shone in the pillar's illumination.

Bastian pointed at the glyphs. "What does this mean?"

"Trouble," Reinhardt snapped back without hesitation. "That's what it means."

"It reads 'Han'Shoden.' That's Jorgan's family name, which means this is their estate." Xander gave his cousin a disappointing look, which was promptly returned in kind for different reasons.

The rhythmic sound of metal clattering against metal grew louder from within the gate. Xander and Reinhardt exchanged an inquisitive glance before Kumori spoke. "Guards are coming!"

Bastian stealthily made his way up a tree.

Reinhardt and Xander looked around for their Nepharen companion, only to find themselves alone. They hobbled toward the stone wall, keeping themselves lower than the decorative foliage obscuring part of the wall.

"I know I heard something." One guard placed a contorted piece of metal into the gate behind the family crest.

"The day we rely on what you know, Korbin, 'll be the day I let 'em string me up by my toes, 'n boil me in oil," his compatriot quipped.

"Well, Trax, you would still taste better than your wife's cookin'!" Korbin pushed forward against the barrier. The emblem separated into two complementary halves, allowing the guards to walk through the open gate.

"I'll have you know my wife makes a perfectly fine bowl of Gelder noodles." Trax looked about, inspecting the shadow-cast areas created by the trees and random obstacles obscuring the lamplight.

"Um, shaat for brains, Gelder noodles come ready to eat from the market."

Trax placed his hand to his heart. " And on my mum's grave, they're the most delicious thing I eat all day."

The two burst into a boisterous laugh, cut short by the sound of large menacing footsteps from within the woodland catty-corner from the gate. The roar of a large jungle beast echoed from beyond the ominously shaded tree line.

"What *was* that?" Trax quivered.

"Nothing I'd care for us to deal with on our own."

The two scurried back through the gate, closing it behind them. They sprinted through the courtyard until they were back into the main house.

Bastian's feet landed soundlessly in the grass beneath his perch. Reinhardt and Xander shuffled from the brush.

Reinhardt turned to Bastian. "Was that you?"

"It was me," a Nepharen accent came from behind the unlikely allies.

All heads turned, each brandishing a confused look toward Kumori's cloaked silhouette. Within the Nepharen's outstretched palm was a dark orange ceramic piece in the shape of a teardrop with holes at either end. Kumori blew into the small end, causing the air around the group to reverberate in the wake of what sounded like a massive jungle beast's roar.

Pushing past his confusion at the situation, Reinhardt spouted. "While I appreciate both the novelty and the utility of this, we need to push on because they're about to return in force, and—" Reinhardt's last words were drowned beneath the wave of a battle horn sounding from the house.

Bastian stepped toward Reinhardt, motioning at Xander. "Give him to me."

"What are you going to do with him?" Reinhardt's tone was infused with a hint of worry.

"Stop him from slowing us down." Bastian reached for Xander's neck.

Reinhardt's hand instinctively met Bastian's forearm in protest. "You can't just kill him. He's my cousin."

Xander looked to Reinhardt. "He's not going to kill me. He's going to carry me."

The mage's face was confident, but his voice cracked with uncertainty. Gently, he guided Reinhardt's arm back down to his side.

"Oh, right. I knew that. I'm not a rutting idiot."

Reinhardt shifted to the side, and Bastian knelt down, draping the mage over his shoulders in a manner that was becoming all-too-familiar for the large Selece.

"Follow me." Kumori passed the Selece to run around the estate's perimeter.

Bastian's foot dug into the ground, shifting the dirt beneath to push off into a jog. The large Selece kept the estate's gate to his right side, staying just a few lengths behind the cloaked Nepharen.

A surprised Reinhardt bumbled forward with a yelled "Hey!" before clapping his own mouth shut. "Wait for me!" he croaked in a voiceless gasp.

Clutching at the hilt of his sword to prevent it from clattering about, he allowed his years of experience running from lords, lovers, and dice throwers to take over. Once he found his stride, he discovered it wasn't too difficult to keep up with the rest, though the terrain was more uneven than he would prefer.

Glancing through the perimeter gate, onto a well-lit courtyard, Reinhardt counted a dozen Han'Shoden soldiers. In unison, they marched toward the front gate. Once through the gate, the armored contingent stepped double time into the wilderness to hunt a deadly beast within the Han'Shoden woods.

Kumori stopped to take a knee. "Do you see it?"

Reinhardt looked puzzled. "See what?"

Bastian knelt silently. "The light ends there."

Kumori reached over Bastian's shoulder, handing Xander another small piece of twig. "I will go. You will chew and rest."

Kumori turned to Bastian. "You will protect them."

"What will I do?" Reinhardt groaned under his breath.

"If we need your help, then all is truly lost." Kumori leveled an intense gaze at Reinhardt.

The Kandari's posh voice strained in frustration. "Hey, I can—"

"I know what you can do." Kumori snapped. "If we need to spill that much blood, we will find ourselves drowning in more trouble than we can swim out of."

Before Reinhardt could reply, Kumori was over the fence. The indigo cloak on the rogue's back faded into the darkness, presenting the illusion of nothing but shadow.

Reinhardt grunted in irritation.

Still suspended on the Selece's hulking shoulders, Xander looked at Reinhardt. "Cousin, we have two goals—clear their names and restore my house's honor and, by proximity, your house as well."

"My house? What does my family's name have to do with this?"

"It's only a matter of time before they draw your family into this because of the alliances and blood shared between our two houses." Xander's face flushed red.

"Xander? What's the matter?" Reinhardt observed cautiously. "Your skin is turning bright red, as though you just bumped into Kera Dar'Banvil in the square."

"My heart is racing. Wait, Kera? Does everyone know—" Xander started gasping heavily.

Bastian spoke before Xander could continue. "What is poking me in the back? Is that your blade handle?"

Xander's gaze fell just below his belt buckle. "I don't carry a blade." His voice came out flat.

Bastian shrugged, rolling Xander backward.

"Just what are you doing?" Reinhardt chided, watching Xander collapse to the ground.

"Your family, your problem."

The three of them looked below Xander's belt.

"You planning ongoing camping, Cousin?" Reinhardt chuckled.

"What is going on?" Xander clutched his knees to his chest.

Bastian sniffed the air before kneeling toward Xander. The Selece drew his nose toward Xander's face.

"What are you doing?" Xander exclaimed, remaining folded in half, clutching at his knees.

"Well, Cousin, you do appear to be in the mood for a kiss," Reinhardt jibed.

Picking up a scent, Bastian pulled his head around. He followed the fragrance to a small half-chewed twig laying on the ground. The three of them looked at the twig before Bastian picked it up by the un-chewed end. He gave it a sniff and let out a small chuckle.

"I don't see what's so funny," Xander lamented.

"The elders in my tribe use something like this to..." Bastian paused to search for words. "Feel young again with their mates."

"Why would Kumori give this to me?" Xander questioned.

"Stand up," Bastian ordered.

"He's injured," Reinhardt insisted.

"Stand. Up," Bastian repeated firmly.

Xander stood tall, looking around inquisitively, as if in search of something he'd lost. "No, Cousin, the pain is gone. All of it."

"All of it? How?" A confused Reinhardt turned to Bastian.

"This twig does many things. Faster Heart." Bastian's fist thudded against his chest. "Faster health for the injured." He held his arms out in front of him, bringing his opened palms in toward his torso, representing general vitality. "And better..." He shook his tightened fist in the air.

"He's right, Cousin. I feel fine." Xander flexed about, admiring his newfound wellbeing.

A horn rang out from within the estate.

Reinhardt's head snapped toward the courtyard. "Just in time, it would seem."

The three crouched to the ground. Bastian peered over the shrubbery. Without warning, he silently dashed toward a tree and climbed.

Reinhardt turned to Xander. "Are you well enough, Cousin?" When Xander's head gave a curt nod, Reinhardt asked, "And your asha?"

"We're about to find out." Xander ran along the perimeter toward the darkness just past the tree Bastian climbed. The preternatural thrum of asha reverberated in the air around him, while aethereal energy coalesced beneath his feet. "Cho'Raka," he said, becoming airborne.

As he coasted over the barrier, one foot clipped a spire on the fence, sending Xander end over end toward the ground. The skilled mage turned the botched spell into a challenging somersault, and he rolled forward into a kneeling position.

Reinhardt quickly came up behind him, with Bastian at the rear. "You planning to propose or fight?"

Xander chauffed at Reinhardt. "How did you—"

Reinhardt interjected, "You think I don't know how to climb a fence?"

"I guess no tall stiff rod is going to stand between Reinhardt and his duchesses."

"Indeed." Reinhardt smirked while they all sprinted toward the main estate house.

Bastian found a set of stones jutting out, working their way up the stone wall. The large Selece secured a footing to ensure the stones would hold him.

"Think you can clear it?" Reinhardt looked at Xander.

Bastian replied first, "Wait here. I'll look inside first."

The Selece climbed the stone wall. Upon reaching the window, he quickly peered inside. After a quick peek, he placed a foot on the open windowsill and vanished into the house.

Reinhardt looked at Xander. "What now?"

Xander shrugged. "We wait, I guess."

"You still…" Reinhardt's gaze shifted below Xander's belt line.

Before the mage could respond, a limp rope spilled from the top window. Xander flinched, arms shielding his face from getting hit. Moments later, the knotted end thudded off Reinhardt's skull.

"Did he just hit me over the head with a rope?" Reinhardt gasped indignantly under his breath.

Holding up the tied bit of rope, Xander pointed to the loose strands at the end. "Nope. A frayed knot." The mage smirked.

"That's it. I'm disowning you. I swear, if I had a crossbow, I'd shoot you square in the face." Reinhardt whined as he climbed up the rope toward the window.

When the elder Kandari reached the window's ledge, a fur-covered hand clasped his forearm to pull him in. After entering, Reinhardt stepped around the rope that Bastian had securely tied around his own waist. The line quivered and jostled with the last member of their party ascending the wall. When Xander's hands clasped onto the windowsill, the two already in the room grabbed on and pulled him in.

"Where is Kumori?" Xander looked from Reinhardt to Bastian.

Bastian held his nose in the air, inhaling deeply through his nostrils. "This way."

The two followed Bastian across the large room, down a corridor, and up a flight of stairs. The stairs led to another long corridor, at the end of which was a heavy wooden door.

"He was like this when I got here," Kumori pleaded from beyond the door.

"Wonderful." Reinhardt drolled, gripping the handle of his long blade.

"What do we do now?" Bastian looked to the Kandari.

"Only one thing to do." Xander sighed, no longer trying to keep the volume out of his voice. "Cha'Sora."

Waves of asha rippled through the air as blue bolts of ashareal energy flew past Reinhardt, slamming into the hinges on the large wooden door.

Upon reaching the door, Reinhardt swiftly thrust his foot into the center of its wooden planks. The door fell forward with a long, slow creak before crashing to the wooden floor. A thunderous echo rumbled in the room before them. Reinhardt strolled into the room, walking on the fallen door. When the dust settled, the blade master stood facing seven guards in light armor surrounding his seated Nepharen companion. The rogue's arms and legs were bound to the wooden chair. An eighth man with a long blond braid lay motionless in the corner, a trail of blood flowing from the corpse to a puddle where the floor dipped just slightly.

The sound of ringing metal resonated through the room as Reinhardt unsheathed his long blade. His face glowed with an impish grin. "Hello, lovelies."

Upon seeing the colors of House Vos'Korendel, the soldiers all took a knee. One remained standing, head slightly bowed. "I am the captain of this guard unit. How can we serve house Vos'Korendel?"

"You can untie my companion there and leave us in peace." Reinhardt's voice had a steady confidence.

The captain nearly choked on his words. "My Lord, this is our patron's killer. We won't just let a red-handed murderer go free."

"I have proof to the contrary. Now, free my companion there, or I'll have to do it myself." Reinhardt's voice radiated with the heat of wrath.

"Han'Shoden guard, stand." The captain unsheathed his sword while the remaining guard shuffled upright.

"If it's a dance you want, I'll insist on leading."

Reinhardt slowed his breathing and with it his pounding heart became steady and even like a smith's hammer against the anvil within his chest.

Time itself came to a crawl, stretching the space between heartbeats from moments to minutes. The young Lord Vos'Korendel relaxed his gaze and examined his adversaries for flaws.

With his sword gripped firm and flexible, Reinhardt advanced gracefully. The captain retreated, maintaining his distance, when two guards came forward to intercept the Kandari swordsman. True to their training, one thrust at Reinhardt's waist while the other soldier's blade swept down at his head. Reinhardt's long blade deflected the thrust upward, binding all three blades together. Reinhardt's off hand pushed his moon-hilted dagger up through one guard's jaw into his skull.

The collapsing soldier's sword reeled toward the other guard. The remaining guard swiped at his ally's blade, allowing Reinhardt to thrust his steel deep into the guard's thigh. With a twist, Reinhardt pulled back on the skewering blade, rending all the flesh between the bone and the soldier's groin. The armored man fell with a scream, blood flowing freely from his leg.

A larger foe flanked Reinhardt from the right side of the room, swiping at the blue-clad noble with an enormous blade, attempting to split him in half at the ribcage. A gust of air blew across Reinhardt's scalp as he ducked beneath the blade into a prone position. Thrust up through his opponent's stomach, Reinhardt sent his blade into the guard's heart, behind his plate armor. The man's face shifted between anguish and confusion before falling to the ground, motionless.

Reinhardt rolled backward, past the chair in the middle of the room. In one motion, he pulled the edge of his crescent-hilted dagger across the rope tied around the chair's arm.

Recovering to his feet, Reinhardt thrust his long blade at the next opponent. The guard successfully parried the attack with an impish grin. Reinhart's blade relented, allowing the guard's sword free to move. The guard slashed. Their crashing blades cried out in a high-pitched ring. Reinhardt maneuvered his blade in a large circle, feigning a retreat before closing the distance. The man's face contorted into a visage of terror, with both blades on either side of his neck. Reinhardt pushed the man away, bringing the blades together. The look of dread forever etched on his opponent's face as his severed head thumped to the floor.

The next guard stepped forward, blade swiping in wild, panicked arcs. Reinhardt slowed his step, allowing the attack to pass in front of him, falling short by a hand's width. He kicked his unbalanced adversary backward into the last guard and lunged forward, thrusting his long steel into the stumbling foe. With another step, Reinhardt pressed his blade through the second guard's neck, and slammed his heel into the skewered pair to pull his long blade free.

Turning to the captain of the guard, Reinhardt launched his moon-handled dagger end over end. The thrown blade went wide by a hair.

The stone-still captain allowed a contemptuous grin to overtake his frown. "You missed."

Reinhardt radiated an expression of satisfaction. "Did I?"

The captain's face contorted into a collage of confused anger when the tip of a blade protruded from the front of his throat. The armored soldier collapsed to his knees, neck sliding off the crescent-hilted dagger held tight in Kumori's hand. A thick gurgle echoed through the room from the gasping captain's blood-filled airway.

Bastian ran to Jorgan's still form lying on the floor. The agitated Selece pushed and pulled at the body, checking for signs of warmth, a pulse, or a breath. Seeing Jorgan's spirit had shuffled off this mortal coil, Bastian turned his heated gaze on Kumori. "What happened here?"

"I didn't do this." Kumori's hands raised in a declaration of innocence.

Xander stood over the corpse. "This doesn't exactly look like innocence." He knelt down to examine the body.

Bastian covered the distance to the Nepharen in a single stride, large, clawed hands clutching forward, only to close around an empty cloak. The confused Selece threw the garment to the floor, spinning about, eyes prowling through the room.

A Nepharen voice echoed from behind Bastian, "This was not my doing."

Bastian turned about, ready to spring at nothing more than air and dust.

Kumori's disembodied whisper reverberated once more, "I found him after he was attacked."

Xander stood. "It's true."

"How can you know this?" Bastian stopped for a breath, turning to Xander.

Xander held out his hands, palms facing up. "Kumori, please hand me your largest blade."

The uncloaked rogue approached from a shadow, calmly displaying two sheathed sets of throwing blades and a curved pair of twin Nepharen short blades. Kumori placed the collection into Xander's outstretched hands. "These are my only blades. I am now unarmed."

Reinhardt's tongue clicked against the roof of his mouth. "Well." He drew out the word longer than was reasonable.

Kumori's hand flicked in a blur. A blade flew end over end

toward Reinhardt's head. The arrogant Kandari remained statuesque, watching the blade spin past. The handle vibrated with a metallic twang when the tip thumped into the wooden shelf behind Reinhardt.

"Now I'm unarmed."

"Good form." Reinhardt reached over and grabbed the handle of his dagger. In line with the blade, he slowly angled the blade up and down before giving it a stiff tug to free it from the furniture.

"Now, I am fully unarmed," Kumori repeated.

Xander's voice trespassed into the tension between his three companions, hoping to maintain their unsteady alliance. "These daggers aren't large enough to have made this wound."

With hesitation, Bastian shifted his gaze toward Jorgan's corpse.

Xander laid the weapon flat against the injury. He compared the entry wound with the base of Kumori's largest blade. "The wound opening is twice the width of those blades."

Bastian growled.

"And even if it weren't..." Xander measured the length of Kumori's weapon. "This blade's length isn't sufficient to leave this exit wound."

"He was stabbed from behind," Reinhardt blurted.

"Way to keep up, master of the blade," Xander mocked.

"What did you say?" Reinhardt asked, heat in his voice.

"I'm simply in awe of your sharp intellect." Xander chuckled.

"Is that another pun? One of these days, I will shoot you square in the face." Reinhardt shook his dagger in Xander's direction.

Hands raised with palms forward, Bastian peacefully padded over to Kumori. "I'm sorry. Please tell us what happened."

Kumori gathered the cloak from the floor, shouldering it into its proper place. "When I entered, he was alone on the floor. I knelt down to ask who attacked him, where my people's bracers are, where the Selece stone is. I don't think he heard me. His last words were, 'I'm sorry, Cousin.'"

Without warning, the sound of armored guards marching down the corridor echoed into the room.

"Time to go." Reinhardt peered out the window. "You must be joking."

Xander's head snapped toward the corridor. "Bastian, the door. Can you put it back in place?"

"To what end?" Reinhardt inquired.

"To buy us time." Xander returned Kumori's blades, locking eyes with the rogue. "You first then Reinhardt. Bastian and I leave last."

"Why—" Reinhardt started to ask.

"Do it before we're forced to fight our way through the front door," Xander snapped.

Kumori secured all eight knives, save for the twin blades, and dove out the window. Once airborne, the Nepharen landed softly on the lower rooftop of the next tower. After finding a secure footing, Kumori scurried down the towers ledges and windowsills before finally reaching the ground.

Reinhardt leapt to the same patch of roof. Landing on a loose shingle, he tumbled into a free fall until his fingers clutched a banner secured over a window. The banner tore at one end, swinging him into a trellis of flowers. Reinhardt clung to the wooden frame, sighing in relief. With a groan, the lattice gave way at the top, landing him on the flat of his back with a gasp. He lay on the ground, hand to his chest, wincing and panting to catch his breath.

"Stop acting like a baby and move. It wasn't even that high." Kumori's Nepharen tone sounded more abrasive than usual.

Bastian looked to Xander. "You go low. I'll go high. I'll meet you at the tree."

Xander gave a swift nod, clasping Bastian on the shoulder. "At the tree."

One of the guard's knocked. "Lord Han'Shoden, are you in there?"

Xander ran toward the opening, jumping off the windowsill with all his might to become airborne. After clearing the closest tower, he focused his will and vibrated the phrase, "Cho'Raka."

Ashareal energy formed around his feet and legs, slowing his fall. Before reaching the ground, he released his focus and landed with a forward roll.

Xander watched Bastian climb up over the tower before bolting toward the shadow at the perimeter. Bastian went in the opposite direction, moving from rooftop to rooftop.

Guards spilled into the room and scrambled to the window. One soldier had the unfortunate luck of being in front. After being shoved through the opening, he bounced off the lower rooftop and landed headfirst on the estate lawn with the sound of armor clattering over a thud and a crunch.

Reinhardt kept pace with Xander until they reached the fence, when the hedonistic young lord went up and over as though he'd done it a hundred times before, running from some jealous noble. Per usual, there was no sign of Kumori. Once at the fence, Xander climbed over rather than wasting ashareal energy. From the other side, Reinhardt reached through the gate to help lift Xander up where the mage could grab a gate spire. Once at the top, Xander used a nearby branch to steady himself before climbing down the tree. The battle horns ringing from within the estate drowned out the sound of Xander's feet thudding clumsily against the ground.

Reinhardt approached. "What do we do now?"

"We wait." Xander's face was fixed in determination.

"Cousin?" Reinhardt pleaded.

"We wait," Xander repeated.

"Fine. At least I know I'm not shifting to the void alone." Reinhardt sighed.

"The void is reserved for traitors and thieves. We're going to Ashara," Xander said confidently.

"You magi and your myths and legends," Reinhardt scoffed.

"Well, I'm going to Ashara," Xander mocked.

"Do you two ever stop?" Kumori snapped.

"No," the cousins answered together.

A sound came from the forest tree line. The three fugitives shifted into defensive stances.

Bastian's head poked through a thick barrier of dark green brush. "Come on. We don't have long."

They bolted forward into the dense woodline while remaining shrouded in stealth. After walking half the night, they came to a clearing with a trail.

Bastian lifted his nose to the air and gave a long inhale. "We're clear of them."

"And if we're upwind?" Reinhardt asked.

"The strongest wind is coming from the direction of the estate." Bastian's ears shifted back and forth.

"It is unlikely they would have made it ahead of us," Kumori added.

"And if they did, I would hear them, so for the moment, we're clear." Bastian growled.

"Where to now?" Xander looked at the other three.

"Now, we find Adriel." Reinhardt started in a direction.

"Adriel?" Kumori inquired.

"He's a friend. He can help." Reinhardt gazed skyward, observing the position of the half-full Evening Moon before his head swiveled back and forth while he contemplated the trail. "Follow me."

19

A man bearing a leathery, olive-toned complexion sat at a corner booth of a busy brewhouse. His rough cut and muscular bulk were attributes shared by many of his fellow patrons. The one obvious difference was that his feet didn't touch the floor from his stool. Securing a shoulder length black head-scarf, he wore a bronze circlet adorned with the embossed image of a single golden eye, affixed with a ruby centerpiece. From his shoulders hung a sand-colored cloak flecking pure white anywhere direct sunlight touched it. His head-dress and band matched the rest of his loose-fitting outfit, all in black, secured by pieces of metallic jewelry shifting between dark amber and bright yellow.

"It's rare that we see one of the Fataak in these parts." The barmaid stood to one side of the table. "What can I get you? A brew? Or maybe something with a bit more bite to it?" She leaned in suggestively.

The Fataak accent came out thick, dripping from the stranger's tongue with dense vowels and heavily rolled softer syllables. "Only water please."

She played at her lip with a finger. "Well, if you want something wet, all you have to do was ask." She swaggered away, hips swaying back and forth, but the Fataak took no notice.

"May I join you?" asked a regal male voice from behind.

"That depends on the weather outside." The Fataak looked around the room.

"It always rains on the blessed." A hulking Kandari walked around the table toward the chair opposite the Fataak. Though dressed in common clothes, his posture was worthy of a king. His essence radiated authority.

"Then may the Great Ashuun bless us all." The Fataak gestured toward the open chair.

The incoming patron was appropriately dressed for the tavern, wearing a green tunic trimmed in a pale green with wooden toggles over light tan pants and black boots. Taking his seat, he carefully positioned his master-crafted sword, brandishing a brass emblem etched with a winged moravian flying away from the sunset. Looking around for the barmaid, he ran his fingers through his neatly groomed short, dark hair, which was styled with oils and cut to precision, causing every strand to fall perfectly in place. His well-maintained hair seamlessly transitioned into his matching beard. It was thick enough to appear intentional, yet short enough to show that it was properly groomed, with whiskers that resembled the color of burnt umber, complimenting his tanned skin, which was the result of spending too many days under the scorching sun.

"The infamous Takesh, I presume?" He lifted his chin inquisitively.

Takesh nodded in acknowledgement. "Certainly, Lord Ser—"

The Kandari interrupted, "Soren. Please refer to me as Soren." Soren held out a cautious hand, palm forward.

"Certainly. Soren." Takesh nodded once again, with a deliberate tilt to one side. "How may I, a humble Fataak, be of service to you? Soren?" The name hung in the air, with deliberate emphasis.

"As you are aware, a dangerous assassin is ravaging the kingdom." Soren interlaced his fingers. He examined the traffic of the patrons in the brewhouse, his calm demeanor unwavering.

"Indeed, I have heard." Takesh sat back, pulling his arms from the table, watching the barmaid approach.

She sat the water down in front of him. His eyes lit up like a small child, gazing upon a harvest day present. He picked up the glass and sipped at the clear, refreshing liquid. Face contorted in shock, he choked on the water before he could get it down. The Fataak slipped off his chair in a coughing fit. His feet thudded on the ground. Standing at full height, he was a head taller than the table.

"It's cold!" the Fataak yelped in confusion. Clearing his throat, he glared at the glass with a caution.

"For certain." Soren gave his drinking companion a confused nod.

"How do you get it cold?" Takesh slid back into his chair in one graceful motion.

"Ice," Soren blurted. "The Monku ship it down from the north with the means to keep it frozen so we can use it."

The bar maid stepped back to the table. "Is something wrong?" Concern etched into her face.

Takesh regained his composure. "Nothing you did." He raised the drink to his lips and took a long, slow sip.

"I'll have the house evening brew. Dark please." Soren placed five uni on the table.

The barmaid took it and wandered off.

"As we were saying..." Soren leaned in toward Takesh. "There is an assassin about. We need the assassin removed."

"Do you? Are you certain?" Takesh shrugged, a nefarious grin growing on his face.

"Undeniably," Soren insisted. "The people are getting restless, and we cannot allow these crimes to go unanswered."

"With that, I agree, but are you sure this is the right answer?" Takesh raised an eyebrow.

"What other choice is there?" Sweeping his gaze around to inspect for zealous ears or wandering eyes, Soren gave a small cough.

"I'm sure you're familiar with the writings of Dorn Strogland."

The Fataak's hands spread open as if he were opening a book.

Soren's tone became indignant. "What are you implying?"

"I'm implying nothing, yet with this particular list of victims, you're a cut above the rest. The people are restless because they want strong leadership to prevent another civil war. They want a leader willing to take bold moves." Takesh looked around the brew house. "This is, indeed, a bold move," he alleged, his arms wide. "Take this gift for what it is."

"This is not a gift. This is treason. The next time you take a breath intending to push such treasonous miasma from your lips, it will be your last." Soren's hand held firm against the table, clenched into a tight fist.

Takesh's shimmering gaze became serious. His voice rolled low with a preternatural echo. "Understood. Your Majesty." The Fataak took in a slow breath while staring deeply at his companion.

Soren gave a long, deep sigh, matching the pace of Takesh's breath. "It does have a ring to it." His gaze drifted off, miles away. With a cough and a sniff, his focus snapped to the meeting at hand. "Before we get ahead of ourselves, we still need to address the immediate situation."

Takesh took another sip from his mug. "This is how we address the situation at hand. We track, observe, and maintain control. This is how we prevent things from straying off the required path. When the time is right, we will be within arm's reach, ready to strike."

"Agreed." The word dripped from Soren's lips like sap from the winter trees.

Takesh's gaze became solemn. "Who is the assassin?"

Soren's face reflected Takesh's stare, interlaced fingers frozen in place. "A Nepharen by the name of Kumori. Bears an indigo cloak, specializes in daggers."

"Man or woman?" Takesh's tongue licked his lips, cool from the chilled drink.

"We're currently unaware and don't consider that critical. As we speak, Kumori is traveling with a group. Two Kandari and a Selece."

"First, we would need to go about finding them." Takesh closed his eyes and took another sip. His face melted into an expression of pure elation.

"That shouldn't be difficult for a hunter of such renown." Soren sat back, providing the barmaid a place to set his brew on the table. He sipped at the mug's frothy top and nodded in satisfaction.

"Will there be anything else?" The barmaid looked between them.

"Only your discretion." Soren held out a single black coin, four red gems glistening from within.

"Yes, of course." Turning her head about, the barmaid inspected the room for onlookers before accepting the coin, subtly slipping it into her small inconspicuous belt pouch. With her reward secure, she flitted away.

"To that end, this should give you a head start." Soren placed a small sheet of parchment before Takesh.

Takesh unfurled the parchment, to examine the Kaanish script. Takesh gave Soren an inquisitive glare. "A Tapi?"

"Of course. Those small glutenous sprites have no end of usefulness." Soren played at the hair on the end of his chin.

"From whom?" Takesh leaned in.

"We've planted an informant in their midst." Soren's gaze swept the room, checking for stares and suspicious glances. "We're on a tight schedule. What's your answer?"

"Regarding my fee, what is your answer?" Takesh's eyebrows lifted.

"We will not press Aestarian men into service to die on Ishtaran soil, but we'll give you enough chen that you can procure twice the men and resources you've requested." Soren's hands folded together tightly.

"Kandari nobility. Always willing to throw money at a problem, never willing to get their own hands dirty." Takesh took the last sip of water, and his face went slack with disappointment. "I agree to the terms."

He held out a hand, and Soren responded with a firm grip, each brandishing a confident smile. Releasing the grip, Soren handed Takesh a small shiny metallic disk.

"A Tapi-lap disk?" Takesh asked.

Soren nodded. "Yes, so you can report your progress. Just place the sweet bit on top, and they will show up to take any single folded piece of parchment to anyone you request. Though you will need to use a name other than Soren to have the message delivered to me."

"Understood." Takesh inspected the disk's every detail. The mirror-polished coin shined brightly. Each side was embossed with interlocked geometric shapes, adorned with arcane glyphs.

"Likewise, when updates become available, we'll convey them to you through a Tapi-gram." Soren lifted his mug. "Oh, one last thing. We'll insist that you work with a contingent of our men." The large Kandari sipped his drink.

"Your men?" Takesh's gaze shifted from the coin back to Soren.

"Is that a problem?" Staring back and the Fataak, Soren's posture shifted.

"A minor inconvenience, but at this price, I'm happy to oblige." Takesh nodded. "As you said, our time here is limited, and now I'm able to send details as the situation blossoms." He floated to the floor with a nimble grace. "I'll leave you to finish your death water in peace."

"Please do. We will send word if and when anything changes." Soren sipped at his house brew.

The Fataak walked past him toward the door.

The Kandari gazed about the room, inspecting for signs of awareness to his presence. Soren sighed. "So, it has come to this."

20

Wearing only one chatta blade, Bastian chopped down a sapling just taller than he was. Using the blade's tip, he carefully played at the bark while he walked, cutting long strands from the fresh length of wood.

Reinhardt's voice echoed over the heavy thudding of footsteps and twisting of branches. "Did no one bring any rations on this bloody trog?"

"Well, Cousin," Xander offered, "if memory serves, we were in jail before we blew it up. Following that, we made a straight shot to the smith's forge. After which, we snuck to Jorgan's estate, where we found only his dead corpse. No Spirit Stone or bracers or any way to clear our names. So, unless you took something from the kitchen at the estate, no. For the fifth time in the past thirty minutes, we have no rations. If anyone had the means to get supplies, it would have been the cock crowing in the courtyard."

Continuing forward, Bastian cut the naked sapling in two, with the bottom thicker piece measuring the length from his elbow to his wrist. He secured the longer piece through his belt, the way a child would sheath a wooden toy sword, and placed the shorter piece in his satchel. With his hands free, he worked at the strands of fibrous bark, twisting and braiding it into a thin rope, all the while not missing a step with the group. Finally, he secured the rope to the end of the shorter stick to make a small loop at the end. Using the remaining cord, he lashed the loop to the stick, just small enough to get two fingers through. He tugged at the rope to check the loop's strength.

From beneath the indigo hood, Kumori peered up at the contraption with an understanding nod. Bastian pulled the long stick from his belt to make a notch in the thicker end. Kumori's suspicions confirmed, the rogue's mouth grew into a smirk.

"The city of Imbros is just northwest of us, yes?" Xander inquired, pushing a branch out of his way to continue down the overgrown path.

"Yes, Cousin, and it would take us half a day's walk out of the way," Reinhardt insisted before turning stone-still.

On the path six lengths ahead stood a full-grown female zelle. She was knee high, with off-white stripes across the back of her hide. The rest of her hair was the color of dried hay, shifting to bright yellow toward her hooved feet. Moments later, a slightly smaller zelle approached with no stripes and a fully grown pair of horns arcing toward the sky.

Reinhardt's face melted into an expression of disappointment at the futility of hunting such a creature without the proper weapon. A thrum echoed through the air, sending the posh Kandari's eyes wide with surprise when a long, thin shaft soared past his chiseled jawline toward the pair of grazing zelle. The shaft landed with the sound of a wet thump echoing off the trees. The startled female darted out of sight in a blur, but it pierced the male, just behind his front quarter. His slack frame went to the ground with a thud.

"Yes!" Reinhardt's excitement overtook him.

Bastian ran ahead of the group to kneel before the animal. He placed his hand over the zelle's eyes and spoke. "Ombatha ja'oor, Ashana Surasha."

The Selece pulled the chatta's razor edge across the beast's throat.

Rising to stand, Bastian turned his gaze to Reinhardt. "We do not celebrate our brother's death. We show thanks for the sacrifice."

"But you missed the big one," Reinhardt complained.

"I don't miss." Bastian's visage became ominous. "If there are young, the father's job is done, and we do not take mothers from their young."

Shame crept onto Reinhardt's face. "I understand."

Bastian positioned the zelle to cut along the stomach. Shaat-filled entrails sloshed against the forest floor, and the Selece took great care to avoid contaminating the meat with their contents. Kumori collected dried twigs, kindling, and fallen branches.

Finding a patch of dry ground, Xander cleared the loose underbrush of debris fallen from the forest canopy. "Cousin, can I borrow your blade?" Xander asked, pulling at the recent growth from the forest floor.

Reinhardt ambled over, producing the handle of his crescent moon-hilted dagger in Xander's direction.

Xander took the blade and began slicing through random plant life to clear the area. "What are you doing anyhow? Aside from lending edged tools and watching everybody else sweat over your dinner?"

"Supervising." Reinhardt chuckled.

"Why don't you supervise yourself by finding some large rocks while I clear the pit?" Xander pointed toward a dip in the forest with a pile of stones roughly the size of a human skull.

"Fine." Reinhardt drew the word out, rolling his eyes into the back of his head.

Bringing the skinned carcass before the group, Bastian stopped, confusion on his face. "What's this?"

Bastian's posture shifted toward the area Xander was clearing. Kumori played at the wood in the fire pit, making a hollow pyramid of dry dead logs over a bundle of small dry twigs and brush.

"Well, we have to cook the meat. We can't just eat it raw." Reinhardt chauffed at Bastian.

Bastian's eyes wandered between traveling companions. His eyes widened in comprehension. "Ahh, medium rare." He grinned at his accomplishment.

"Sure, if that's how you'd like yours." Reinhardt grunted with the effort of hauling the last skull-sized stone to the fire pit.

"No thanks. I'll take mine fresh, but you can cook yours."

Bastian sat the animal's body down, with nothing but the hide preventing it from touching the dirt. He used his chatta blade to cut off a single hind quarter. He set it aside on the edge of the bloody pelt. Unsure what to do next, he turned to Kumori and shrugged.

Kumori walked over with a long stick and knelt before the kill. "May I?"

Bastian nodded. "The rites are done. It is ready."

Kumori ran the wooden skewer through the beast, from front to back, before lifting it by the stick. The rogue place their soon-to-be dinner onto the spit over the fire pit. They built the spit from two strad pieces of wood thrust into the ground. Kneeling down to the firewood below, Kumori pulled a small bent piece of metal and scraped the two ends against each other. Sparks flew into the dry brush, and Kumori blew until the smoldering smoke grew into a small flame. The flame grew under the spit while Kumori turned the small handle that had grown naturally from one end. Bastian hung the pelt over a branch two lengths above the flames. Xander cleared out the remaining greenery from around the firepit, removing any sticks or sharp rocks.

The four travelers sat around the fire, three of them picking meat from the spit. Bastian, already done with his share, used his chatta blade to whittle at an ivory zelle horn. The sky went lavender, bidding the sun its daily farewell.

"Kumori, what was the herb you gave my cousin?" Reinhardt's gaze fell on the cloaked rogue.

Kumori continued chewing at a bit of recently pulled zelle meat. "Which one?"

Taken off-guard by the question, the confused young noble's eyelashes fluttered. "Well, both."

Bastian looked on in confusion before leveling a serious glare toward Reinhardt. "We do not speak with our mouths full, here in civilized country."

All three heads slowly turned toward Bastian, as though he'd just grown a second pair of arms. Kumori let out a cough to avoid choking on a small piece of meat. Reinhardt and Xander let out a jubilant belly laugh.

The confused Selece asked, "What's funny?"

"Sitting in the back woods of nowhere, west of the Katlus river, half a day from the nearest city isn't exactly civilization," Xander said through a mouth full of meat.

"That and you sound like my father. Next, you're going to tell me to use the large strad on the right for meat and the small strad on the left for vegetables." Reinhardt passed Kumori's drinking skin to Bastian. "It's fine, just a bit ironic to be scolded about Alabaster's formalities by a Selece while sitting in the back country."

"Alabaster's formalities?" Bastian questioned.

Xander played at the seams of his robe. "Alabaster was the royal adviser ages ago who decided what is and is not proper etiquette for the royal table."

Reinhardt continued, "Eventually, the nobles all followed suit before it trickled down to the common folk, who did their best to follow the rules of etiquette with no formal training."

Xander sighed. "Reinhardt and I have endured years of formal training on Alabaster's rules of etiquette and still can't remember all of them."

"Small strad on the left, large strad on the right. Goblet on the left, knife on the right," Reinhardt mocked.

"Knife on the left," Xander challenged.

"Which knife?" Reinhardt jested.

The pair of them pantomimed placing formal dinner settings in the air in front of them before rolling backward in laughter.

"What's in this?" Bastian held up the drinking skin.

"Just water." Kumori shrugged.

Reinhardt sat up, face serious. "To the subject at hand. The herbs," he said, leveling his gaze on Kumori.

Kumori relented with a sigh. "The first was SoShi. This is used to dull the pain. The second is tsutaki. It will increase heart rate and blood flow to the whole body."

"So we noticed," Xander scoffed.

"Increased blood flow means increased healing. Increased blood flow balances the four key elements of health within the body. So-shara and so-asha balanced with the Ak-shara and ak-asha. This brings the body into harmony, allowing it to heal itself," Kumori patiently explained.

"And the..." Reinhardt gestured below Xander's belt. "Other benefits?"

Kumori shrugged. "That is the Ak-Asha at work. Now it's my turn to ask a question."

Reinhardt and Xander exchanged a curious glance. Reinhardt shrugged, spreading his arms wide in submission. "Ask what you'd like."

The rogue's voice was low and firm. "What is the ceremony of sorrows?"

Reinhardt's mouth shifted into a curious pucker before nodding at Xander. "I believe this is your area, Cousin."

"It's the ceremony where an acolyte becomes a full magus." Xander answered.

The still silence radiating from the young mage was deafening. A light breeze blew, thick with night air and the campfire aroma.

Leaves rustled in the wind. Bitty little bugs chirped for what felt like an eternity.

Reinhardt's slack hand waved through the air toward Xander with a flourish. "And there you have it."

"That only tells part of the story. Why is it called the ceremony of sorrows?" Kumori insisted.

Xander continued hesitantly, "The Archanium's three head magi oversee the ceremony of sorrows—Prima Aeternum, Sera Aeternum, and Terra Aeternum—in addition to three other magi of their choosing."

Kumori nodded. "If someone is becoming a mage, why is there sorrow?"

Reinhardt began. "Not all—"

Xander abruptly cleared his throat. "Not everyone who enters the chamber leaves alive." His eyes glassed over, gaze fixed on nothing in the far-off distance. "They..." Xander paused. "Pull..." He hesitated again. "Some of our soul from Ashana into the realm of Ashara."

"And this is why so many mages are required? Because of the ceremony's delicate nature?" Kumori ran the edge of a knife along the wide side of a sharpening stone.

"It is." Xander picked up a small stick and began doodling on the blank soil.

"And the surge," Reinhardt blurted out.

"Surge?" Kumori froze mid-stroke, halting the blade against the stone with a coarse scrape.

"Do you ever shut up, Cousin?" A glass-eyed Xander made to no effort to hide the frustration in his voice.

"Sorry." Reinhardt shrugged.

Xander's gaze returned to Kumori. "If the ceremony is successful, the transition opens a portal within the new magus, which causes immense power and grants immediate access to layers of magic and power for which the new mage is not yet prepared to control individually."

"Are the head magi required to close the portal?" Kumori continued sharpening.

"From what I've read, no. The portal closes on its own, never to be reopened, but they must prevent the newly awakened mage from destroying the Archanium and everyone and everything in it. Originally, the ceremony was administered by the head magus. Eventually, they decided more magi were required to shield the chamber, the building, and everything in it from the ashareal portal's destructive potential."

"And who did you lose?" Kumori changed blades, wetting the stone with a glob of spit before scraping the new blade's edge over the rough surface.

Xander tried to speak. Unable to shake the quiver from his voice, he nodded to Reinhardt.

"His elder brother, Zarius." Reinhardt's voice was soft.

Kumori's visage became curious. "This isn't required for the disciples of DoTotSu."

"This isn't required for the *Nepharen* disciples of DoTotSu," Xander corrected. "If I were to follow the path of DoTotSu, I would still require the ceremony to become a full disciple."

"This is what happens when you tamper with forces that you do not fully understand." Kumori snorted.

"This is what we must do to have an equal contribution to the world." Xander's hands ran through his hair in frustration.

"If the Kandari people are happy to throw their children at the wall and see what sticks like a fresh-cooked noodle, who am I, or the rest of Ashana, to say no?" Kumori re-sheathed the second knife.

"What did you say, thief?" Xander stood tall, circling the fire.

Kumori floated upward into a defensive posture, retreating to maintain the distance.

"I hate to be accused of being the voice of reason here," Reinhardt interjected, placing a hand on Xander's shoulder, "but perhaps we should all get some rest."

Xander shrugged off his cousin's grip, continuing forward.

Bastian stood to intercept the infuriated Kandari. The Selece gently placed a hand on Xander's chest in a gesture of peace. "Please."

Xander stopped. Eyes now wet with sorrow, he looked up to meet Bastian's gaze.

The young Selece looked down softly on Xander's grief-stricken visage. "Please."

Without a sound, Xander turned and walked away toward the large nearby tree. He removed his purple robes trimmed with silver lining and slumped down against the trunk. The young acolyte laid the fabric over himself, turning it into a makeshift blanket before yielding to exhaustion.

Bastian scowled at Kumori. "You know you went too far."

"Maybe, but someone needs to." Kumori strode away, vanishing into the darkness.

21

A small girl of five or six cycles hid crouched in front of a large wooden desk. The glow of her ivory skin was in stark contrast to the dark hardwood furniture. Her hair was the color of light beach sand cut short enough it danced on the shoulders of her pink nightdress. The furnishing was constructed of ancient hard wood embossed with polished engravings, flourishes, and scenes from ancient lore.

"Daddy, read me a bedtime story," the little girl pleaded to her father from the other side of his elaborate desk. Her half-hidden eyes peered over the edge.

"Where is mistress, Maven?" he stated with a playful pomp in his rich baritone, an eastern lilt the way his S's slid through his teeth.

"Her stories are boring and put me to sleep." The little girl's eyelashes fluttered.

"Well, isn't that the whole idea of a bedtime story?" He shuffled his papers into a neat stack before securing his ink-stained quill into its stand.

"But your stories are fun and give me the sweetest dreams," she implored.

Her father stood tall, pressing the backs of his legs against the dark, ornately carved wooden chair. The furniture groaned beneath him as the wooden legs scooted across the wood floor. Candlelight glinted from the gold trim of his crimson doublet. Stroking his clean-shaven jawline, he sighed. "Okay young lady, but you best go right to sleep. Do you hear me, Inara?"

"Yes, Father." Her voice was sweeter than a meadowlark's call on a morning windowsill.

When he stepped past the girl, she wrapped her hand around his index finger, following his lead from the room. They kept a steady pace, just fast enough for the corridor air to lift the ends of her hair from her shoulders. At the end of the passage was a large, dark hardwood door. Standing on either side were two men, each armed with a long sword. The soldiers wore red uniforms trimmed in gold, embroidered with the royal seal of Aestaria on their right breast. When the man and his daughter stopped, both men stomped a foot in unison. One politely opened the door.

"Your Majesty," the guard said, shutting the door behind them.

"All right, Inara, which one would you like tonight?" the king asked.

"I want the story about the princess and the warlord." She got under the covers and pulled them up tight.

Tucking the princess's blanket around her shoulders, the king began, "A long time ago, in a land far, far away, there was an evil overlord named Vathred. He ruled his lands harshly with a steel fist. The evil overlord was told that a band of local rebels were making a plan to destroy his new castle, so he led a contingent of guards to capture them and find the spell they had stolen, which would allow them to destroy his new fortress. Vathred and his guards dispatched every rebel except one. She was a princess and the daughter of the one true queen."

Inara's eyes fluttered shut, and the stillness of sleep overtook her. Sitting on her bedside, her father brushed her bangs from her eyes the way fathers often do, when he noticed his daughter's blanket had become unusually still.

"Inara?" The king reached for her shoulder to stir her awake.

The color drained from her skin, fading to a pale grey.

"Inara?" Her father's voice shook with worry.

The little girl's cheeks became gaunt and sunken.

"No!" the king yelled. "No! I can't lose you!"

The king embraced his daughter's frail body as it crumbled to ash in his arms. He clutched her covers and blankets, screaming into them.

"No! Come back!" He rolled himself inside of them. "Come back!" the king wailed repeatedly. "Come back! Come back! Come back to me!"

A familiar voice unexpectedly came from beyond the covers. "Your Majesty." The feminine voice was silken with a soothing air of maturity. "Your Majesty," the voice continued from beyond the covers.

The king pulled the covers down from around his face to be assaulted by the light of dawn. Looking around, he found himself lying in his own bed.

"King Dailan." A pale face beneath dark hair and with soft golden eyes and sharp features looked down at him. His eyes were red with sorrow and wet with sadness. "I miss her too," the voice said reassuringly.

"Oh, Maven, I don't know what to do without her."

The king's arms wrapped around the woman, pulling her close. His nose nestled neatly into the base of her neck. She used one middle finger to trace a line over his ear through his dark brown hair and rest on his jawline.

The two shared a moment of sorrow before the lady pulled away to stand upright and regain her composure. "You're going to do what you've always done. You're going to stand tall, remembering there are countless fathers and daughters in this kingdom, and each one of them needs their king. You've entrusted me with the royal seal for sound reason. You know that of all these bootlickers and nanny wallers around this castle, I'm the one who's going to tell you what you need to hear whether you want to hear it or not. She's gone. Ashana knows I've cried myself to sleep every night for the past year, and I'll cry myself to sleep every night until the day I die over that fact because I love you both until my dying breath. But this kingdom needs their king, and my king needs his kingdom."

"You're right, Maven, as always." The king reluctantly sat up and donned a red silk night shirt trimmed in gold.

"Not often enough," she whispered to herself, eyes glassing over.

A knock sounded, echoing through the room.

Maven walked over and opened the door. She allowed the king's attendants to enter before exiting the king's bedchamber. Upon reentering, she averted her eyes. King Dailan stood bare behind a dressing panel.

"Your Majesty, I've been notified that Archon Serantes has arrived."

"Advise him to wait in my study. I will be with him presently."

The king's attendants stood with him behind the panel, poking and prodding at his wardrobe to ensure every fold was straight, every seam in place. The gold trim glimmered brightly against the deep red of his royal attire.

Serantes sat calmly in his majesty's personal study. When the doors opened, Serantes rose. Seeing the king, Serantes took a knee, averting his gaze toward the ground while shielding his eyes with a forearm. "Your Majesty!"

"Arise, Serantes. How many times must I tell you that this is unnecessary when we're alone?" The king played at a stack of parchments on his large, elaborate wood desk before walking around to the other side.

"Your Majesty, as you are aware, only those with the royal seal can speak and act freely before the king," Serantes insisted.

"As you keep reminding me." The king stood before his chair and gracefully lowered himself into it.

Serantes' sense of propriety pulled him down into the chair

behind him. "Your Majesty, I have news. Jorgan Han'Shoden has fallen." His face twitched with discomfort.

"My deepest condolences. I know how much your cousin meant to you. The sacrifices he's made for this kingdom will never be forgotten. What of the murderers?" The king folded his hands, listening inquisitively.

"They have eluded capture for the time, but we have the means to track them. My agents are in pursuit as we speak."

The king leveled the archon with a grave look. "We have a serious problem. The kingdom is in a state of unrest with the falling of four major household lords, and now it will only get worse with the death of Lord Han'Shoden's most promising heir. The people of Aestaria need assurances the situation is in hand."

"I understand, Majesty." Serantes tone projected a confidence only gained from years of experience.

"Do you? Do you know what they're saying? They're talking about a resurgence of the Trillium wars. They're afraid if the kingdom splits, they will have to sacrifice more sons and brothers, husbands, and fa..." The king's voice shook, eyes glassing over.

His gaze fell to a small drawing on a scrap of paper with a scribble of two stick figures holding hands. The tall one with a large, pointed crown was next to a smaller figure wearing a little triangle dress.

Maven's words echoed through King Dailan's mind. *There are countless fathers and daughters in this kingdom, and each one of them needs their king.*

Dailan's voice pierced the silence with royal poise. "And fathers. You claimed to have a strategy, and I agreed that, so long as that strategy worked, we would move forward as you recommended. Did I misplace my trust in you?"

"No, Majesty." Serantes laid a small bit of curled parchment before King Dailan.

The king read the parchment aloud. "They are currently headed northwest from Aestaria Una, toward Imbros. They have just crossed the Katlus River." King Dailan settled back with a sigh. "Who is your source?"

"Agents of the crown are tracking them this very moment." Serantes crossed one leg over the other, placing his interlaced fingers proudly on one knee.

"Serantes, you serve the crown well, and this revelation provides a modicum of confidence, yet any mistake made here will have ultimately been my doing as it was I who put my trust in you. I hold the members of my court accountable for the consequences of their actions. You will bring this situation to heel, or I will personally intercede." When the king stood, his heavy chair's wooden legs groaned across the floor.

Serantes rose, hand on his heart, before leaning at the waist with a solemn bow of his head. "Your Majesty, I swear it will be done."

Serantes strode toward the door with a confidence befitting a king. He gave the door three rapid knocks and waited. Moments later, the door opened, and guards snapped to attention.

Their words resonated in one voice, "Hail, Archon Serantes!"

When the high lord marched forward, they shut the door behind him.

The king sat back at his desk, overtaken by the exhaustion from the simple meeting. He picked up the paper and held it just in front of his face. Lips closed, he inhaled deeply, taking in the scent. The fragrance of garden flowers seemed as fresh as the day she handed it to him. The king's eyes glassed over wet at the conversation echoing through his mind.

Daddy, why did Mummy leave us?

Mummy went to Ashara, Princess, to make sure it was ready for us when we get there.

Promise you won't leave me like she did.

Inara, I'll never leave you.

Promise me, Daddy.

I promise.

A single tear slid down the king's cheek.

22

Xander continued trogging forward on the half-worn dirt trail, with Reinhardt leading just in front of Kumori and Bastian at the rear. The young mage looked skyward where an oran was gliding on the breeze. Shuddering at the wind's touch, a row of red-tipped feathers edged the cloud-white bird's massive wingspan. Crimson lines painted on the bird's long pointed amber beak matched its wing-tipped accents. Pulling its massive wingspan back into a narrow swooping position, the oran thrust its gracefully elongated neck toward the ground. The diving raptor's slender beak plunged through a smaller bird, which gave no more than a bitty squawk. With a single flap of its wings, the air trembled, and the oran ascended once more. The majestic beast tilted north, soaring back to the nest with its prey.

Bastian quickened his step, approaching Xander from behind, both keeping pace with the others down a long woodland road. "You said you carry no blade." His voice had more gravel than usual. He hadn't spoken much since breakfast.

Xander nodded. "I usually have no need for one."

Bastian held up a horn-handled blade, secured by a zelle pelt sheath, and offered the piece to Xander. "This is for you, so you can eat or cut things without having to borrow from the fancy man."

Xander carefully took the gift with a chuckle. "The fancy man. I like that. I think I'll use it."

Goosebumps ran down Xander's spine when he considered the time and attention Bastian had put into the piece, the whole time planning to give it away.

Pulling the handle revealed a pearlescent blade made from the same horned material. He plucked at the edge. *Not quite good enough for shaving*, Xander considered, *but close.*

"I couldn't possibly take this. I have nothing to give you in return," Xander attempted to hand the piece back to Bastian.

"Without your magic, I would still be stuck in a cage. Please take this gift to make us level." Bastian's forearm gently nudged the sheathed blade in Xander's fist.

"Are you two going to keep up? Or just stay back and hand clap Miss Monku songs all day?" Reinhardt's pompous tenor echoed from six or seven lengths ahead on the trail.

"Thank you." Xander nodded graciously.

Bastian's head motioned to the others up ahead, beckoning Xander to join him in a light jog.

"I haven't clapped out a Miss Monku rhyme in ages." Xander's voice was unsteady. "Care to give it a go?" he asked, hands held out toward Reinhardt, one horizontal, one vertical.

Reinhardt chuckled, swiping Xander's hands out of the air. "We have serious business to attend to. This road may be better than the last shaat trail, but this is where we need to be on the lookout."

"Lookout indeed." A voice came from beyond the tree line on the path ahead.

Moments later, a tall stranger stepped onto the trail. Half a head taller than Reinhardt, the lithe figure donned a long grey cloak, hood pulled back, revealing a shoulder-length mane of dark wavy hair streaking white. The stranger's pale skin intensified the piercing gaze of his bronze eyes, flecked with ruby. Beneath the grey cloak, he wore a black tunic over green pants held by a black leather belt.

Strutting forward, the stranger brandished a pair of well-kept black leather boots, matching his belt. "What are you..." The stranger paused to inspect the travelers. "...tender feet... doing so far from civilization?"

Xander began to approach. "We're on a quest to restore the sacred relics of Theshana, and—"

The stranger's words echoed in a thick baritone, lowered from age and the occasional pipe. "A quest? How noble of you. Your quest ends here." The words were laced with sufficient authority to stop the mage in his tracks. After pulling a long steel from under his cloak, he pointed the blade in the direction from which they'd traveled. "Turn back now before someone gets hurt."

Xander's hands came together, eyes half closed, focusing his will to bring forth the Asha within.

Bastian advanced, placing a hand on Xander's shoulder. "Save your strength, mage." He sauntered forward, addressing the stranger, "You will not stop us." The heat in his growl was palpable.

"Certainly." Reinhardt nudged his way past the Selece. "But this one's mine."

Searching for Kumori, Bastian turned to find the rogue leaning against a tree, arms folded. He gave Kumori an inquisitive shrug. The Nepharen returned the shrug and pulled a small piece of dried zelle meat from a pouch. Kumori started chewing, giving Bastian a nod toward the impending duel.

Pulled from its ornate sheath, Reinhardt's long steel rang. His breathing slowed with his pounding heart. The blood flowing through his veins surged. Falling leaves drifted to a gentle glide before hanging in midair.

Reinhardt lunged, slashing deliberately short of his target. The stranger intercepted the attack, binding their blades. Reinhardt broke free, stepping wide to find an opening in the cloaked swordsman's guard. The stranger thrust his tip toward Reinhardt's head. Reinhardt swiped the long steel clear. With his feet in perfect position, spine straight, elbow high, the young noble thrust forward and hit nothing but air.

Ducking low, the stranger shifted his foot behind the young swordsman's ankle and surged forward with a shoulder. Reinhardt flew off his feet with a gasp, slamming to the ground with the flat of his back, abruptly forcing any remaining air from his lungs. With a firm thrust, the tip of the stranger's blade pierced the dirt next to Reinhardt's head. The young noble sighed in relief.

Bastian and Xander bucked with intention to engage the stranger. Both stopped in response to something tugging at the back of their clothes. When the pair turned to find a meddling Kumori, their faces became etched with curiosity.

"What?" Xander raised his hands with a confused gasp.

"Why are..." Bastian relented.

Kumori's head shook with disappointment. "Look." The rogue's head jutted toward the ground where Reinhardt lay.

"You've gotten better." The stranger leaned forward, offering an open hand to his defenseless opponent.

"Thanks. Glad it shows," Reinhardt squeaked out, gripping the stranger's forearm.

"What..." Xander stepped forward.

"Happened?" Taken aback, Bastian's eyes flickered between Kumori and the stranger.

Reinhardt shuffled about, regaining his balance. "Cousin, I'd like to introduce you to—"

"Adriel," Xander interjected with a smirk, drawing the word out the way his cousin often did.

"Took you long enough," Kumori scoffed from under the shade of the indigo hood.

"You knew?" Bastian turned to Kumori.

Pulling away from the tree, Kumori chauffed at the forest canopy, "Anybody who didn't know wasn't paying attention."

"Who are you talking to?" Reinhardt chauffed at Kumori.

"No one in particular." Kumori walked past the group.

"Where are you going?" Reinhardt looked over his shoulder toward the hooded Nepharen.

"Forward," Kumori chirped without looking back.

"Aye! Please, come. Tell me about your journey and rest at my lodge. It's cozy, but it will serve." Adriel walked in step with Kumori. "How do you know where to go?"

Kumori pressed on. "Your boots are too clean. You have not gone far from the road. You were ahead of us. That means you came from the opposite direction. You have no mount, so you didn't intend to go far. Without some magical method, you wouldn't know we were coming. I hope we're not interrupting anything important."

"The Nepharen always were a clever lot. No, nothing overly important." Adriel ran a hand through his thick, wild hair.

After taking a long trail from the main road, the group came to a large clearing. Around the clearing was a circular garden lush with fruits and vegetables. The clearing's centerpiece was a cabin two floors in height and eight or nine lengths across by Bastian's measure.

Xander gasped. "Cozy?" he asked, mouth agape.

"You didn't tell them?" Adriel looked at Reinhardt.

"Didn't want to ruin the surprise." Reinhardt smirked.

"I was always told you didn't like company." Xander shot Reinhardt a side-long glance.

"I don't. Not strictly speaking, anyhow. I prefer to avoid the trappings of formal civilization and arguing about which side of the plate the knife and strad go on." Adriel took the lead, walking toward the house.

Xander and Reinhardt pantomimed setting up placement settings before glancing at each other with a chuckle. Bastian pointed at the two and laughed.

Adriel ascended the two steps to the wraparound porch before taking off his boots in front of the door.

Lost in the scent of a log house with a well-used fireplace, Bastian drifted into a memory of other recent friends.

Adriel poked his head out the door, watching the large Selece stare off into nothing. "You're welcome to come in. We're not that way here."

Bastian's eyes and face went slack at the shattered memory. "What way?" he inquired, walking toward the door.

"Oh, nothing. Forget I said anything." Adriel stepped aside, sweeping his arm through the air in a welcoming gesture toward the house's interior.

Bastian stepped inside the two-story log cabin, walking immediately into an open living area. Inside sat two chairs, each large enough to hold two fully grown Selece. Set back between the seats was a long piece of furniture wider than both of its shorter counterparts combined. All three pieces were upholstered in rough tan fabric trimmed with a forest green and framed in a light brown wood. Between them was a large ornately carved table sitting knee-high, topped with a dark wood and light wood trim throughout. The whole oval-shaped piece was near the full length of a Selece at its two farthest points. A rocking chair sat in the far corner framed in dark wood, a lighter wood for the dowels and trim.

Farther in, a cooking stove sat in a separate open room. Preparation surfaces, cabinets, and cupboards surrounded the stove, except where the flue vented out smoke. Directly to Bastian's right was a window frame with latches set to open outward. A netting over the window prevented insects from getting in while allowing those inside an unobstructed view of the woods and wildlife beyond.

Before the kitchen on the far side of the room was a set of stairs leading up to the next floor. Two other doors were visible from where Bastian stood, one up to the left behind the rocking chair, the other on his left, halfway to the next wall.

"What's for supper?" Reinhardt looked around, focusing on the cooking area.

"Do you ever think with anything that isn't on either side of your belt?" Adriel removed his cloak, hanging it on a rack.

"Do you know Reinhardt?" Xander chuckled, finding a place to rest on the longer piece of furniture.

"There's fresh-cooked swine on the counter. Help yourself." Adriel pointed toward the countertop next to the stove.

Bastian eyed a familiar object on the far wall.

"Uni for your thoughts?" Adriel inquired.

"Just remembering home." Bastian turned to Adriel with a toothy smile.

Reinhardt came back into the sitting area carrying a platter of swine and steamed vegetables. In his other hand was a wooden mug of dark evening brew fresh from the barrel. Reinhardt sat on the long furniture directly facing the window and placed his food and drink down on the table. Bastian's eyes lit up at the sight of steaming greens on Reinhardt's plate.

Giving him a firm pat on the back, Adriel regarded Bastian with a warm smile. "Help yourself. My home is your home while you're here." Adriel pointed at Reinhardt. "You!" Adriel dropped his voice an octave. The rich baritone reverberated off the walls in Reinhardt's direction. "Don't even think of taking another rutting bite until you tell me what you're doing here."

Bastian froze, checking back over his shoulder in Adriel's direction.

"Go on, friend. It's just that way. Please do help yourself." The natural lilt of Adriel's voice danced across the hairs of Bastian's mane.

Reinhardt froze mid-bite. Putting down the hot pink swine meat in his hands, he chewed timidly until his mouth was clear. "Yes, Rector. Have you heard of the murders?"

"I heard about Duke and Duchess Han'Durial." Adriel walked through the room. Passing the window, he pushed a set of levers and the windowpanes opened outward. Only the netting remained between those in the room and the natural landscape outside.

"It's worse than that. It's been five of the seven major noble households." Reinhardt used his crescent-hilted dagger to play at the swine flesh, frustration setting on his face.

"Which two have eluded assassination thus far?" Adriel walked to the shelf above the rocking chair to reach for an ornately carved dark wooden box engraved with flourishes. Each corner and crevice of the box was oil-polished to a shine. He pulled the box down from where it sat next to a lit candle held in a tin jar. Adriel slowly lowered himself into the rocking chair and carefully placed the box on his lap.

"Houses Vos'Gannon and Vos'Korendel." Reinhardt cut the pieces of swine on his plate, separating the fat from the lean.

Adriel opened the box and pulled out a dark wood pipe. The piece's distinct curve suggested the stem, and the ridged bowl were carved from a single flowing piece. The flourished etching throughout gleamed in the candlelight. Putting the bit between his teeth, he pulled a small purple bag from the box and opened it carefully. Adriel took a pinch of crushed smoke leaves from the bag and gently stuffed them into the bowl's packing chamber. He cautiously closed the bag and set it back in the box before returning the box to the shelf. After taking a stick from a small pile next to the candle, he held the stick over the lit flame and waited for it to ignite. Once lit, he sat down, putting the flame to the smoke leaves in the bowl.

Adriel took a long draw from the pipe and responded through the smoke curling from his mouth and nostrils, "I understand. What information do they have on the suspect?"

Reinhart's words drew out with a sigh, all the pomp deflated from his ego. "A hooded figure in a dark cloak, able to climb walls, with a mastery of small blades."

Adriel's gaze slowly shifted to the floor before shaking his head. The smoke curled up around his face and hair. "What were you thinking coming here?"

Reinhardt looked down at the perfectly cooked meat, and his stomach grumbled. He placed the piece back on the plate with the rest. "Rector Eldrogan, Xander is my cousin. Beyond that, I wasn't thinking."

"Thank Ashana you realize that much." Adriel took another small pull from his pipe before speaking through the smoke. "Everyone, come sit."

The smoke, carried by a cross breeze, slowly wafted out the window. Kumori sat in the chair closest to the front door. Xander and Bastian walked out from the cooking area, each with a mouth full of food, bantering back and forth about Xander's earlier embarrassment with the Nepharen herbs. Their expressions turned serious, seeing Adriel's solemn visage.

"What's the..." The Selece's words fell into the open air, like small helpless animals dropping off a cliff. Bastian's voice echoing off the wall was the only sound in the room. The sudden stillness created a palpable awkward tension that grew thicker by the moment.

"What's your part in this?" Adriel's gaze fixed on Bastian.

"A group of Kandari stole the Spirit Stone from my tribe. I was hunting Jorgan to find the stone when my pouch was taken by a cloaked rogue. Chasing the rogue got me locked in a cage." Bastian ran a paw through his mane before slipping a hand into his pouch.

"Jorgan?" Adriel turned his gaze to Reinhardt.

"Han'Shoden." Reinhardt cleaned the swine fat off of his blade before putting it back in its sheath.

"Kotch." Adriel's eyes fell to the floor, smoke curling up around his face and hair. "What's your place in this?" His head turned to Kumori.

The words came out in a thick Nepharen accent. "The Healing Bracers of Theshana were stolen from my people by the Kandari. I tracked them to Aestaria Una. Needing to eat, I took the money from the Selece. I thought none would care if a Selece reported it to the authorities." Kumori's face turned to one of sorrow. Eyes glassy with moisture, the rogue's hands came together in a reverent gesture, before solemnly bowing to Bastian to beseech absolution, "I am forever ashamed without your forgiveness."

"It is given only Once," Bastian growled through clenched teeth.

The Kandari elder lackadaisically threw one leg over the other, eyes flickering to Xander. "Your turn, kiddo."

Xander walked to the chair by the far wall near the rocker and eased himself down. "I was walking home with a box of supplies for a lab assignment from my professor. They crashed into me, destroying everything. I chased them to get reimbursed for what they'd destroyed. I cast two Cha'Sora spells and an On'Daka spell before the Kalash interceded with a brilliance spell."

"Flag?" Adriel gave Reinhardt a curious glance.

"Red," Reinhardt answered.

Adriel's eyebrows shot high. "You freely engaged in a brawl with two foreigners in a red zone and openly used magic. You're brave, stupid, or both."

Xander's arms flailed in frustration. "Well, the next thing I knew, we woke up in a prison."

"Where you," Adriel said, pointing the stem of his pipe at Reinhardt, "happen to be a guard."

"Yes, Rector." Reinhardt hung his head.

Xander's voice radiated with an angry heat. "Now the

Tor'Quari thinks I commissioned the rogue to assassinate the court members to elevate the status of my household."

"Let no disaster go to waste," Adriel said under his breath.

"Rector?" Reinhardt questioned.

"It's an old phrase from an old book, Of Kings and Tyrants, by Dorn Strogland." Adriel's gaze shifted about the room to each of them. "Where are the relics now? Does Jorgan still have them?"

"No, Rector. We went to recover them from Jorgan's estate." Reinhardt's demeanor resembled that of a small child awaiting the instructions to get a switch from the nearest sapling. "When we arrived, he had already shifted to the void."

"As such, none were able to speak with him." Adriel took another pull from his pipe.

Kumori looked up. "I spoke with him. He was not completely gone when I found him. He said, 'I'm sorry, Cousin.' Those were his last words."

Adriel looked toward Reinhardt. "And we know that Archon Serantes is the son of Count Han'Shoden." He ran one hand through the thick waves of his salt and pepper hair. "Jorgan, however, was the son of Duke Han'Shoden."

"What are you saying?" Bastian squinted in confusion.

Reinhardt answered, "The head of House Han'Shoden is a duke, who had two sons. The eldest becomes a duke, while the younger remains a count. When they have children, the younger son's eldest children will always become a count, while the eldest of the older will become a duke."

Xander interjected, "Unless the count becomes an archon and removes the heads of all the families."

Adriel spoke through a thick haze of smoke. "If Archon Serantes kills King Dailan, he can become king with no one to stop him."

"But who is doing the actual killing?" Reinhardt looked toward Adriel.

"That, I fear, is the worst part. Let me show you." Adriel sat the pipe down on a small stand before walking to the closed door behind the rocking chair, entering the small room and closing the door behind him. Moments later, he came out with two books.

Reinhardt accepted the first of the two books and read the title aloud. "The Tome of Origins. Is this going to be an Emsday School lesson?"

Xander reached out, taking the second book. '*The Ascension of Theshana*'. He started leafing through the pages and whispered, "The Chakeraut."

Reinhardt's face was blank with confusion. "The what? Excuse me?"

Adriel pulled his pipe from the shelf. "Yes. Continue." Taking a long pull, he sat back down in his chair.

Xander continued scanning the pages faster than he could talk. "The Asharaut is the tree of life. It is the core of everything good and righteous within the ancient tomes and scrolls."

"Right, so an Emsday school lesson," Reinhardt scoffed.

"No, Cousin. They don't teach the Chakeraut in Emsday school. This is the tree of death." Xander examined the tome, carefully inspecting its cover and binding.

"All right, I'm game. What *is* the tree of death?" Reinhardt inquired.

Adriel interjected, "Not everything in the ancient scrolls and texts is sunshine and rainbows. There are things buried in the past that are not discussed. These are the fruit of the Chakeraut." He puffed at his pipe. "The Asharaut teaches that the mighty Ashuun rescued Theshana from the invincible Kaitans before giving her thirteen gifts in gratitude. In exchange, she agreed to become his wife, but that isn't the entire story."

Bastian's gravelly voice echoed through the room. "What is the entire story?"

Adriel's response shifted the cloud of smoke drifting out the window. "The gifts weren't given in gratitude. They were given out of desperation. It's true that, after her rescue, they fell in love and spent aeons together, yet in the end, Theshana was the last of the Kaitans. Her kin were a cruel lot, consumed by power. After the Ashuun destroyed them, she was the lone survivor belonging to that mighty pantheon of gods. His gifts were a plea, imploring her not to ask him to end her life. She became overwhelmed by the solitude, so overwhelmed that her sorrow was greater than her love for him."

Xander read aloud, "'The Ashuun granted thirteen gifts, pleading his love not to shift. He knew if she enters the void, his heart would shift and be destroyed.'"

"Well done, Xander. What does it say of the fourth gift?" Adriel rocked slowly in his chair, pulling the pipe from his mouth.

"'The Soul Blade,'" Xander read.

"What is the Soul Blade?" Kumori's question hung in the air, pulling everyone's attention in the Nepharen's direction.

Xander read, "'The handle shaped of Kaitan mour. A blade forged of Kaitan ore. The weapon's edge brings death to all, even those who cannot fall.'" Xander squinted up at Adriel. "Mour?"

"The ancient Kaitan word for bone. It's a weapon created to destroy gods." Adriel spoke through clenched teeth, tightly gripping the pipe's end.

"Why kill the gods?" Reinhardt leaned forward, anticipating an answer.

"What were the first three gifts?" Adriel glanced back toward Xander.

Xander flipped back and forth through the pages, and pointed to the letters inscribed on the parchment. *The Stone of the Spirits.'*

"The Spirit Stone?" Bastian nearly stepped on Reinhardt,

climbing over the long furniture to kneel next to Xander's chair.

Xander's eyes shot wide. "Well, I don't have it with me."

"Show me!" The growl in Bastian's voice echoed throughout the room.

Xander pointed at the inked glyphs staining the aged parchment. 'Stone of the Spirits'.

Bastian examined the unique shapes arranged in Kaanish. "Why?"

"It's one of three keys." Adriel stood to pace, pipe in hand. "When brought together, it's said they open a portal through which the bearer can retrieve the Soul Blade. Xander, please continue."

"'The Bracers of Life and the Crown of Wisdom,'" Xander read.

Kumori stood. "The bracers are a key to this Soul Blade? Why? And when will they open the portal?"

Adriel leveled a serious gaze at Kumori. "Unless I miss my guess, they already have it. It's likely they had it before you ever entered Aestaria, given how their targets have been dying."

Kumori returned Adriel's solemn stare. "They are not killing gods. They are killing men."

"Indeed. That's where things become complicated. The Ashino were an infamous clan of assassins. They brought the blade before the mighty Vasuum and attempted to use it in a bargain for immortality. Their wish was granted after being warped beyond their expectation. The wish came at the cost of an immortal curse. The details are sparse, but the wielder of the blade can command these shadow assassins to kill anyone."

"Anyone?" Reinhardt sat straight up, eyes wide.

"Well, almost anyone," Adriel answered. "The legend says they can only attack if no one is watching. Even if the victim sees them, they are immediately banished back to the shadows."

"So, they would need to be stabbed in the back." Kumori leaned forward in thought.

"To be clear, we're saying that this is Serantes' play in an attempt to consolidate power for himself and overthrow the king?" Xander looked up from the book, eyes set on the pacing elder Kandari.

Adriel took a puff from his pipe. "According to the facts, it's him or one of you," he uttered, speaking into the smoke through clenched teeth.

"Why has he not killed us?" Reinhardt stood to walk behind the long furniture.

"It's my assumption that some of you are still of use," Adriel replied, drawing out the last few words.

"And that's his guiding star, isn't it? What's *of use*?" Heated emphasis rolled off Reinhardt's last two words. "Rector, you still have yet to answer the question. Why kill the gods?"

"The only Kaitan the mighty Ashuun regretted destroying was Oritheus, Theshana's brother," Adriel responded. "The first three gifts would let her speak to the spirits, restore their bodies, and give her the knowledge to return their souls."

"And the blade?" Kumori's arms spread inquisitively.

"In the event he needed to be killed again, the blade would allow her to defend herself." Adriel sighed, sitting back down in the rocking chair.

"Did she summon Oritheus?" Reinhardt questioned.

"How did the Ashino corrupt the blade?" Xander followed.

"Regarding Oritheus, the books don't say," Adriel replied. "As for the latter question, I can only point you in a direction to get an answer. That, though, will be for tomorrow. I, myself, have not yet had supper and should do so before the night comes. Reinhardt, bring me a full plate and a brew. The lot of you can stay in one of the open rooms on the second floor once you've had your fill."

Xander walked upstairs in front of Bastian to the second floor. A scrummage table sat in the upper levels open area, a set of eleven hardened ceramic balls positioned on a field of green felt—one white ball, one black ball, seven grey balls, one black and grey, and one white and grey. Each ball was roughly the diameter of a Kandari fist.

"Scrummage!" Xander ran to the table.

Bastian ascended the stairs to the second floor. "Scrummage?"

The table was nearly one length by half a length in size. A border stood around the outer edge with two pairs of pegs at each end of the table, set just far enough apart that one ball could roll between. The grey balls were set into a diamond in the table's center, with the multi-shaded balls at each end of the diamond. The black ball and the white ball were sitting between the wooden pegs at opposing sides.

"Yes, it's great fun. Grab a stick, and I'll teach you." Xander went to the lance rack mounted on the wall. "The stick is your lance. We each have one king ball and one archer ball. I'll be dark. You can be light. Your archer ball is white and grey. Mine is black and grey. We share the soldier balls across the green. Here, just use your lance to hit the white ball into the diamond at the center as hard as you can, and I'll show you the rest." Xander pointed at the collection of balls in the middle to be clear on Bastian's target. "First to ten goals wins."

In the room below, Reinhardt brought Adriel a platter of swine and vegetables with a mug of evening brew. "Rector, I have a bad feeling about all of this." He sat the meal down before his teacher.

"As you should."

The sound of clattering balls echoed down from the second floor while Xander murmured something instructional to Bastian.

Adriel looked around the open area to confirm they were alone. Noting a presence missing, he shot Reinhardt a curious glance.

Reinhardt looked around. "Yeah, that. You don't really get used to it, but eventually it stops being a surprise."

"Clever that one and no signs of guilt." Adriel chewed at a small piece of swine before washing it down with a sip.

"None that I've seen. Wrong place, wrong time." Reinhardt started to sit.

"Don't get comfortable down here. I intend to eat in peace. Go and join your friends up the stairs." Adriel cut at the meat on the plate.

Reinhardt walked to the stairs, floor creaking underfoot in the still evening air.

"And remember, there's no such thing as coincidence."

Reinhardt froze mid-climb. "Yes, Rector." Moments later, he reached the second floor. "Is he as bad at this as he's always been?"

"You only win when you cheat," Xander responded.

Over the log cabin, a newly risen Evening Moon hung low in the sky with its silver light shining down on a patch of freshly sprouted herbs infusing the evening breeze with their refreshing bouquet. Next to a shrub at the edge of the clearing, a kneeling Kumori gazed down on a wiry little knee-high sprite. The creature's lavender skin was glowing from its toes up to its head, from which sprouted long black hair. Reaching down, the creature took a small piece of candy from a silver disk sitting on the ground. After securing the sweets, it accepted a small, curled piece of parchment from the cloaked rogue. With the wave of the sprite's hand, a clap echoed and a glowing purple line appeared in the empty air between them. The line grew into a swirling amethyst portal, and the creature jumped through with a hiss and a pop. The small mirror polished token gleaming in the moonlight, the only evidence it was ever there.

Kumori sucked in a deep breath of cold night air, and the

pungent odor of pipe smoke wafting in the breeze caused the rogue's nose to twitch.

"Well, isn't this interesting? I wasn't aware the Nepharen people benefited from working with Tapi-lap sprites." Leaves crunched beneath Adriel's boots as he approached, maintaining a healthy distance between himself and the rogue.

"We are not all stuck in the old ways." Kumori collected a few sundries from the ground and placed them into pouches and bags.

"That appears to be so. In any case, it would be best if you stay with your companions, two on watch, two asleep. That's the best way to stay alive." Adriel puffed at his pipe.

Kumori walked past Adriel toward the cabin. "Agreed."

"Oh, by the way..." Adriel turned to follow, only to notice he was alone. "Surprising indeed."

Kumori climbed in through a window and walked down a hallway to an open room.

Xander sat watching over his sleeping cousin and the large Selece. "Glad you could join us."

"I had personal matters to tend." Kumori took a seat across from Xander, while their slumbering companions slept between them.

"We're all in this for you. You could be a little more appreciative," Xander stated flatly.

"You're in this to clear your own name. You're not the saint you make yourself out to be in your mind." Kumori pulled out a small blade in one hand and a sharpening stone in the other.

"Well, we're in this because of—" Xander started.

A mature baritone interjected from the hall, "You're in this because evil men did evil things and brought you into the midst of their iron-shard tempest. Remember this: If you fight, they win. Now let everyone else rest until it's your turn."

"He's right. My apologies." Xander offered Kumori a slight nod.

"Understood." After returning the gesture, Kumori's gaze fell on Reinhart's sleeping face.

Reinhardt's eyes twitched, while the sleeping Kandari mouthed three breathless words. "Yes, Lord Archon."

23

Reinhardt suddenly found himself standing in a hallway outside the magistrate's office within the Magistrate's Hall of Justice.

"Come in, Reinhardt!" a voice rang out from the office.

Reinhardt entered the office, feet snapping to attention. "Yes, Magistrate."

Just beyond an ornate hardwood desk sat an average-looking man dressed in red robes trimmed in gold, wearing a red cap edged with gold trim covering his bald pate. The elaborately carved furnishing was stained blonde with a thick, shiny coat of lacquer.

Without looking up, the magistrate scrolled an ink-tipped quill across the parchment. "You have been requested in the royal delegation office down the hall," he resonated in a nasal monotone.

"I have?" Reinhardt's eyes went wide with confusion.

"Did I stammer?" The magistrate dipped the quill back into the ink before tapping it twice into a small bowl. Minuscule droplets of excessive ink splattered in the bowl, and the magistrate continued inking his calligraphy onto the parchment.

"Why have I be—" Reinhardt's mouth snapped shut, almost as quickly as it had opened, but not quickly enough.

"Is this what we're doing?" The magistrate wiped the ink from the quill with a smudged cloth before placing it inside the hole of a polished wooden block. "Playing switch rolls? Now I'm the cadet and you're the magistrate?" He stood and walked around from behind the desk. He was just tall enough that the top of his head was level with Reinhardt's eye.

"No, Magistrate." Reinhardt's throat shifted with an uncomfortable swallow.

"Then who answers to whom?" The insipid figure walked around the young cadet.

"I answer to you, Magistrate." Reinhardt's eyes strained to keep track of the man while the rest of him remained statuesque.

"In that case, report as directed before I have you beaten for sport." The magistrate ambled over to his chair. The wooden legs groaned while he pulled the seats cushion beneath him.

"Yes, Magistrate." Reinhardt looked forward without moving.

"To the task!" the magistrate barked.

"Yes, Magistrate." Reinhardt snapped around toward the magistrate's door and left. In a light jog down the corridor, Reinhardt made his way to a sign which read, *'Royal Delegation Office'*.

Reinhardt knocked on the door, to which an imposing baritone responded, "Enter." The simple word rang with an air of authority, devoid of any emphasis or aggression.

Opening the door, Reinhardt entered to find an ominous figure sitting at a dark hardwood desk. The varnish on the simple furnishing highlighted the thick sinews of natural wood grain. The figure behind it had short dark hair, trimmed long enough to fall freely, transitioning into a short, groomed beard highlighting his chiseled jawline. His attire was a traditional Aestarian red trimmed in gold around the seams and edges. From his neck, the mirror-polished archon's medallion hung from a thick chain. The man smiled with his eyes as he stood, crow's feet cracking above his well-tanned cheek bones.

Reinhardt immediately took a knee, shielding his eyes with a guarded forearm. "Archon Serantes, how may I serve?"

"Reinhardt, please rise." The archon's voice was a soothing

baritone with rounded consonants that come from long travel to distant lands. Archon Serantes gestured to the chair in front of the cadet. "Please, sit with me. We have important business to discuss."

"Important business?" Reinhardt walked around the furniture cautiously and lowered himself into the wooden chair that matched the desk. The dark brown leather-covered padding gave a slow hiss under the cadet's weight.

"If I didn't know better, I'd say you were questioning my orders." The smile behind the archon's eyes fractured ever so slightly.

"No, Your Grace. It's simply that I didn't expect that I would be worthy of such service so soon." Reinhardt fought the urge to squirm in his chair.

"Situations being what they are, you're in great demand." The archon folded his hands on the desk.

"How may I be of service?" Reinhardt looked on, deflecting his gaze just over the royal delegate's head.

Studying a set of parchments before him, the archon took a deep breath. "According to the house of records, Xander Vos'Gannon is your cousin from your mother's side. Yes?" The smile returned to Archon Serantes' face.

"Truly, Your Grace. Our mothers are sisters," Reinhardt answered.

"Well, it turns out he's found himself in the magistrate's custody." The archon inspected Reinhardt's demeanor for any signs of treachery.

Reinhardt's mouth fell agape. "I, uh... How does this concern me?" he stammered.

"We know you've been to see him." The archon leaned back in his chair.

"I don't—" Reinhardt contested.

"Do not insult my intelligence, cadet," the archon interjected.

Reinhardt's demeanor shifted, and he calmly leaned back in his chair. Through a soft gaze, the young nobleman looked directly forward, meeting the archon's eyes. "Of course, Your Grace. How may I be of service to his majesty's highest officer?" The young lord's voice came out smooth as warm honey. His posh tone reflected no dishonor while infused with a hint of arrogance.

Archon Serantes' chest rumbled with a drone of satisfaction. "There you are. As I was saying, your cousin is in custody, and we have a task for you."

"The anticipation is stifling." Reinhardt shrugged with a smirk.

"You will help free your cousin and the companions with whom he's been caught." Serantes' words hung in the air.

Reinhardt raised his brows, tracing a circle in the air with his finger, requesting further elaboration. "And?"

The archon shook his head with a chuckle of masked frustration. "The boat anchors on you, boy. I don't know how you walk around without a wheelbarrow."

"I manage." Reinhardt grinned. "You were saying?"

Heat grew on the archon's visage before his bright smile returned. "You will follow your cousin and his new companions and report their whereabouts during the journey."

"And why would I do this?" Reinhardt's expression was that of a master toying with a novice on the tress board. *Archon four, to magus two, and it's an imminent yield.* Reinhardt contemplated a traditional tress maneuver.

"Because I know your family secret." The archon grinned with renewed pleasure.

A hidden rogue's gambit deflection? I'm all in; Reinhardt mused. "And what secret would that be?"

"You're not the child of Lord Vos'Korendel, thereby having no claim to the Vos'Korendel estate or title."

Rogue three to Praetorian five with an imminent yield.

"If I'm not the child of my father, Lord Vos'Korendel, then who's to be my father?" Reinhardt took a breath, somewhere between a yawn and a sign.

"What? Can't you tell?" Archon Serantes puffed his chest, flexing his jaw to one side, holding his bearded chin between his forefinger and thumb. "Chiseled jaw, piercing gaze... Isn't it obvious?"

Reinhardt's eyes shot wide in surprise. "No!" He sat back in his chair.

The archon chuckled. "No, you're right. If you were mine, I'd have bog-sacked you at birth like the rest of my bastards. Lucky for you, that honor went to another, yet, as I've stated, it wasn't the venerable Lord Vos'Korendel."

"And if I decide to do otherwise?" Reinhardt sighed in a mild relief.

"As any proper asset, you'll do as you're told. Elsewise, I'll be obligated to restore honor to the realm through the purification of House Vos'Korendel. Your mother will be stripped of her title for her indiscretions, and you'll be branded a bastard." The archon slowly interlaced his fingers, a crescent grin growing on his face. "But if instead you were to demonstrate your loyalty to the realm, it would be obvious that these rumors were entirely lacking in merit and permanently dismissed. The decision is yours, but now it's time for me to rest."

"The decision is yours!" Reinhardt groaned.

"Reinhardt, it's my turn to rest." Xander nudged his sleeping cousin.

"The decision is yours!" Reinhardt repeated.

"C'mon, Reinhardt, my turn!" Xander sighed while Kumori nudged Bastian's shoulder.

"It's your decision!" Reinhardt blurted in a startled shout, shooting up into a sitting position.

"What's my decision?" Xander looked on in bewilderment. The two were so close their noses nearly touched.

Reinhardt lurched forward, embracing his cousin tightly. "I'm so sorry, Cousin!" His tears fell onto Xander's shoulder. "I'll make it right. I promise I will."

"It's all right, Cousin. It was just a dream. Stop blubbering on like one of the fallen. Everything will be fine. The last thing we need is your frozen tears setting us on a course straight for the void." Xander's voice came out flat with exhaustion.

Reinhardt sat back with his hands clutching either side of Xander's face. "It may be the void for me, but if it's the last thing I do, I'll take you to Ashara myself."

"I appreciate it, but not too soon, Cousin. We still have much to do." Xander chuckled.

Reinhardt's solemn gaze locked onto Xander's eyes. "Agreed."

After he got to his feet to make room for Xander on the pallet of bedding, Reinhardt looked across the room where Bastian and Kumori switched places with nothing more than silent nods of acknowledgement. Moments later Reinhardt and the Selece sat quietly looking at each other while their companions drifted off.

"You realize this is likely unnecessary for now? So long as we're still useful to them, they'll keep us alive." Reinhardt took a small sip from a drinking skin.

"Best to practice now. I don't think they'll let us know when we're not 'of use.'" Bastian shifted into a more comfortable sitting position.

"I suppose we'll see." Reinhardt stared at his Selece travel companion as echoes of his dream ran through his mind.

Minutes became hours until rays of sunlight crept into the room, gradually pushing back the darkness.

Adriel's voice echoed through the room. "Come on, tilonka heads. Beauty rest only works in mora tales."

"Tilonka?" Bastian raised an eyebrow at Xander.

Xander shuffled about, cleaning up after himself. "Giant animals raised as livestock. We raise them to eat them. They sleep a lot."

Wiping the weariness from his eyes, Reinhardt chimed in, "They really do have the best of us. All they do all day is sleep, eat, and ka—"

"Crash!" Xander interjected. "The males butt heads over the females before eating some more and going back to sleep. The calves are adorable, though."

"Sure! Nearly as adorable as their parents are delicious." Reinhardt took in a long breath in through his nose. "Speaking of delicious, what's that in the air?"

"Eggs and breakfast meat. Likely tilonka sausage."

The four companions secured their gear before stampeding down the stairs into the kitchen. The aroma of pipe smoke and hot morning brew wafted through the air, intermingled with the fragrances of scrambled canter eggs and spiced sausage. Adriel was already sitting in his chair with a plate empty of everything but a single strad, morning mug in one hand, pipe in the other. Three of his four guests were piling plates high, while Bastian stood unsure of how to proceed.

"Your plate is here, Bastian," Adriel announced through teeth clenched around a pipe bit.

Bastian padded into the open area where four packs sat on the table, already prepped for a long journey. At the corner of the table was a plate without a strad covered in a sizeable chunk of raw pink meat. Next to the plate was a pair of small bowls. The first had steamed fruits, the other fresh water.

Bastian sat on the ground in front of the meat, mouth wet with anticipation. Taking each thick slice one by one, he devoured them quickly, extracting as much flavor from the meat as possible.

He slowly sipped at the water before moving to the steamed fruits.

"Why do you eat the meat raw?" Reinhardt inquired, pushing his strad into the bit of sausage.

"This is the way Ashana intended the Selece to eat meat. Fresh," Bastian mumbled around the flesh, jaw moving up and down, separating the sinew.

"And yet, you cook your fruits and vegetables," Reinhardt said between bites.

"Selece who eat cooked meat or uncooked vegetables, become ill. This tells us Ashana wants us to eat our meat fresh, and our plants bathed in flame." Bastian picked up two more pieces of meat between the claws of his thumb and forefinger and flicked them into his mouth.

Reinhardt looked on, imitating the urge to gag in jest.

Adriel stood, gesturing toward the table with his pipe. "You have a long journey ahead. Too much to do with such little time. Xander and Reinhardt, I've prepped packs for each of you. They include a proper bed roll, a meal kit, small dagger, water skins, rope, spark stones, rations, and torches. I've replaced any insufficient gear that you had, leaving all your superior equipment alone. For our Nepharen and Selece friends, I've left your packs intact, only adding rations and a few additional supplies."

Xander entered the room with a plate full of eggs and sausage. "Where are we to go?"

Adriel turned to Xander. "You'll be traveling to Kharsus Centra."

Reinhardt's head snapped over. "What's in Kharsus?" A small bit of egg rolled out of his mouth down his tunic.

"This may not be the king's court, but you will afford me sufficient respect as to keep your food in your mouth." Adriel shook his head and took a disgruntled pull from his pipe. "And it's not what, but who. You'll be traveling to visit an old friend by the name of Takala Teki. When you see her, you can provide this to her as payment."

Adriel held out his hand, unfurling his fingers to reveal an amulet. Reinhardt took the piece and examined the mirror-polished chain. The beautiful ornament's unique center piece was a multifaceted dark blue stone socketed into a golden circle, adorned with arcane glyphs at the outer edges. Reinhardt tilted his hand forward and backward, watching the stone shimmer between blue and purple. A preternatural feeling thrummed through his hand into his arm. Reinhardt flinched, and the necklace fell.

Adriel's hand flew through the air and snagged the piece by the chain. "Best let the mage handle the arcane objects." He walked over to Xander and offered the piece of jewelry. "Keep it safe in a pocket."

Xander took the piece and secured it in the inner pocket of his robe. "Agreed."

"You'll need to hurry and be off before the sun rises any higher in the sky. There's much ground to cover." Pipe smoke wafted through the air with Adriel's gesture toward the morning sun.

The four guests quickly downed the rest of their meals before dashing toward the stairs.

Adriel cleared his throat with purpose. "Excuse me!" The four froze mid-stride before looking back. "Reinhardt, can you fetch your servant girl for me?"

"Beg your pardon?" Reinhardt's face betrayed his confusion.

"Your servant girl, can you fetch her, please?" Adriel took a pull from his pipe.

"But, Rector, she's at least four days' travel from here," Reinhardt pleaded.

"Then perhaps you and your companions should clean up behind yourselves. I said you should make haste. I don't recall

saying anything about being so quick you forget your manners."
Adriel gestured about to the mess, pointing at the place settings
with the bit of his pipe.

"Yes, Rector." Reinhardt gestured about, and they worked
together to take their dishes and place settings into the kitchen.

Adriel's voice rang out toward the kitchen. "Bastian, Kumori,
I think those two can handle the workload on their own. Besides,
they're family, and you're our honored guests."

The large Selece and the Nepharen hesitantly walked into the
open room. Bastian froze in place at the site of the object in
Adriel's hands.

"I noticed you eyeing it before, and it's better in your hands
anyhow. I can barely pull it back to a full draw, if I'm honest."
Adriel offered a wooden bow and quiver full of fully fletched
arrows to Bastian.

The Selece lowered his head in reverence and accepted the
weapon from Adriel. With both sets of hands on the bow, there
was a slight shake of acknowledgement between them before
Adriel's fingers slipped away.

Bastian examined the weapon before looking into the quiver
where two bow strings sat tucked inside. Setting the quiver down,
he leveraged the bow between his legs and slipped a string loop
onto each end. He gave the string a mild pull, testing the limbs
without fully drawing it.

"This was made by a master. I will make sure I treat it
accordingly."

"I have no doubt." Adriel reached into a pouch on his belt,
pulling out a spool half the size of his own fist before turning his
attention to Kumori. "For you, I have this small gift to assist you."
The elder Kandari offered the spool to his Nepharen guest.
Kumori examined the spool with a curious disbelief. "Do you
know what it is?"

"Is this really..." Kumori started.

"Indeed. It's a full spool of silver silk." Adriel's lips curled up into the slightest smirk.

"Where would you get silver silk?" Kumori looked up at Adriel with curiosity.

"Well, there's only one place to acquire silver silk, isn't there? So, the question isn't really where but how, and that secret is one I'll be keeping."

"You're welcome to keep your secrets if I can keep the spool." Kumori held the roll in the air, inspecting the thread against the light in disbelief.

"As I said, it's yours. A gift between new friends." Adriel bit at the pipe end.

"All finished." Reinhardt sauntered into the main room, taking in the exchange, when a curious look grew on his face. "What's this about?"

"Nothing nefarious, just making sure you two aren't the only ones with new gear." Adriel clasped Kumori on the shoulder. "I've gifted some trinkets to your companions to help you on your journey."

"Speaking of which, things are tidied up, so it's best we be off before the sun gets too much higher." Reinhardt wiped his damp hands on a small bit of cloth.

The four took to the stairs, bounding about on the second floor, collecting their sundries and bobbles. Moments later, they descended again, ready for the road. Each picked up their packs, and exited the door, Reinhardt last in line until Adriel came over to follow close behind.

Adriel looked down from the porch over the other three travelers. "May the Ashuun guide you on your travels and give you the strength to keep yourselves safe."

Turning to Reinhardt, he offered his hand. The two exchanged a grip of the forearm before embracing each other with the opposite arm.

"Stay safe. Ashana bless you, and Ashara keep you. Or take you peacefully into her bosom," Adriel muttered quietly.

Reinhardt failed to cover the break in his voice. "Me? What about you? At least I have travel mates to keep me company."

Adriel grinned. "I've got all the company I need. That I promise you. Now fortify up and start walking before I decide it's time for another lesson." Adriel patted Reinhardt on the shoulder reassuringly.

Reinhardt walked toward the road in the company of his travel companions.

"Remember, go to Kharsus and ask for Takala Teki. She won't be hard to find."

Reinhardt turned to face his mentor, walking backward. "Takala Teki."

Xander popped his head around. "Kharsus Centra. Understood."

24

Finding the main road, the four travelers turned toward the north.

"Does anyone have a plan?" Reinhardt gestured to the group.

"The plan is to go to Kharsus Centra," Bastian stated matter-of-factly.

"Yes, of this we are all aware. I'm asking if any of us has an understanding on how we're going to get there." Reinhardt's last three words were slow and deliberate.

"Walking." Bastian shrugged, uncertain of Reinhardt's confusion.

Reinhardt smacked the flat of his palm against his forehead with a sharp crack. "If I have to go through four more days of this, just smash my head with a melon hammer."

"What my cousin is asking," Xander said, scowling at Reinhardt, "is which direction is best to travel and what roads will offer the straightest journey and least resistance."

Bastian gave a thoughtful nod.

Xander pointed toward the setting sun. "Currently, the sun is just an hour off the horizon. The North Strad between Imbros and Andros leads directly to Kharsus Centra by way of Ky-Ra. We should be able to pass the outskirts of Imbros before mid-morning, reaching the northern pass to Ky-Ra by nightfall."

Bastian looked between his companions. "How does this help me retrieve the Spirit Stone and save my people?"

Kumori placed a gentle hand on Bastian's forearm. "If we know why they stole our relics, we can find who has them and where they are now."

"After which, we clear your names and our own," Reinhardt droned. "Does anyone have any—"

Xander's hand snapped out. The knuckles of his clenched fist thudded against Reinhardt's chest. The whining noble looked down to find Xander holding a pouch of dried meat.

Xander dropped the bag into his cousin's hand. "Now shove those in your pie hole and leave us alone about your grumbling stomach."

At the sound of clattering hooves and wagon wheels coming from behind, the four moved to one side of the road. Two dark steeds pulled a covered wagon with a dark wood frame and a bonnet that was likely pure white before being tainted by exposure and trail dust. The driver was a husky man in a light brown vest over a green tunic with grey trousers. Age had moved the bulk of his dark brown hair from his head to his face, his complexion made dark from years of exposure to the sun. Beside him sat a woman, appearing similar in age, with a wiry frame. She wore a light green headscarf over golden locks draping down over her weathered yellow travel dress edged with a light blue trim to match her kerchief.

The four travelers slowed, allowing the wagon to pass. Xander politely locked eyes with the driver before they exchanged a curt nod.

Moments later, the wagon came to a leisurely halt. The driver peaked his head around to one side. "Where ya headed?" His northern brogue was loud and slightly higher pitch than would have been expected from such a burly figure.

The four stood around looking at each other, uncertain of what to do. Bastian started toward the front of the wagon before Xander grabbed him, urging him to hold.

"They're offering to help." Bastian pulled his arm from Xander's grasp.

"We don't know who they are," Reinhardt pleaded.

"We have to remember we're wanted criminals, and they could be the king's men." Reinhardt gestured toward the waggoners.

"But one of them is a woman," Bastian insisted. "How can she be the king's man?"

Reinhardt's eyes rolled. "Serantes doesn't discriminate when it comes to hiring assassins."

"Daddy, why have we stopped?" A little girl, no more than five cycles old, poked her head from the back of the wagon's bonnet. Her dark hair contrasted against the wagon's cover's pale background. A little doll's head popped out from around the corner with her before flopping over the edge onto the dirty road.

"Kayti!" the little girl yelped.

"Is Serantes in the habit of hiring little girls to do his killing for him?" Kumori walked over to pick up the doll and handed it to the child.

Xander chuckled.

Reinhardt shook his head. "Not likely, I suppose. However, I wouldn't put it past him if he considered it an effective means to an end."

Xander walked toward the wagon's driver's seat. "Good day to you both."

The wagon driver looked down to his left, inspecting Xander carefully. "Where ya headin'? You must have been travelin' for weeks as there's nothin' out here for the length of a buzzard's gaze."

"We're traveling to Kharsus Centra by way of the north strad passage." Xander gestured down the road.

"We're headin' to Ky-Ra." The reins were slack in the driver's hands. The large dark mounts stood statuesque, awaiting his guidance. "We could take ya as far as the eastern strad into Ky-Ra, and that could take a few days off your journey."

Xander's face lit up with excitement. "That would be greatly appreciated."

The woman next to the driver pulled gently on his elbow. "We could take 'em into Ky-Ra where they could catch the Estrobi river ferry right into Kharsus Centra."

"That's a grand idea, wife. If they don't mind the river boat." The driver shot Xander an inquisitive glance.

"I don't think we mind the river boat." Xander checked with his companions, all of which were nodding in affirmation save for Bastian, who stood with the look of a lost puppy.

"River boat?" the large Selece inquired.

"You'll be fine. You'll see when we get there. Besides, it's the fastest way to recover your Spirit Stone," Reinhardt assured him.

Bastian replied with a confident nod, "The river boat, then."

"Feel free to hop into the back, and we'll be there straight away." The driver pointed a thumb toward the back of the wagon. "These are our daughters. The little one's Serina, and the one with a stick up her bum is Tayra."

"I don't have a stick up m' bum." The girl's irritation rode through the air like a shaat odor on a hot, windy day. Tayra had one small hook in each hand, with two spools of yarn. She glared at the knotwork, stitching and knotting together as she twisted the hooks around each other.

The inside was a large open crate on wheels with no built-in seating, walled up with four vertical wooden slats as simple borders to prevent anything from falling over the side. Clothing chests arranged into makeshift barriers established the girls' personal territories. Tayra sat in the section closest to her parents, appearing to be eighteen cycles. She had long, light brown hair tousled from road travel and wore a white dress trimmed in yellow. Little Serina wore a matching dress. The little girl sat to the back of the wagon playing with her dolls, putting on some wonderfully dramatic production where Kayti was the star. Her shoulder-length dark brown hair fell slack in front of her emerald green eyes.

"Pardon my husband. Where are our manners?" The Kandari

woman next to the driver turned around. Her joyous voice resonated with a melodic soprano brogue. "This is Dalmer, and I'm Lyrial."

Xander entered first to sit across from a small boy slumped in the corner. The child had short auburn hair, tousled about and unkept, and wore a short sleeve tunic above newly sewn oversized brown pants. Peeking out from beneath his clothes were cuts and bruises. He rocked back and forth, staring out into nothing, and mumbled beneath his breath.

"And who's this?" Xander gestured to the small, pale child.

Lyrial looked toward the child. "We've taken to calling him Toli, and he doesn't speak much."

"Or at all, really," Dalmer interjected.

"We found him in the middle of a roadside massacre a few days back," she continued. "We're taking him to an orphanage in Ky-Ra where Dalmer's sister, Verna, is the headmistress."

One after another, the other travelers piled into the carriage, ducking underneath the bonnet and stepping carefully to navigate the crowded wagon while finding a place to sit.

"All secure?" Dalmer inquired with a shout.

"All seems to be secure." Lyrial placed a hand on his shoulder.

With a flourish, he popped the reins. The wagon heaved forward under the power of the team of walking horses. Before too long, they picked up the pace to a trot, and the wagon bumped along.

Xander's head turned to Tayra. "May I ask what you're weaving?"

"It's gonna to be a hat when I'm done." Each word came out short and sullen.

"For whom, if I may ask." Xander played at his pant leg, brushing off a bit of debris from the cart.

"For Mum, or Da, or whoever wants to purchase it if they have the chen." She made a drastic flurry of movements, pulling one hook around the other while the violet and light grey threads pulled together, forming an interwoven pattern.

"Has the boy said anything of note since you found him?" Kumori's voice came out from beneath the cloaks hood.

"Is that a Nepharen accent?" Dalmer shouted back into the wagon.

"Aye. I hope that's not a problem." Reinhardt situated his pack, attempting to make the wooden boards he was sitting against more comfortable.

"Not at all. Just making conversation. We're happy to be neighborly to any fellow travelers on the road." Dalmer pulled at the reins, guiding the horses around a stack of logs in the road ahead. "An' aside from mumblin' to himself, Toli hadn't made more th'n a peep."

"It just so happens I have some spare chen, and I could likely use a hat as I don't currently have one." Xander pointed to the spools of yarn. "And coincidentally, purple and grey are my—"

Reinhardt kicked the young mage's shin. "Favorite colors," Reinhardt blurted, taking his turn to give Xander a disapproving gaze.

"That they are." Xander looked at Reinhardt with the slightest shrug, only to have it answered with the curt shake of the head.

"So what's your business in Kharsus Centra?" Lyrial inquired.

Reinhardt spoke first. "My cousin here is going to university. He'll be starting his first cycle of studies shortly."

"In what discipline?" Dalmer asked.

"Cartography," Xander yelped as the wagon jostled over a hard bump.

"A map maker? Can't have too many o' them about," Dalmer replied.

"Nibblings anyone?" Lyrial hobbled into the back wagon to

open a chest. After securing a set of pouches, she passed around small cloth bags.

Reinhardt untied the draw string of his little yellow sack and peered inside. Turning the bag over, he poured a pile of nuts and dried berries into his hand. "This looks delicious. Thank you."

"Oh, you're certainly welcome."

Lyrial stooped down by Toli, pulling out bits from the bag she didn't pass out. She carefully placed the food into his mouth. Instinctively, the small boy chewed and swallowed, one piece at a time. After the bits of food were gone, Lyrial moved back up to the driver's bench next to Dalmer.

Travel continued on with little more conversation, and the rhythm of the road overtook their power to stay conscious.

"Ho!" Dalmer shouted, pulling on the reins. The wagon lurched to a crawl.

Reinhardt and Xander jolted awake. Reinhardt went for his blade. Xander's shifted his hands to summon the asha from within. Looking around, they noticed everything was mostly the same save for the sun being long out of the sky. Reinhardt let an audible sigh and slid his fingers from the handle of his dagger. Picking up a small pebble from the corner, he threw the stone and hit Bastian on the head.

"Where are we?" Xander asked.

"Currently, you're in me wagon." Dalmer chuckled.

Lyrial playfully slapped her hand against her husband's chest. "We're just east of the east strad pass on the road to Ky-Ra. The horses need ta' rest, and there's a clearing up ahead we use coming through these parts."

Dalmer played at the reins, urging the horses forward off the well-worn path in a careful walk. The wagon wheels jostled over the unsteady terrain.

Xander peaked his head out from the wagon bonnet. The area

had nothing more than the remnants of campfires, lean-tos, and tent ropes from long abandoned camp sites. "Looks lovely!" His voice cracked.

Moments later, the wagon stopped. One after another, everyone save for Toli piled out of the back. Serina began dancing as soon as her feet hit the ground, Kayti in one hand, another unnamed doll in the other. Reinhardt and Xander stepped down last, their Kandari bones stiff from sitting too long in the same position.

"Well, it's nightfall. We should get the tents up and fire lit." Lyrial moved into the back, began rifling through chests, and handed down pieces of gear to her waiting husband.

"Will do, love." Dalmer took the pile of gear, carrying it toward a long dead fire pit. Surrounding the circle of ash and stones were half a dozen squat logs for sitting on.

Before long, they finished setting up the tents, and the lot was sitting around the roaring bonfire. Dalmer was recounting stories of his youth in the big tent show as a strong man until he met Lyrial, who gave him two very good reasons to settle down. Lyrial told stories of her years being a merchant's daughter, learning the craft of bartering and trading. Now, they and their family traveled from town to town, finding things other towns are short on or have a heavy stock of. They buy the goods in quantity, keeping them until they can find a place in need, and charge accordingly.

After not too long, the fire died out, and everyone took to their sleeping arrangements. Toli shared a tent with Dalmer and Lyrial. They slung a rope around Dalmer's ankle, tying the other end to Toli's ankle, so he didn't wander off in the night and get lost. Serina and Tayra were set up in a tent near their parents.

Bastian set up his hammock in the lowest tree he could find. Kumori took position at a similar height in the nook of a tree just across from Bastian. Xander and Reinhardt nestled up in their sleeping rolls against a tree between their two companions. The Selece and Nepharen took first watch, keeping an eye on each other and their Kandari travel mates. Late night turned to early morning, and the dark grew cold in the nighttime breeze.

When the time came to switch shifts, Bastian and Kumori shuffled down to awaken their companions. A high-pitched scream from the larger merchant's tent shattered the stillness of the night. Lyrial ran from the shelter wearing a white sleeping gown and white woolen knickers, both soiled so thick with blood it was difficult to tell if it belonged to her or another. Lyrial's pleading gaze landed on Reinhardt.

A wiry form slid behind her through the darkness. The moist sound of rending flesh defiled the still morning air. Three long thick talons protruded from her stomach, needle-thin tips dripping red. Trying to scream, Lyrial forced a wet muffled gurgle that popped with desperation, and her gaze went flat.

The creature's howling screech tore through the chaos as it jumped high into the air, obscuring itself in the darkness. From the girls' tent echoed a shrill cry of dread cut short, sending Reinhardt's eyes wide with terror. He sprinted toward the tent, when a set of Kumori's spinning daggers flashed by, thudding into a tree. The creature's slender body maneuvered around the incoming blades, and Bastian clawed his way up the tallest tree he could find.

"Ashino?" blurted a distraught Reinhardt on the move.

"Something else!" Xander summoned the asha from within.

Reinhardt positioned himself to intercept the obsidian beast, naturally concealed from sight, within the shroud of darkness. Xander held the words on the tip of his tongue. Kumori continued throwing daggers, one after another.

When the creature was within Reinhardt's range, Xander unleashed the asha from within. "Daka On'Kada!"

The barrier surrounded Reinhardt, crackling to life with

ashareal energy arcing light blue from the impact. The creature bounced, propelling itself upward.

Bastian dove into a free fall. The sound of two massive bodies colliding midair reverberated from the trees. The freefalling creature released an earsplitting shriek from between two rows of razor-sharp teeth stained red. Bastian's knees and chatta blades drove down into the creature's back. On impact, the Selece warrior rolled forward after slamming the beast into the ground.

"Cha'Sora!" A bolt of blue energy flew from Xander's hands into the creature's chest, slamming into dead tissue.

"I think that's it, Cousin." Reinhardt's cautious voice was devoid of its usual arrogant undertone.

They watched the dead body's shrinking bones pop and crackle into place under tightening skin. When the creature's monstrous complexion drained of darkness, a frail minor form, pale as the winter snow, was all that remained. The three looked at each other in horror, faced with the difficulty of acknowledging the truth before them.

"Is that..." Reinhardt asked.

"Toli?" Xander's eyes went wide, mouth agape.

Bastian covered the boy's lifeless form with a nearby piece of tent canvas.

A muffled sound approached from behind. The three turned, ready to fight. Kumori stood before them, carrying the still body of a small child with a doll on top, both covered in blood.

Reinhardt choked out a sound. "No!"

"She'll live but requires much care." Kumori walked between them, carrying the girl toward the smoldering fire.

"Dalmer? Tayra?" Xander made the name a question.

Kumori froze. The cloak's hood shook slowly, and the rogue continued forward.

Xander looked to Reinhardt. "What now?"

"Now, we move." Reinhardt started collecting anything salvageable from the carnage.

Bastian landed next to the fire pit with a muted thud. "How can I help?"

Kumori used a piece of tattered fabric to wipe the blood from Serina's face. "I need water."

Bastian handed Kumori a nearly full drinking skin. Kumori doused the fabric before running the cool liquid through the girl's soiled hair. Her breathing was shallow but steady.

Reinhardt approached. "What's her condition? We can't take her if she was infected by that beast."

Kumori applied salve to the back of Serina's head. "Her head was bashed. There's no reason to think she's infected, but she requires time to heal." The Nepharen wrapped the injury with a length of flexible fabric.

Reinhardt knelt down to inspect. "How long before she can move?"

"Ten, maybe twenty minutes," Kumori answered.

"Were moving in fifteen." Reinhardt stood and walked away.

"Cousin, we know what did this." Xander gestured to the carnage. "The danger has passed."

"We don't know that, and even if we did, what are we to do? Sleep in this?" A flustered Reinhardt mirrored the gesture. "We have two options. We sleep, or we move. I propose we move."

"And what do we do with the other bodies?"

"You know what needs doing." Reinhardt's head tilted toward the campfire.

"This isn't right. They deserve a proper burial," Xander protested.

"Righteousness and necessity won't always agree, and when they don't, necessity should prevail." Reinhardt started pulling the fallen victim's bodies toward the firepit.

Kumori finished bandaging the little girl before looking up at Bastian. "You should carry her. She needs to be kept steady."

Bastian nodded.

Xander finished helping his cousin pull the bodies into the firepit. "How do we say we were attacked by an omni'sr—"

"We don't." Reinhardt interrupted. "Unless you're looking forward to a lifetime in a padded cell reserved for slug-heads and those touched by the void."

"But it was right in front of us. We saw it," Xander objected.

"We don't say a word. Not one rutting breath of it," Reinhardt insisted.

On the far side of the camp, Kumori gathered any sundries overlooked by the Kandari.

With the wagon packed, they took to the road. Reinhardt drove the horses forward, accompanied up front by his cousin. Kumori and Bastian did their best to make Serina's motionless body comfortable for the journey. Occasionally, they hovered a finger over her face, letting the warmth of her breath on their fingers reassure them that she was still alive.

Once they reached the city of Ky-Ra, there was little in the way of protection. Two guards stood on either side of a rundown city entrance protected by a moderate wall topped with three ramshackle guard towers. One guard wore a black uniform with yellow trim, typical of a Kharisian honor guard. The other was in medium plate with a medium trigger bow in one hand and an Aestarian long sword sheathed at his side.

The guard in black and yellow held up a hand. "What's your business in Ky-Ra?" The intensity of his uniform reinforced the seriousness in his voice.

"We're here to see Mistress Verna in the orphanage," Reinhardt answered.

"Orphanage is full. Move along!" the guard protested.

"We have her niece with us. She was injured in an attack," Xander explained.

"What kind of attack?" the second guard inquired.

Reinhardt interjected, "Bandits... set on us as we slept. We were traveling with her family, and she was the only survivor." He gestured with the reins. "May we continue?"

"Let's have a look at the girl," the honor guard insisted.

Reinhardt and Xander dismounted the bench to accompany the guard. The armored soldier moved to the back of the wagon and looked inside. The injured child was lying in Bastian's arms.

"Captain, you should see this!" the armored guard yelled.

"Yes, soldier?" the captain shouted.

"It looks bad, captain." The guard gestured toward the back of the wagon.

After walking to the wagon's rear, the captain peered inside before turning back to the guard. "Agreed. Get them an escort to the orphanage and summon the medicus immediately."

The captain returned to the front of the wagon and gestured to the guard in the tower beyond the gate. In response, the tower guard jerked on the bell rope, summoning a piercing resonance that rippled on both sides of the wall. Moments later, a pair of guards arrived on horseback, both lightly covered in dark plate armor over black tunics trimmed in yellow.

The captain approached the mounted soldiers, giving them separate commands. "Escort this wagon to the orphanage. Summon the medicus for aid immediately."

Each mounted soldier gripped a horn slung at his side. Pressing their lips to a small opening, the horns created a dissonant reverberation, shaking everything in their path.

"Let's make haste, Cousin." Reinhardt bolted to the driver's seat.

Xander ran to the other side. The mounted soldiers made a

path, and Reinhardt snapped the reins to follow. They weaved through the bustling crowd on the thoroughfare behind their armored escorts. Reinhardt followed the guard up one street and down another, passing brown wooden street signs painted with yellow letters, *'Chondura', 'Bayleal', 'Armdale'.*

Their attending guard shouted over the crowd, "Make way for the royal guard!"

Placing his lips to the horn's mouthpiece, he let loose a burst of air. When the distinctly ominous sound rode the air like an invisible flame, everyone in its path pushed and shoved at one another to scramble hurriedly from the street.

They continued forward, stopping four lengths from the other guard's horse, standing before a large white building crowned with a brown roof trimmed in red accents featuring three stories of arched windows. The guard aided an elderly, disheveled figure down from a steed. The figure collected herself, grabbed a black bag in each hand, and stood upright. She came up a head shorter than Xander, with close cut salt and pepper hair betraying her age. The woman wore layers of long, flowing white robes accented in dark purple at the bottom, with lavender seams throughout.

"I can take those for you, madam!" her guard offered.

"I'm quite capable of managing myself. Thank you all the same. Where is my patient?"

The guard gestured to the rear of the wagon, where Bastian was slowly exiting with the child in his arms. The medicus gasped, dashing to the injured girl. Immediately, she lifted the child's arm, lightly touching the demure wrist with her index and middle finger. In that moment, she froze, all focus on the girl's pulse.

"Get her inside immediately." The medicus pointed to the orphanage door.

Walking up the stairs, Bastian came face to face with a woman exiting the front door to the landing. Her dark red hair was well kept, thick curls held tight to her head by a dozen metal pins. She wore an elaborate dress layered in shades of green, from tea leaf to dark emerald, starting from a high-necked collar down past her ankles.

"What's the commotion?" the woman inquired.

"Verna, we need an empty first floor bed immediately." The robed lady bustled up the stairs behind Bastian.

"Of course, Amil. Down the main hall, third door, no! Fourth door on the right." Verna held the door for Bastian as he crossed the threshold with the child. "Who's the child?"

"My patient," the medicus snapped.

Reinhardt approached the porch. "Are you—"

"Headmistress Verna," she interjected. The woman straightened her posture, pulled up by an invisible thread of propriety.

"I should handle this, Cousin," Xander insisted.

"A mage?" The tone in the headmistress's voice betrayed her enthusiasm.

"How did you?" Xander began.

"You look the part. Now state your business," she insisted.

"You're Dalmer's sister. Yes?" It was difficult for Xander to conceal the sadness in his voice.

"Yes, I'm expecting him shortly. Have you heard from him?" She looked past the young mage, hoping to see her brother coming down the road.

"Is there somewhere we can sit and talk?" Xander gestured toward the front entrance.

Small lines grew on Verna's forehead. "Speak plain, or be on about your way."

"Cousin?" Xander nudged Reinhardt.

"On it." Reinhardt casually walked off.

"I really must insist," Xander pleaded.

"Guard!" Verna motioned toward one of the mounted soldiers.

"Your brother isn't coming." Looking toward the door, Xander was unable to hide his sorrow.

Verna's eyes went wide with comprehension. She looked at the door and back at Xander. She gasped. Her knees went weak. Already in position, Reinhardt gently helped lower the headmistress to the floor of the porch landing. "Lyrial? Tayra?" she asked.

Reinhardt sank to the floor with her, positioning her against the wall for support. "Only Serina, I'm afraid." His voiceless breath came out soft.

Burying her eyes in his shoulder, the grief-stricken woman soaked his shirt beneath her muffled sobs.

With a sigh, Xander leaned against a column supporting the awning. "I'm so sorry to put all this on you, but she needs you now more than ever." His eyes went to the door.

"You're right." The words came out matter-of-fact.

After finding her feet, she used a small handkerchief to clean up her face. Gathering her poise, she walked through the front door. Xander and Reinhardt followed. Upon reaching the fourth door on the right, Verna knocked. Amil solemnly exited the room and Verna's eyes fell on the medicus in a silent plea.

"She needs rest now, but you can go in and sit with her." The medicus looked at the three standing in the hall. "I'd recommend only one of you."

"Amil." A tear fell down Verna's cheek. "What's the cause?"

"The girl took a nasty blow to the back of the head. I've stopped the bleeding and mended all that can be mended. The rest is between her and the Ashuun." The medicus started to walk away before pulling something from her bag and turning back toward the headmistress. Amil held out a small clear vial, just large enough that her fingers fit all the way around it. Exchanging a sincere look with the medicus, Verna thoughtfully held the healer's clenched fist. "One dropper at sunrise and one at sunset. That's the best I can offer." Amil whispered.

Their hands slowly separated, connecting at the tips until the last possible moment. With that, the healer walked down the hall and exited through the front door.

"Please tell me what happened." Verna's gaze fell on Xander and Reinhardt.

"We were set on by—" Xander began.

"Bandits in the night," Reinhardt interrupted.

Xander shot Reinhardt a surprised glance. "Bandits! Yes, we were set on by bandits."

Verna looked between the two of them. "Well, where are they now? And where are the rest of my family's bodies?"

"We made camp at a site Dalmer said they'd used before when traveling this direction." Xander gave Reinhardt a side-long glance, wondering when he would interrupt again. "Dalmer insisted on taking first watch. By the time the noise startled us awake, your brother, Lyrial, and Tayra were already fatally wounded. We engaged the bandits in an attempt to restrain them, but they were too many."

Reinhardt interjected, "I battled their leader, a large burly man with no hair in rough cut leathers wielding two enormous swords. After a brief exchange, I dealt a critical blow. His men set to tending to his wounds, allowing us to escape. We found Serina still barely breathing in her tent, so our Selece companion scooped her up and put her in the wagon." He regarded Xander, unsure of how to continue.

"We recalled Dalmer saying that they were coming here to bring you a small orphan boy," Xander continued.

"Yes, Toli. I had received word from the Tapi-lap that they were bringing him. Where is he now?" Verna inquired.

"Gone," Reinhardt stated flatly. "We think the bandits were following the boy, and that's why they set on your brother's family."

"Once we were clear of the trouble and thinking straight, we knew we had to bring her to her aunt at the orphanage. We've had much time to ponder what happened during the journey. In all honesty, most of it has been useless speculation," Xander said.

Kumori entered the orphanage, cloak waving in the wind through the threshold.

Xander looked past Verna. "This is our Nepharen companion, Kumori." He raised his hands in curiosity. "What were you doing? Where have you been?"

"Checking the city's border. Making sure nothing followed us." Kumori pulled the hood down to reveal a grave visage.

Xander's gaze fell to Verna. "We were just telling Verna about what happened."

Kumori's gaze shifted to the floor. "About the omni'sryth?"

The mistress's head shot toward the Nepharen. "What are you talking about?" Verna's head snapped to Xander and Reinhardt. "What's this?"

"I didn't—" Reinhardt croaked.

"We weren't—" Xander uttered, slapping his face with his palm.

"Come!" Verna started away from them down the hall.

The three hesitated momentarily

"You rutting fool." Reinhardt glared at Kumori.

Verna picked up a whistle hanging around her neck, puffing a quick burst of air into the mouthpiece. The three recoiled from the sound, overcome by the feeling of spikes piercing their skulls through their ears.

"What was that?" Xander groped uselessly at his ears.

"That was my training whistle. Come!" She started forward again, and the three immediately followed.

"Bastian?" Reinhardt inquired.

"In the room watching the girl if I recall," Xander responded.

Verna led them up a flight of stairs and down two corridors into a small office cluttered with stacks of organized paper. The mistress walked behind the desk and sat calmly.

"Speak." The headmistress's glare radiated a raging heat.

Reinhardt spread his arms wide in a show of uncertainty. "I don't know—"

"The truth," Verna interjected.

"That's a difficult proposition given the nature of the truth." Xander folded his hands.

"Let me make it less difficult for you. Either provide me with the truth now, or I'll have *you,* arrested for the murders."

Reinhardt glared at his Nepharen companion. "The truth is, we met your brother and his wife while walking east toward Imbros. We told them we were going to Kharsus, and they allowed us to travel with them as far as Ky-Ra because they were bringing a boy here to you. They told us Toli's family had been attacked and killed. He still had the wounds from that attack and was unresponsive to everything save being spoon-fed by Lyrial. We camped at the site they used before. Two of us were standing watch when we saw Lyrial run from the tent screaming when an omn..." He hesitated. "A beast..."

"A beast?" Verna questioned.

"A beast." Reinhardt nodded. "It ran its claws through her. We fought the beast and killed it. Everyone was mortally wounded with the sole exception of Serina, who we've brought to you."

Verna stood and turned to face the window. "You're trying to tell me that a mora tale monster killed my brother, his wife, and their oldest child?"

"I told you we were attacked by bandits because it was easier to believe than this horrible truth." Reinhardt's face hardened with determination.

"And how do I know you didn't do this yourselves?" she alleged, staring out the window.

"What would be the point? Why harm the three of them only to bring you everything they own and their surviving child?" Reinhardt asked.

"Guilt?" Verna replied.

"For what?" Xander stood. "We did nothing!" His defiant voice was infused with anger.

"Sit!" Verna commanded.

"No!" Xander replied.

Verna picked up the whistle, placing it to her lips.

Xander summoned the Asha within. Thrusting his hands toward Verna, he shouted, "Daka On'Kada."

A blue sphere surrounded the headmistress. The Ashareal sound waves reverberated around within the magical barrier. She fell to her knees, holding her hands over her ears to no effect.

Xander whispered, "So'Lesh," and the aethereal field dissipated.

Walking toward the headmistress, Reinhardt clenched the whistle tightly. "We appreciate your grief, but we are not your dogs to command."

Overwhelmed by exhaustion and anguish, she relented. With a quick tug, the chain around Verna's neck snapped. Reinhardt threw the whistle into the air.

Xander chanted, "Tu'Razo."

In a flash, the blue ashareal blade split the metallic bobble into two even halves.

Kumori and Xander exited the room, leaving only Reinhardt and the headmistress, with the desk between them.

"Bandits or mora tales, believe what you want, Headmistress. We've done our part here." Reinhardt spun and followed his companion's lead.

They went back down the hall to return to the room where Bastian was with Serina.

Kumori knocked softly at the door. Moments later, Bastian opened it a crack.

"We need to go," the rogue insisted. "They will care for her, but we have much to do."

Bastian looked back to Serina and peered through the door. "She is not yet well."

"We cannot wait until she is well to leave. It will take much time for her wounds to heal. She is here with her people, and your people need you. We cannot delay any longer. They will look after her now."

Bastian nodded and opened the door wide. He turned for one last glimpse, watching the sleeping child's blanket rise and fall. Kumori walked down the corridor, through the front door, and Bastian followed.

"Now what are we to do?" Bastian looked to the other three for an answer.

"Now we make for the dock and ferry up to Kharsus. We put this whole blasted nightmare behind us." Reinhardt handed Bastian his satchel and weapons.

"The river should be in this direction." Xander returned Kumori's satchel.

The four followed Xander north toward the river, walking along the riverbank before finding the docks. The ferry was floating at the end of the dock. A toll-man stood at the post behind a booth on the riverbank.

Reinhardt approached the booth. "We're seeking passage on the ferry to Kharsus. When does it leave?"

"How many?" the toll-man asked.

"Four."

"That will be eight chen for the lot." The toll-man held out a hand.

Reinhardt handed the man eight chen. "Thank you, and when does it leave?" He drew out the last word, uncertain of what to say next. "I'm sorry. Your name please?"

"I am called Willem, and the ferry leaves first thing at dawn." The toll-man took the money and provided four small metallic coins embossed with the image of a boat.

"Much appreciated." Reinhardt took the tokens and passed them out to his fellow travelers.

They walked up the dock and onto the boat.

Of the lot, Bastian seemed extremely apprehensive. "Is this the only way to Kharsus?"

"What's the problem?" Xander slowed his pace to match Bastian's hesitant stride.

"This is a boat?" Bastian pointed at the deck.

"It is. Do the Selece not use boats?" Xander asked.

"We don't float on the water. If we were intended to float, we would be made of wood," Bastian snarled.

"This is the best way to Kharsus. I promise it's safe." Xander awkwardly attempted to comfort a Selece nearly twice his size. Gently, he took Bastian's arm and eased him along until they were on the boat. The hair on the back of Bastian's neck stood on end. "Everything will be all right," Xander reassured him.

The attendant on the ferry took their coins and escorted them to their cabins. The quarters were small but not uncomfortably so. Each had two beds on either side and a small closet with a shelf for sundries.

"We still need to stand watch," Reinhardt stated. "Xander and I can take first watch, unless there are any objections."

No one raised any objections.

The two Kandari sat facing each other. After a while, Xander held out a fist. With a sigh of comprehension, Reinhardt did the same. They shook their fists three times and, on the third shake, held out several fingers.

"Water douses fire." Xander chuckled, holding up four fingers, comparing it to Reinhardt's lone extended index finger. Reinhardt flipped him one uni.

Again, they shook their fists.

"Fire scorches Ashana." Reinhardt grinned, examining his cousins extended index and ring finger.

Xander flipped the uni back to his cousin with a snicker.

They continued long into the night while watching over their traveling companions. Bastian and Kumori drifted off for the first peaceful night's rest since Adriel's cabin. Come early morning, the pairs changed duties, and Kumori and Bastian sat in stillness awaiting the dawn.

25

The boat launched on schedule at the newly cresting sun's first light. In the daylight, Xander and his traveling companions gawked at the vessel's true enormity. By Bastian's count, the deck was over ten lengths wide and more than twice as long. The deck was constructed of thick timbers, with every surface painted white save for the blue trim. In the center of the deck was a raised platform enclosed within four walls, where a man stood tending to a large, spoked wheel. Bastian kept to the middle, hoping to reduce his discomfort at the unnatural situation. The boat had no apparent mechanism to push it forward save for enormous clouds of smoke coming from the water directly from the rear.

Shortly after finishing their morning rations, the four stood on the deck.

Looking across the bow, Kumori pointed to something in the distance. "There appears to be a bridge ahead."

Three minutes downstream was a large cobblestone bridge supported by two massive stone pylons spanning the delta of the river.

Xander nodded. "Yes, that's the bridge we would have had to cross if we'd have taken the road to Kharsus Centra by foot."

"What's that on the bridge?" Reinhardt pointed just over one of the keystones. He squinted to bring the sight into focus. "Are those people?"

"Why would they?" Xander asked to no one in particular.

"Bandits," Kumori replied.

"Friends of yours?" Reinhardt patted the rogue on the back.

"Be glad I'm on your side. For now," Kumori returned with a smirk.

Continuing down the river revealed a group of seven bandits covered head to toe in dark garments. When the boat passed under the bridge, the bandits jumped toward the ferry two at a time. Missing the boat entirely, the first two splashed into the river. Another pair landed sideways on the roof above the captain's head before falling face first onto the deck, unconscious. Thinking better of it, the last pair opted not to jump at all, leaving the seventh bandit to jump alone. A small squad of soldiers in Kharisian uniforms swiftly captured him and the other two inept raiders.

"It appears they have things well in hand here." Reinhardt chuckled. He bit into a fresh turandi.

"Where are they taking them?" Bastian pointed to the soldiers escorting the bandits away.

"Likely to the brig," Reinhardt answered.

"Brig?"

Reinhardt turned his gaze to Bastian. "A below deck holding quarters for criminals or passengers who pose a danger to themselves or others."

Bastian and Reinhardt looked on, watching the soldiers escort the bandit below deck. For the rest of the journey, they and their companions relaxed to the best of their ability, given the circumstances.

Over the next few days, Bastian became slightly more comfortable on the floating craft. Before he could become truly at ease, the boat approached a gargantuan wall in the distance. At first glance, it appeared to be five lengths in height. When they got closer, Bastian was in awe of the massive wall thirty lengths high topped with enormous, mechanized bows loaded with giant spears each twice the length of a Selece. Beautifully elaborate obsidians and gold stones, laid in a pattern on the wall, created an enormous image of a golden crown with golden wings on a black background.

"It's a picture." Bastian gestured to the wall, looking at Reinhardt.

"That's the flag of Kharsus." Reinhardt patted the Selece on the shoulder and made his way toward the cabins below deck. The other two joined him while Bastian stood staring.

After gathering their belongings, the lot made their way topside to the deck and queued up to exit. Reinhardt handed Bastian his bow with his satchel and other belongings hanging from the weapon like a yoke for livestock. Still distracted by the mosaic stonework, Bastian nearly dropped the whole mess. In a lithe display of grace, Bastian slid the bag to the floor and anchored the other belongings onto his body. With a flick of his ankle, he sent the satchel airborne, letting the strap fall around him.

"Show off!" Reinhardt said without looking back.

Xander snickered. "Admit it, Cousin, you're just upset at anyone more impressive than you, and I must confess, that was impressive."

Turning toward the queue, Reinhardt gestured at the indigo cloak ahead. "How did Kumori get ahead of us?" He scoffed.

"I'm not a big, dumb animal." Kumori chuckled.

Xander threw his hands into the air. "Kumori, that's no way to talk about Bastian."

"I wasn't." Kumori shrugged, giving Reinhardt a mischievous grin.

Once they hit solid land, the four gazed upward, slowly spinning about, taking in the magnificent grandeur of it all.

"An entrance!" Kumori pointed, walking toward the droves of people lined up awaiting their turn to enter the city.

"Wait for us!" Xander urged Bastian forward, while Reinhardt followed lazily from the rear.

The sun drifted an hour closer to the horizon before they

finished shuffling toward the archway to enter the walled city. Upon reaching the corridor door, a guard fully covered in black plate mail trimmed in gold approached the travelers.

The guard settled his gaze on Bastian. "Greetings and welcome to Kharsus Centra."

Bastian stared back at the guard. Unsure what to say, he looked to Xander and Reinhardt.

Following the Selece's gaze, the guard did the same. "I'm sorry. Does he not speak Kaanish?"

Reinhardt straightened his posture before pushing forward past his cousin. "In fact, he does, but the grandiose nature of your fine city has him awestruck at the moment."

"Well, I'd love to hear him speak Kaanish. We see so few Selece this side of the river." The guard returned his gaze to Bastian.

"Go on, Bastian. There is no reason to worry," Xander assured him.

"Greetings. My name is Bastian, and I have come searching for the Spirit Stone," the Selece rumbled in his gravelly baritone.

The guard scoffed. "What's a Spirit Stone?"

Reinhardt interjected, "We come on behalf of Duke Vos'Korendel in search of precious Kharisian art and relics for his collection."

"Do tell, what are you to the Duke of House Vos'Korendel?" the guard countered.

"I'm his son." Reinhardt pulled out a medallion displaying the image of a black raptor gripping a white serpent in its talons against a field of royal blue.

"No garments of nobility?" The guard inspected the young noble, pointing at his faded black vest over a dull blue tunic and grey trousers, all held together by a travel worn leather belt.

"These are my travel clothes." Reinhardt straightened his collar.

A second guard approached, wearing a black jerkin over a bright yellow doublet trimmed in black with gold toggles over dark grey trousers. He had a matching hat holding a large black feather sweeping back from the hat. "What seems to be the problem here?"

The armored guard snapped to attention. "Captain Hamish, these travelers have a Selece companion and claim to be journeying on behalf of Lord Vos'Korendel of Aestaria Una to collect art."

The new arrival looked the party over before turning his attention to Reinhardt's medallion. "In which case, it would be in our best interest to grant them passage into our city so they can squander their chen on whatever trinkets tickle their noble fancies." The captain turned to Reinhardt. "My deepest apologies, good sir." The captain held out a small tome with a column of empty slots and a quill.

Reinhardt placed his hand over his heart with the slightest bow. "Think nothing of it, good sir. I'll sign here for the lot."

"Jolly good." The captain nodded.

Reinhardt scrawled all four names with the quill and sauntered onward past the guard clad in black plate armor.

Making their way through arches, Bastian moved to the front of the group. "Where do we find the Spirit Stone?"

Reinhardt gently placed the back of his hand on Bastian's chest. "Easy, friend. All in due time. We are famished and in need of rest and a good meal."

Xander stepped forward. "Bastian, the Spirit Stone's not here."

Reinhardt slapped his palm against his forehead.

Bastian's eyes went wide. "If the stone is not here, why are we here?"

Kumori stepped forward, removing the cloak's hood. "We are being hunted, my friend, by creatures we cannot stop. We have come to speak with an ancient sorceress, who can help us find a way to stop these creatures."

"If we don't stop them?" A perplexed Bastian ran his hands through his mane.

"If we don't stop them—" Reinhardt started.

"We die, and if we die—" Xander continued.

"We fail," Reinhardt concluded.

Bastian nodded in comprehension.

"Now, let's find a brew house." Reinhardt started forward down the brick road.

The manufactured stones were made of various shades of pink, red and brown, set into intricate geometric patterns highlighted by the brilliant white mortar bringing them together.

"Is that a brew house?" Bastian pointed to a tavern with a faded red sign with white letters, *The Soaring Oran'*.

"Well spotted!" Reinhardt clapped him on the back before dashing forward.

Xander followed closely, with Kumori and Bastian trailing behind in hesitation.

Bastian looked to Kumori. "What should we expect?"

Kumori answered, "Always hope for peace and plan for trouble."

Upon entering the tavern, Kumori gazed around the room. To the right was a long wooden bar stained the color of red tree sap with golden yellow streaks of the natural grain showing through. On the left was a section with round tables, each occupied by patrons, most of whom were dressed well enough to be merchants rather than wealth or nobility. In the middle of the room stood four men throwing small knives at a target hanging on the wall opposite the bar. Every time a knife sank, they scratched a mark on the blackboard nearby. Mounted to the far wall was a rack holding a set of sticks. Beneath it was a large table with blue felt.

It looked similar to the scrummage table at Adriel's cabin, except this table had only red and black balls with no pegs sticking up to interfere with the ceramic spheres rolling about. The table had six holes, one in each corner and two on either side.

Xander and Reinhardt walked over to stand near the table, observing intently. Kumori approached from behind to stand quietly while the cousins commented on the game.

"It appears as though each player is assigned a single color to hit the white quarrel ball into." Reinhardt pointed toward the table.

"So why is neither opponent putting any of their balls into the holes?" Xander asked.

"Excuse me." Reinhardt raised his arm toward an idle player holding a stick. "Why is no one trying to score?"

The man, dressed in a nature-toned pallet of moderate means, mostly green and brown over grey, looked up at Reinhardt. "The point isn't to score. It's to make your opponent score. First player with no balls left loses."

"Curious." Reinhardt stroked his chin. "Can you please explain?"

The man straightened with a sigh, thudding his stick into the tavern's wood floor. "Aye. Each shooters' turn, they strike the quarrel ball across the table's center line, hitting one of their own balls. That ball must bank off the felt walls two or more times. Miss any three, and their opponent can place any ball on the table into any pocket."

"Even their opponent's ball?" Xander's squinted in confusion.

"Any ball on the table." The player took a few steps before leaning over and taking a shot. The quarrel ball hit a black ball. That black ball banked off the side wall and smacked into a red ball before resting up against a second felt wall. The black ball eased into a side pocket.

"Wait." Reinhardt threw his hands up. "Your ball hit his ball before it hit the second wall."

The man chuckled. "Fair play. It crossed the center line and hit two felt walls, or cushions, as we call 'em. The first player with all of their balls in the pockets loses."

"And what do you call this game?" Reinhardt began walking around the table, analyzing the players' strategic options.

"Eunuch." The man took his shot.

Xander barked out a laugh.

Both players jerked their heads in Xander's direction. "What?" they asked in unison.

"Well, it sounds like—" Xander started.

"We know what it sounds like, shaat-head. How do you think it got the name?" the second man scoffed. Taking notice of his appearance, Xander realized noble attire was a touch more regal than his fellow patrons.

Reinhardt bowed slightly. "Well, gentlemen, it's been a pleasure, but we really must take a table and rest from the road."

The two turned and jumped back in surprise, confronted by Kumori and Bastian hovering behind them.

"What the shaat?" Reinhardt yelped.

"It looks fun. Like scrummage." Bastian stared at the table over Reinhardt's shoulder.

"A bit," Reinhardt replied, "but we really should eat and set off to this sorceress."

One of the men barked, "Come on back if you ever want to lose some chen."

Reinhardt's face twitched at the challenge.

"Rye, no!" Xander scolded, to which Reinhardt answered with a disappointed look. "No..." Xander stretched the word as if to warn a defiant pet.

Reinhardt turned to the table. "I'll return for you shortly."

The four continued to a round table in the dining area. The road-weary companions shuffled about their chairs. Moments later, they were met by a sturdy built barmaid, standing taller than Xander but just shorter than Reinhardt. She wore a black apron over a green ankle-length skirt, contrasting her beige bodice, over a color best described as a manly shade of salmon. her soft pale face had an alluringly pleasant asymmetry, her naturally dark red hair embellished by two streaks of dark gold from overexposure to the sun.

"What'll it be tonight, loves?" Her festive words rolled out in a high alto brogue.

All save for the Selece sat awestruck silence by her radiant presence.

"While you're taking your time to think, I'll bring four evenin' brews, yeah? Pale or dark?"

Xander raised his hand. "I'll have a dark morning brew, please."

She drew her lips to one side of her face. "Morning brew in the evenin'? What do you think this is? They call it evenin' brew for a reason, darlin'."

"Water then." He put his hand back down on the table in defeat.

"I'll have a green leaf tea if you have it." Kumori pantomimed holding a teacup.

She gave a quirky frown. "No green leaf here, love. We have black leaf and red leaf if you're into that sort of thing."

"Red will do fine, thank you," Kumori answered, brandishing a shaat-eating grin.

"Two evening brews then?" She looked at Reinhardt.

"Sure, but then what would my friend here drink?" he asked with a classic smile.

"Oh, mister, with wit like that, I can see why you're single."

She shot a sarcastic wink his way.

"Well done. Two evening brews then. One for me and one for my friend." Reinhardt gestured at Bastian.

"Evening brew?" Bastian asked.

"Trust me, you'll need it after that boat ride." Reinhardt elbowed the Selece playfully.

"I'm bringing four specials, with two evening brews, a red leaf tea, and a water."

"What's the special?" Xander raised his hand again.

"Well, aren't you just the most polite student in the whole entire class?" she fawned. "Smoked pheasant with a side of raw house greens."

"Could you please bring one of those with raw pheasant and cooked house greens?" Reinhardt gestured at Bastian. "For my friend."

"Likely we can accommodate." She turned away, talking over her shoulder. "The names Maully. Just call me Maulz if you need anything." She sauntered away with a confident stride.

"Friend?" Bastian gave Reinhardt a side-long glance.

"Friend." Reinhardt nodded with pride.

Minutes later, Maulz brought out four drinking goblets, each paired with a platter. They hit the table, and she was off.

Reinhardt tore into his steaming pheasant, chewing only to weed out the little bones. Bastian started into his evening brew and choked, spitting it onto the floor. Reinhardt restrained a chuckle.

"Take it one sip at a time." Reinhardt demonstrated with a single sip.

Maulz brought a mop and bucket.

Bastian smacked his lips, allowing the flavor to settle in. Slowly, he sipped at the goblet before sinking his teeth into the raw pheasant breast.

Reinhardt finished his food with a vengeance. After wiping his hands with his setting cloth, he stood to walk back toward the object of his desire.

"Rye! This is a bad idea, Cousin!" Xander shouted after him.

"Most fun ones are," Reinhardt shot back over his shoulder, passing by their ginger waitress.

The lot continued at their food. Shortly after they finished enjoying their meals, Reinhardt returned. A pouch of ceramic tiles hit the table with a notable thud.

Xander washed down his food with a gulp of water. "You're feeding the beast, which is best left to starve."

"I feed the beast with the greatest hunger." Reinhardt retook his chair and sipped this evening brew. "Besides, I'm undefeatable with a lance in hand."

"If the best you've got to offer is a lance in hand, then you've already lost, love." Maully swooped in from behind, picking up dirty plates and used silverware. "Will that be all for my favorite weary crew?"

"How much for the best room you've got and the meals?" Reinhardt picked up the pouch.

"Four uni per meal, three chen for the room." She held out a hand.

"Call it seven chen, and maybe you'll come keep me company?" He dropped the coin into her hands.

Maulz blushed. "M'Lord, I'm an honest woman and a married one, moreover." She pointed toward the bar where an unusually tall Kandari stood behind the bar wearing all black. "That's my husband, Marsden. He's the bar owner here. Besides—" She lifted his hands, holding them delicately as she inspected. "Your hands are far too smooth for my liking." She sauntered away with a chuckle.

In his hand sat a small wooden placard engraved with the number ten. Attached was a long brass key.

"Let's get to rest." Turning toward the table, Reinhardt faced a set of empty chairs.

Xander sputtered a cough from behind. "We're waiting on you."

Covering his mouth with a cupped fist, Reinhardt rolled his eyes before pushing to the lead. Walking down the hallway, both Kandari read the numbers on each door aloud until they reached door ten. The large room had two sets of bunk beds with overly thin mattresses.

"Better than the ground." Xander patted the bedding, watching the dust waft into the air.

Once the four situated themselves, Xander and Reinhardt faced off, placing a tight fist over a flat hand. Their fists smacked against their flat hands.

"One, two, three, shoot!"

"Water douses fire!" Xander cheered. "Any other volunteers?"

"I'll take first watch with Stick Boy," Kumori mumbled, climbing to the top bunk nearest the far wall.

"Stick Boy?" Reinhardt scoffed. "I'll have you know, scrummage is a gentlemen's game!"

Once settled, Kumori and Reinhardt stayed up comparing blade sharpening techniques, while a deep sleep quickly overcame Bastian and Xander.

26

It was mid-morning when the sound of a wooden mug slamming against a hardwood table echoed from the small window of a local pub.

Xander glared across the table at Reinhardt, the morning brew in Xander's mug still rippling from the shock. "What the shaat are we still doing here, Rye? It's been days, and we've seen not hide nor hair of this sorceress Adriel spoke of."

Reinhardt placed his hand over his cousin's mug. "Calm yourself. If Adriel said she's here, then she's here. Besides, I don't see you proposing a better plan?"

"We know Serantes has two artifacts, and the last was the crown. That's our evidence." After peeling Reinhardt's fingers from the mug, Xander stared down into the hot black liquid and confronted the wrath of his own gaze. His voice softened. "She's not here, Rye. As much as I want her to be, there's no sign. We've looked everywhere."

"You have yet to look in between."

The small voice came from a short little man appearing old enough to be a grandfather. He stood no taller than the table. The figure hopped up on a chair. He wore an orange vest over a white tunic. His black belt held up light brown pants. His appearance looked so natural they almost didn't notice that his feet were bare.

"In between what?" Reinhardt scoffed.

"You have to look in between if you're going to find Takala Teki." The petite figure's thumbs pulled at the holes of his sleeveless vest.

With the swiftness of a lightning bolt, Reinhardt lunged at the figure, his hands whipping out to meet each other in a single, fluid motion. To his dismay, his grasp found nothing but empty air.

"Well, that's no way to treat a friend offering to help." The character stood on the chair across the table.

Inhaling slowly, Reinhardt closed his eyes before pushing a slow, deep breath through pursed lips. "My apologies. It's been a challenging few days. Can you please help us find her?" Reinhardt calmly placed his hands on the table in front of him, and his fingertips explored the nooks and crevices of the rough wooden surface.

"That there's your first problem." With a feline agility, the figure fell to the floor. His movements would have appeared almost clumsy if not for a powerful air of confidence and his graceful ability to find his feet beneath him with only a muffled thump.

Xander's eyes shot wide in surprise. "First problem?"

"Most certainly!" The figure looked up, holding out a hand. "You don't find Takala Teki. She finds you."

Reinhardt's hand audibly smacked against his head.

"Name's Damil Botomb, at your service."

"The pleasure is ours." Xander reached down to shake Damil's hand. Damil's grip was supple yet firm. "So you'll help us find her?"

Retracting his hand, Damil chauffed. "Maybe you didn't hear me. You don't find her. She finds you. You've been so busy looking for her you've not spent enough time letting her find you, but now she has, so it's not you I'm helping. It's her." With a knowing smile, he turned toward the door and strutted forward. "Onward, weary travelers. Your journey has yet to truly begin."

The two cousins scrambled awkwardly after their new little guide, while Bastian and Kumori followed with more grace and ease than their Kandari counterparts. Damil was short, but what he lacked in height, he made up for in speed. They exited the pub and through the congested barren district, taking mostly back alleyways until they reached midtown. They took a right down the finely cobbled Taldain street, heading north toward the high quarter. To their left, they approached a well-kept park with large wooden obstacle courses. Laughter came from the play sets as the children jumped from one log to another, swinging on ropes from one set to the next. Between the collection of wooden structures was a series of vertical wooden posts with cord strung between them, fashioning a type of labyrinth.

Following Damil, the group moved swiftly toward the center of the park, dodging the gaggles of children frolicking about. One child hurled through the air at another, colliding with a smack before they crashed to the ground with a solid thud. "Tag, you're it," one of them groaned. The group went into one of the labyrinth's entrances.

"Where are we going? This doesn't make any sense," Reinhardt complained without losing a step.

With focused determination, Damil continued pressing forward. "I've already made this perfectly clear. We're going in between."

Reinhardt chauffed. "Yes, that clears everything right up. Much obliged."

Damil snapped his head to one side. "Happy to be of service."

Reinhardt rolled his eyes.

When Xander looked up, the sky was no longer visible, and the sounds of children playing around them became a distant murmur. Reinhardt stopped so abruptly that Xander nearly crashed into him. Before them was a door, not overly large but not so small it would be difficult for most of them to fit through. It was golden hard wood, well finished with a brass door knocker in the center and no handle. From the door knocker hung a small piece of thin cord.

Damil reached up and grabbed the cord. Swinging it back and forth, he made a rhythmic beat against the door in patterns of three. After a moment's pause, he swung the cord again, repeating the pattern.

Kumori looked over at Damil. "What happens now?"

Damil stroked an invisible beard at the edge of his smooth jawline. "Now, we wait."

"Where are we?" Xander turned about slowly, trying to make out the distorted shapes likely to be children playing in the park.

"Hmm?" Damil chirped. "We are in between."

Kumori peered from underneath the hood. "Yes, but how did we get here?"

Damil turned to the Nepharen. "We walked."

At that, Bastian nodded, holding out a gesturing hand toward Damil. "That is true."

From that remark grew a still silence that stretched for an aeon.

With a creak, the door opened slowly toward the confused company of weary travelers. A hooded figure of medium size accompanied by a fair woman with long silver hair came through the door. The hooded figure wore a gold cloak trimmed in midnight blue. The silver-haired woman wore armor so well fitted it looked like a second skin, with a long sword on her hip and a short sword over her shoulder. Secured to her arm was a perfectly fitted Ivaness buckler, with razor-sharp edges.

Once the doorway cleared, a shrill voice echoed from within, "Well, come in if you're coming, and stop letting the dilly-drifters in."

"Yes, my love." Damil entered.

Upon crossing the threshold, his clothing dissolved into glittering dust, replaced by a thick coat of white fur. Where his trousers were just concealing his bottom was a thick furry tail as long as he was tall. Damil walked forward toward a similar-looking figure with open arms. When they embraced, their tails intertwined overhead.

"I found them for you, Taka," he said.

Following Reinhardt, they entered one after another. Kumori trailed behind Xander, slowing only to stop from colliding into the distracted young mage. Bastian crouched slightly to get through the door frame. The four stood upright, turning about, eyes wide, mouths agape in amazement of the wide-open space, not unlike a large festival tent with canvas composed of a shimmering twilight dusk. Beneath their shuffling feet was a lawn made of grass softer than silk. The well-furnished area had all the trimmings of a house with an open floor plan. At the center was a large, elaborate rug. The woven piece was busy with ornately curved lines and intersecting geometric patterns. Prismatic lights danced over the shapes, shifting from shades of pink to hues of blue and violet. In the middle of the iridescent rug was Damil, newly covered in a thick layer of white fur. Beside him stood a slightly smaller, more effeminate figure, equally covered in white fur. The wisdom of time lined her smooth hairless face.

"He's a Monku?" Reinhardt gasped.

"Obviously," Xander replied, patting his cousin on the back with a stiff thud.

Reinhardt turned about slowly, his gaping mouth betraying his sense of awe. "I don't believe my eyes."

The female Monku approached. "If your eyes disagree with reality, you need to reevaluate your eyes or reevaluate your reality." She stopped and straightened, bending forward at the waist with the greatest of subtlety.

"Takala Teki?" Reinhardt's inflection raised with a lilt to match the movement of his brow.

"Aye, child." The diminutive figure stepped back.

Xander gave the slightest bow, matching her gesture. His companions followed in kind.

Their hosts' faces softened considerably, and they began moving about the space freely. The Monku bustled about, pulling down pillows and retrieving a black crystal orb from a large wooden chest.

Xander stood upright. "We have come—"

"I know why you've come," she snapped. Her voice was shrill with age over the warm resonance of affectionate wisdom. One after the other, she regarded each of them with a grave look through the center of their eyes, into their very souls. "The threads of your fate have been interwoven into the tapestry of destiny."

She turned and arranged a sitting circle with the orb at the center on its own pillow.

"Sit." Takala gestured to the circle.

Each of the weary travelers grabbed a cushion to sit on, shifting back and forth until they were comfortable. Damil quietly took a seat between Reinhardt and Bastian.

The wise Monku sorcerer sat comfortably on the empty pillow between Xander and Kumori. She stared off into the distance, looking at nothing in particular. "Ask your question."

Xander cleared his throat. "What is the origin of the Soul Blade?"

Takala's eyes glowed white before fading to an empty abyssal obsidian. The room's iridescent light faded to nothing. From the orb came amorphous swirls of dark blues and light greens drifting out into the circle. The nebulous spectral clouds materialized into solid shapes, forming a desolate woodland clearing surrounded by mysterious arcane artifacts. A malicious mist fell across the ethereal woodland floor. The group sat amongst an assembly of a dozen night-clad assassins transporting themselves through an abyssal vortex to a forest not meant to be seen by mortal eyes.

Takala's hand drifted upward, finger pointing at one of the figures. "That is Surashi."

Surashi and his coterie stood in the oblivion of that forsaken forest, surrounded by overgrown vines of viscous pitch that brandished dark thorns discharging a black ichor from their razor tips. The orb before them could be called black by those with a diminished capacity for observation. In truth, it was a sphere of nothing, where all essence of light and vitality merely cease to exist. When the sphere vibrated, every member of the assassin company struck their right fists to their chest, covering the Ashino order emblem embossed in the center of their stygian leather armor. The impact resonated through the forest, and the pressure of forces unseen compelled the unwilling clan members to one knee.

The vibrating sphere's metallic tones shifted into comprehensive words from the Nepharen language. After each Nepharen phrase, the ominous words echoed in Kaanish. "What do you seek?"

"We seek immortality and invincibility, great Vasuum." The words came from Surashi's lips, gaze averted to the base of the pedestal holding the orb.

Vasuum's voice reverberated again. "What do you offer?"

"You may take any of my followers' lives, great Vasuum." Surashi's hesitation betrayed the lack of confidence in his words.

"Where did you find that blade, Surashi?" The pedestal holding the orb shuddered.

"It is one of the thirteen treasures of Theshana." The assassin drew the blade and presented it to the orb.

"You offer what is not yours to give, keeping the best for yourself." The arcane weapon levitated into the air, hovering before the pedestal in an orbital spin.

"Many apologies, great Vasuum." The assassin quivered.

The darkness around the orb trembled. "I will grant your request."

Surashi's head jerked up in enthusiastic surprise.

The mystically suspended dagger fell from the air, blade piercing the desecrated soil.

"And yet, the cost will be greater than you were prepared to pay."

Arterial strands of darkness erupted from the orb, latching onto the master assassin. Surashi's ethereal doppelgänger levitated over his mortal coil, and he watched his own corpse slump to the ground. The dark, swirling mist surrounding his spectral form pulled his phantasmal essence into the arcane blade, piercing the Darkthorne forest floor.

The defiled blade penetrating the ground thrummed in the darkness. Abyssal tendrils lashed out into the rest of the deadly company, leaching the essence of their vitality into the blade. Moments later, the spectral tentacles retracted, having littered the ground with the assassins' tattered shadows of their former selves, leaving every member of clan Ashino both invincible and immortal, precisely as they had requested.

The orb vibrated. "You will obey the one who wields the Soul Blade. It is their will which shall be done!"

The sun's rays pierced the woodland canopy, chasing away the darkness to illuminate the forest floor. In the daylight, the obsidian spectral wraiths retreated into the shadows, moving unseen through the forest. The only evidence of the encounter was a small empty hole where the Soul Blade had pierced the ground.

The ethereal forest faded away.

Reinhardt stood. "What was that?" The terror in his words betrayed the anxiety crawling under his skin, into his bones.

"That..." Takala raised her arms, spreading her hands to

gesture toward the room's center, once again peacefully encircled in a tapestry of twilight dusk. "...was the distant past." Her voice was warm and calm, with a hint of shrill betraying her age.

Reinhardt paced, his eyes flitting about. "Please explain how we saw into the distant past."

"It's magic, Rye." Xander walked over to place a hand on his cousin on the back.

Reinhardt startled at the touch. "Don't," he snapped, shifting in discomfort. "That's what we're facing?" He thrust his hands toward the empty space recently occupied by images of phantasmal assassins.

"We will find a way through this." Kumori calmly assured, from beneath the cloak's shadow.

"This is why we've come." Bastian stepped forward. "To face this together."

"But how do we defend against mystical assassins that can become shadow, swimming through it like fish in the sea?" Reinhardt's hand clasped his moon-hilted dagger.

Unexpectedly, a small hand grasped two of his fingers, overtaking the anxious Kandari with a calm he'd not known in months. Not since before he had helped his cousins escape from that cell. Reinhardt chuckled at the thought. He remembered seeing his cousin's name on the jailer's roster, and figured he'd go have a laugh. How naïve he had been to assume he could just walk him out of that brick building as easy as buying a piece of fruit from the market. The tears overtook his face, and he slumped to the floor.

The elder Monku wrapped her arms and tail around this giant being and rocked him back and forth. "All will be well. In time, this too shall pass." The words came out a lullaby of silken syllables.

A solemn stillness consumed those in the room as they

acknowledged the daunting task before them and the challenges they would have to overcome to succeed.

"The most important thing, dear, is that you never stop pushing forward. Even when you think… Especially when you think you've lost. Push forward because on the other side of that loss is victory. So long as you never accept defeat, you will be victorious."

Swollen with sadness, the Kandari's wet eyes looked up at the elder Monku sorceress.

"Just remember, every victory has a price, and you must be willing to pay it when the time comes."

Reinhardt nodded. "Indeed."

Takala unwrapped her arms and tail from around the crumpled Kandari and backed away slowly. "Now, to make a plan."

"Yes. What is the plan?" Bastian inquired.

The Monku, clad in white fur, sprang to the furniture on one side of the room. She was opening and closing drawers.

Kumori strode up behind the small Monku figure. "What are you searching for?"

"The Eye of Aramis," she stated flatly, continuing to search the drawers. "Now, what did I do with that trinket?"

Damil stroked his chin with his thumb and forefinger. "Didn't you lose that old bobble in a game of shackul almost a decade back?"

"Blast, I think you're right." She thrust the drawer forward, slamming it shut with the sound of finality.

Reinhardt's head shook. "I knew it. We're rutted. All shoe-horned into the same barrel."

Kumori glanced over casually. "You see what's coming. How could you not?"

Reinhardt turned to Kumori. "Who are you talking to?"

Kumori's head shook with disappointment.

Xander ran his hands through his hair. "What does it look like? The Eye of Aramis?"

"What?" Takala's face distorted in tumultuous contemplation.

"The eye. What does it look like?" Xander repeated.

Takala's gaze drifted off into the distance. "It's a shimmering orudite stone set into a gold circle engraved with magical glyphs. Last I saw, it was set on a master-crafted chain." The elder Monku took a deep breath.

Before the Monku could let out a sigh, Xander pulled a hand from his robe, holding a gold master-crafted chain wrapped around his thumb and fingers. From the chain, a shimmering orudite stone, set in a magical gold circle between engravings of magical glyphs, swung side to side.

"Ka bata latika chakata ka ooki cheetaki tuka!" The small voice erupted into a shrill tone, shattering the silence and any sense of calm within.

"What are you— Reinhardt blurted.

"That's it!" Takala pointed at the bobble hanging from Xander's clenched fist. She approached, mouth agape. "Where did you get this? I lost this in a game of Shackul to a scamming cheater an age ago."

"Adriel said you were friends," Reinhardt mumbled in an uncertain tone.

The Monku pulled on the chain, easing it from Xander's grasp. "How do you know that name?"

"He's my master." Reinhardt's eyes gleamed with conviction.

"It was he who sent us," Xander interjected.

Bastian continued, "He said you could help us in our quest."

"How did you know we were here if he did not send a Tapi?" Kumori inquired.

Takala chirped in a huff, crossing her arms. "To answer the first, we are friends, but he's still a lying, cheating shaat-head.

Two, I don't need a Tapi to tell me that four bumbling bartle-beaks are shouting my name all over town. And last..." She lifted the amulet. "All the help I can give you, you already have." The little sorceress paced about, examining the bobble, an expression of disbelief etched into her face.

"Already have?" Reinhardt shrugged in confusion.

"This *is* the Eye of Aramis." She pointed to the orudite stone.

"What does it do?" Reinhardt's brows furrowed.

"What does an eye do?" the Monku countered.

A sigh pulled their attention in Kumori's direction. Looking over, the Nepharen stood there, eyes rolled, hood back. "It sees," Kumori stated flatly.

"Yeah? So?" Reinhardt replied.

"It *sees*," Kumori repeated with a heavy inflection through the Nepharen accent.

Reinhardt's eyes went wide in comprehension. "It sees? It sees! What does it see?"

"Everything." The Monku walked over and handed the chain back to Xander.

Reinhardt stomped toward Xander. Grabbing his collar, he shook the mage with excitement. "You mean I could have slept this entire time?"

"How was I to know?" Xander pulled himself from his cousin's grip.

"What do we do now?" Bastian stepped forward, posing the obvious question.

"And why did Adriel send us here with his if he knows what it does?" Xander offered to the room.

"The eye has many uses. He was likely unaware that it would hold the Ashino at bay," the Monku answered.

"What was his use for it?" Reinhardt asked.

"That is between him, myself, and Aramis. Who sent the

Ashino against you?" Takala gestured back to the pillows in the center of the room.

The group recounted the details of their meeting and Serantes' plot.

"This is bad." Takala gazed off into the distance.

"We realize." Kumori nodded.

"No, you don't. The sovereigns won't accept Serantes. Everything will fall, rekindling the fires of the Trillium wars." Her voice shook with trepidation.

"What comes next?" Bastian asked.

"At first light, you return to stop Serantes. All of Aestaria will not withstand this plot," Takala answered.

Takala led the group of traveling companions to an empty corner of her aethereal domicile. There, she spread her hands, from which spectral mist drifted forward into solid posts and poles with sacks of down for sleeping.

Bastian gazed uncomfortably at the bed in front of him. He grunted in dismay.

Takala looked over to find the problem. "Oh, my mistake."

She lifted her hands, putting her fingers together and drawing them apart. The bed split into two halves, shifting into solid posts. Between the posts, a set of lights intersected into a prismatic webbing and settled into the shape of a hammock.

Bastian took to his phantasmal sleeping arrangements, joining his companions in the first restful slumber they've had in weeks.

27

The thin whisper of a blade separating flesh drifted into the obsidian silence. Gurgles and pops from the struggle for life echoed through the air, bouncing off walls laden with ornate tapestries obscured by the veil of night. Moments later, the macabre symphony was accompanied by splatters falling from the bed against the surrounding floorboards.

A window opened slowly, its hinges silenced by the viscosity of Hesheim grease. A squat, hulking figure exited the window and closed it before descending the manor's ornate walls. With no sound underfoot despite his bulky frame and hulking muscle, the cloaked assailant dashed toward the estate's border. The assassin navigated through the perimeter wall, unseen by the centurion guards overlooking the courtyard.

Once he was clear, the surreal sound of a loud tap followed by a high-pitched tone and a woosh ending in an abrupt clap startled him, and he pulled back the hood of his cloak. Beside him stood a spritely figure just under knee high with glowing lavender skin.

The Tapi lifted a hand toward the Fataak, holding a small scroll skyward. "For Takesh El Hesheim."

Takesh took the scroll with a grin. "A few minutes sooner, friend, and you would have had me hung from the ramparts."

The Tapi-Lap turned to draw an azure line in the air that swirled into a portal. After the Tapi plunged forward, the portal closed with the sounds of a tapping whirring and pop.

Takesh opened the scroll and read, "They are visiting a friend between the veil in Kharsus centra."

Takesh used his quill and ink to sign the scroll, "Takesh." He pulled out a silver coin and laid it on the ground, placing a small cube of sugar on the silver piece. Soon after, a small lavender sprite approached. "Greetings," The Tapi's voice came out a pleasantly high-pitched soprano.

"This is to go to Kasaam El Hesheim."

The sprite nodded before departing through an aethereal vortex. Sliding through a labyrinth of prismatic tunnels, the small lavender sprite navigated the aethereal veins of Ashana until it found the one glowing sky blue. After plunging through the ashareal whirlpool, the Tapi was suddenly in the middle of a dark woodland landscape. Approaching the lavender sprite was an olive-skinned figure clad in robes walking toward a bonfire.

Upon seeing the pixie, he stopped to hold out a hand. "You have something for me?"

The Tapi lifted the scroll. "For Kasaam El Hesheim."

With the message delivered, the Tapi dove through a newly manifested portal.

Kasaam continued toward the bonfire. Sitting on a stump under the dark of night before a roaring campfire, he poked the logs curiously with a long thin stick, twisting to apply leverage to shift the logs with minimal effort. Torrid flames licked at the air above, provoking shadows to flicker and dance across a youthful male face. Shimmering firelight gleamed off the whites of his almond-shaped eyes. His abyssal robes hung loose about his frame, obscuring a hulking figure beneath.

Hagan confidently strode forward toward the fire. Beneath his long jet-black hair, muscles flexed, putting tension against the dark leather straps of his attire. Standing only a few steps behind Kasaam, the mercenary contemplated what must be done. The words rolled off his tongue, breaking the silence like a distant thunder on a mild summer's day. "The men keep asking me a question, and I'm starting to ask myself the same thing more and more each day."

Continuing to poke at the fire, Kasaam's words rolled out in a heavy breath, barely above a whisper. "And what question is that?"

"Why are we following you?" Hagan's words released a palpable tension which hung in the air like dirty laundry on the line.

"Because my wisdom is superior to your brute force." Kasaam poked the stick between two logs, twisting his elbow to set one atop another. New flames licked at the fresh air between the logs.

"How do you figure?" Hagan force through gritted teeth.

"I see what is coming before anyone else." Kasaam's hand flexed around his stick, to adjust a piece of wood standing in the fire, causing the glowing log to teeter unsteadily.

The air grew still. Hagan's right hand clenched the handle of his curved blade, chipped and marred through years of service. The warrior's arm moved like lightning. The blade's edge rent through meat and separated bone where Kasaam sat at the fire. A smack echoed off the trees as cloth-covered flesh sloshed to the ground with the sound of a wet sack.

The fire made a rumbling crackle when the log tottered over, throwing hot embers into the air with a poof.

"Didn't see that coming." Hagan's words rumbled into the darkness, lips growing into a smirk.

A sharp chill overwhelmed the hulking man's right shoulder and his swordhand went slack. The sound of metal scraping stone rang out when his blade fell against a nearby rock.

Kasaam's voice crept from the shadows." I saw that coming even before *you* did."

Sweat beaded on the crest of Hagan's forehead. "How?"

Kasaam stepped out from the shadows and kicked the unidentified remains into the fire.

They stood silent for a long moment until the smaller man, clad in dark robes, moved around, eyes locked on Hagan. He poked at the fire with his stick once more while the aroma of burning flesh wafted through the air into their nostrils.

"Because my wisdom is greater than your brute strength. Let's not have this conversation again. Now go eat with the others."

"But my arm." The large man quivered.

"It will be restored after you regain my trust. Until then, you're left handed. Now go."

Hagan slogged back toward the fire at the center of camp. The force of his feet hitting the ground shook the leaves from the smaller trees in his wake. When Hagan reached the center campfire, his men's boisterous exuberance faded to a hushed murmur.

Upon sitting in the circle of mercenaries and warriors, one of them asked, "What happened?"

"Did you do it?" one of his fellow chen-blades whispered.

Hagan lowered his head. "It didn't go as planned. Where's Karth? We need to move forward as instructed."

The men looked around puzzled, heads darting back and forth. Hagan's cousin, Karth, was nowhere to be seen.

Sitting before the fire, Kasaam drew a map into the dirt, identifying all the towns between Kharsus Centra and Aestaria Una. He visualized the roads with caravans and the river with boats. The mystic contemplated the needs and desires of his prey before stabbing the point of his firestick into one of the dirt circles.

"That's where I'll find you." He stood and approached Hagan with a casual grace. "Ready the men to break camp. We leave tonight."

"Where to?" Hagan flinched at the question.

"You're paid too well to ask so many questions." With his abyssal robes wafting in the breeze, Kasaam returned to the fire.

28

Traveling southeast on the Estrobi river, the large craft bucked against the wind and waves, rocking the boat this way and that. Bastian hung his head over the side of the riverboat, a lurching growl forcing itself out before the water answered with the splatter.

Xander looked at Reinhardt. "We could have taken the river boat all the way from Kharsus Centra to Aestaria Una. Why didn't we?"

Kumori gestured at Bastian. "We would have ended up one short, I think."

"Ya think?" Reinhardt chuckled.

"I will go attend to him, to get him upright." Kumori approached the Selece. Reaching into a pocket, the Nepharen pulled out some leaves and crushed them. After adding a small bit of water from the waterskin, the rogue turned the mixture into a little ball. Kumori held a hand up to Bastian's face. "Smell these."

Bastian placed his nose over the concoction and drew in a large breath.

"Set them inside your cheek, and don't swallow. Just suck on them. It will help," the Nepharen instructed.

With one hand supporting his stomach, Bastian used his free hand to take the small ball of herbs and firmly placed them into his right cheek. As he continued to breathe, a sense of calm washed over his face, overtaking his whole body. "I feel better. Thank you."

Kumori nodded and walked back to Xander. "Why are we going to Imbros?"

Xander took out his water skin. "The southern Imbros is the

fiefdom of Count Han'Shoden. It's the most likely place Serantes would use to coordinate his plotting. We're expecting he would be too cunning to leave anything about the royal accommodations within the castle walls."

"How close will the river take us?" Kumori inquired.

Xander lifted his water skin and popped the cork. "A good bit of the way. The ferry will dock at Andros, and we can head west from there." The mage took a gulp, replaced the cork, and dropped the water skin to dangle from its cord.

Kumori became overwhelmed with worry. "Head west? By carriage?"

Xander reassuringly patted Kumori's shoulder. "We'll take a proper caravan this time."

"Good to hear." The fear faded from the rogue's face.

Days later, the ferry docked at Port Satarin. The large bell atop the ferry rang out, swinging back and forth while the steam horns sounded. The four disembarked from the boat, walking down a large ramp beneath a massive wooden sign which read, *'Port Satarin'*.

Once his feet were on solid ground, Bastian looked around with a curious squint. There were no city walls, only farmland off into the horizon. Between the fields of vegetables was a wide road where the other travelers herded in droves toward the town.

"No guards? No walls?" he grunted in a Selece growl.

Reinhardt sauntered forward, hand resting on his blade. "Andros is a much different city than Kharsus Centra and Aestaria Una. Those are capital cities, each a proper metropolis. The outer territories are each quartered off. West Andros is the territory of... oh, dear me."

"What is it now?" Xander stopped.

"Nothing. Let's carry on." Reinhardt snapped.

"Rye!" Xander raised his voice, infusing it with the heat of impatience.

"Cous—" Reinhardt started.

"Don't you 'Cousin' me! Tell me now!" Xander pointed his finger toward Reinhardt.

Bastian crouched down to whisper in Kumori's direction. "What's happening?"

"Can't say why yet, but it looks like they're fighting." Kumori looked on, chewing on a ration of meet.

Hands raised in submission, Reinhardt took a breath and sighed. "It's just that this is the domain of Lord Ras'Burges."

"And?" Xander glared. "You didn't!"

Reinhardt shrugged in admission. "I... It... We just... I..."

"'I it we just I.' Is that what works on the ladies in this age? The silk-tongued Reinhardt Vos'Korendel going from window to window with 'I it we just I,'" Xander chided. "You will keep your head low in this town while we search for a caravan to Imbros, or I will shove a spell so far up your shaat spout you'll taste magic for a month!"

"Yes, Cousin." The deflated swordsman glowered.

With Xander in the lead, the four made their way from the port through the fields of wheat and other assortments of unharvested stalks. They passed by diligent farm hands working at the behest of expecting farmers. Bastian's visage soured at the aroma of fresh vegetables wafting through the air.

Pressing forward, they made their way to the outskirts of Andros. There was no wall to speak of but a gradual encountering of shops and merchants. The first merchants down this alley were the meat shops. On either side of them hung dozens of red wet carcasses slung up to drain, airing out before being sold to local pubs and taverns.

At the sound of Bastian's lips smacking, Xander's head snapped around. "You do have rations!"

Bastian gazed longingly at the fresh flesh. "Yes, but it's fresh."

"We'll get something in town when we're' closer to our destination." Xander glared at Reinhardt. "We need to be out of this town with all due haste."

"Can't we at least—" Reinhardt started.

"Not one second more than needed." Xander's hand raised, index finger pointed skyward. "Not one kotching moment!"

Closer to the city's center, the quality of the merchants improved. Coincidentally, so did the guards, or at least they appeared to, based on their armor and conduct. The guards nearest the city's capitol building stood still as statues until needed and were more refined than the guards in the outer areas, where their heads turned at the first sign of a nice dress or low-cut skirt. The guards in the city's center had cleaner, better kept uniforms in the colors of yellow trimmed in black, representing house Ras'Burgess.

Pressing forward through the town, Kumori kept pace on Xander's right, with the other two behind. Without even an upward glance, they passed the thoroughfare and the town's midway without acknowledging the capital or any such grandiose structures, not that there were many.

At the first hint of dusk, the quality of the merchants and the guards began to wane.

Xander stopped so abruptly the two behind nearly crashed into him and Kumori.

"What now, Cousin?"

"Wait here." Xander walked up to a local guard eyeing a group of women passing by. "Sorry to bother you. Which way to the caravans?"

The guard coughed out a muffled sound, finger pointed down the road. "That way till you hit En'Tari lane. Turn left on En'Tari then take a right once you've come to Ivaness Boulevard. Can't miss it. There's a sign on the corner, Nocturnum's magical tomes."

"Much obliged." Xander made his way back to the group. "I have our heading. The first small pub we see, we'll stop in and take a proper meal."

Following the guard's directions, they passed by each of the expected landmarks until they stumbled across a small tavern. The walls appeared as though they were about to cave in, but the scent of hot food wafting out through the window drew them closer. A sign hung over the entrance, "The White Horse."

The night sky was pitch black when they left the pub with full bellies and rested feet.

Kumori looked up at Bastian under the lamplight and pointed at the corner of Bastian's mouth. "You have something, just there."

Bastian pulled the back of a paw across his lips, wiping away a dribble of red juices lining his snout with remnants of fresh meat.

"It should be dark enough that no one should notice us now." Reinhardt picked at his teeth with a small sliver of wood.

"Let us pray, Cousin." Xander pushed forward. "The caravan drivers should be gathered down at the end of this road if I heard that guard correctly."

Arriving at the end of Ivaness Boulevard, they came to a courtyard filled with covered wagons with a large stable on the far side. Between the group and the wagons was a merchant's booth, constructed of assorted wood covered in a fine cotton cloth, doing its best impression of a more expensive silk draping. Standing behind the bench, an Ignatian Kandari hovered over a drawer likely filled with chen. His ebony skin glistened from the illumination offered by lamp lights on either side of the bench. He wore a fitted ensemble made of fine cloth with a vest of crushed black velvet against a light blue silk shirt and matching pants. He walked with a cane and tipped his tall, crushed velvet black hat as he approached.

"Good evening, weary travelers. Mathías Locque at your service." His moderate tenor was infused with a smooth eastern lilt of the Ignatian people.

Xander stated the obvious, "A caravan?"

"My deepest apologies." The Ignatian's face became fraught with disappointment. The dapper gentleman glanced back at a fleet of wagons and horses and then shifted his gaze to a collection of waggoners sitting on stools playing cards. The light blue ribbon over the brim of his hat glistened in the lamplight. "We're all out."

"You've got to be kidding me." Xander chauffed at the man. "There's an entire army of wagons and horses behind you."

"Well, they're all in for the night." The man's lips grew into a sly smirk.

"We're stuck here for the night?" Xander ran his hand through his hair in frustration.

"I may still be able to assist, but it would require you pay double for the extra effort. What is your desired destination?" The man looked down at the map on his bench.

"We're set to travel to Imbros," Xander answered.

"I see, in which case, we'll need..." The man contemplated, furiously putting inked quill to parchment, scribbling and scratching. "Three sune."

"Three sune?" Reinhardt shouted. "That's thirty chen!"

Looking at Xander, the man grinned, "Your friend knows the maths." Head turning to Reinhardt, he gave a slow, silent clap. "Well done. As I was saying, that's three sune per driver."

"Per driver?" Reinhardt's arms went up in frustration.

The Ignatian nodded. "This is a four-day run at minimum. Unless you're willing to help drive the horses." Mathías raised eye eyebrow.

Kumori placed six sune on the bench. "We should leave before we cause a scene."

"Well said." The man glanced back. "Madradors!"

A large elderly gentleman rose from a table surrounded by fellow drivers. The large wagoner strode forward, followed by a larger, younger man. It quickly became obvious that the first stood just a finger's width taller than Bastian, the second four fingers' widths taller. The larger man wore a simple grey tunic with light brown pants and a black belt. He had no hair visible anywhere on his body, and one of his eyes was blue, while the other was a dark brown. The older man's head was covered in white hair pulled back tight. A thin sheen of road dust covered the upper half of his pale face, the lower half concealed by a long thick white beard a few shades lighter than his cream-colored vest worn over a red tunic.

In stark contrast to Mathías' proper posh lilt, the man's thick northern brogue radiated from his medium pitch. "How may I be of service, Mathías?"

"These good people here want to travel to Imbros this evening. The drive is yours if you desire." Mathías shuffled around four of the sune' coins in his hand.

"What's the split?" Mr. Madrador nodded toward Mathías' hand.

"Four, two, your favor. Do consider, though, that I will require your presence by the weekend for the Elias Family." He gave the caravan driver a curious squint. "You're the only ones I can count on to service the Elias family without costing me an earful and a morning lost from an unending diatribe. If it's your preference, I can offer Taran—"

The large Northman snatched the coins from Mathías' palm like a viper taking a mouse. "I'll do it. If nothing else, just to watch that halfwit Taran squirm."

"What is it with you two?" Mathías straightened his hat.

"That'll be a tale for another time." The waggoner shuffled

around and addressed his new patrons, "Name's Borden Madrador. This is my larger, quieter brother, Leland. Do as I say when I say, or we'll kick you to the ditch and leave you to the sunava. We clear?"

"Crystal," Reinhardt and Xander replied in unison.

The giant man's grunt shifted upward joyously. "Excellent."

Without another word, the waggoners turned and strode away. The four followed the brothers to a large black steed and observed while they hitched up to a modest wagon. The beast was dark enough to be mistaken for a moravian steed save for the soft sheen of its coat. One by one, they stepped up and in.

Their departure went perfectly smooth, but the remainder of the journey was unnecessarily turbulent as the Madrador brothers made haste a top priority. The pair drove for three days and three nights, taking turns at the reins. Stopping only for uneventful water breaks and to allow someone to use the nearest bush, they reached a large stone archway when the taller brother was driving. The large man pulled the wagon to a patch of flat ground. The brothers escorted their charges from the wagon. With no pomp or circumstance, the elder Madrador said farewell and began the return trip.

"Ashana bless you," Bastian mumbled quietly into the darkness at the departing wagon.

"The stone arch of Imbros, once the pride of Central Aestaria." Reinhardt gestured to the large archway made of hundreds of medium and large stones fit so tightly they appeared to have been melted together.

The four stood in awe of the structure's simple complexity.

Bastian spoke first. "What do we do now?"

"We get Serantes to return our relics so we can return to our people," Kumori answered.

Bastian shrugged. "How will we find him?"

Reinhardt gestured toward the city walls ahead by forty or strides. "The Han'Shoden family isn't known for its modesty. Look for the most extravagant estate in the best part of town, and we'll be in the right place."

"And when we find him?" Xander chimed in.

The noble swordsman rounded on the group. "We'll have one opportunity to get what we've come for and clear our names. The best strategy here is to attack quickly from every direction. We'll be outnumbered ten to one, but I still believe we can succeed."

"Based on what?" Xander chauffed.

With a solemn gaze, Reinhardt pointed to each of them as he spoke. "With Kumori's stealth, your magic, Bastian's strength, and my steel, we may stand a chance." Reinhardt's face overcome with realization. "We'll need to stop at a weapons shop, so I can pick up a set of crossbows."

Kumori drew a small pistol crossbow from inside the cloak. "Is this good?"

"This is perfect. Do you have a second?"

Kumori brandished a spare blade the length of Reinhardt's forearm and offered it handle first to the posh blade master.

"Where did you get these?" Reinhardt hooked the crossbow to his belt and accepted the blade. He removed it from the sheath embossed with the Ganoshian royal seal.

"Six men came at me in Ganos. One of them carried this." Kumori frowned at the memory of what had to be done to escape from the Ganoshian guard. The rogue's face betrayed a struggle with the conflict between enjoying the thrill of mortal combat and facing the sorrow that comes with taking a life. With a brisk head shake, Kumori banished the thought.

"Unarmed indeed," the Kandari jeered, balancing the hilt of the long knife on his index finger.

With a flourish, he rolled it through his remaining fingers

before flipping it over the back of his hand. He grasped the spinning blade so abruptly the metal thrummed in the air when it stopped. The blade's mirror sheen in the light revealed the character, *six*, etched in elder numeric form.

"I can make this work." He sheathed the blade and belted the sheath. "We're all agreed?"

Everyone nodded before pushing forward toward the city. Attending the gate were four guards, only one of which appeared to be conscious.

The guard approached, wearing light plate armor over a green tunic with grey trim and black pants held up by a black leather strap. His hair was obscured by a helmet bearing the silhouette of a winged moravian against the setting sun.

"What's the business of such an unlikely collection of travelers as we have here?"

Xander stepped forward. "We're merchants with money to buy goods, which we will sell abroad."

After looking them over, the guard waved a hand toward the open gate, constructed of solid interwoven steel bars tipped with sharp ends ready to pierce the soil below. The thick, sturdy walls stood only two lengths tall by Bastian's measure, which was quite underwhelming after having confronted the barriers to Aestaria Una and Kharsus Centra.

Xander pressed forward beside Kumori. "You've traveled through many Aestarian cities in your quest?"

Keeping pace, Kumori replied, "I have."

"How do you find your way around a new city?" Xander asked.

"Your cities are not built for the ease of visitors, yet they are easy to read when you see that they are built to show the gaps in the layers of society," Kumori answered.

"I see," Reinhardt remarked from behind. "We've lived in it so long we just never realized it."

"Or thought there was another way," Xander continued.

"You'll always find the wealthiest closest to the capital, while the merchants live in the center ring, and the poorest remain at the outer edges. The only exceptions are the estate houses some nobility have far away from the inner city," Kumori commented from under the hood.

"And where do you think we would find Serantes?" Reinhardt inquired.

"That depends on what kind of man he is," Kumori replied. "Does he value knowledge and power over privacy and security?"

"Knowledge and power," the cousins answered simultaneously.

"Who built the house?" Bastian mumbled timidly.

"Beg your pardon?" Reinhardt questioned.

"No, Cousin, he's right." Xander smirked. "Please, Bastian, go on."

"Who built the house?" Bastian repeated with more confidence. "Did Serantes build the house?"

"No, his father built the house." Reinhardt sighed with a dejected glare, piercing the ground. "And his father, Count Han'Shoden, was a man who valued security and privacy." He clapped Bastian on the back. "Well done."

Kumori started taking longer strides, leading them through back alleys and dark passageways. "If that's true, we'll find his estate in the outer section beyond the farmland. Unless Imbros is different from Pax, Aeternum Centra, Bellum, Ganos—"

"We get it." Reinhardt groaned. "You've been taking the scenic tour of Aestaria."

Xander's head turned to Kumori. "What's the plan when we get there?"

"Why are you asking the rogue?" Reinhardt's face twisted into an indignant visage.

"Stick Boy is right." Kumori chuckled. "I'll leave the plan of attack to the soldier."

"Fine." Xander sighed. "What's our plan?"

With Kumori leading them toward Serantes' estate, Reinhardt outlined the strategy. Xander fell to the rear, keeping pace with Bastian as they continued closer to their quarry with every step. On the far side of Imbros, they turned from a back alley to a stone-cobbled road. The sign on the road was clear, "Han'Shoden Court."

"I wonder if we're heading the right direction," Reinhardt scoffed.

"His hubris will be the end of him." Xander sneered.

Reinhardt gave Xander a side-long glance. "Oh, Kettle, Mr. Pott has a Tapi-gram for you. It reads—"

"I get it." Xander interjected. "I've seen a few roads named after my family also, but I'm not the one trying to usurp a kingdom."

"Fair play, Cousin," Reinhardt relented. "The match is yours."

The only thing faster than their banter was their feet while they made their way to the estate. They moved as fast as they could without arousing suspicion.

"There it is," Reinhardt declared in an intense whisper, nodding toward the gate.

The distance of a tangu field in front of them, or just over fifteen lengths by Bastian's count, stood a robust black gate with iron bars crested with polished bronze letters glinting in the lamp light, "Han'Shoden."

"It's the same from Jorgan's house," Bastian stated flatly.

"They were family. They share this name." Reinhardt looked over at his cousin, eyebrows raised. "Well, Cousin, you're up."

"Aye."

Guided by the Nepharen, Xander and Bastian stepped into the shadows.

Watching them all fade into the darkness, Reinhardt waited. Moments dragged on into eternity. The young noble bided his time, examining the four soldiers guarding the Han'Shoden estate. One older, two middle aged, one younger, two of them right handed. One middle-aged guard favored his left foot slightly, shuffling from one side of the gate to the other. They didn't appear to have rigorous marching or standing orders like the royal guard, but if your only order was to stay in front of a gate and watch, walking around seemed the thing to do.

Reinhardt contemplated the men's lives. What did they do every day when they returned home? Did they kiss their wives and daughters? Would they playfully ruffle their son's hair? Were they caring providers or harsh men abusing their authority over those whom they were charged with protecting and providing for?

An ashareal bolt struck the tallest roof spire, illuminating the air over the house. Reinhardt surged to life at the sight.

"Well done, Cousin," Reinhardt whispered. Moments later, he openly charged at the four guards, giving them time to ready their blades before he closed the distance.

Three of the four guards drew their swords. The youngest of them struggled to unsheathe his weapon. Reinhardt pressed his charge, loaded crossbow in one hand, Ganoshian short blade launching from the other. The slick sound of a splitting melon came from the young guard's face, dagger buried to the hilt. The guard collapsed near the gate, fingers still twitching around the unsheathed blade.

Reinhardt pulled the trigger, and a whistling bolt skewered the old soldier's throat. To no avail, he clutched at his neck, body slumping to the ground. The two remaining guards approached, taking coordinated offensive stances. One attacked high, while the other attacked low. Reinhardt dove between the swords, narrowly avoiding each. Rolling forward, he grabbed the Ganoshian blade's handle. Regaining his feet, he freed the dagger from the young guard's head in time to parry one attack with his long blade, intercepting the other with the dagger.

Pushing both enemies away, Reinhardt sidestepped, putting one soldier behind the other. The closest guard slashed down heavily. Reinhardt bound the edge with the Ganoshian dagger, sliding his long blade into a gap under the man's breastplate. The soldier's gaze went flat. Unable to withdraw his imbedded blade, Reinhardt thrust a foot forward, freeing the steel from the fallen man's body.

Moonlight glinted off the remaining guard's sword, flashing through the air before it clattered against the armor of his defeated ally. Reinhardt jabbed with his tip, and the guard parried, shuffling to the side in a low crouch. The man's limp suddenly disappeared as he thrust forward and swiped the edge at his lithe opponent. After deflecting the strike, Reinhard shifted off the centerline and flicked downward at his opponent's wrist. The soldier parried the attack and slashed wide. The young master swordsman intercepted the attack, sending it high, before drawing his blade's razor edge across his opponent's throat. The man fell with the sound of wet air popping and gurgling from the slit in his neck.

With all haste, Reinhardt wiped and sheathed his weapons. He then pulled the bodies behind the ornate topiaries beside the gate. Marching toward the estate, he pulled at the string and loaded a bolt into the small trigger bow. After hanging the weapon from his belt, Reinhardt sprinted in a dead run toward the estate's main entrance.

Shortly after, Reinhardt encountered two additional Han'Shoden guards. His opponents unsheathed their swords with expert proficiency. The adversary on the left swiped, while the shorter man on the right lunged. Evading the assault, Reinhardt intercepted the swiping blade. With a flick of his wrist, he directed the edge of the taller guard's steel towards the shorter man's neck. As the smaller adversary defended, Reinhardt plunged his dagger through the shorter guard's inner thigh, creating a wide gash. Disarming the fallen soldier, Reinhardt readied himself for an imminent attack. His lower sword clanged against his opponent's blade while the edge of his offhand weapon cut a narrow crimson line across his adversary's throat. The guard collapsed to the ground, eyes rolling back.

Reinhardt entered the Han'Shoden house through a pair of large ornately carved wooden doors, blades out, ready for combat to find his allies engaged in a fierce battle. Xander backed in through the right corridor, thrusting bolts of ashareal energy and deflecting attacks from blades and bows with aethereal shields. Kumori was on the upper foyer beyond the stairs, blades in hand trading blows with two guards, deflecting edges with the impenetrable cloak while finding openings in their armor to weaken them with every strike. From the left corridor, Bastian rolled under a swiping blade and stood, chatta ready. He used one claw to bind a blade and deflected another. Quickly, Bastian answered the attacks with a blurred jab into both guards' chests, sending the chatta blades through each breastplate, impaling the men to a wall.

Moments after Reinhardt entered, the din of combat became nothing more than the hushed whisper of death rattles escaping the Han'Shoden guard's fragile corpses. His comrades looked tired, appearing no worse for the wear. All looked able to move about freely without any sign of severe injury.

A heavy sigh of remorse escaped the young noble's lips. "Well done. I realize this is a heavy burden, but we're almost through it now. Any sign of Serantes?"

Bastian shrugged, gesturing toward the wing behind him. "This area is empty."

In a quick jerk, Kumori flicked any blood off the daggers. "I see no trace here."

Xander slumped back against a wall in exhaustion. "He's not here."

A macabre voice reverberating from the walls echoed through the house. "Did you think it would be that easy? You would come here to find your prey waiting, a helpless victim ready to fall on your blade."

Moments later, mercenaries closed in from the corridors, and the large wooden doors of the estate's main entrance opened. A hulking Kandari with long midnight dark hair, standing a head taller than Reinhardt, stepped through. His upper body was covered only by the straps that held his blades. Each band strained against the mercenary's massive, chiseled form. The rest of him was covered in dark leather, down to his boots.

His enormous voice bellowed in a northern brogue smoothed out with a western lilt, "Tonight, you will feast with the Ashuun."

The warrior-for-hire drew his blades and attacked. Reinhardt drew his sword, but instead of clashing blade against blade, he locked their forearms together, preventing his opponent from swinging down.

Against this larger enemy, speed and leverage were Reinhardt's only advantages. *I only hope it's enough,* he thought.

On the upper foyer, half a dozen bandits surrounded Kumori, three on either side. Bolting to the right, the rogue dove low into a roll before jumping into a tumble. The erratic movements caught the mercenaries off guard, allowing Kumori a path between the three enemies impotently blocking the passageway. The cloaked Nepharen used the mercenary's bulky size against them, fighting each one individually when they entered the tight passageway.

Bastian's chatta blades tore through his opponent's flesh.

Confronted from all sides, the large Selece stepped in a circular form, attacking low, dodging to the side, crouching down, and slashing high, constantly shifting the path of his attacks. Binding a sword between his chatta, the Selece blocked an incoming strike with the opponent's weapon. Bastian's second chatta blades separated the mercenary from his arm with a wet thump. He ducked beneath another slash, pulling the bound swordsman into a roll and pinning his arm. Bastian twisted, forcing the mercenary's shoulder to crunch in the wrong direction. With a forward jab, he pressed his chatta through a man's thigh. When he retracted his arm, his enemy collapsed to the floor. A metal blade bit into the thick fur covering Bastian's shoulder. The Selece lurched forward to escape the pain of a razor-sharp edge being pulled down across his back.

"I got him!" the attacker yelled.

His compatriots roared with excitement.

Xander thrust an aethereal blade forward into his opponent's stomach and deflected an incoming attack with an ashareal shield on his other arm.

Reinhardt parried an incoming axe from behind while dodging the largest mercenaries' off-hand sword. "I didn't realize you could use two at once like that."

"Neither did I until I wasn't given a choice," Xander grunted, slamming the edge of the ashareal shield into his opponent's throat.

The mercenary shuffled back, grabbing at his neck with a muffled choke. Stumbling backward over his comrade's body, he crashed to the floor.

The steel of Reinhardt's blade drew a thin red line across the larger mercenary's forearm. The giant man's dominant weapon dropped to the floor.

With a quick pivot, Xander avoided a slash while thrusting his phantasmal azure blade forward into an opponent. Without warning, the sting of cold steel jolted through the mage's abdomen, dropping him to a knee. Xander brought his magical shield up to encounter a second strike from the same foe.

"Xan!" Reinhardt yelled, pulling his sword from his smaller attacker's heart.

He shifted his feet to get a clear line of sight and flicked his moon-hilted dagger at Xander's adversary, giving his larger opponent his back. Reinhardt's dagger landed home, skewering his target's throat.

The large mercenary wrapped an arm around the noble swordsman from behind, squeezing Reinhardt's neck tight inside the crook of his muscular elbow. Pulling at the hulking arm, Reinhardt squatted low and twisted, tossing his enormous enemy forward end over end.

Bastian turned to the side as the Kandari mercenary standing over him cleaved forward slamming his blade so deep into the hard wooden floor the man struggled to pull it out. Bastian slid his feet along the floor kicking the mercenary's legs out from under him. The Selece rolled forward, thrusting his chatta blades into the fallen man's chest and recovered his stance.

Kumori tumbled along the upper floor railing to sidestep an opponent. The rogue whirled around a banister pole, plunging a Nepharen short blade into the final mercenary's spine.

The walls of the estate reverberated with an ominous echo. "It appears I must handle this myself." An abyssal figure cloaked in robes of shadow dropped from the ceiling.

"Ashino!" Reinhardt yelled.

"Wha... How?" Xander stood with a groan.

"No." The stygian figure pulled back his hood, revealing the face of a young Fataak. "They would be too quick and not have nearly as much fun."

Kasaam turned slowly, gazing in disgust at the fallen mercenaries from the north. With a glance, he thrust his cloak of shadow at the balcony, sliding a spectral ebony blade between Kumori's ribs. The cloak's abyssal tendrils swiped Xander's legs out from under him. The Fataak twirled with intense flare. From Kasaam's cloak, long razor-sharp onyx shadows streaked toward Bastian. Both Selece chatta blades blurred through the air, partially deflecting the attack. A gash in Bastian's arm sent one of the blades crashing to the floor.

The dark mage lashed a phantasmal tendril around Reinhardt's neck, lifting him toward the ceiling. "This ends now."

A small glass vial clattered down from the second story.

"I agree," Reinhardt croaked out.

The glass rang out, breaking with a high-pitched 'ping'!, followed by a deafening explosion. Kasaam drew the cloak of shadow up around himself, shielding against the chaotic inferno. Reinhardt pulled the hand bow's trigger, sending the bolt screaming into the abyssal cloak. The tendril loosened, dropping Reinhardt to his feet. He kicked at the dark figure and watched it slump to the floor. Part of the cloak shifted away to reveal Xander's face beneath.

"What? No!" Reinhardt's gaze flickered to the empty patch of floor where Xander had fallen. Dropping to his knees, Reinhardt pulled at the layers of shadowy cloak disintegrating into abyssal mist. He glanced around quickly searching the room but saw no trace of the malevolent sorcerer.

Kumori hobbled down the stairs, hand covering a stomach wound beneath the cloak. "What happened?"

"I don't know." Reinhardt cried. "By the Ashuun, I don't know! I pointed the bolt at that kotching sorcerer and pulled the trigger. Somehow, it struck Xander."

"You need to work on your aim." Xander coughed, clutching his chest, fingers laced around the bolt.

Reinhardt smiled through his tears. "Holy Ashana, you're all right!"

"No, Cousin," Xander sputtered, a red droplet falling from the corner of his mouth. "I can already see Ashara."

Reinhardt looked to Kumori. "The twig." His eyes brimmed with hope.

Kumori's head shook. "No. The wound is too deep. It's no good to make a bleeding heart pump faster." The rogue pulled out a small pouch. "I can give him this. It will slow the heart and make him sleep until we can find a healer."

"No, it was supposed to be me!" Reinhardt choked out. "I have to tell you before you go. I did this. It was all me!"

"What was all you?" Xander's mouth opened.

Kumori sprinkled a pinch of powder under the injured Kandari's tongue. He winced at the bitterness overwhelming his senses.

"Serantes told me I had to follow you and report everything. He threatened my family. He threatened to tell—" the dark-haired Kandari pleaded.

"You what?" Kumori glared with indignation.

"How could you?" The confused Selece picked up his fallen chatta blade and secured it to his side.

"I was going to turn it around. I had a..." Reinhardt reached out for his cousin. "I had a plan," the elder cousin implored, hands together beseeching forgiveness. "It was never supposed to turn out this way."

Xander closed his eyes. "I was wrong, Cousin. Your aim was perfect." He turned his head away from his dishonorable kinsman.

"Please!" Reinhardt implored.

"Go!" Xander coughed, more crimson fluid spilling from his lips.

"You should go. We will tend to him." Bastian's neutral voice concealed a deep rage within.

Reinhardt fled.

"Thank you, Brother." Xander placed a hand over a cut on Bastian's forearm.

The large Selece flinched at the freshly disturbed open wound as a memory trickled in from his past. Bastian's head spun to Kumori. "We must leave."

Kumori gestured at the chaos and the flames from a fallen candle beginning to consume a curtain at the top of the stairs. "What was your first clue?"

"We need to go far away." With one arm, Bastian picked up the limp Kandari mage, cradling him to avoid upsetting his wound.

The three left through the east wings.

Kumori struggled to open the large door. "What is your plan?" With a groan, the door relented.

"We need to go somewhere far away, but it will take days." Bastian followed, cradling his charge.

"I'm not sure I have days," Xander choked out before being overtaken by the powder.

Kumori pressed forward. "I have an idea. Follow me." The Nepharen trudged around behind the mansion. "I saw this when I entered the house from the rear estate grounds."

Kumori led them past a herd of corralled horses to a set of stables in the rear.

"He can't ride in this condition," Bastian contended.

"No." Kumori agreed, "but can he fly?"

Kumori stopped at the last stable. There stood a massive steed clad in natural kaitanous armor, more than twice the size of a large horse. The evening moonlight glistened from the mirror-smooth surface of the moravian's natural obsidian armor. The beast reared back, spreading its enormous leathery wings.

"I don't know how to fly this," Bastian contended.

"It's this or nothing," Kumori said, gesturing to Xander, "and he dies!"

Bastian gently placed an unconscious Xander into a hay-filled feeding trough. Exuding an essence of calm serenity, Bastian slowly approached the creature. The beast stomped and snorted before taking a step back. Bastian pressed forward, and the moravian quieted.

"We need your help now. I have a friend... a brother to save," Bastian pleaded with the winged steed.

The ruby embers within its eyes pierced Bastian as though the creature saw through him, saw into him. The winged beast hung its head in consent. Bastian lifted Xander from the hay. The moravian's legs knelt until its stomach touched the ground. Kumori threw the gate wide and removed the restraining lines.

Bastian placed Xander in the middle of the creatures back, looking over at Kumori. "You sit behind him. Stop him from falling."

Kumori nodded, securing the gate open. As the rogue mounted the saddle-shaped plates on the moravian's back, the cobalt cloak billowed in the breeze. "Let's fly."

Bastian held the reins as a matter of propriety, but they were unnecessary. He leaned forward, and it moved. He tilted slightly right, and the creature turned as the Selece directed while trotting toward a large clearing.

The house began falling under an all-consuming fire while guards rushed toward the engulfed estate. Bastian leaned forward, and the steed trotted to a canter until it tilted into a full gallop. In the span of four strides, the moravian spread its wings, lifting them into the air. Every flap of its wings clapped thunderously against the air with furious energy. Every thrust against the air sent them reeling skyward. Its body remained horizontal while pressing its vertical ascent. The soldiers beneath them shrank to the size of little bugs, and the ground at their feet disappeared. Houses became smaller than tree nuts on the forest floor. Bastian leaned forward toward the right, and the soaring steed tilted accordingly, flying away from the city. As it flew, the wings puffed up with the air beneath them. Whenever they lost altitude, the beast would once again push furiously against the wind.

Using the Evening Moon's position and the Qalderian star form, Bastian continued guiding the beast through the cool midnight air. For hours, they soared north and west, searching for a small light near the forest tree line.

"It's there." Bastian pointed to the small, well-lit cabin near the trees.

Kumori shouted over the wind, "How do we land?"

"We'll soon find out!" Bastian urged the massive beast down toward the log cabin in the distance.

From the ground came an ever repeating, "Yip! Yip! Yip!"

Bastian kept his gaze focused on the open clearing in front of the house. The moravian pulled its wings back, plunging into a dive toward a spot just in front of Bastian's chosen target.

"What's goin' on out here?" An older man exited the house, coming out to the wraparound porch.

When the moravian was only a few lengths from the ground, it popped opened its wings. The sheer force pulled at the riders' stomachs. Moments later, the moravian's talons landed gently on the soft patch of grass.

"Ma!" the man called from the porch.

Bastian dismounted from the dark-winged steed.

The stout woman came out to investigate the commotion. "Oh, my."

Bastian pulled his companion from the moravian and approached the stairs. With his injuries, the feral warrior's arms strained to keep the Kandari aloft.

With his eyes glassed over, Bastian looked up at the elderly couple. "Help?"

29

Kumori gazed out the window at the approaching dawn, left hand playing at the slashed cloak seam. At Kumori's back, Bastian stood watching Maxina. The old woman sat crossed-legged next to Xander's still form. Between them, the blood-soaked bolt lay on the floor. Immediately after its removal, the small stout lady had replaced it with her hand, pouring luminescent green ashareal energy into the wound. Bastian wasn't sure how many hours had passed since then. The only sign Xander wasn't a statue on the floor was the shallow rise and fall of his chest.

Daybreak cracked through the window when the thrum of aethereal energy faded.

Bastian took a half step forward. "Is he healed? Will he live?"

Kumori turned to examine Maxina's face as their hostess rose from the floor.

Maxina shrugged. "That's up to him now. I've done all I can for the time being. Come, let's tend to you."

"Ma!" Urma protested.

"You hush up now. I have more than enough vigor to tend these scrapes."

She ambled over to Bastian, examining for cuts and lacerations and gently drawing her hand down his back. Green light poured from her palm into the wound. His thick Selece hide shifted and rippled until his laceration melded into a patchwork of undulating flesh. Maxina placed her hand over his upper arm, and he pulled lightly at her wrist in protest.

"My friend first." Bastian nodded at Kumori.

"Oh, don't you worry." She ignored his plea. "I'll have enough to tend that wound, too."

The aethereal echo thrummed across the air. Green prismatic energy radiating from her hand mended the separated flesh across the upper section of the Selece's hulking harm.

Moments later, Maxina patted the marred sections of Bastian's newly mended hide. "Not to worry. We'll pull the rest of it together later," she said, before walking toward the rogue.

Kumori retreated from the hostess's approach. "No, thank you."

"You'll be fine," Maxina insisted. "Now let me see that cut before it sours."

The rogue relented, allowing the healer to approach. Maxina found the wound, and her new patient sighed as the sharp pain subsided, leaving only a dull ache.

Maxina withdrew her hand, brushing it along the edge of Kumori's cloak. "This is silver silk from the Nepharen frost worm."

"How do you know of the frost worm?" Kumori questioned.

"I know a thing or two," the woman replied.

"Because she's seen a thing or two," Urma echoed from the next room.

Kumori's eyes rolled in dismay. "Everyone's a bard."

"No," Urma replied. "We're farmers."

"Anyhow." Maxina rolled her eyes. "I have some Theeshan steel spider silk that will fix that right up."

"You don't—" Kumori protested.

"I insist." Maxina wandered off to fetch a small box from the corner of the sitting room. "You don't even need to remove it. You just stay still."

She plunged the enchanted thread through the needle's eye and knotted it before pulling the fabric together stich by stitch. With a swift twist and a tug, Maxina tied off the thread, pulling it with two special plyers. After a few more pokes and stitches, she hid the ends of the thread into the cloak's seam without cutting it, making the patchwork near invisible.

"See? Almost good as new."

Kumori flapped the cloak, unable to find where it had been cut. "I'm very thankful."

"Now tell me, what cuts through fabric made from Nepharen silver silk?" Maxina gave the Nepharen an expectant look.

"A cloak of shadow," Bastian growled in a muffled tone.

"What cloak of shadow?" Urma walked into the room.

"There was a small man, just taller than her." Bastian pointed at Maxina. "He was wearing a cloak made from shadow."

"Not just shadow," Kumori added. "It was made from the void itself."

Maxina turned to Urma. "This means the Hesheim have escaped Izhtar and brought the knowledge of Ka'Seth with them. I won't go back."

Urma approached his wife, pulling her into a soft embrace. The old Kandari comforted his wife. "All will be fine."

"Back?" Kumori inquired.

"She's Fataak, like the enemy you met, but she has pledged her life to Ashara after escaping Izhtar's curse." Holding her gently in his arms, Urma continued rubbing his wife's back. "You go rest. We'll take care of things here."

Maxina walked off into the bedroom.

"I don't understand." Kumori sat in the large chair in the center of the room.

Careful not to disturb Xander, Urma sat in the other chair near the hearth. "The Fataak have lived on the continent of Izhtar for centuries, but a millennia ago, they originated from the deserts of central Aestaria until the Ashuun guided them to the land of Izhtar to protect them from the rest of the world. Or to protect the rest of the world from them. It was ages ago. There is no telling how much truth was lost to the sands of time." The man cleared his throat. "What we do know is the entire continent is infested with Kaltusaam."

"What are Kaltusaam?" Bastian took a seat on the remaining empty piece of furniture.

"Bringers of death," Urma answered. "Huge sand fish with rows of giant teeth. They swim through the beach sand or soar in the air with giant wing fins. They kill anyone trying to leave or enter Izhtar."

"And Maxina is Fataak?" Kumori asked.

"Yes, indeed. She is a disciple of Kaltukeer."

"Kaltukeer?" Bastian asked.

"Bringers of life. After finding their new land, many Fataak turned to Ashara, though they refer to Ashara as Izhtar. They've pledged their lives to her and to use the Ashuun's gifts to heal. Those healers are called the Kaltukeer, in honor of the first giver of life with that same name."

The three sat, continuing their conversation long into the evening. They carefully moved Xander onto a pallet of padding and quilts they had stretched out onto the floor. Once the other two succumbed to sleep on the furniture near the fireplace, Urma moseyed into the bedroom.

The next morning, they woke to the aroma of freshly cooked meat and vegetables in the kitchen, but Bastian sat watching over Xander while the rest of them ate.

Urma followed Maxina out into the sitting room. "You're not gonna do any good worrying over him," he urged Bastian.

"The old man's right," his wife agreed.

Bastian sat up straight in the chair, overcome with agitation. "I need to know he will live." Bastian ran his hands through his mane.

"He's strong. I'm sure he'll fight through." Standing eyelevel with Bastian, Maxina pulled at the back of his head to envelope him in a warm embrace. Running her fingers through his mane, she gave Urma a sorrowful look, shaking her head ever so slightly.

Later that day, Kumori sat nearby while Maxina continued tending to Xander. Her steady finger wet the young mage's lips with a damp cloth before squeezing liquid droplets into his mouth. The Nepharen silently observed while the Fataak healer summoned green aethereal energy forward into Xander's wound. A flash of home ran through the rogue's mind, accompanied by a single tear.

Just outside the window, Bastian pushed a squeaking wheelbarrow full of hay toward the moravian.

"Why do you think she stayed?" Urma asked.

"I think it's because we know each other," Kumori overheard Bastian's reply.

"Know?" Urma scrapped the pitchfork against the wheelbarrow.

"We think the same." Bastian's hand reached up to the kaitanous plates, rubbing the moravian's head between its eyes.

"Oh!" Urma's eyebrows shot up in comprehension. "Understand."

"No. We understand each other, but also we think the same." Bastian agreed.

"What's her name?" A confused Urma picked up some loose hay from the ground and put it into the feeding trough.

Bastian's gaze became distant. "When I look into her glowing eyes, I hear the name, 'Sarabi,' so that's what I call her." He grabbed the wheelbarrow and started toward the tool shed.

Urma stood statuesque for a moment and then nodded. "Good name. Good reason."

After tending to Sarabi, the two climbed to the roof, stomping around directly above Maxina and Kumori to repair a patch of loose boards and tattered shingles.

Before nightfall, the healer tended to Bastian and Kumori's wounds, smoothing the flesh and tightening the mend. Patches of Bastian's fur was already growing over his previously marred arm. Meanwhile, Kumori's dull ache diminished to a moderate throbbing.

The two elders fed their company supper as any good host and hostess would, before everyone saw to their sleeping arrangements. Bastian and Kumori slept in the sitting room, using the furniture on either side of their fallen friend.

The following day, the four were eating lunch together. Bastian was chewing on a raw piece of small game he caught that morning.

Urma took a drink from his cup and cleared his throat. "Soon enough, you're gonna have to make a plan."

"Plan?" Bastian asked through a full mouth.

Maxina answered, "What will you do if your friend doesn't wake up? Or what will you do if he does?"

Urma scooped up a bite of vegetables onto his strad. "From what you said, you still have Serantes to contend with and the Ashino hunting you. Not to mention what ever became of the Hesheim." The old Kandari chewed at the food, awaiting an answer.

Kumori finished chewing a bite. "We don't know. Somehow, he switched places with Xander and vanished."

Bastian dropped the bone, now picked clean. "Whatever happens, my people need the Spirit Stone." His gaze shifted to Kumori. "Your people need the healing armor."

"So where would you reckon those two things are?" Urma questioned.

"With Serantes," Bastian answered. "We need to find Serantes."

Urma nodded.

Bastian played at his food. "But first, we must know if Xander will live. This was difficult with four. We're undone with two."

Later that night, Maxina lay in bed next to her husband. "The boy is getting worse."

Urma stroked his wife's hair. "I know, Ma', I know. I just don't know how to lay it out in front o' that boy. He's hard as a ripe paani-melon on the outside and just as soft on the inside."

The following day, Kumori assisted with the chores, while Maxina continued working with Xander. Bastian and Urma cleared the back forty, a brush covered area furthest from the log house, to make space for a new farming plot. Time dragged on as they toiled away, under a scorching sun.

After lunch was served, Bastian and Kumori rested in the sitting room.

"We will not leave him." Bastian's words were flat and confident.

"Not if we still have hope," Kumori assured.

Stopping only for a light supper, they worked until sundown. When Bastian and Urma finished tilling the soil, the two tended to Sarabi's trough and water bucket before moving inside for the evening.

Maxina sat on the floor with Xander lying between her and the fire. She alternated between infusing his wound with ashareal energy and stroking his hair. The din of nature from outside the window dwindled to a hushed whisper. The moravian bucked and grunted in the stillness. A shallow whisper escaped Xander's lips, and his chest fell. Moments stretched into minutes with his chest remaining motionless. When Maxina looked up, a tear streaked down her face, eyes glassing over with sorrow. A low growl resonating from the Selece's chest accompanied the echoes of Sarabi's rearing and snarling in the night's unnatural stillness.

From beyond the silence rumbled the sound of uncountable

hooves heralding a squadron of horses. The echo of thundering steeds grew louder until the regiment closed in on the house.

Bastian looked at Urma. "Stay here. We'll take care of this."

Followed by Kumori, the large Selece, padded to the back of the house through the rear door. The two slipped around under the cover of shadow. Staying close to the walls, they crept toward the kaitanous winged steed, stopping when they reached the front corner. Forty soldiers on horseback gathered in front of the house, led by a Fataak whose face had leathered with age and time in the sun. His figure was rough cut, displaying muscular bulk beneath a black cloth draped over his head held tight by a shimmering bronze circlet. On his shoulders were pauldrons made from the shell of a spined kortoise. Beneath the armor, his upper body was bare, save for the beach sand-colored cloak covering a set of brown glossy straps securing his weapons. To one side of the Fataak towered the large barbarian Hagan, the glimmer of a familiar crescent trinket tucked into his belt. Upon seeing the sinister figure on Takesh's left, a jolt of pain surged beneath Kumori's recently healed wound. Kasaam's cloak of spectral shadow bellowed in the wind.

"We're stuck." Bastian pulled his head back around the corner.

Kumori's head hung in defeat. "We need to get to the moravian and hope to lead them away."

"If they don't pursue?" Bastian insisted.

"If we sit here shaating about it, they go in the house and kill everyone," Kumori answered.

Bastian grunted. "You go left. I'll go right. We'll divide them and meet at Sarabi."

By the time they sprang from the shadows, half of the soldiers had dismounted. The other half were steady on their horses with the focus of purpose. Four mounted soldiers had bows and arrows. With flicks of their wrists, cloth-covered arrow's tip lit ablaze. The mounted archers loosed their fiery shafts, landing scorching flames in the roof's pitch to lick at the newly placed shingles.

Kumori tumbled forward into the regiment of foot soldiers, rolling low and attacking upward. With fatal accuracy, the Nepharen delivered a blade to one soldier's gut, while another felt the sting of the rogue's sharp steel thrust between his ribs.

Bastian bolted forward on all fours and climbed up a small farming wagon. Moments later, the Selece soared into a group of mounted horsemen. Midair, Bastian pulled the chatta blades across two soldier's necks. One fell over, clutching at the wound in a useless effort to keep his lifeblood in his body. The other's head bobbled over, hanging by sinew and tendons. On his way to the ground, Bastian pushed the chatta forward into the chest of a mounted archer. The archer's flaming arrow pierced the back of a fellow soldier, now riding a bucking mount trying to escape the flame.

Navigating the chaos, the pair found their way onto Sarabi. Within moments, Bastian tilted, and she galloped forward becoming airborne. The sound of thunder cracked over the din of clamoring soldiers when a tendril of shadow lashed forward, carving through Sarabi's wing. The moravian jilted in pain and toppled through the air. Kumori and Bastian vaulted from the falling beast before she crashed to the ground. Bastian hit the dirt and rolled forward.

The Selece turned to find himself face to face with his new friend. He opened her eyes and saw the embers glowing dimly within. "Will you be all right?"

The steed flexed her neck, nodding in affirmation.

Bastian sighed in relief before sprinting away toward her tail and jumping over Kasaam. The airborne Selece slashed down at the dark figure with his chatta, and the Fataak sorcerer deflected them with shadow. Pushing the abyssal cloth forward, he sent

Bastian sprawling toward a group of soldiers. The large feral warrior landed awkwardly, hitting the ground hard. Before he could recover, Hagan removed his chatta blades, and the men bound his hands with rope. He struggled as they brought him up to place another rope around his neck. Pulling him toward the closest tree, the soldiers threw the other end of the rope over a large branch and tied it to a horse.

The Nepharen rogue sprinted toward Takesh's back, blades out. Takesh sidestepped the attack, pulling out two medium-length curved blades, thicker at the top than at the hilt. The Fataak pressed forward, swinging the blades in constant arcs, each blade slashing high then low before switching places with its twin. Pressing forward, the Fataak mumbled something under his breath. The method of movement didn't appear unnecessarily flamboyant save for how the sword's polished edges glinted off the ambient light. The razor-sharp blade's glowing edges swirled up and down, back and forth.

Tracers of light swam in Kumori's vision, creating a blinding flash and everything faded to black. Moments later, when Kumori's vision came surging back, everything in sight glowed painfully bright. An avalanche of sound echoed in roaring waves.

Kumori looked down to find Takesh's blade plunged deep. The rogue's knives thudded against the dirt. Takesh kicked the Nepharen's limp body to the ground, pulling the slick blade from Kumori's chest with a wet sucking sound.

A thin leather strap cracked against a horse's hind quarter, causing the steed to spring into a gallop. The rope snapped tight, jerking the large Selece from the ground by the neck. Bastian tucked his chin, trying to hold the noose steady, struggling for room to breathe. Celebrating his defeat, the soldiers cheered, watching the Selece struggle against his own weight. Bastian's sight faded to black.

Closer to the house, Takesh ordered the men to fan out before marching them in lock step toward the silent abode. When they approached, a torrent of thunderous ashareal lightning flashed through every open surface, forcing the soldiers to shield their eyes and cover their ears. After the echoes faded, an iridescent blue light streaked with prismatic veins of pure white and sky blue radiated from within.

Moments later, a blinding luminescent figure crashed through the roof, unleashing cobalt waves of arcane force that extinguished the rooftop flames. Azure ripples of aethereal energy formed phantasmal tendrils that ripped through the approaching soldiers.

Takesh dove forward, taking solace in the shadow's safety, while the men under his charge were rent asunder. Beyond them, cerulean asha transformed into spectral tentacles that thrashed wildly, bisecting the men standing around Bastian's still hanging body.

Hagan threw himself into a mound of brush. The Kandari was thankful to be alive until he looked down at the carnage to discover he's now half the soldier he once was. The dismembered mercenary glanced up as a stray lash of energy severed the rope holding the Selece aloft, causing Bastian's wilted form to collapse into the shadow behind the tree.

The glowing figure floated forward, projecting azure waves of mystical energy, annihilating any living being in their wake. The white iridescent glow faded while the form slowly drifted to the ground, leaving an exhausted Xander lying in place of the irradiant phantasm.

A tenebrous form clad in abyssal shadows writhed in anticipation upon approaching the fallen mage.

Kasaam gazed down longingly on his enemy, consumed with the desire to extinguish that magical spark within and watch his eyes go flat. "The omnipotent mage finally comes into his power, only to exhaust his energy, finding himself all alone."

"Never alone," declared a posh Kandari voice from behind the dark sorcerer.

Kasaam looked down at the slick sound of a blade piercing flesh to find the crimson tip of a Kandari long steel protruding from his chest. The abyssal mage drew his arms in to coil himself within his umbral cloak.

"Not this time!" barked the voice, thrusting the blade farther in with a twist. The swordsman pushed the handle in at an awkward angle and pulled up and out.

Kasaam's body collapsed with the sloshing thud of a sack filled with over-ripe melons. Reinhardt stood victorious over his enemy, watching the abyssal cloak dissolve into a shadowy mist, leaving a half-naked Fataak covered in arcane tattoos.

The ring of naked steel from behind prompted Reinhardt to turn, sword ready, handle high. Intercepting the assault from Takesh's curved sword, Reinhardt instinctively grabbed for his moon-hilted dagger, only to find himself clutching the air with his off hand. Using the advantage of his blade length, Reinhardt fought to control the distance while the assassin's dual curved blades swirled through the air, pressing forward to set the pace.

Takesh, noticing an oncoming attack from a large feral opponent, shifted off the centerline. Side by side, Bastian and Reinhardt towered over their adversary, blades ready. The Fataak murmured something before bringing his blades together. Sparks flew, igniting the air in a white-hot explosion. The two lifted their hands, shielding their eyes. When they peered out, the Fataak was riding away on horseback.

Bastian turned to give chase until Reinhardt pulled on his arm. "No, we need to see to ours!"

Securing his single chatta blade with a feral grunt, Bastian nodded, stepping forward into the carnage. Reinhardt turned to find his cousin nowhere in sight.

Wandering the battlefield, Bastian found Kumori's still body lying on the ground. The large Selece crouched to inspect his Nepharen friend for any signs of life.

"No!" Bastian lifted his fallen ally, pulling Kumori's body into his lap and stroking at the dark strands of hair beneath the hood.

Xander approached, gazing down on the mourning Selece.

Bastian looked up. "Gone," he whispered.

The mage knelt to meet Bastian's eyes. "No. This is only an illusion. So long as the portal to Ashara is open, our friend is not gone. Only sleeping."

Xander rested his hands on Kumori's chest, pouring in the last remnants of raw ashareal energy from the ever-closing vortex within. With a crack of thunder, Kumori's heart pounded, and the rogue's body jolted to life.

Having spent the last of the raw asha, Xander rocked backward onto the dirt when Reinhardt approached, hand outstretched. Staring at his cousin's hand for a long moment, Xander's gaze became curious noticing Reinhardt was clad in the attire of the royal guard. "Interesting attire for this particular party." Xander's visage softened, and the tension broke as he accepted the offer of assistance, pulling himself up into a familial embrace.

"Thank you Cousin, for not staying away." Xander pushed forward, holding Reinhardt at arm's length, eyes locked, staring. "You made the wrong choice, but you did it for the right reasons. For now, I understand, and in time, I may forgive." Again, Xander pulled his cousin closer and whispered, "But right now, I'm just thankful you saved my life."

Reinhardt's eyes glassed over. "I never—"

"I know." Xander nodded. "But right now, there's work to be done."

The four stood amidst the carnage.

Bastian looked to Reinhardt. "How did you find us?"

Reinhardt pointed toward the newly mangled mercenary. "He ran to Takesh after leaving the HanShoden estate. I fell in with the squadron of soldiers charged with this assignment."

"What do we do now?" Kumori asked.

"We take that one in as proof." Bastian pointed at Hagan, slinking away.

The newly retired chen-blade was missing one arm from the elbow down and one leg just above the knee. His damaged flesh had melted into a tapestry of pinks and red by the heat of the energy, embroidered with black scabs in between.

The Selece walked over and clutched the straps around the Kandari mercenary's chest. He slogged back to the group, dragging the flailing wretch behind him. Moments later, he let go, sending the languid Kandari to the ground with a thud. "He was with those that took my tribe's Spirit Stone."

Reinhardt looked down curiously. "I'll take that."

He pulled the moon-hilted dagger from Hagan's belt and placed it into its proper sheath at his side. Using chains and manacles from the tool shed, Reinhardt secured the former mercenary to a large tree by his remaining wrist.

"In the near future," Reinhardt said, latching and locking the manacles, "you and I will go toe-to-toe in an ass kicking contest." He walked away, shaking his head and clicking his tongue against the roof of his mouth.

"Was that a pun?" Xander chastised.

"Shut it!" Reinhardt continued walking.

The four of them walked back into the cabin to find Urma standing in front of the fireplace gawking up through a giant hole he recalled recently patching.

The old man gave Xander an flat look. "You put a hole in my roof."

Xander stared back, uncertain how to respond. "Yes." He drew out the end of the word longer than required.

"He lives!" Maxina tackled the young mage, abruptly replacing excitement with awkwardness.

"Yes." Xander grunted. "Sort of," he croaked.

The small Fataak woman glanced up. "What do you mean 'sort of?'" Xander winced as she released her constricting embrace. "Oh! You four go rest up. We will take care of this."

"What of Sarabi?" Bastian asked, walking toward the room.

"We'll see that she's all right. You just do what Ma' said."

The exhaustion from the events of the evening had already settled in. Too weary from their battle to argue, the four wandered off to the largest bedroom and collapsed from fatigue.

"Now where are we going to sleep?" Urma bickered at his wife, gazing at the hole in the ceiling.

"Anywhere we want." She chuckled.

30

It wasn't long before the sun rose on a quiet cabin sitting on a plot of land covered in death and blood, having dried a murky brown over the soldiers' green tunics trimmed in grey. Bastian and his companions continued their slumber through the day to wake early the following morning. Just after sunrise, Xander and Reinhardt took shovels from the tool shed to the back forty and dug graves for the fallen soldiers just short of the wood line.

Reinhardt slammed the shovel into a fresh patch of grass. "Why are we digging graves for our enemies?"

From deep in the next grave, Xander's voice echoed. "They weren't evil. They just didn't know which side they were on."

"What was it like?" Reinhardt questioned.

"What?" Xander deflected.

"Going. Coming back. Being in Ashara." Reinhardt flung a bit of dirt over his shoulder.

"Not sure." Xander's shovel hit another rock. "I don't quite remember much." His tone was rigid, certain. It was as though he'd repeated it to himself ten thousand times.

After they finished digging, the mage hopped out of the hole to gaze toward the cabin where Urma and Bastian worked at the roof.

Urma knelt down over the gaping absence of shingles and wood, ready with a hammer and nail. "I feel like we've done this before." Urma chuckled.

Bastian steadied a wooden brace, giving Urma enough room to nail it to the roof joist.

"So, what's your plan?" Urma inquired through a nail between his teeth.

Bastian secured the next brace. "Take Hagan to your king. Remove Serantes. Take the Spirit Stone back to my tribe." He stared off at the tree trunk in the distance, watching the dismembered Kandari lap water from a rusty bucket. "It's better than he deserves."

"Sure enough." Urma set another brace with a final nail. "But you need him healthy enough to talk in front of the king."

Bastian's gaze shifted to the trough Sarabi was eating from while Maxine and Kumori worked on her wing. The Fataak healer projected green luminescent energy into the severed leathery hide of the moravian's wounded wing.

Kumori applied a salve to the top of Sarabi's wing. "We appreciate your help."

"Oh, it's no problem at all, dear," Maxine said in fluent Nephari.

Kumori stopped in surprise. "You speak Nephari?" the rogue questioned in the same tongue.

"I once stayed with the Okutakana of southern Yukari," Maxina said in Kumori's native language.

"When? For how long?" Kumori inquired.

"Oh, that was ages ago. I simply wanted you to know the reverence and respect I have for you and your people." Maxina brought her hands together, bowing slightly, as was appropriate in the traditional Nepharen custom. Kumori returned the gesture.

Once the sun climbed to the center of the sky, they gathered in the dining room for lunch.

After swallowing a large bite of vegetables, Reinhardt cleared his throat. "While we appreciate the hospitality, we will need to leave first thing in the morning."

"Agreed." Xander nodded.

Urma wiped his mouth with his napkin. "We know the stakes here. You're welcome to leave after lunch, if that's what's best."

"We can take care of the rest," Maxina agreed.

"Are you sure?" Bastian gave Urma a concerned look.

"We can clean up the yard. You're the ones gonna clean up a castle. I wouldn't trade places if I had a choice." Urma took another bite of meat from the leg bone.

"It's settled then?" Xander looked around the table, shooting a Reinhardt a concerned glance. "Not all of us will fit on the moravian. Even if we could, she's not likely up for flying. And even if she were—"

Urma cut Xander off. "Take the spare wagon. She'll hitch up to that just fine."

Xander bowed his head graciously. "Much appreciated."

After finishing their plates, they set up their packs to travel. Bastian and Urma put the top cover on the wagon. The old Kandari checked the wheels and axles. He handed Bastian some extra-long leather straps with a set of buckles.

"You'll need to secure her good and tight for the hitch."

They fastened the straps, securing the hitch to each side. Bastian kept looking forward toward Sarabi's head to make sure there was no discomfort.

I'm not in any pain, a delicate, unfamiliar voice floated into his mind.

Sarabi? he thought inquisitively.

The moravian nodded.

"We don't have a moravian bridle." Urma set the last buckle. "Do you want me to rig something up?"

"I don't think we'll need it." A curious grin grew on his lips.

Near the tree, Reinhardt was making a ruckus. "You're going to do what we say when we say, or I will slit your mother-rutting throat. Are we clear?"

The slender swordsman had Hagan by the collar. Reinhardt lifted him up, bringing them nose to nose. The mutilated barbarian could taste the food on Reinhardt's breath. Reinhardt opened his hand and sent the mercenary reeling backward.

His head thudded against the tree trunk. "Yes, M'Lord," the barbarian conceded in a pathetic whimper.

Urma came out to interject. "Now is that rea—"

"Pa!" Maxina's hand cut through the air with an audible snap. The old man's mouth closed before the echo faded. Maxine covered the distance of ten paces between her and her husband in three quick steps and pointed at Hagan. "That animal knows nothing but violence and, were he fully able, would kill us all." Her seething breath drifted toward her husband. "They are the ones with a week's travel beside that monster, and this is how they make sure to live through it."

"I know." Urma sighed. "But I don't have to like it."

"Like it? None of us like it," she seethed. "But it's not ours to rut it up."

Bastian and Reinhardt secured the large barbarian with ropes, binding his elbows from behind like a plucked hen ready for the fire. Once settled in the wagon, they latched his foot to a board with a bolt and chain.

"Will this be good enough?" Xander inspected.

"It's not like he has two good hands to unbolt it with." Reinhardt chuckled.

The rest hopped into the wagon, with Bastian and Reinhardt on the bench, while Kumori and Xander sat in the back with the prisoner.

Bastian brought a single word to mind. *Forward.* The cart lurched as Sarabi started a slow trot.

Maxina and Urma watched their former house guests begin their drive toward the capital city. From the porch steps, the pair looked on reverently, each of them tracing circles in the air. Their fingers completed circles before tracing down to touch the center of the invisible sphere. "Ashana bless you."

The rolling wagon jostled and jilted down the road. Hours passed, and Reinhardt broke the silence. "Are you the only one able to drive the wagon?"

"I don't know." Bastian's brow rose with curiosity, and he closed his eyes. *Can you hear others? Can others hear you?*

I only hear you. If you need rest, others can sit on my back and guide me, Sarabi replied.

Bastian gestured to the kaitanous plates on Sarabi's back, naturally contoured, resembling a large, bisected horse's saddle. "If I'm not in front, someone would need to guide her from there."

Reinhardt nodded.

Days on the road passed without incident. Hagan, being sufficiently broken, did as he was told, including rest stops and wash breaks. They traded drivers, allowing Bastian to rest a few hours every day while the sun was at its highest, and drove through the night, which he preferred.

It was their fourth or fifth twilight dusk on the road. By now, Xander had lost count. Bastian sat in the driver's seat next to Kumori while the two Kandari rested in the back next to Hagan to the degree that one could rest when sleeping next to a murderous beast who would kill you at the first opportunity regardless of how well they were secured.

Xander sat in endless contemplation of his new connection to Ashara. He had lost something that night but had gained something else. The power reverberating through his chest surged in ways he'd never known. The thrum of asha reverberated with every heartbeat. He thought, if he willed it, he could make his heartbeat hard enough to push through his chest. Bringing his fingers together, he sent the crackling asha arcing effortlessly between them.

Suddenly, the sight of a familiar landmark outside caught his attention, showing they were approaching the city of Niru.

"Shaat." Xander jolted upright.

The commotion startled Hagan long enough that he stopped mumbling to himself.

"What now, Cousin?" Reinhardt groaned.

"How are we getting into the city?" Xander asked.

"Oh," Reinhardt said flatly.

"Were we really that naïve? We just thought that they were going to let us through the front gate?" Xander chided.

"What's wrong?" Kumori's head poked through the canvas draping at the front of the wagon.

"We have no way into the city," Xander answered.

"We—" Reinhardt started.

"The moment we hit the front gate, we'll be locked down tighter than Hagan over there." Xander gestured to the mutilated mercenary.

The three sat and collaborated.

Xander stepped up front. "Bastian."

Bastian nodded in acknowledgement.

Xander hesitated. "Is she ready to fly?"

Bastian paused a moment before responding, "No. It's too soon."

"Then we'll need you to turn left at the river after we cross the Nirulian bridge." Xander pointed forward, toward the bridge.

"Nirulian bridge?" Bastian's eyes went wide, giving Xander a side-long glance.

Xander sighed. "Go forward until we cross any bridge over a river. Turn left, and stay along the river. The trail will be narrow, but it's there."

Bastian nodded.

Xander slunk back into the covered wagon to continue plotting with the others.

Hours later, the wagon jostled and jilted Reinhardt awake.

"What in Ashana is happening?"

"We're on the Nirulian river trail," Xander bemoaned. "I can't sleep either."

The journey continued for four more days. That morning, Reinhardt was only an hour into guiding Sarabi when the wagon came to a crashing halt. Reinhardt bucked forward, gripping the moravian tightly to stay on. After steadying himself, he patted Sarabi on the neck and dismounted. Bastian and Kumori came out of the wagon first, each stepping awkwardly to exit the lopsided carriage. Walking to the back of the wagon, they found the axle had detached from the wheel.

"I thought Urma inspected this," Reinhardt complained.

"It wasn't made for a trail this rough," Xander answered. "Perhaps, Cousin, if we had a better plan before setting out, he could have reinforced it knowing we'd be taking such a shaat rout."

"You joke now. Wait until you're waste deep in it," Reinhardt bickered.

"Waste deep in what?" Bastian asked.

"Does he not know the plan?" Reinhardt pointed to Bastian.

"Plan?" Bastian innocently inquired.

"What do we do with *him*?" Xander nodded to Hagan.

"Unfortunately, he's the lucky one. He gets to ride Sarabi while the rest of us walk," Reinhardt answered.

"I will ride with him to keep him upright," Bastian added.

After Bastian and Reinhardt unhitched Sarabi, the four secured their packs and pressed forward. Shortly after midday, they reached the aqueduct, where the city sewage ran into the river. It was little more than a manmade drainage ditch slagged with stone and mortar.

Reinhardt looked at Bastian. "She should stay here until she can fly or until we can come get her."

Bastian dismounted. "How will Hagan travel?"

"We'll need you to carry him the rest of the way." Reinhardt frowned.

Taking a deep breath, Bastian nodded. He went to Hagan and hefted the lame Kandari over his shoulders like a prize game.

The five of them pressed forward to find a large, circular drain. Blocking the drain was a gate of flat steel bars latticed together and forged welded to a steel circle the size of the hole.

Reinhardt looked to Xander. "Well, Cousin, I do believe this is your aria."

Xander stepped forward, centering himself in front of the gate. He pulled the asha to his fingers and swirled it into a vortex. He shifted the vortex into a spinning sphere and launched it toward the bolted latch. The latch turned molten red, dripping into the water with a hiss. As the metal cooled, the gate creaked open.

"Show off." Reinhardt chuckled.

Xander shook his head with a sigh. "If you only knew, Cousin. If you only knew."

The four of them pressed through the tunnels when they were startled by a horse rearing in the streets above. Following the whinny and snort of a prize stallion, Lord Han'Shoden's pompous laugh rang out at the sight of a dozen frightened peasants scattering in the streets.

Reinhardt looked at Xander, eyes wide. The taller Kandari leaned over toward his cousin, speaking in a heavy, voiceless breath. "What's the goal here?"

"To get him in front of King Dailan and expose Serantes," Xander replied in a similar tone.

"Right. I have an acquaintance that can help us do just that," Reinhardt replied.

"And, Cousin, who precisely is this untapped resource?" Xander's one eyebrow raised in anticipation.

"Well..." Reinhardt blushed. "I wouldn't say she's an untapped resource."

"Oh Ashara, are you really going there?" Xander scolded.

"Listen. She trusts me, and she has connections. Wait here for one hour. Give me..." Reinhardt stopped. "Us. Give us one hour, and we'll have everything we need."

"Us?" Xander inquired.

Reinhardt grabbed Kumori around the shoulder. "Yeah, us."

"Why us?" Kumori gave Reinhardt a confused look.

"Because you're an expert in getting into places, and I need to get into a place." Reinhardt grinned.

"Rye!" Xander chided.

"Not that place!" his cousin objected. "We have actual work to do. One hour." He pressed forward, and Kumori followed with a determined sigh.

By Xander's count, an hour had passed, then two, and eventually, he would have sworn it was five. The sound of boots sloshing in the waste echoed through the drains. Xander readied a bolt of Ashareal force, placing Bastian and Hagan behind him.

Ahead of Kumori, Reinhardt rounded the corner to find himself face to face with the business end of a magical bolt. "Would you put that thing away?"

"I could have killed you." Xander released the magical energy, allowing the asha to dissolve into the aether.

"But you didn't," Reinhardt quipped.

Kumori stepped around the squabbling cousins to Bastian. "All is well?"

Bastian nodded. "Tired but well."

"You should have said it was you." Xander threw his hands up. "It's been five hours."

"No!" Reinhardt protested. "It's been two and a half."

"That's still longer than one." Xander paced back and forth, frustration etched on his face. "And what did we get for our two and a half hours?"

"A meeting with Maven," Reinhardt boasted.

"Mistress Maven?" Xander's mouth was agape in surprise.

"The same." Reinhardt's lips grew into an impish grin.

"Who's Mistress Maven?" Bastian inquired.

"Only the most trusted advisor to King Dailan himself. She'll meet with us to hear us out. If she believes our claims hold merit, she'll bring us to His Majesty." Reinhardt postured like a cock, finding his crow for the first time.

"And where is this meeting to take place?" Xander shrugged.

"We set the meeting at the northern temple of Inara. We are to be offered sanctuary in the profits quarter, where Maven will grant us an audience," Reinhardt answered.

"Temple of Inara?" Bastian questioned.

"The temple of the Ashiere of Air," Xander replied.

"Thank you. We refer to her as Othura." Bastian gestured toward the sky.

"And we call her TsukiYue," added Kumori.

"By whatever name, that is where we meet this night. We're due there in three hours and are still at the top of the shift list for all of Aestaria." Reinhardt pantomimed running his finger down a list of names on parchment.

"The top?" Xander barked.

"Yes, the top, and they will shift us all right to the void to interrogate our dead corpses after if we don't make haste."

Reinhardt turned and took the lead. Two and three-quarter hours later, the five of them exited the aqueduct tunnel near the Temple of Inara.

Reinhardt approached Kumori, placing a gentle hand on the rogue's shoulder. "The shadows are yours. We follow you."

With a nod, Kumori crept forward toward the temple through

the cover of night. A bright lamplight hanging on the road allowed an obstruction to cast an overdark shadow. Kumori froze, hands out, signaling to stop. Two guards were patrolling in the next alleyway. Kumori's arm went up in anticipation. The guards continued their patrol and fell out of sight. Kumori's hand dropped, and the group sprinted through the darkness, crossing the road to a shrouded corner of the temple. They stuck to the walls skulking carefully, turning one corner and another to find an arch stone doorway as the rear entrance. Reinhardt rapped a pattern against the large wooden door with no handle.

A bald man wearing orange robes embellished with yellow scarves opened the door, eyes locked on Reinhardt. "From where does the truth come?"

"From the light of the Ashuun through the spirit of Inara," Reinhardt answered. He looked back to find a shocked audience, mouths agape. "Don't look so surprised. It's a line I just memorized when we made this plan." He pointed at Kumori. "You were there. I'm just repeating what the baroness told me to say."

"I'm afraid it's true," Kumori confirmed. "He wouldn't know the spirit of the Ashuun if it kicked him in the face." The rogue chuckled.

"Hey," Reinhardt protested. "I resemble that remark!" He chuckled.

"Enough games," the new stranger barked. "Inside."

He held the door open and led them through a hall and down a spiral staircase to a large open room. By Bastian's measure, the room was eight lengths by twelve lengths and three lengths high. The walls were painted yellow, decorated with orange curtains and tapestries embroidered with large archaic white glyphs.

They followed him to the middle of the room. There sat a woman in an ornate wooden chair placed before an elaborate hanging tapestry. She was a woman of demure stature, who, nonetheless, commanded enormous respect. She wore a dress of deep red crushed velvet with bands of gold around the seam at the bottom, and two more gold ribbon bands evenly spaced from the lowest. Gold ribbon edged the high neckline, tracing down the arms and around the long-sleeve cuffs. Around her neck hung a slender golden chain carrying a gold key, its handle displaying the royal seal of Aestaria in stained glass.

At either side of the woman's chair, standing a finger's width shorter than Bastian, were two Kandari soldiers similarly outfitted in red and gold under moderate plate armor. Each of them held upright large wooden glaives composed of thick poles and long, heavy, elaborately engraved razor-sharp blades pointing toward the ceiling. Their weapons resembled something between a hunting spear and an oversized fishing harpoon with a single edge. The four stood stone-still, Bastian still carrying Hagan over his shoulders.

When she pushed the slightest cough, the soldier on her left slammed his glaive against the floor. Resonating off the walls with the authority of a magistrate's gavel, the sound summoned a regiment of half a dozen Aestarian soldiers in through the corridors.

Xander's heated gaze fell on Reinhardt. "What the shaat is this?"

"I didn't do this!" Reinhardt protested. His eyes hardened on Maven. "What is this?"

"He is correct. He did not do this." Her voice came out warm and silky smooth as freshly squeezed honey milk hot off the stove. Her accent was posh, with the faintest inflection betraying the likelihood of an underprivileged upbringing. "These men..." She gestured at the soldiers. "...are a part of my contingency plan. If your tale does not ring with the light of truth, they will take you to the authorities. You have until the end of the next hour to convince me to bring your case before His Majesty."

Reinhardt stepped forward, gaze flicking to Bastian. "Mistress Maven, I am Reinhardt Vos'Korendel."

Maven nodded. "I know who you are. Do not waste your time telling me things I already know."

Reinhardt cleared his throat. "This is my traveling companion and friend, Bastian. Our tale begins with him and the death of his father and Selece chieftain." He stepped back, tilting his head, a signal for Bastian to step forward.

Bastian stepped forward. "Mistress Maven, I am Bastian, new chieftain of the northern Selece and son of a murdered father, Nuratha. This man killed my father." He knelt forward, sloughing Hagan off his shoulders. The mutilated mercenary collapsed to the floor at Bastian's feet. "He and a team of mercenaries worked with Jorgan Han'Shoden to steal an ancient relic from my people."

Over the course of the next hour, they all recalled their stories. Kumori told of the theft of the healing bracers and a journey north through Ganos.

"So, it was you giving the Ganosians so much trouble," Maven remarked with an impish grin. "Well done."

The Kandari nobles told of their meeting in the prison and how their fates became entangled with these strangers turned friends now thought of as kin from foreign lands.

"You say that you consider them family?" Maven inquired.

Reinhardt stepped forward proudly. "Yes! Your Grace."

"Why?" she inquired.

Reinhardt nodded. "Sometimes blood shed together is stronger than blood shared."

"Indeed," a disembodied baritone voice resonated through the room.

The soldiers at Maven's side appeared shaken. Uncertain what to do, they both stamped their glaives clumsily against the floor.

Maven's eyes rolled, and another two dozen soldiers entered the room from behind tapestries and through corridors.

"What now?" the cousins said to each other.

Maven sighed. "These are *his*... security force."

A man stepped out from the tapestry behind Maven's chair. "I've heard enough."

He smiled confidently, strolling past the towering guard. The man wore a perfectly tailored red velvet doublet trimmed in gold under a red velvet jerkin vest embroidered with golden thread woven to form a pattern of intricate diamonds. His lower half brandished a pair of loose-fitting slop trousers stopping just over the knee, primarily red with vertical lines of gold peeking through from the layer folded beneath the seam. At his waist, a thick strap of black leather secured a scabbard which held an Aestarian long blade, the pommel brandishing the royal seal of Aestaria, a golden castle tower with a pair of golden Ashuun wings set on a field of red. His thick mahogany hair fell symmetrically to the edge of his chiseled clean-shaven jawline, each strand held in place by the golden royal circlet resting on his head. The large ruby set in the apex was the crown's keystone with smaller rubies imbedded in the six smaller peaks encircling His Majesty's head.

Reinhardt and Xander immediately took a knee, each averting their respective gazes to the floor.

"Do rise," the king's rich baritone echoed with elated undertones.

The pair of cousins stood attentively while the king loomed over the pathetic heap on the floor known as Hagan.

"You stole the Spirit Stone from the Selece?" The king's voice resonated with the authority of one reared by kings and the institutions that make kings. The dejected cutthroat's head nodded lazily, his shameful gaze averted. "And it was at Serantes' instruction?"

"Well…" the barbarian started, "it was at Jorgan's instruction, but we all knew he was working for his kinsman."

The king snapped, "Ondrus."

One guard next to Maven snapped to attention.

"Where is Serantes now?"

"Somewhere between his quarters in the palace and the royal hall. Most likely in the courtyard in between at this moment," Ondrus said, his consistent tenor resonating with confidence.

"Take ten men, and secure him."

Reinhardt advanced to interject. "Your majesty! We've been pursuing him since the start of our quest. We humbly request to see this through."

The king's majestic gaze regarded the young noble. "I understand your concern. But this has become a matter for the crown and must be handled accordingly. I hope that you understand."

Reinhardt nodded reverently. "Yes, Your Majesty."

King Dailan's gaze turned to Ondrus. "As you were. Find him, and place him in holding to await an appointment with the Tor'Quari," the king ordered.

Xander winced at the mention of the name. A surge of adrenaline pushed through his veins, causing his heart to skip a beat. He breathed hard through tightly pursed lips until his heart steadied, bringing the thrum of the asha to a murmur.

"Keldrin," the king called.

The soldier on Maven's left snapped to attention. "Your Majesty."

"Take six men, and search Serantes' palace quarters. Bring what you find to my royal estate room." The king looked on at Xander. "I understand you recently had a run it with the…" He stopped himself before he finished the sentence. "I understand, and I'm sorry you had to go through that, yet occasionally it's necessary to get to the truth."

"Your Majesty." Keldrin bowed, dismissing himself with six other guards.

"Now for the unfortunate bit." The king sighed.

"Unfortunate?" Kumori questioned.

The king nodded at a set of guards. A pair of soldiers came and picked up Hagan, bringing him to his feet. He languidly hobbled off under their direction.

"I would be remiss if I simply allowed you to run rampant in the city at this juncture." The king paced back and forth. "And I wouldn't want to think of you as being ill-treated." He sighed. "As such, for the time being, I'll have to place you in the tower until I can validate your claims."

The two cousins looked at each other and tension grew between them, while Bastian's visage betrayed his confusion.

"Now, I understand that we could have an epic battle here, under the halls of the temple of Inari, but I would hope that you would see reason and logic in my words and know that I will make a just decision."

Maven approached. "Your Majesty, if I may."

"Maven?" The king glanced toward his advisor.

"What if we were to remand them to the palace grounds?" she suggested. "In all honesty, a Selece, a Nepharen and a mage, if he has truly achieved grand magus... The tower would only hold them by their honor."

"What about me?" Reinhardt contended.

"Psh!" Maven's piercing gaze stared daggers into Reinhardt's soul.

He staggered back a half step. There was no magic in it, just the pure understanding that this woman's authority would not tolerate insolence.

"Agreed." The king nodded. "Please be my guests in the royal palace grounds. You will be free to wander about per your desire, so long as you give your word, you won't leave the grounds until this matter is resolved."

Xander and Reinhardt nodded at each other.

Xander walked over to Bastian and Kumori. "We still need to find the Spirit Stone and bracers. This will give us time and opportunity to accomplish that."

Bastian and Kumori nodded.

Reading the room, Reinhardt broke the silence. "We agree, Your Majesty."

"Wonderful," the king cheered. "Being that the alternative was significantly less pleasant."

A contingent of guards escorted Mistress Maven and King Dailan through a rear corridor. A

separate set of guards ushered Kumori and company from the temple to the Aestarian Palace.

31

Every corner of the extravagant estate room was decorated in royal blue, with white walls trimmed in black. Over the fireplace, against the far wall, hung the Vos'Korendel coat of arms, a black raptor driving a white serpent in its talons against a field of royal blue.

Bastian and Xander stood in the middle of the room, examining the large elaborate tapestry.

"What does it mean?" Bastian asked, gesturing to the crest.

"Mean?" Xander questioned.

The Selece elaborated, "What story does it tell?"

"I'm starving," Reinhardt moaned, lying on the overlarge mattress and tugging lazily at the bell rope.

"I think it's a story of good triumphing over evil," Xander answered. "What do you see?"

Bastian paused in contemplation. "The serpent isn't evil. It kills on instinct. It doesn't choose to bite, just as you don't choose to breathe. The raptor is a symbol of order and ascension, but it has no more choice to dive and attack than the serpent does to strike. It shows the battle within each of us."

The door opened and Reinhardt bolted toward the door, stopping just short of crashing into Mistress Maven. The mistress wore a slightly less ornate gown than when they had first met, still maintaining the royal colors of house San'Durin.

"You're not Tobin," Reinhardt complained.

"Is that a problem?" Maven heckled.

"I've been ringing the bell. I'm starving," Reinhardt pleaded.

"For now, your stomach will have to wait," she instructed.

"For what?" Reinhardt chauffed at Maven.

"His Majesty." Maven crept forward a half step, arms down, eyes forward.

Reinhardt relented like a submissive pet, taking half a step back to stand rigidly upright.

"Where's the Nepharen?" Maven looked around. Her gaze fell on Xander and Bastian, who were giggling like school kids at an obedient Reinhardt.

As if on cue, the cloaked Nepharen ran into the room, glowing with delight. "I have great news."

"The bracers?" Xander inquired.

"The stone?" Bastian looked between Xander and Kumori.

"No—" the Nepharen started to answer.

"Actually—" Maven started.

"I have new friends," Kumori shouted.

"Friends?" Reinhardt's head turned curiously toward the cloaked rogue. "Where?"

"The Tolabri's caravan was traveling through the royal courtyard, showing off to the attending nobles." Kumori's face glowed with excitement.

Xander and Reinhardt's hands slapped against their respective foreheads while groaning together.

"What—" Xander started.

"I—" Maven tried to interject.

"Did you get—" Reinhardt continued.

"We—" Maven again failed to interject.

"From the Tolabri's caravan?" Xander finished.

"Friends!"

From a pouch beneath the cloak, Kumori brought out two slender furry creatures with soft coats the color of winter frost, tipped in shades of pot ash save for their stubby charcoal legs. They had long necks, at the end of which two short pink and white ears stood over white faces with black fur masks and pink noses.

"No," Reinhardt groaned.

"They're adorable!" Xander fawned.

"And smart. Watch."

Kumori excitedly threw out two little cloth sacks filled with dried beans. The pair of small creatures spiraled down the rogue's legs and scurried across the floor. Once secured, they returned with the bounty to get their reward. Kumori gave each a small pellet of food.

"What are their names?" Bastian stepped forward inquisitively.

"This one's Fanty." Kumori pointed at one. "And that's Mingo."

"How can you tell?" Xander squinted, shifting his gaze between them.

"And why do you care?" Reinhardt's confused gaze fell on the large Selece.

"Because we don't name food," Bastian answered plainly.

The room exploded in laughter save for Maven, whose expression could have melted glass.

"We have your treasures!" Maven screamed with a stomp of her foot, and the silence that followed consumed the room. The mistress cleared her throat before releasing a whisper, "His majesty has commanded an audience."

The four stood straight. Fanty and Mingo vanished into the cloak.

Maven knocked on the door, and the guard opened it. The four kept pace while maintaining a reasonable distance as they marched down a long corridor. Three rights, two lefts, and one more right later, they stood at the throne room's grand entrance.

A pair of royal guards, clad in red and gold, stood before an enormous set of doors already opened inward toward the grand throne room where the high king sat poised on one of two golden thrones. To King Dailan's right, the dais was empty. To his left, an extravagantly crafted gold chair with red upholstery and a single red velvet pillow sat unoccupied. Beyond the vacant throne stood an unknown individual with no hair and a neatly kept beard, wearing a golden advisor's mantle over the expected honorary colors of the kingdom.

The king stood, and Maven bowed along with her company.

"Do rise." King Dailan nodded, courteously raising a hand in vestigial humility.

The five of them stood and Maven led the way forward, making her way toward the dais. Moments later, she turned to them, bowing slightly before moving to stand at the king's right side.

King Dailan approached, waving a hand to beckon the closest guard. A large Kandari entered holding a cushion covered with a red silk draping. Behind him walked another guard, carrying a similar cushion. The king gestured toward their guests, and the guards advanced accordingly.

"I believe these belong to you."

The guards removed the cloth coverings, and before Bastian was a stone shimmering between iridescent amber and glistening gold, embellished with arcane carvings. In front of Kumori was a set of bracers.

"The Bracers of Theshana." The Nepharen gasped.

With a solemn visage, Kumori reached for the mystical armor antiqued in dark green tarnish over bronze and imbedded with light green stones shaped into arcane glyphs set into ornate designs throughout. On the bottoms were leather straps to fasten them into place. Kumori placed them into a leather satchel beneath the cloak.

Bastian reverently looked on. Slowly, he picked up the stone etched with ancient symbols. "The Spirit Stone," he rumbled under his breath.

"So that's it." Xander shrugged, a morose expression on his face.

"Where were they?" Reinhardt inquired.

"Found in Serantes' bed chamber," the king answered.

"And Serantes?" Xander asked.

"Captured by Ondrus and his guard, now awaiting his appointment for questioning," the king replied. "So, what will you do now?"

"We will restore them to their rightful place." Bastian bowed slightly.

"Indeed." The king nodded and returned to his throne. "If I can be of service, you have only to ask."

"You are dismissed," Maven instructed.

The four bowed before turning and exiting the throne room. When they entered the Vos'Korendel estate quarters, Bastian and Kumori remained silent, consumed by their own reverent thoughts.

"Then this is the end?" Xander's words cut through the stillness.

"What else is there?" Reinhardt shrugged and pointed to Bastian. "He will return the Spirit Stone, and Kumori will take the bracers to the Nepharen."

"I feel like this is too important for one person to do on their own." Xander sat in a royal-blue reading chair. "What if we went in pairs?"

"Pairs?" Bastian's eyes went up.

"Yes," Xander answered. "You and I can return the Spirit Stone to your people. Reinhardt and Kumori can return the bracers to the Nepharen people."

"Well, Cousin, that depends. Will they have us?"

Bastian and Kumori exchanged amusing looks.

Bastian answered. "I could use the company."

"Do I have to take Stick Boy?" Kumori complained.

"Stick Boy?" Reinhardt objected.

"Let's pack." Xander began moving around the room, sorting and securing weapons and gear.

"We're still staying for supper, right?" Reinhardt pleaded.

"We can leave in the morning. Until then, I'll speak to Maven about the supplies we're missing."

Xander continued shifting about. Fanty and Mingo ran across his feet, passing a ball back and forth.

A knock rapped at the door. Xander opened it, and Tobin stepped through. He wore a grey tunic under a red and gold vest over grey trousers, which complemented his short dark hair. In his hands sat a wooden tray filled with finely cooked game meats and an assortment of cheeses.

Reinhardt crashed into the unexpecting attendant. "Food!" He shouted, stumbling about to rescue the tray and its contents.

Xander helped the man to his feet, assisting him out of the room. "My apologies for my cousin's behavior." He looked at the guard through the open door. "Can you please tell Maven I'm requesting an audience?"

"I'll send for her immediately." The guard marched down the hall.

The next morning, Bastian and Kumori were the first to wake just before the dawn. They checked their travel packs, confirming that their respective relics were accounted for. Each of them sighed, releasing the weight of anticipation.

Xander and Reinhardt woke just after sunrise. They prepared for their respective long journeys.

"Are you going to survive without me, Cousin?" Reinhardt jeered.

"I was going to ask you the same thing. Who's going to save you now that I'm going west?" Xander teased.

"I do believe it was me who saved you last." Reinhardt tilted his head to the left, eyebrows raised.

"You're right, Cousin. This match goes to you," Xander answered.

The four met in the royal stables. Xander and Bastian stood over Sarabi's hay-filled trough.

"Well, this is it for now." Xander's somber gaze wandered between his friends.

Xander and Reinhardt gripped arms, pulling each other in close for a solid embrace.

"No goodbyes! I'll see you after," Reinhardt said under his breath.

Kumori walked over to Bastian. "Don't let anything eat him. He's too squishy for the wild."

"It won't be easy," Bastian agreed, "but I'll keep him alive."

A sudden pop followed by whooshing sounds drew their attention away from each other and the mounts.

A small Tapi strode up to Reinhardt. "Reinhardt Vos'Korendel?" the small pixie asked knowingly.

Reinhardt nodded before taking a small scroll. The pixie turned and plunged through a new vortex. Reinhardt opened the scroll, and his eyes glassed over.

"Rye, what's wrong?" Xander took the scroll from Reinhardt's fumbling hands.

"What?" Kumori inquired.

Xander sighed. "Lord Vos'Korendel has passed. Assassinated days ago by an unnamed assassin."

Reinhardt grabbed a wooden stool from the ground and slammed it against the stone wall, shattering it into pieces. "That bastard!" He thrust a finger in Xander's face. "He didn't deserve this."

"None of them did, Cousin," Xander implored.

"I must go." Reinhardt picked up his pack before turning to Kumori. "Stay with them. Stay together. Stay close."

Kumori nodded.

"What do we do now?" Bastian asked Reinhardt.

"I'm going to attend to matters at the Vos'Korendel estate. You're going to return the Spirit Stone, followed by the bracers."

Reinhardt opened the stable gate holding a large brown mustang. He secured his pack and guided the horse from the stable before mounting the steed and pushing it to a trot. Moments later, the horse galloped off into the distance.

"To your tribe, then?" Xander asked Bastian.

The Selece nodded. "To my tribe."

"Can she fly yet?" Kumori asked Bastian.

Bastian looked to Kumori. "Can you use the bracers?"

"That honor has not been passed to me." Kumori nodded reverently.

"Then we will ride to visit Maxine and Urma. I'm sure she'll be ready to fly after a day or two there," Bastian answered.

Their packs secure, they mounted the moravian steed, and Sarabi trotted to the western river bridge.

32

King Dailan stood at the window of his royal estate room with the light of the full Evening Moon shining brightly upon his face. In a dark corner at the opposite end of the room crouched a stocky figure wearing a bronze circlet over a black headscarf. Dailan looked down in contemplation of recent events.

Takesh moved forward in absolute stealth under the shroud of darkness. Standing an arm's length from Dailan, Takesh broke the silence. "It is done."

Dailan took a long, deep breath before sighing heavily. "As it should be. Serantes' fate?"

"It appears as though he hanged himself with the fabric from his own tunic before the Tor'Quari could perform their interrogation," Takesh answered.

"How original. Now there's only one other matter to wrap up." The king's silhouette was dark against the moonlight filled window.

"Agreed." Takesh nodded.

Eyes closed. Fingers held tight around a shrouded obsidian dagger. The blade's hilt was set with an iridescent stone shimmering between dark amethyst and lavender, brandishing preternaturally sharp edges undulating from the hilt to the tip. Without warning, the slick sound of a blade pushing through flesh echoed off the chamber walls.

"Wha..." the Fataak choked out over the sound of an abyssal blade pushing into his back.

The tip of a phantasmal blade tinted red, protruding from Takesh's sternum, and he sank to the floor. His fallen body left nothing standing between the High King of Aestaria and the

Ashino hovering three heads taller directly behind the Kandari ruler. Dailan loosened his grip on the Soul Blade, and the Ashino was sucked backward into a spectral vortex.

Dailan placed the blade into a secret compartment hidden behind his ornate hardwood chair.

A metallic tone resonated through the room, modulating into separate sounds. The reverberation caused Dailan's skin to crawl with discomfort, as though it didn't fit on his body. His heart skipped a beat, and his chest felt tight.

"Now that the Pillars of Ashana have fallen, you must deplete the wells of Ashara," the voice crackled. The spectral form of a black orb reflected back at him through the pane.

"As you command, Vasuum. As things stand, this will take years to complete."

Vasuum's ominous voice resonated, sending a crack through the glass, "I have slumbered for aeons. What you call years are mere moments."

Dailan swallowed hard, voice stuck in his throat. "Mighty Vasuum, I have upheld my end of the bargain."

Vasuum's voice thrummed, "And I shall uphold mine. After you deplete the wells of Ashara."

One final wave of fluctuating metallic resonance echoed off the walls, sending the room into an anxious silence.

A single tear rolled down Dailan's cheek. "I will hold you again, my dearest Inara, whatever the cost."

About The Author

Jay Roland is an up-and-coming author in the Dark Epic Fantasy genre with the release of this first novel "Shadow of the Soul Blade". The first of the Dark Thorne Chronicles. Jay is a devoted, caring husband of sixteen years to his wife Nyssa, and loving father to their five wonderful children.

As a lifelong tabletop RPG gamer and storyteller across many platforms, he's often found weaving intricate tales of intrigue, or impending doom for his family and friends. During the day, Jay is a technology professional, leading teams and departments to overcome unique technical and logistical challenges. But now, after decades of telling stories around the gaming table, he has finally decided to craft the first of many books to come.